Defending the Future: Advancing U.S. Cyberspace Security Cooperation in the Post-Ukraine War Era

www.defending-the-future.com

Disclaimer

The views expressed in this publication are those of the author and do not necessarily reflect the official policy or position of the Department of Defense or the U.S. government. The public release clearance of this publication by the Department of Defense does not imply the Department of Defense endorsement or factual accuracy of the material.

Table of Contents

Dedication

To my family,

This book is dedicated to the unwavering support and love you have shown me throughout my life. Your encouragement and belief in my dreams have been the driving force behind my journey, and I am eternally grateful for everything you have done for me.

As an immigrant and first-generation American, I carried with me the dreams I had since I was a young boy. Growing up, I aspired to become a G.I. Joe, "America's fighting man," who wanted to make the world a better place. Little did I know that my path would indeed lead me to become just that.

My journey has been filled with challenges and adversity in both my military and civilian career. However, your support and unwavering belief in me have been my constant source of strength. You taught me the values of hard work, perseverance, and the importance of making a difference in the world.

This book is a testament to my efforts to make the world a better place despite the obstacles that stood in my way. It is a reflection of the sacrifices you made and the sacrifices we endured as a family. It is a tribute to the resilience and determination that runs in our blood, passed down through generations.

Thank you for standing by me, for believing in my dreams, and for being the foundation upon which I built my life. This book is as much yours as it is mine, and I hope it serves as a reminder that with love, support, and determination, we can overcome anything life throws our way.

With all my love and gratitude,

Mohamed Amer.

About The Author

Mohamed Amer is a Cyber Capacity Building SME with over twenty years of experience in cyber strategy, defensive cyber operations (DCO), and military intelligence (MI), as well as security cooperation (SC) and assistance as it relates to cyberspace. Mohamed possesses extensive expertise, spanning fifteen years, in various cyber security domains within the U.S. Department of Defense (DOD) and Intelligence Community (IC). His areas of specialization include cyberspace security cooperation, indications and warnings, threat hunting, incident response, risk assessment, penetration testing, intrusion detection, and malware forensics. Mohamed served as a Cyberspace Security Cooperation Advisor to the U.S. European Command (USEUCOM or EUCOM) in Germany.[i] He has experience working closely with foreign Ministries of Defense and Cyber Commands, U.S. Embassies, and Country Team leadership to ensure security cooperation objectives are met. As a Cyberspace Security Cooperation Advisor to the U.S. European Command, Mohamed was part of the first USEUCOM-led cyber exercise, Cyber Unity, dedicated to Military CISRTS of NATO Allies, sponsored by Luxembourg's Directorate of Defence and NATO Support and Procurement Agency (NSPA).[ii]

Prior to his EUCOM role, Mohamed spent eight years supporting the U.S. Army Europe and Africa (USAREUR-AF) and U.S. Army Cyber Command (ARCYBER). In addition, for six years, Mohamed served as a cyber threat and intelligence Analyst in the U.S. Army at the Cyber Battalion at Fort Eisenhower in Georgia. Mohamed holds a Master of Science degree (MSc) in Information Assurance and Security from Western Governors University in Utah.

In his free time, Mohamed develops open-source software to protect non-profit organizations from ransomware attacks through an anti-ransomware detection tool designed to search and identify phishing campaigns and legitimate MITRE ATT&CK tools that are hard to detect. The open-source scanner also scrutinizes foreign-made software and highlights its impact on organizations' security posture.[iii]

Preface

Welcome to "Defending The Future: Advancing U.S. Cyberspace Security Cooperation in the Post-Ukraine War Era." This book is an essential resource born out of a pressing need in the market for comprehensive guides and references on cyberspace security cooperation. Its aim is to fill the gap and provide practitioners with a valuable tool for navigating the complexities of this field.

One of the primary motivations behind writing this book is the lack of available resources and practical guides that specifically address the intricacies of cyberspace security cooperation within U.S. foreign policy. As cyber threats continue to evolve and intensify, the importance of collaboration across borders has become paramount. Yet, there has been a dearth of comprehensive guidance for newcomers and even seasoned practitioners with limited cyber experience. This book endeavors to be the first of its kind, incorporating everything one needs to know about U.S. cyberspace security cooperation, making it accessible to individuals from diverse backgrounds.

Within the pages of this book, we cover a wide range of topics critical to understanding and effectively engaging in cyberspace security cooperation. We explore the concept of integrated deterrence in cyberspace, examine the strategies and techniques of Advise & Assist (A&A), and delve into the complexities of Hunt Forward Operations (HFOs). Additionally, we address key aspects such as DOD's Title 10 and DoS's Title 22, cyberspace security cooperation force providers and stakeholders, Foreign Military Sales (FMS),

Foreign Military Financing (FMF), Computer Security Incident Response Team (CSIRT) Assistance Programs, and the FBI Cyber Action Team (CAT), as well as Significant Security Cooperation Initiatives (SSCIs) Assessment, Monitoring, and Evaluation (AM&E) activities. By encompassing these essential elements, this resource aims to equip readers with a comprehensive understanding and practical guide of the field.

The book caters to two distinct audiences: newcomers entering the field of cyberspace security cooperation and experienced policymakers and practitioners. For those new to the field, we provide a solid foundation by explaining fundamental concepts, terminologies, and challenges in the cyberspace domain. Our goal is to demystify complex technical jargon and make the core principles of cyberspace security cooperation accessible to individuals new to the field.

For experienced policymakers and practitioners, this book goes beyond the basics. We explore advanced strategies, emerging trends, and international best practices in cyber capacity building and international cooperation. Through the insights of renowned contributors, we offer numerous case studies and valuable insights that can inform decision-making processes and enhance the effectiveness of seasoned professionals supporting security cooperation roles within the DOD and beyond.

Throughout the book, we emphasize the real-world applicability of cyberspace security cooperation. We address the geopolitical considerations that shape international collaborations, delve into the legal frameworks governing cyber investment and cooperation activities, and discuss the role of technical innovations and emerging technologies in bolstering cyber defenses. By grounding our discussions in practicality, we seek to equip readers with the knowledge and tools necessary to navigate the ever-evolving landscape of cyberspace security cooperation.

We acknowledge that cyberspace security cooperation comes with its own set of challenges. Conflicting national interests, divergent legal frameworks, and political influences can complicate efforts to forge effective partnerships. To address these complexities, we present nuanced discussions that encourage critical thinking and foster informed dialogue. By exploring the intersection of national defense strategies and security considerations, we aim to guide policymakers and practitioners in navigating the intricate trade-offs inherent in this field.

To newcomers, we extend our warmest welcome and encourage you to embrace the exciting and ever-evolving field of cyberspace security cooperation. For experienced practitioners and policymakers, we express our gratitude for your dedication and unwavering commitment to defending our digital future.

We hope that "Defending the Future: U.S. Cyberspace Security Cooperation Post the Ukraine War Era" serves as a valuable companion on your journey. May its insights inspire collaboration, foster innovative approaches, and empower individuals and organizations to effectively address the challenges of our interconnected world. Together, let us embark on this vital mission to safeguard our digital landscape for generations to come.

Chapter 1:
Capacity Building Investment in the Context of the Current International Order in Cyberspace

Introduction

Cyber capacity building is a crucial undertaking that requires a thorough understanding of the evolving threats and the current state of the international order in cyberspace. As technology continues to progress at a rapid pace, the cyberspace landscape becomes increasingly intricate, presenting significant challenges to the security of nations and their critical infrastructure. Policymakers, senior cyber advisors, and country desk officers involved in supporting cyberspace security cooperation missions play a pivotal role in fostering collaboration and strengthening cybersecurity capabilities among Allies and partners. By comprehending the threats and the dynamics of the international order in cyberspace, these individuals can effectively allocate resources, develop strategic partnerships, and implement measures that enhance resilience and deter malicious cyber activities. Ultimately, their dedication to understanding the multifaceted nature of cyberspace ensures the success of capacity-building efforts and the safeguarding of national and international security interests.

The evolving dynamics of conflict in cyberspace are increasingly influenced by the growing recognition and acceptance of certain norms and rules. As digital interconnectedness expands, so does the urgency of developing and adhering to standards that ensure the security and stability of our online world. This chapter explores the key trends we can anticipate in cyberspace conflict for 2023 and beyond, based on recent developments in the acceptance of specific norms and rules, as well as real-world incidents disrupting these norms. We also delve into the investment needed for cyberspace capacity building to support these standards. By understanding what we need to protect the most, we can work towards a cyberspace that is resilient, secure, and characterized by cooperation rather than conflict.

Protecting the Public Core of the Internet

The recognition of the norm that the general integrity and availability of the public core of the internet should be safeguarded is gaining momentum. This is an encouraging trend, as it indicates a growing collective dedication to preserving the fundamental infrastructure that underlies the internet. A concrete illustration of the significance of this norm can be observed in the widespread disruption caused by the 2016 Dyn cyber attack. This distributed denial-of-service (DDoS) attack targeted the domain name system (DNS) services of Dyn, a pivotal component of the internet's infrastructure, and resulted in extensive outages for numerous popular websites. The increasing embrace of this norm signifies a commitment to preventing similar incidents in the future.

Furthermore, it is crucial to acknowledge and address the potential risks linked to the integration of 5G networks and the subsea cables ecosystem, particularly with the involvement of Chinese telecom giants like Huawei and ZTE. 5G networks hold the promise of transformative advancements in speed and connectivity, yet they also introduce new vulnerabilities. These networks will play an integral role in a broad spectrum of essential services and infrastructures, rendering them attractive targets for cyber attacks. Concerns have been raised about the potential exploitation of equipment from Huawei or ZTE by the Chinese government for espionage or the disruption of critical infrastructure in light of China's 2017 National Intelligence Law. This law essentially mandates Chinese entities and citizens to cooperate in state intelligence activities, heightening apprehensions that Huawei or ZTE might be coerced into embedding backdoors or other vulnerabilities into their equipment. Similarly, the subsea cables ecosystem, which constitutes the foundation of global communications by carrying the majority of the world's data across oceans, exposes potential vulnerabilities. Huawei Marine, formerly a subsidiary of Huawei, has participated in numerous submarine cable projects globally, giving rise to concerns that these undersea cables could also be exploited for espionage or sabotage. As we strive to safeguard the public core of the internet, it is imperative to prudently manage these risks. Striking a balance between potential security threats and the benefits of cost-effective technological advancements from companies like Huawei or ZTE is paramount.

Geopolitical Shifts and Undersea Cables

Recent major geopolitical developments, such as Russia's 2022 invasion of Ukraine, China's aggressive stance on unifying with Taiwan, and deteriorating US-China relations, have prompted countries to engage in physical security attacks on submarine cable systems. These attacks aim to disrupt cable operations and covertly intercept data flow for national security and economic espionage purposes. In a real-world incident that underscores these concerns, Norway's government reported that a submarine cable connecting its mainland to the Svalbard archipelago was severed on the night of January 7, 2022, which law enforcement investigators determined to be the result of "human impact.".[iv]

While state actors remain the primary threat due to their advanced expertise and capacity for strategic disruption, non-state actors also contribute to these disruptions, often targeting more easily repairable nearshore locations. An example of such actions includes a 2013 attempt by three divers to cut the SEA-ME-WE 4[v] submarine cable off the coast of Alexandria, Egypt.[vi] The complex landscape of undersea cable security calls for comprehensive measures to safeguard these critical communication pathways and mitigate the potential cascading effects of deliberate sabotage or accidental damage.

The geopolitical landscape shift caused by Russia's invasion of Ukraine and China's preparations for Taiwan's unification has reshaped the threat scenario for submarine cables. Russia, aligned with its hybrid warfare strategy, is the most probable direct threat, especially in the North Sea region. If China were to invade Taiwan, its already established capability for damaging cables connected to the island would escalate the danger to submarine cables in the immediate vicinity, propelled by its various maritime assets capable of accessing deep-sea cable locations.[vii]

Fostering Internet Security Initiatives and Investments to Mitigate Disruptions

In response to these geopolitical threats, anticipate a wave of initiatives that will strive to fortify the critical components of the internet, safeguarding it against physical security attacks and cyber threats. These initiatives encompass a multifaceted approach, combining reinforced cyber and physical security protocols, substantial investments in cutting-edge technology, and the strengthening of international collaboration between nations.

A notable aspect of this evolving landscape is the growing spirit of collaboration between nations. The realization that cyber threats are not confined by geographical boundaries has prompted unprecedented international cooperation. Countries are sharing intelligence, expertise, and best practices to create a collective defense against cyber adversaries. Forums for diplomatic negotiations and collaborative agreements are being established to ensure that responses to cyber incidents are swift, effective, and harmonized.

While these proactive measures may not entirely eliminate the risk of conflicts in cyberspace, they are expected to substantially diminish the potential for widespread disruptions to the internet's core functionalities. The goal is to create a secure and resilient digital environment that can withstand the challenges of a rapidly evolving threat landscape. As these initiatives gain momentum, a safer digital future becomes attainable, fostering trust, stability, and innovation in the global digital ecosystem.

Securing Electoral Infrastructure and Public Confidence

The increasing recognition of the norm to safeguard electoral infrastructure against cyber threats indicates a growing awareness of the potential for cyber interference in democratic processes. This trend is likely to result in comprehensive measures aimed at securing electoral systems, encompassing improved cybersecurity protocols for voting systems, heightened scrutiny of social media platforms, and enhanced digital literacy programs to assist the public in identifying and countering disinformation campaigns.

As recognition of the norm of safeguarding electoral infrastructure expands, there is an uptick in endeavors to protect electoral systems from cyber threats. For instance, following allegations of Russian interference in the 2016 US presidential elections, numerous countries have bolstered their defenses against analogous attacks. In the US, the Department of Homeland Security has classified election systems as critical infrastructure, and multiple steps have been taken to fortify the voting process against cyber threats. The 2022 US elections were no different, with an intensified focus on securing electoral processes and infrastructure against potential cyber threats, which will be elaborated upon in the subsequent section.

Ransomware Attacks and the 2022 US Elections

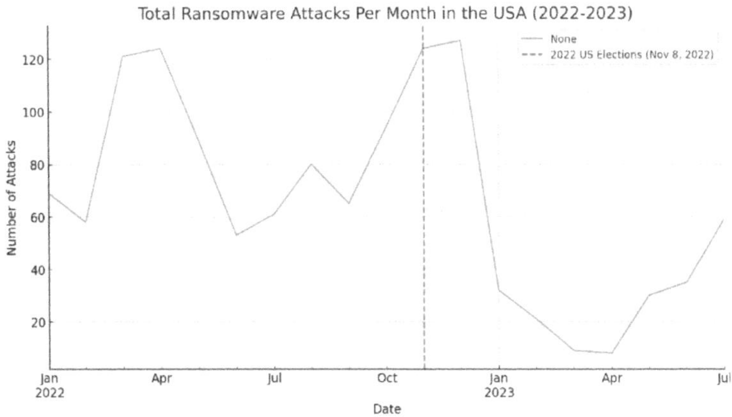

Figure 1: This graph pinpoints the 2022 US elections held on November 8, 2022. The red dashed line indicates the date of the elections, providing context to the spike in attacks around that time.

In today's digitally-driven world, cybersecurity assumes a pivotal role in ensuring the conduct of free and fair elections. This significance has been magnified due to the increasing reliance on digital platforms for various electoral functions, including voter registration, ballot casting, and vote tallying. The 2022 United States midterm elections, held on November 8, 2022, exemplified this trend, witnessing an intensified focus on securing the electoral machinery and critical infrastructure against potential cyber threats, including ransomware attacks.

The graph in Figure 1 illustrates the total ransomware attacks per month in the USA for 2022-2023[viii], demonstrating a notable upswing in attacks around November 2022, closely aligned with the timing of the 2022 US elections. This surge in ransomware attacks wasn't a random occurrence but is regarded with concern as a potential element of influence operations. Cyber adversaries might have strategically employed ransomware attacks to target not only the electoral systems but also vital state and local services, government bodies, political entities, and public utilities. The purpose behind these orchestrated attacks could have been to introduce confusion, undermine trust, and sow chaos, thus manipulating public sentiment and influencing voting behavior.

The synchronization of this increase in attacks with a pivotal democratic event that garners global attention, such as the US midterm elections, underscores the vulnerability of democratic practices in the face of sophisticated cyber threats. This underscores the necessity for a comprehensive and vigilant cybersecurity approach, encompassing transparency, international collaboration, and an unwavering commitment to preserving the integrity of democratic processes and institutions.

The Role of Non-State Actors

As recognition wanes for the norm that non-state actors ought not to engage in offensive cyber operations, we encounter an escalating threat from entities lying beyond the jurisdiction of national governments. This includes rogue hacktivist groups, criminal organizations, and state-sponsored cyber militias.

The diminishing acceptance of the norm that non-state actors should abstain from offensive cyber operations is a disconcerting trend. This decline is highlighted by several high-profile incidents involving non-state actors.

One such incident is the 2021 Colonial Pipeline ransomware attack. The Colonial Pipeline, a major fuel conduit in the United States, fell prey to a cybercriminal group known as DarkSide. The attack prompted the pipeline to halt its operations, causing significant disruption in the gasoline supply across the southeastern United States. The incident underscored the capability of non-state actors to profoundly disturb critical infrastructure and functioned as a clarion call for the necessity of enhanced security measures in safeguarding such vital infrastructures.

Furthermore, it's crucial to acknowledge the role of the private sector in countering these cyber threats. Many non-state actors, including hacktivist groups and cyber criminals, target private companies. Collaborative efforts between the private sector and other stakeholders are essential in addressing these challenges. Private companies possess technological expertise, real-time threat intelligence, and critical infrastructure. This collaboration can facilitate proactive defense, timely reporting of incidents, and the development of effective countermeasures.

In response to this trend, governments may need to allocate greater resources to counter these threats. This could encompass establishing dedicated cybersecurity units and implementing more stringent legislation. An example of this is the recent announcement by the U.S. Department of Justice regarding the formation of the National Security Cyber Section, or NatSec Cyber, within its National Security Division. This development, sanctioned by Congress, was prompted by findings from the Comprehensive Cyber Review in 2022. NatSec Cyber is designed to fortify the Justice Department's capacity to counter and respond to malicious cyber activity with regard to national security. The newly established section will amplify the Department's ability to prosecute nation-state threat actors, state-sponsored cybercriminals, and other cyber-enabled threats to national security with greater speed and on a larger scale.

This initiative underscores the acknowledgment that grappling with highly intricate cyber threats frequently demands substantial time and resources. As such, NatSec Cyber is positioned to function as an incubator, investing in the intricate investigative work required for early-stage cases. The establishment of NatSec Cyber builds upon recent triumphs in identifying, addressing, and neutralizing national security cyber threats. These successes encompass charging an alleged cybercriminal with ransomware attacks against U.S. critical infrastructure and disrupting the primary cyber espionage malware tool of the Russian government. Through initiatives such as NatSec Cyber, the Justice Department perpetuates its endeavors to preserve national security in the realm of cyberspace.

Ransomware Attacks and Non-State Actors

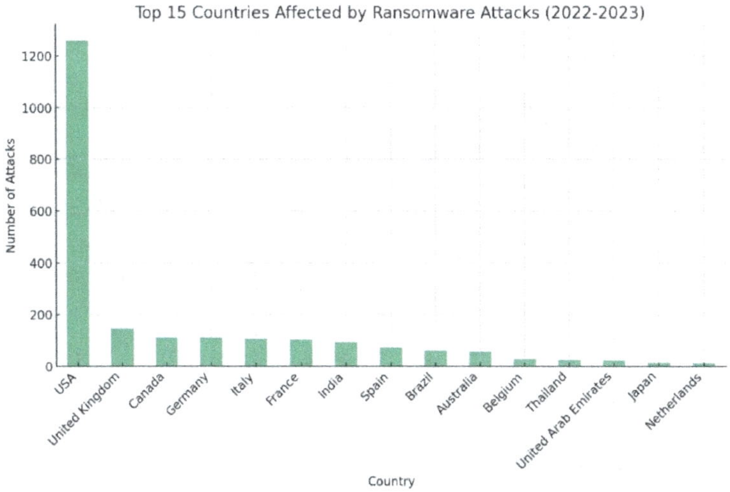

Figure 2: The bar chart above highlights the top 15 countries affected by ransomware attacks from 2022 to 2023. The USA is the most targeted country, followed by the UK, Canada, Germany, Italy, France, and other countries.

The graph above illustrates the top 15 countries affected by ransomware attacks from 2022 to 2023.[ix] It provides a clear view of the geographical distribution of these cyber threats, highlighting the nations that have faced the highest number of attacks. The USA stands out as the most targeted country, followed by other major economies and technologically advanced nations.

USA: The United States tops the list, experiencing the highest number of ransomware attacks. This emphasizes the country's position as a major target for cybercriminals.

UK: The United Kingdom follows as the second most affected country, reflecting its significance in the global economy and technology landscape.

Canada: Ranking third, Canada's presence on the list highlights its susceptibility to ransomware threats.

Germany: As a leading European nation, Germany's position in the top five underscores the importance of cybersecurity in the region.

Italy: Italy is also a notable target, ranking fourth in the number of ransomware attacks.

The remaining countries in the top 15, including France, India, Spain, Brazil, Australia, and others, underscore the widespread nature of ransomware threats, affecting nations across different continents and economic standings.

The prevalence of ransomware attacks across various countries, as depicted in the graph, underscores the global challenge posed by non-state actors. These actors, often operating in loosely affiliated groups or as independent cybercriminals, exploit vulnerabilities in cyberinfrastructure to launch ransomware attacks without direct state sponsorship or control. In countries heavily targeted by ransomware, these non-state actors can have a substantial impact on critical infrastructure, industries, and public services. They may act out of financial motives, ideological or political beliefs, or simply to create chaos and undermine confidence in digital systems. The diverse and often anonymous nature of these actors makes it challenging for governments and organizations to defend against their activities. The graph emphasizes the need for international cooperation, robust cybersecurity measures, and a comprehensive understanding of the complex landscape of non-state actors. By recognizing the global reach and persistent threat of ransomware attacks, nations can better coordinate efforts to detect, prevent, and respond to these malicious activities, safeguarding their citizens and critical systems.

Protecting State Critical Infrastructure

Undoubtedly, the 2016 Dyn cyber attack stands as a stark reminder of the imperative to safeguard the public core of the internet. This audacious attack, targeting the domain name system (DNS) services of Dyn, a pivotal component of the internet's infrastructure, triggered widespread disruptions, leaving a multitude of popular websites inaccessible. This incident vividly illustrates the vulnerability of the very backbone that supports our interconnected digital world. By exploiting the fragility of the DNS, cyber adversaries wielded the power to plunge a vast portion of the online realm into darkness. Such a brazen intrusion not only disrupted businesses and individuals but also exposed the potential to disrupt essential services, communication channels, and even democratic processes. In the aftermath of the Dyn cyber attack, the importance of protecting the public core of the internet assumes a heightened significance. As the reliance on digital interconnectedness continues to deepen, the imperative to shield the foundational infrastructure of the internet from malevolent forces becomes paramount, ensuring the sustained functionality, resilience, and security of the global digital landscape.

In parallel, the growing consensus surrounding the imperative to safeguard state critical infrastructure from cyber attacks is a positive stride forward. This heralds a future wherein critical services like power, water, and healthcare assume a diminished vulnerability to disruptive cyber assaults.

The increasing recognition of the norm to protect state critical infrastructure is heartening. A vivid illustration of the significance of this norm can be witnessed in the 2015 cyber attack on Ukraine's power grid, which plunged a substantial portion of the nation into darkness. This incident underscored the potential of cyber attacks to induce tangible real-world harm and disruption. In response to this looming threat, governments and private sector entities are investing in measures aimed at fortifying critical infrastructure. This encompasses the implementation of robust cybersecurity standards and the sharing of threat intelligence.

The embrace of this norm is poised to stimulate endeavors to augment the security of critical infrastructure. This is likely to encompass the enforcement of stringent cybersecurity standards, an escalated exchange of threat intelligence, and the establishment of dedicated cyber defense units within both government and industry. This collaborative approach acknowledges that the protection of state critical infrastructure is not the responsibility of governments alone but requires collective action involving various stakeholders to effectively counter the evolving landscape of cyber threats. The concerted efforts to safeguard both the public core of the internet and state critical infrastructure serve as crucial components in upholding the security and functionality of our interconnected digital world.

Ransomware Attacks and Critical Infrastructure

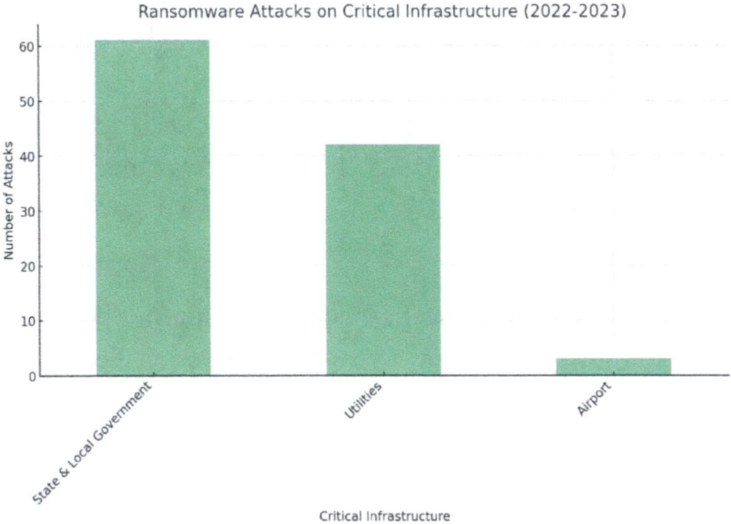

Figure 3: The graph above highlights ransomware attacks on critical infrastructure, specifically focusing on "State & Local Government," "Utilities," and "Airports" sectors from 2022 to 2023. The bars represent the number of ransomware attacks on these essential services, illustrating their susceptibility to cyber threats.

Safeguarding state critical infrastructure is of paramount importance, particularly in developing countries where such infrastructure may be more vulnerable to cyber threats. Sectors like State & Local Government, Public Utilities, and Airports form the bedrock of a nation's development and societal well-being. In developing countries, where resources may be limited, a ransomware attack on these essential services can have devastating effects, crippling the already fragile systems and leading to widespread disruptions.

The significance of protecting critical infrastructure in developing nations extends beyond maintaining service continuity. It's a matter of national resilience, economic stability, and public trust. Developing countries may lack the advanced technological defenses and expert manpower required to fend off sophisticated cyber threats, making them more susceptible to attacks that can hinder economic growth and social progress.

Efforts to protect critical infrastructure in developing countries must be tailored to the unique challenges and constraints they face. This includes cyber capacity building, investing in cybersecurity education, fostering public-private partnerships and international cooperation, and adopting international best practices. Implementing resilient systems that are both secure and adaptable to the local context is paramount.

In summary, safeguarding state critical infrastructure in developing countries is not merely a technical issue but a strategic imperative for national development. Ensuring the security and resilience of these vital sectors is foundational to achieving sustainable growth, social stability and enhancing the quality of life for citizens. The stakes are high, and the commitment to this endeavor must be unwavering, recognizing the critical role that infrastructure plays in shaping the future of developing nations.

The Adoption of Protective Measures

The growth in acceptance of rules regarding the protection of the internet's public core, the limitation of private sector hack-backs, and the protection of critical infrastructure is a pivotal development. This trend signifies a move towards a more regulated cyberspace, where states and non-state actors alike are held to account for their actions.

For instance, the Active Cyber Defence (ACD) program implemented by the UK's National Cyber Security Centre (NCSC) is a proactive government-led initiative designed to protect the country from high-volume commodity attacks that affect people's everyday lives. The ACD's approach is rooted in the belief that many cyber threats, even sophisticated ones, exploit basic vulnerabilities. By addressing these fundamental issues at scale, the NCSC aims to protect a vast number of users.

Similarly, the US Active Cyber Defense Certainty Act is a piece of legislation that clarifies the legalities where the conduct constituting an offense involves a response to, or defense against, a cyber intrusion. This legislation created clearer boundaries for both public and private sector entities, including the establishment of attribution for criminal activity, the disruption of unauthorized activity against the defender's own network, and the monitoring of the behavior of an attacker to assist in developing future intrusion prevention or cyber defense techniques.[x]

The Fight Against Ransomware

The spike in ransomware attacks during the 2022 US elections, discussed earlier, underscores the multifaceted challenges of securing democratic processes in a digital age. Key protective countermeasures and controls may include:

• Holistic Security Measures: Safeguarding the cybersecurity of elections necessitates an all-encompassing strategy. This approach must extend beyond the protection of voting systems to include public utilities, airports, and other vital infrastructure that the public relies on. The objective is to prevent any influence on public opinion and confidence in the current administration, factors that can ultimately sway voting decisions.

• Threat Intelligence and Collaboration: Proactive monitoring, threat intelligence sharing, and collaboration among federal, state, local authorities, and the private sector are vital for early detection and mitigation of ransomware attacks.

• Public Awareness and Education: Educating voters, election officials, and other stakeholders about potential cyber threats, including ransomware, helps build resilience and promotes responsible digital behavior.

• Legal and Regulatory Frameworks: Developing and enforcing robust legal and regulatory frameworks can deter cybercriminal activities, facilitate prosecution, and support international cooperation.

The increase in ransomware attacks during the 2022 US elections serves as a stark reminder of the evolving cyber threat landscape. As democratic processes continue to embrace digital technologies, a concerted effort from governments, industry, academia, and civil society is essential to safeguard the integrity, transparency, and inclusiveness of elections.

The experience of the 2022 US elections offers valuable insights and lessons that can inform future electoral cybersecurity strategies, not only in the United States but globally. By recognizing the interplay between political events and cyber threats, societies can better anticipate, prepare for, and respond to the dynamic challenges of the digital era.

Whole of Government (WoG) Approach

The White House's National Cybersecurity Strategy Implementation Plan (NCSIP), released this year, is a prime example of these protective measures. Among other things, it identifies ransomware as a major concern throughout the country and a significant national security threat. The Defense Department (DOD) is a key player in this strategy, focusing on countering, disrupting, and deterring destabilizing cyber behavior while preserving U.S. superiority in cyberspace. [xi]

Additionally, the U.S. Justice Department's Whole-of-Government (WoG) approach to combating cyber threats by integrating the team responsible for investigating criminal cases related to cryptocurrency into its cybercrime division is a significant step in the right direction. This integration consolidates the capabilities required for investigating the complete life cycle of ransomware attacks, spanning from the initial breach to the payment of ransomware.[xii]

The strong correlation between ransomware and cryptocurrency has been recognized for an extended period. Some experts assert that the proliferation of ransomware can be largely attributed to the expansion of cryptocurrencies such as Bitcoin, Ethereum, and Monero.

In a report issued last year, the U.S. Senate's Committee on Homeland Security and Governmental Affairs emphasized that "the use of cryptocurrencies has further facilitated ransomware attacks, primarily due to the decentralized and distributed nature of cryptocurrency, which enables malicious actors to obscure transactions and make them more difficult to trace." [xiii]

Embracing the UK's 'Early Warning' Defense

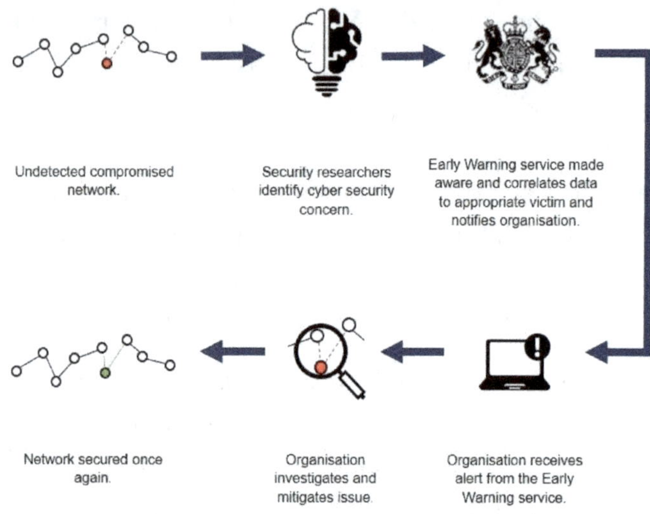

Figure 4: Process flow for the UK Early Warning service

Across the Atlantic, the increasing sophistication and frequency of ransomware attacks are prompting nations to take proactive cybersecurity measures. These measures are becoming essential for both public and private organizations worldwide.

The UK government has exemplified a proactive approach in this arena. They've introduced a commendable system called "Early Warning," overseen by the National Cyber Security Centre (NCSC), an extension of GCHQ. This innovative system is crafted to preemptively notify organizations about looming cyber threats before they burgeon into significant incidents.[xiv]

A hallmark of Early Warning is its ability to monitor a vast array of information feeds, some of which are exclusive to the system. By correlating millions of daily events, it pinpoints potential threats tailored to specific organizations. The system categorizes its alerts into daily threat notifications and weekly vulnerability bulletins, which provide insights into potential system breaches, malicious network activities, and vulnerabilities within network services. Such timely notifications equip organizations to swiftly address and neutralize identified risks.

A testament to its efficacy is an incident involving a critical infrastructure owner in the UK. Utilizing Early Warning, they were swiftly alerted to a concealed web shell associated with the 2021 Exchange vulnerabilities. This crucial intel allowed the organization to thwart a cyber attack that might have otherwise gone unnoticed, thereby averting a potentially massive data breach.

Considering the tangible benefits and success narratives linked with Early Warning, there's a pressing need for governments globally to implement systems with similar capabilities. Adopting such systems not only bolsters an organization's defensive mechanisms against emerging threats but also instills renewed confidence in the integrity of their network security. In a world where cyber adversaries are perpetually refining their strategies, it's pivotal for governments to remain ahead of the curve, making tools like Early Warning an indispensable asset in their cybersecurity arsenal.

In summary, the recent adoption of these cutting-edge measures and legislations marks a promising step forward in the realm of cyberspace security. Their primary aim is to curtail the severity and frequency of cyber conflicts, which have been on the rise globally, threatening not only individual entities but also national securities.

For these measures to be effective, it is imperative to establish robust enforcement mechanisms. This means creating dedicated agencies or task forces equipped with the necessary tools and expertise to monitor, identify, and respond to cyber attacks promptly. These bodies will play a critical role in ensuring that all entities, foreign or domestic, adhere to the set guidelines and that any breaches are met with appropriate consequences.

Furthermore, ambiguity in cyberspace can often be a catalyst for unintentional conflicts or misinterpretations. Hence, clear definitions of what constitutes acceptable and unacceptable behavior in the digital domain are paramount. This clarity will provide a framework for entities to operate within and will reduce the chances of inadvertent transgressions.

Lastly, the intricate nature of cyberspace means no single entity can navigate its challenges alone. Therefore, a commitment to transparency and cooperation is vital. All involved parties, be they nations, organizations, or corporations, must actively share information, best practices, and threat intelligence. Joint training exercises, shared research initiatives, and collaborative response strategies can foster a sense of unity and mutual trust. By doing so, not only can we anticipate and counter threats more effectively, but we can also create an environment where actors think twice before engaging in malicious cyber activities.

In essence, while the new measures and legislations lay a strong foundation for a safer cyberspace, their success hinges on the collective will, cooperation, and dedication of all stakeholders involved.

Cyber Capacity Building Investment Needs

Cyberspace Capacity Building Investment is a critical element in the current international order, given the increasing importance of cybersecurity in maintaining global stability. As our reliance on digital technologies grows, so does the threat of cyber attacks that could disrupt not only individual nations but the interconnected global community. The investment in building cyber capacities – which includes strengthening cyber defenses, enhancing the skills and knowledge of cyber professionals, and improving incident response capabilities – is thus essential. By promoting cooperation and shared learning, such investments can help to level the playing field, providing even those nations with less developed digital infrastructures a fighting chance against increasingly sophisticated cyber threats. In the context of the current international order, such capacity building is not just a matter of national security but a crucial component of global resilience.

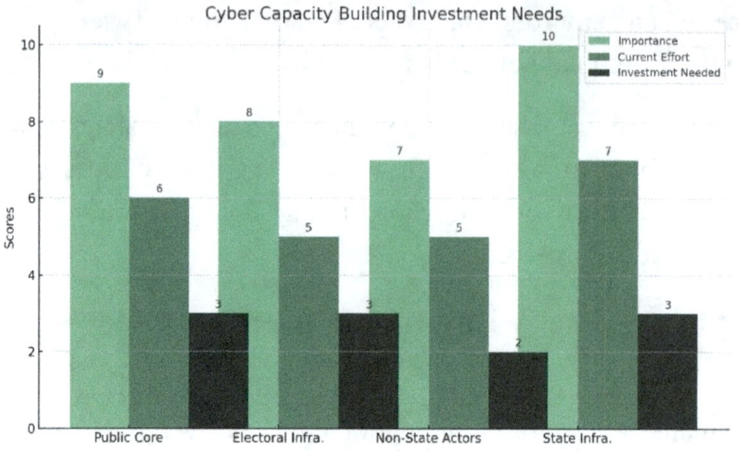

The graph above illustrates estimates of cyberspace capacity-building investment across different areas from 2023 to 2024. The areas considered are:

Protection of the public core of the internet.

Protection of electoral infrastructure.

Regulation of non-state actors.

Protection of state critical infrastructure.

We will use a qualitative approach to rate the four areas discussed earlier on a scale from 1 to 10 based on their perceived importance and the current level of effort. We based this assessment on some of the real-world incidents and efforts we observed in each area.

Protection of the public core of the Internet: Importance = 9, Current Effort = 6.

Protection of Electoral Infrastructure: Importance = 8, Current Effort = 5.

Regulation of Non-State Actors: Importance = 7, Current Effort = 5.

Protection of State Critical Infrastructure: Importance = 10, Current Effort = 7.

The "gap" between importance and current effort could be used as a measure of where more investment is needed.

As you can see, it is estimated that there will be an overall increase in cyber investments across all areas from 2023 to 2024. The most significant increase is projected for 'State Critical Infrastructure,' followed by 'Public Core of Internet,' 'Electoral Infrastructure,' and 'Regulation of Non-State Actors.'

These estimations align with the trends discussed earlier, where emphasis is placed on protecting the internet's core, safeguarding electoral systems, and ensuring the security of critical state infrastructure. Regulation of non-state actors also receives significant investment, highlighting the importance of this aspect in maintaining a secure cyberspace.

Conclusion

In the final analysis, while the trends identified in this chapter paint a promising picture for the future of conflict in cyberspace, they are not without challenges. Achieving these goals will require substantial effort, investment, and collaboration on a global scale, especially in cyberspace security cooperation.

The trends outlined above indicate a changing landscape in cyberspace conflict. While the acceptance of these norms and rules is a promising development, the implementation will require global cooperation and concerted effort. By continuously working towards these norms and rules, we can build a more resilient, secure, and cooperative cyberspace.

Chapter 2:

Assessing the Trends of Conflict in Cyberspace: A Glimpse into 2023 and Beyond

Introduction

As we venture deeper into the digital age, the landscape of conflict in cyberspace continues to evolve. Our comprehension of this landscape is influenced by several pivotal indicators: the intentions of states, perceptions of interstate tensions, the capacity for cyber warfare, and the activities unfolding within the realm of cyberspace. In this chapter, we will evaluate these factors and delve into their implications for the future of conflict in cyberspace.[xv]

Intentions: A Push for Transparency in Offensive Cyber Capabilities

The diminishing threat associated with states disclosing their offensive cyber capabilities signifies an emerging trend toward transparency. This is a positive development as increased transparency can help avert misunderstandings that could potentially lead to unnecessary escalation. An exemplary instance of this shift can be observed in the US Department of Defense's 2018 Cyber Strategy, which openly discusses the nation's offensive cyber capabilities to a greater extent than previous iterations.

Another manifestation of this trend is evident in the joint advisories of the United States' Cybersecurity and Infrastructure Security Agency (CISA) and the Federal Bureau of Investigation (FBI) in 2022. These advisories offer insights into the cyber threats posed by foreign state-sponsored actors, providing a degree of transparency regarding the nature of these threats and the measures being taken to counter them.

Nonetheless, it is crucial to emphasize that transparency alone does not guarantee stability and must be coupled with responsible behavior and adherence to agreed-upon norms.

Perceptions: Escalating Interstate Tensions in Cyberspace

The escalating concern surrounding perceptions of heightened interstate tensions in cyberspace has emerged as a significant global issue, warranting careful attention and strategic foresight. This trend underscores an increasing sense of vulnerability felt by nations, potentially leading to a worrisome cyber arms race. To shed light on this phenomenon, a compelling real-world case is the ongoing cyber confrontation between the United States and China. This scenario stands as a compelling example of how heightened political tension, coupled with responsive actions, can rapidly trigger a perilous cycle of escalation within the digital realm.

The implications of such escalations extend beyond the virtual world and have tangible effects on national security, diplomatic relations, and global stability. This mounting apprehension stems from the realization that the potential consequences of cyber conflict are no longer confined to bits and bytes but have real-world impacts that can disrupt critical infrastructure, compromise sensitive information, and even spark conflicts with physical consequences.

The United States' decisions to prioritize the protection of its national security interests in cyberspace are fundamentally grounded in the need to safeguard its economic prosperity, technological advantage, and critical infrastructure. The actions taken to strengthen cybersecurity defenses, develop response capabilities, and engage in diplomatic dialogues regarding responsible behavior in cyberspace are not only prudent but essential to maintaining a secure digital landscape. By actively responding to cyber threats while also advocating for international norms and cooperation, the United States aims to mitigate the escalation of tensions and create a more stable environment in cyberspace.

The significance of managing interstate tensions is further underscored by the war between Russia and Ukraine. In 2022, this war bore witness to a significant upsurge in cyber attacks, coupled with spillover attacks that reverberated not only within Ukraine but also across the globe.[xvi] Russian hackers wreaked havoc as their actions extended beyond Ukrainian borders, illustrating the alarming potential of cyber conflicts to disrupt international stability and security. These instances of cyber aggression accentuate the necessity of preemptive and measured actions to prevent further escalation.

In conclusion, the growing threat posed by perceptions of escalating interstate tensions in cyberspace demands a proactive and measured response from the international community. The examples of the United States' engagement with China, as well as the tensions between Russia and Ukraine, underscore the significance of managing these tensions to avert potential escalation in the digital domain. By engaging in robust cybersecurity measures, advocating for international norms, and fostering diplomatic dialogue, the United States aims to not only protect its own national security but also contribute to a safer and more secure global cyber landscape.

Capacity: Cyber Military Spending and National Cybersecurity

Divergent trends in cyber military spending and national cybersecurity and counter-cybercrime expenditures unveil a potential imbalance between offensive and defensive capacities within the realm of cyberspace. The allocation of resources in this context serves as a critical indicator of a nation's priorities and strategic posture in the digital age. In 2022, a series of intriguing developments shed light on these trends, underlining the intricacies shaping global cyber power dynamics.

China, in its bid to solidify its standing as a digital superpower, demonstrated a clear commitment to amplifying its military capabilities in cyberspace. Evidenced by a significant augmentation in its military budget, China directed considerable funds towards the advancement of its cyber capabilities. This upsurge in spending reflects the nation's unwavering pursuit of technological superiority, seeking to establish its dominance not just within traditional military domains but also in the increasingly influential cyber domain.

Conversely, other nations, such as Australia and Canada, opted for a distinct approach in 2022, signaling a pronounced emphasis on fortifying their defensive cyber capabilities. These countries chose to allocate more substantial portions of their budgets towards enhancing cybersecurity measures and countering cybercrime. This strategic direction showcases a commitment to safeguarding critical infrastructure, sensitive data, and national interests from the ever-growing spectrum of cyber threats.

However, an intricate challenge emerges when the growth in offensive cyber capabilities outpaces the augmentation of defensive measures. This potential disparity in cyber spending could give rise to a lopsided power balance within the digital arena. A scenario where offensive capabilities overshadow defensive preparedness not only escalates the risk of state-sponsored cyber conflicts but also creates an environment ripe for non-state actors and cybercriminals to exploit vulnerabilities.

The delicate equilibrium between offensive and defensive cyber capacities is crucial for maintaining stability and minimizing the likelihood of cyber conflicts. Ensuring parity between the two is pivotal to prevent any single entity from wielding disproportionate influence within the virtual realm. Striking the right balance entails not just investing in the tools of cyber offense but also in bolstering cybersecurity, developing response strategies, and fostering international cooperation to establish norms of responsible behavior.

In conclusion, the divergent trends in cyber military spending and national cybersecurity efforts underscore the multifaceted landscape of contemporary geopolitics. These trends illustrate the varying strategies nations adopt to navigate the evolving challenges of the digital age. Achieving equilibrium between offensive and defensive capabilities is imperative for cultivating a secure and stable cyberspace, where the potential for conflicts is mitigated and cooperation thrives.

Activity: Cyber-Enabled Espionage, Attacks, and Disinformation Campaigns

The evolving landscape of cyber activities portrays a complex and multifaceted panorama. As the digital world becomes increasingly intertwined with global affairs, a deeper analysis of recent trends in the cyber domain reveals a mixture of consistent patterns and disruptive incidents that shape the contemporary state of cybersecurity.

Among the persistent trends is the undeniable reality of cyber-enabled espionage, which continues to pose a considerable threat on the international stage. State-led cyber espionage remains a prevalent concern, and indications suggest that these activities are likely to persist at their current pace. This form of cyber operation, often characterized by its covert nature, aims to infiltrate and compromise sensitive systems to glean valuable information for intelligence purposes. Such persistent threats hint at the enduring nature of espionage in the digital era.

In the year 2022, the global cybersecurity landscape experienced a significant surge in activity, adding another layer of complexity to the ongoing narrative. One noteworthy example that showcases the heightened level of cyber activity is the Microsoft Exchange Servers breach by Chinese state-sponsored hackers who were implicated in exploiting vulnerabilities within what is considered one of the most widely used email platforms in the world. This campaign of cyber intrusion was alleged to have resulted in the theft of sensitive data from high-profile targets in the United States and Europe.

The Microsoft Exchange Servers attack epitomizes the sophistication and audacity of state-sponsored cyber actors, who consistently seek to capitalize on vulnerabilities for intelligence and potentially disruptive purposes. Such instances underscore the gravity of the cybersecurity challenges faced by governments, organizations, and individuals worldwide. The far-reaching consequences of these cyber intrusions emphasize the urgent need for robust defense mechanisms, international cooperation, and stringent cybersecurity protocols.[xvii]

On the flip side, a contrasting trend emerged as the threat level associated with cyber-enabled attacks and disinformation campaigns continued to escalate, pointing to a notable increase in these malicious activities. This evolution in the digital landscape raised concerns about the efficacy of defensive measures and the potential for broader societal impacts. Incidents that unfolded over recent years provided poignant examples of the extent to which these activities could influence global events and disrupt the fabric of modern societies.

The 2020 SolarWinds hack stood as a chilling case in point, attributed to sophisticated Russian state actors. This cyber attack reverberated across government agencies and major corporations, underscoring the audacity of such operations. The incident exposed vulnerabilities in software supply chains, revealing the potential for a single breach to cascade into widespread compromise. The key concern lingered that the same access that had given the Russians the ability to steal data could have also allowed them to alter or destroy it.[xviii]

Similarly, the manipulation of information in the 2016 U.S. Presidential elections unveiled the dark underbelly of disinformation campaigns. The pervasive use of false narratives and misleading content demonstrated how such tactics could influence public sentiment and decision-making processes, impacting the foundation of democratic systems.

Fast-forwarding to 2022, the trend persisted and even intensified. The ransomware attack on Ireland's Health Service Executive served as a stark reminder of the real-world consequences of cyber-enabled attacks. The disruption of healthcare services underscored the vulnerabilities of critical infrastructure to cyber intrusions, with potentially life-threatening ramifications.

Simultaneously, the pattern of disinformation continued to thrive. The campaigns surrounding COVID-19 and vaccination efforts spotlighted the extent of the challenge posed by information warfare. The spread of misleading or false information could erode trust in public health measures, hinder efforts to combat the pandemic and create divisions within societies.

The multifaceted nature of these trends underscored the need for a comprehensive approach to cybersecurity and information integrity. It was no longer solely a matter of protecting data; it was about safeguarding the very foundations of societies. As cyber-attacks and disinformation campaigns became more intricate and impactful, a proactive stance was imperative. This included bolstering defensive measures, enhancing international collaboration, and cultivating media literacy to empower individuals against the manipulation of information.

In essence, the surge in cyber-enabled attacks and disinformation campaigns reflected the evolving landscape of global conflicts, where the frontlines were not marked by physical borders but by bits and bytes. Navigating this landscape necessitated resilience, adaptability, and a collective effort to fortify digital societies against the ever-shifting tide of cyber threats and information manipulation.

Global Ransomware Attacks in 2022-2023

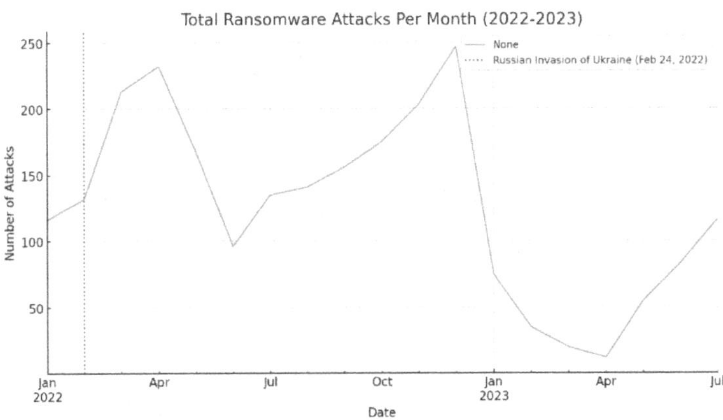

Figure 5: This graph highlights the date of the Russian invasion of Ukraine on February 24, 2022. The blue dashed line represents this significant geopolitical event, offering insight into the fluctuation in ransomware attacks during that period.

The graph displaying total monthly ransomware attacks for 2022-2023, shown above, provides significant insights into the cyber threat landscape.[xix] It clearly illustrates the surge in cyber-enabled attacks following the Russian invasion of Ukraine on February 24, 2022. The blue dotted line denotes this pivotal geopolitical event, which appears to coincide with a spike in ransomware activity. The post-invasion increase in ransomware attacks suggests a potential strategic exploitation of global turmoil and heightened tensions by cybercriminals, including potentially state-affiliated actors. These attacks, targeting various sectors and regions, might have aimed to capitalize on vulnerabilities, sow discord, or achieve political or financial gains. The correlation between the invasion date and the rise in ransomware attacks underscores the intricate connection between geopolitical dynamics and cyber threats, highlighting the imperative need for vigilant and coordinated cybersecurity efforts during times of international crisis.

Visualizing the Trends: A Comparative Analysis

To better understand the changing landscape of conflict in cyberspace, let's consider the following graph:

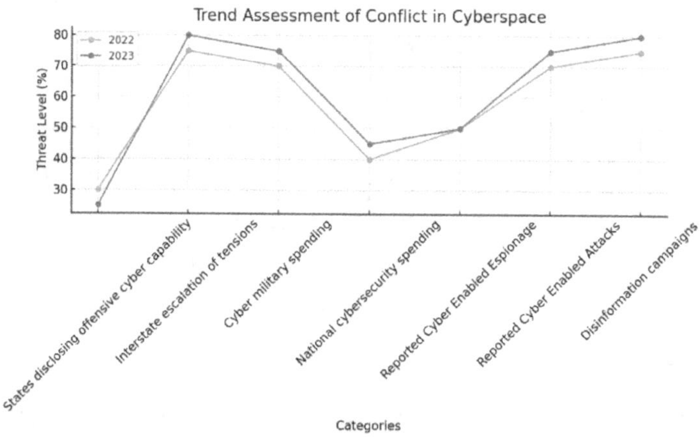

Figure 6: Trend Assessment of Conflict in Cyberspace

In this graph, the y-axis represents the threat level for each category, while the x-axis lists the categories under evaluation. The 2022 line serves as the baseline for each category, and the

2023 line projects the anticipated threat level for each category in 2023.

As evident from the graph, the threat level for most categories is expected to rise from 2022 to 2023, except for "States disclosing offensive cyber capability," which is anticipated to decrease. The threat level for "Reported Cyber-Enabled Espionage" is projected to remain stable. These trends underscore the evolving nature of conflict in cyberspace, characterized by increased transparency but also escalating tensions, the potential for a cyber arms race, and a rise in cyber attacks and information warfare.

Forecasting Ransomware Attacks for 2023-2024

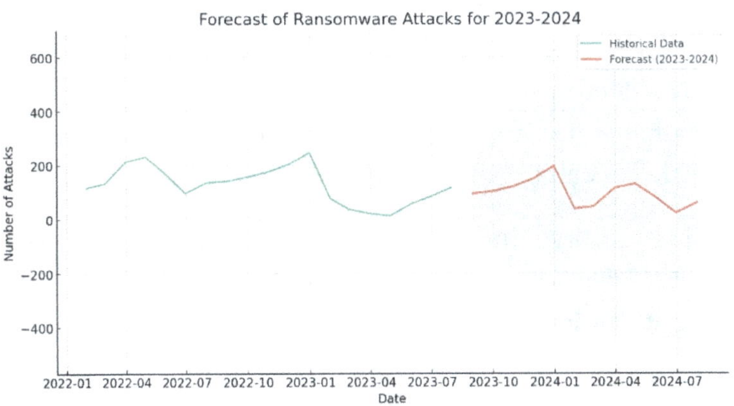

Figure 7: The forecast plot above illustrates the predicted trend of ransomware attacks for 2023-2024. This forecast, based on historical data from 2022 to 2023, provides insights into the expected number of ransomware attacks in the coming year.

In our endeavor to predict ransomware attacks for the years 2023 and 2024, we employ the advanced SARIMAX model

(Seasonal AutoRegressive Integrated Moving Average with eXogenous variables), a sophisticated technique for time series forecasting. The plot presented above provides a glimpse into the projected ransomware attack trends for 2024, meticulously derived from historical data spanning 2022 to 2023.[xx] The forecasted trend is depicted by the crimson line, while the enveloping azure-shaded region delineates the corresponding confidence interval. The plot underscores the anticipated undulation of ransomware attacks, a manifestation of their inherent seasonality (e.g., the 2024 United States elections) and the fluid nature of cyber threats. This dynamic trend intimates that significant geopolitical, economic, or societal events might trigger fluctuations in the frequency and intensity of such attacks. Consequently, there exists a paramount need for unwavering vigilance and adaptable security measures. This forecast stands as an invaluable instrument for premeditating forthcoming patterns and devising efficacious cybersecurity strategies to curtail potential hazards.

The upsurge in ransomware attacks subsequent to the Ukraine War, involving both state and non-state entities, spotlights an intricate and evolving landscape of threats. The projection for 2024 corroborates the persistence of this trend, thereby accentuating the urgency for astute cybersecurity measures, international synergy, and strategic investments. Governments, industries, and organizations must grasp the interconnected fabric of cyber threats, laboring collectively to ameliorate risks and bolster resilience. The insights gleaned from this analysis can furnish blueprints for policies, strategies, and decisive actions aimed at confronting the ransomware conundrum and its Allied cyber perils within an ever-fluctuating global milieu.

Conclusion

In summation, as we cast our gaze towards the horizon of 2023 and beyond, these trends portend an environment of cyberspace growing progressively intricate and volatile. While encouraging strides are discernible, such as heightened transparency in nations' cyber capabilities, the mounting tensions, escalating offensive potential, and the burgeoning deluge of cyber incursions and disinformation campaigns usher in substantial trials. Navigating these trials mandates united international endeavors, including the formulation and enforcement of mutually agreed norms of conduct, confidence-fostering measures, and cooperative security pacts. Armed with comprehension of these trends, we stand poised to navigate the future contours of cyber conflict adeptly.

Chapter 3:

Navigating Hybrid Conflict: Strategies for Cyberspace Security Cooperation

Introduction

Understanding the current landscape of hybrid threats is crucial for effective cyberspace security cooperation. Hybrid conflict, with its blend of conventional and unconventional methods of warfare, has become a defining feature of the global security environment. This type of conflict includes not just traditional military engagement but also economic coercion, disinformation campaigns, political interference, and cyber attacks on critical infrastructure. In this complex landscape, cyberspace has emerged as a key battleground.

State and non-state actors alike exploit the digital domain to carry out disruptive activities, often blurring the lines between peacetime and war. As these threats grow in scale and sophistication, it is crucial that nations cooperate in enhancing their defensive capacities, sharing intelligence, and establishing norms for responsible behavior in cyberspace. This collective approach is vital in mitigating the risks of hybrid threats and ensuring a stable and secure cyberspace. This chapter delves into key trends in hybrid conflict and offers an assessment for 2023 and the foreseeable future. [xxi]

Increasing Perception and Use of Hybrid Warfare

There is a noticeable upward trend in how states perceive hybrid conflict as a threat to their national security. This trend suggests that countries are becoming increasingly aware of and concerned about the dangers posed by hybrid warfare. Moreover, there is a growing inclination among states to incorporate hybrid methods into their defense strategies. This inclination could signify a broader acceptance and adoption of hybrid warfare tactics within defense strategies.

The escalating recognition of hybrid conflict as a national security threat indicates that countries are not only gaining a deeper understanding of the perils associated with hybrid warfare but are also actively seeking ways to counter these threats. This heightened awareness is evident in policy documents like the US National Security Strategy of 2017 and 2022, which openly acknowledge the risks posed by hybrid warfare. Furthermore, the fact that states are increasingly considering the use of hybrid methods as part of their defense strategies may indicate a shift toward a more adaptable and multifaceted approach to national defense.

For example, countries such as Russia and China have gained notoriety for their application of hybrid warfare tactics. These strategies often combine elements of conventional warfare, cyber attacks, information warfare, and economic tools to achieve strategic objectives, all while avoiding outright war. These countries employ these tactics to exploit vulnerabilities in their rivals, disrupt alliances, and shape global narratives in their favor.

In response to this evolving threat landscape, nations worldwide are compelled to develop more comprehensive and flexible defense strategies capable of effectively addressing the multifaceted nature of hybrid warfare. This includes strengthening cyber defenses, enhancing information security, investing in cutting-edge technology, and bolstering economic resilience. It also necessitates robust international cooperation and intelligence sharing, as hybrid threats frequently transcend national borders.

Therefore, as hybrid warfare continues to redefine the global security environment, nations must continue to adapt their defense strategies to keep pace. Recognizing and understanding the growing trend in states' perception of hybrid conflict, along with the corresponding shift in defense strategies, constitutes a critical first step in this ongoing process.

Growing Capability to Engage in Hybrid Conflict

The capability of nations to both participate in and counter hybrid conflicts is on the rise. This trend indicates that countries are actively investing in the capacity to conduct hybrid operations or defend against them. This is readily apparent in the ongoing military modernization efforts of many nations, where elements of hybrid warfare are increasingly integrated. Notably, countries like China and Russia are incorporating cyber and information warfare capabilities into their military strategies.

This growing state's capacity to engage in hybrid conflict underscores the evolving nature of 21st-century global security challenges. Hybrid warfare, characterized by a fusion of traditional and unconventional tactics, necessitates a multifaceted and adaptable response. Consequently, nations are making substantial investments in various capabilities, spanning from cyber defense and information warfare to economic coercion and political influence operations. The objective is not merely to match potential threats but to proactively anticipate and counter them.

In the cases of China and Russia, these endeavors are part of a broader strategy aimed at asserting their influence on the global stage. By integrating cyber and information warfare capabilities into their military strategies, they gain the ability to project power beyond their borders, manipulate narratives in their favor, and exploit vulnerabilities in adversaries' critical infrastructure and information systems. These capabilities enable them to conduct operations that can disrupt, degrade, or deny an adversary's effectiveness in the information environment.

Simultaneously, the inclusion of hybrid tactics within military strategies reflects an understanding that the future battlefield is as much digital as it is physical. Cyber attacks, disinformation campaigns, and other forms of information warfare can achieve strategic objectives without the need for conventional military force. They have the potential to sow discord, erode trust, disrupt economies, and undermine democratic processes.

In response, nations are not only bolstering their offensive capabilities but also investing in defensive measures to safeguard critical infrastructure, digital networks, and societal cohesion from hybrid threats. This comprehensive approach involves enhancing cybersecurity, infusing resilience into information systems, promoting digital literacy and fortifying institutions to withstand political interference.

Nevertheless, the increasing capacity of states to engage in and respond to hybrid conflict also raises crucial questions about the rules of engagement in this new domain of warfare, the balance between security and privacy in the digital age, and the potential for escalation and unintended consequences. As nations navigate this intricate and rapidly evolving landscape, international cooperation and dialogue will be paramount in establishing norms and preventing conflicts.

Rising Military Activity

The use of proxies by state actors in third-party military conflicts, military exercises near borders, and aerial and maritime intrusions are all showing an increasing trend. This highlights the growing complexity of military conflicts and the broadening scope of activities that can be considered part of hybrid warfare.

For instance, Russia's deployment of mercenary forces, such as the Wagner Group, in the Ukraine war and Syria serve as examples of the use of proxies.

Furthermore, over the past decade, Russia's annual strategic military exercises (KAVKAZ, ZAPAD, VOSTOK, and TSENTR) have demonstrated a noticeable increase in scale and suggest a geographical expansion, covering various strategic directions, including the Caucasus, West, East, and Center. This could indicate an intention to maintain readiness on multiple fronts and in diverse environments. If this trend continues, future exercises might encompass even more varied terrains or involve operations in multiple strategic directions simultaneously.

As warfare continues to evolve, exercises may increasingly integrate operations across multiple domains, including cyber, space, and electronic warfare. These exercises could also involve a larger number of or more active roles for Allies and partners, signaling Russia's intent to strengthen military ties and cooperation with other countries, such as China or Belarus.

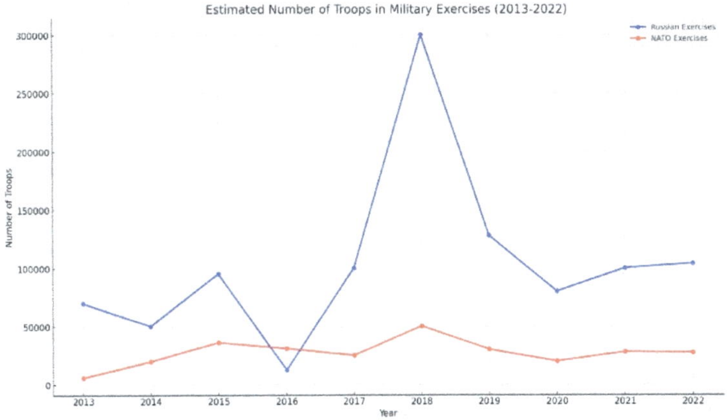

Figure 8: Comparative Scale of Major Military Exercises: Russia vs. NATO (2013-2022)

This graph illustrates the observed trend in Russia's annual strategic exercises compared to NATO exercises from 2013 to 2022, leading up to the Ukraine war. The y-axis represents the number of troops, while the x-axis represents the years.[xxii]

Russia: The graph shows that Russia has generally been conducting military exercises on a larger scale compared to NATO during this period. The peak was observed in 2018, when Russia reportedly held its largest-ever military exercise, "Vostok-2018," with around 300,000 troops.

NATO: NATO's exercises, as visualized, tend to be more consistent in scale, with a notable peak in 2018, corresponding to the "Trident Juncture" exercise, which involved about 50,000 troops.

In another region of global contention, China has been regularly conducting military maneuvers with fellow Indo-Pacific nations to bolster its security presence in the area. A notable instance of this occurred when China initiated a military drill involving various ASEAN countries, conspicuously excluding the Philippines. The Philippines had previously filed a complaint with the Permanent Court of Arbitration in The Hague, expressing their objections to China's activities.

In response to a demonstration of naval power by the U.S. Navy under Freedom of Navigation Operations (FONOPs) in the same area in October 2019, China conducted its own military exercise to emphasize its control over the South China Sea.

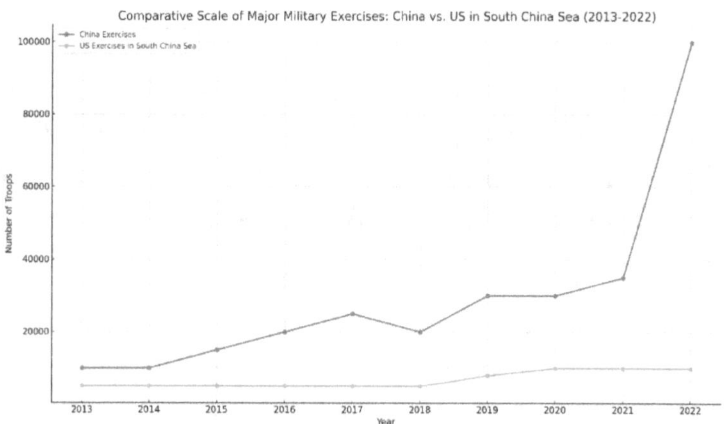

Figure 9: Comparative Scale of Major Military Exercises: China vs. U.S. in the South China Sea (2013-2022)

This graph provides a visual representation of the estimated number of troops involved in major military exercises conducted by China and the U.S. in the South China Sea from 2013 to 2022.[xxiii]

China: The graph shows a consistent increase in the scale of China's military exercises over the years, showcasing the nation's focus on bolstering its military capabilities and presence, particularly in the South China Sea. The gradual uptick in troop involvement reaches its height in 2021, reflecting China's growing assertiveness in regional matters.

U.S. in the South China Sea: The U.S., on the other hand, has maintained a relatively consistent presence in the South China Sea over the years, as seen by the steady troop numbers. There's a noticeable increase in 2019 and onward, which can be attributed to the U.S.'s intentions to counterbalance China's growing influence and to ensure freedom of navigation in the contested waters.

Political Interference on the Rise

There is a discernible increase in external interference in domestic politics, indicating that states are progressively employing hybrid warfare tactics to influence political outcomes in other countries.

The ascent of digital technologies and social media has fueled a growing trend of external meddling in domestic politics, underscoring a heightened reliance on hybrid warfare strategies to shape foreign political landscapes. These tactics, which merge conventional and unconventional methods, are becoming more intricate and widespread.

One of the most prominent instances of this phenomenon was the alleged Russian interference in the 2016 US presidential election. However, this is far from an isolated occurrence. The issue has evolved into a global concern, with numerous reports of foreign interference emerging from various regions worldwide.

In Europe, allegations of Russian interference surfaced in connection with the Brexit referendum in the UK in 2016, as well as in various national elections across EU member states. European democracies have grappled with cyber attacks, disinformation campaigns, and other covert methods of influence aimed at sowing discord and undermining democratic processes.

Across the Atlantic, countries in Latin America, including Mexico and Brazil, have also expressed concerns about foreign interference in their elections. In Africa, the political landscapes of countries like South Africa and Kenya have been targeted by external disinformation campaigns aimed at shaping election outcomes.

Moreover, in the Asia-Pacific region, countries like Australia and Taiwan have raised alarms regarding instances of foreign interference, particularly linked to the dissemination of disinformation and cyber attacks targeting critical infrastructure.

These instances underscore the grave threat that external interference in domestic politics poses to the sovereignty of nations and the integrity of democratic processes. They emphasize the pressing need for international cooperation to establish clear norms, deter such behavior, and enhance resilience against these forms of hybrid warfare.

Economic Coercion as a Tool of Conflict

Economic coercion is indeed becoming an increasingly prevalent element of global hybrid conflict strategies. It is also gaining prominence as a fundamental tool of contemporary diplomacy and conflict resolution, showcasing the adept utilization of economic power to pursue strategic objectives.

A clear illustration of this trend can be found in the strategic application of economic sanctions by the United States against countries like Iran and North Korea. These sanctions are not arbitrary punitive measures; rather, they are part of a deliberate effort to maintain global peace and security by discouraging behaviors that challenge international norms.

In addition to sanctions, the United States has effectively employed other means of economic influence. The trade negotiations initiated with China in 2018 represent a proactive stance aimed at addressing longstanding trade imbalances and alleged unfair practices. In doing so, the United States is not only safeguarding its economic interests but also setting a precedent for equitable trade practices on a global scale.

Furthermore, the United States' approach to securing its technological edge and national security, as evidenced by restrictions imposed on Chinese tech firms like Huawei and ZTE, underscores the convergence of economic policy with national security considerations. This approach signals a proactive effort to protect the nation's technological infrastructure from potential foreign interference.

Economic Coercion through CAATSA: Leveraging Sanctions in U.S. Foreign Policy

The Countering America's Adversaries Through Sanctions Act (CAATSA), enacted by the United States in 2017, serves as a potent instrument for economic coercion, primarily aimed at Russia, Iran, and North Korea, in response to various transgressions, including alleged election interference, human rights abuses, and missile testing. This legislation empowers the U.S. government to impose punitive economic measures, including freezing assets, limiting access to the U.S. financial system, and restricting trade against entities and individuals from these countries, as well as third-party entities that engage in significant transactions with them. By leveraging its economic might and the centrality of the U.S. dollar in global finance, the U.S. uses CAATSA to exert pressure on adversarial states, compelling them to alter behaviors deemed hostile or threatening to U.S. interests. This approach underscores the strategic use of economic tools in pursuing foreign policy objectives, demonstrating how economic measures can be employed as an alternative to military intervention to achieve geopolitical goals and maintain global hegemony.

In summary, the United States' use of economic coercion as a component of its foreign policy toolkit demonstrates its dedication to safeguarding its national interests and upholding international standards. It exemplifies the strategic harnessing of economic strength to navigate complex global dynamics and reflects the evolving nature of international relations in the 21st century.

Information Warfare: The Rise of Disinformation Campaigns

There is a noticeable upward trend in disinformation campaigns, underscoring the growing importance of information warfare in hybrid conflict. The Ukraine war, in particular, has witnessed a surge in disinformation campaigns, frequently orchestrated by state actors with the aim of sowing discord and confusion among Allies and partners. These campaigns transcend the battlefield and permeate various information channels, including social media and news outlets, skillfully manipulating narratives to advance strategic objectives. They exploit existing divisions, fuel tensions, and promote conspiracy theories, thereby shaping public opinion and eroding trust in institutions.

For instance, false narratives regarding the conduct of Ukrainian forces, the portrayal of Russian actions as defensive, and the exaggeration of threats from NATO have been recurrent themes. These disinformation efforts are designed not only to influence the international perception of the conflict but also to instill fear and uncertainty within Ukraine itself, weakening its resolve and resistance.

The digital age has amplified the reach and impact of these campaigns, rendering them a cost-effective tool for hybrid warfare. They can be disseminated widely and rapidly, often surpassing the capacity of fact-checkers and counter-propaganda initiatives to respond. Furthermore, the anonymity and plausible deniability afforded by the online environment render these campaigns challenging to definitively attribute and counter effectively.

Looking ahead, comprehending and addressing the use of disinformation in hybrid warfare is of paramount importance. It necessitates not only technological solutions for detecting and countering disinformation but also endeavors to foster resilience among populations and to preserve the integrity of information spaces. The growing trend of disinformation campaigns underscores the evolving nature of hybrid conflict and underscores the imperative for comprehensive strategies to confront these emerging threats.

Cyber Attacks on Critical Infrastructure

The surge in cyber attacks targeting critical infrastructure is becoming an alarming trend, indicating an elevated risk to civilian systems from the utilization of hybrid warfare tactics. Hybrid warfare, characterized by a combination of conventional and non-conventional conflict methods, is increasingly being employed by various actors to exploit vulnerabilities within the interconnected digital infrastructure upon which modern societies heavily rely.

In this section, we will delve into two real-world instances of nation-state influence operations carried out through cyber attacks on Information and Communications Technology (ICT) infrastructure. These examples provide insight into the strategic motivations and consequences of cyber operations on critical infrastructure, underscoring the challenges that governments and organizations encounter in securing their digital domains.

Case 1: Kenya ICT Cyber Attack by Anonymous Sudan (a front for Russian intelligence services)

In July 2023, a nation-state cyber operation targeted Kenya's ICT infrastructure, specifically focusing on the eCitizen portal, a crucial platform for Kenyans to access government services online. The perpetrators, initially identifying themselves as "Anonymous Sudan," were subsequently linked to Russian intelligence services. The attack utilized distributed denial-of-service (DDoS) tactics to disrupt the eCitizen portal, resulting in widespread service unavailability and significant inconvenience for citizens.

The motivation behind this operation likely stemmed from Kenya's President William Ruto's decision to decline participation in the Russo-African summit. President Ruto had expressed concerns about taking sides in Russia's conflict. "Anonymous Sudan" aimed to exert pressure on Kenya and convey a message regarding its stance on Russia's actions, particularly its non-participation in the Russo-African summit.[xxiv]

Case 2: Albania's Cyber Attack by Iranian Hackers

In July 2022, Albania faced a severe cyber attack attributed to Iranian hackers. The attackers targeted critical government websites, including those providing essential services such as utilities and driver's licenses. This cyber assault significantly disrupted daily operations across the country, underscoring the potential consequences of cyber operations on a nation's functionality.

While the attack had significant ramifications, Albania refrained from invoking NATO's Article 5, which would trigger collective defense measures, as a strategic decision to avoid escalation and potential strain on diplomatic relations with powerful Allies. The decision highlighted the complexities surrounding the threshold for a cyber attack to trigger a full NATO collective defense response.

Despite the severity of the attack, which was likened to "bombing a country" in its impact, Albania's smaller size in terms of geography and population, coupled with the fact that no lives were lost or permanent infrastructure destroyed, made invoking Article 5 less likely. This case study reflects the complex decision-making processes surrounding cyber incidents on critical infrastructure, as the threshold for activating collective defense measures remains ambiguous.[xxv]

These two real-world examples of nation-state influence operations through cyber attacks on critical ICT infrastructure underscore the growing utilization of cyber capabilities to achieve strategic objectives. The interconnected nature of modern societies renders critical infrastructure an attractive target for hybrid warfare tactics. As cyber threats continue to evolve and intensify, governments and organizations must remain vigilant and proactive in bolstering their cyber defenses.

Furthermore, this chapter sheds light on the increasing significance of cyber operations within the realm of international relations and national security, emphasizing the imperative for robust cybersecurity measures to safeguard critical infrastructure from potential cyber adversaries.

Another notable illustration of this growing threat is the cyber attack on Viasat's infrastructure in Ukraine in February 2023. This attack involved the use of a new malware named "AcidRain," resulting in wide-ranging effects, including rendering Viasat KA-SAT modems inoperable in Ukraine, causing malfunctions in wind turbines in Germany, and disrupting satellite internet services across Europe. This attack underscored the interconnectedness of cyberspace, highlighting how an attack in one area can have far-reaching consequences. The United States assessed that "Russia launched cyber attacks in late February against commercial satellite communications networks to disrupt Ukrainian command and control during the invasion, and those actions had spillover impacts into other European countries."[xxvi]

Another example of attacks on homeland infrastructure is the Colonial Pipeline ransomware attack in May 2021, which led to significant disruptions in fuel supply across the Eastern United States, vividly demonstrating the real-world impacts of such cyber threats.

Furthermore, the Oldsmar water treatment facility incident in February 2021, where hackers attempted to manipulate chemical levels in the water supply, serves as another stark example of how critical infrastructure can be targeted with potentially devastating impacts on public health and safety.[xxvii]

These incidents underscore the urgent need for stronger cybersecurity defenses and enhanced international cooperation. As our world becomes increasingly networked and digital, ensuring the security of our critical infrastructure is not just a national security issue but also a matter of public safety and societal resilience in the face of escalating hybrid threats.

Visualizing Trends in Hybrid Conflict

Now, let's generate a visual graph to illustrate these trends. Using a quantitative approach from previous incidents in each category, we can create a radar chart to visualize the relative intensity of the trends. We assigned the following scores on a scale from 1 to 10:

1. Perception: 8

2. Capability: 8

3. Military Activity: 9

4. Political Activity: 7

5. Economic Activity: 7

6. Information Activity: 8

7. Civil Activity: 9

The scale from 1 to 10 in the context of the assigned scores represents a quantitative measure of the relative intensity of each trend category. A score of 1 would indicate that a particular trend category is very weak, while a score of 10 suggests that the trend is extremely strong. These scores are based on a quantitative assessment of each category's impact, with higher scores indicating a greater level of influence in the analysis of the trends.

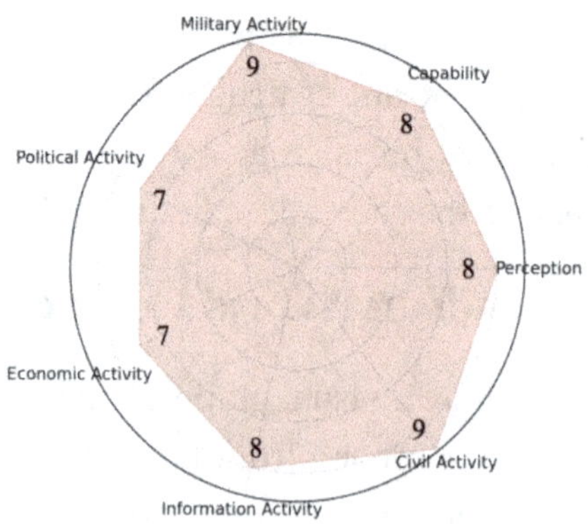

Figure 10: Trends in Hybrid Conflict in 2023 and Beyond

This radar chart illustrates the relative intensity of trends in various categories of hybrid conflict. The chart is constructed based on the number of real-world incidents observed in each category[xxviii], revealing that "Military Activity" and "Civil Activity" (such as cyber attacks on critical infrastructure) exhibit the most pronounced intensity trends. Following closely behind are "Perception," "Capability," and "Information Activity." "Political Activity" and "Economic Activity" also display noteworthy trends, albeit at a slightly lower intensity.

Conclusion

The contemporary landscape of hybrid threats underscores the necessity for robust cooperation in securing cyberspace effectively. Characterized by a fusion of conventional and unconventional tactics, hybrid conflict has become a defining aspect of global security. This form of conflict encompasses not only traditional military strategies but also economic coercion, disinformation campaigns, political meddling, and cyber assaults on critical infrastructure. Within this intricate environment, cyberspace has emerged as a pivotal battleground.

Both state and non-state entities exploit the digital realm to execute disruptive actions, frequently blurring the boundaries between peace and warfare. As these threats escalate in magnitude and complexity, collaborative efforts among nations are imperative to bolster defensive capabilities, share intelligence, and establish norms governing responsible conduct in cyberspace. Such a collective approach is essential in mitigating the perils posed by hybrid threats and ensuring the stability and security of cyberspace.

Chapter 4:

Introducing Integrated Deterrence in Cyberspace with Allies and Partners

Introduction

The United States is currently navigating a complex strategic landscape, marked by the persistent military threat posed by Russia, the rise of China as a great power, and the evolving challenges presented by countries like Iran and North Korea. In addition, the emergence of offensive cyber capabilities has further compounded the threat landscape. To safeguard its homeland and global interests, the United States must deter aggression from two nuclear-armed great-power adversaries while also addressing the growing menace of offensive cyber capabilities. However, the U.S. faces significant challenges, including limited capacity, capability, and readiness to effectively counter multiple advanced threats and crises. In response, the U.S. Department of Defense (DOD) introduced integrated deterrence in the 2022 National Defense Strategy (NDS). Integrated deterrence emphasizes the fusion of all national powers across domains, geographies, and the spectrum of conflict while fostering close collaboration with Allies and partners.

Integrated deterrence has emerged as a pivotal concept in modern strategic thought, adapting the timeless principle of deterrence to the multifaceted and dynamic nature of contemporary security challenges. At its core, integrated deterrence weaves together strategies from various domains, such as land, air, sea, space, and particularly cyberspace, to dissuade adversaries from initiating hostile actions. In an era dominated by technology, cyber threats are prolific and can undermine national security in insidious ways, necessitating a nuanced approach to deterrence that extends beyond conventional military capabilities.

Integrated Deterrence: A Key Pillar of the 2022 National Defense Strategy (NDS)

In the 2022 NDS, "integrated deterrence" is articulated as "the seamless combination of capabilities to convince potential adversaries that the costs of their hostile activities outweigh their benefits." This approach necessitates integration across domains, regions, the spectrum of conflict, the U.S. government, and its Allies and partners. The 2022 NDS Fact Sheet outlines three primary avenues for advancing Department of Defense goals: integrated deterrence, campaigning, and building enduring advantages. Specifically addressing integrated deterrence, the fact sheet states:

"Integrated deterrence entails developing and combining our strengths to maximum effect by working seamlessly across warfighting domains, theaters, the spectrum of conflict, other instruments of U.S. national power, and our unmatched network of Alliances and partnerships. Integrated deterrence is enabled by combat-credible forces, backstopped by a safe, secure, and effective nuclear deterrent."

These national strategies explicitly enumerate the essential components of integrated deterrence, including the nuclear deterrent, cross-domain and cross-aspect interagency efforts, and cooperation with alliances and partners.

The essence of integrated deterrence is the synergy achieved through coordinating efforts across these diverse domains, creating a resilient and adaptive posture capable of addressing both conventional and unconventional threats. The inclusion of cyber threats in this framework is especially crucial, given their capacity to transcend physical boundaries and disrupt societies, economies, and governance structures, accentuating the importance of developing robust cyber capabilities, policies, and doctrines. Cross-domain deterrence is instrumental in this framework, allowing states to apply pressure or create effects in one domain, such as cyberspace, to influence behavior in another.

Moreover, the role of asymmetric warfare and hybrid threats is significant in the realm of integrated deterrence, with states recognizing the need to counter a blend of military and non-military conventional and unconventional threats, including cyber attacks and information warfare. Addressing these threats necessitates the leveraging of multi-domain operations and proactive measures to present adversaries with multiple dilemmas and complicate their decision-making processes. The focus is not solely on reactionary postures but also on shaping activities, engagement, and presence aimed at influencing the security environment and adversary behavior in peacetime.

In addition to military and cyber strategies, integrated deterrence also emphasizes the importance of diplomatic engagement, alliances, and economic leverage. The forging of strong alliances and partnerships and the effective use of diplomatic channels are vital for collective security and resilience against common threats, including those emanating from the cyber domain. Economic tools such as sanctions and trade controls are deployed to impact adversaries' economic interests and capabilities, thereby influencing their decisions and behaviors.

Strategic communications play a crucial role in conveying intent, resolve, and the willingness to employ various forms of power to deter adversaries. Clear and consistent communication is fundamental for signaling to third parties, shaping international perceptions and narratives, and reinforcing the credibility and resolve essential for the success of integrated deterrence strategies. Controlling escalation and managing the intensity and scope of conflict is also paramount to prevent conflicts from spiraling out of control and to avoid unintended consequences, especially when dealing with the complexities of cyber threats.

The objective of the integrated deterrence strategy is to implement deterrence effectively, utilizing relevant resources and support from various domains and aspects. The proposed framework aims to provide a platform that fosters flexibility in executing deterrence in the contemporary era, where the cyber or virtual world coexists with the physical. A key emphasis is placed on the application of deterrence in both the cyber and physical realms.

In summary, integrated deterrence represents a holistic, nuanced approach to contemporary security, emphasizing the importance of integrating various elements of national power to deter across a wide spectrum of conflict. The focus on cyber threats within this framework is indicative of the evolving nature of warfare and conflict, requiring adaptative, multifaceted strategies to address the challenges posed by the interconnected, digital global landscape. Theoretical terms and concepts embedded in integrated deterrence, such as cross-domain deterrence, asymmetric warfare, and hybrid threats, provide a structured lens through which policymakers and strategists can navigate the complexities of modern security environments, ensuring a balanced, robust, and resilient defense posture in the face of emerging cyber threats.

Integrated Deterrence Framework

To translate the concept of integrated deterrence into practical terms and ensure its successful implementation, this chapter proposes a framework for the DOD to guide its strategy in cyberspace security cooperation with Allies and partners. The framework envisions a striking imagery of three pyramids elegantly stacked on top of each other, forming a formidable spear. Within this conceptual architecture lies a systematic identification of three crucial levels of integration between the United States and its esteemed Allies and partners: strategic, institutional, and tactical. Each level is critical in fostering effective collaboration and achieving integrated deterrence.

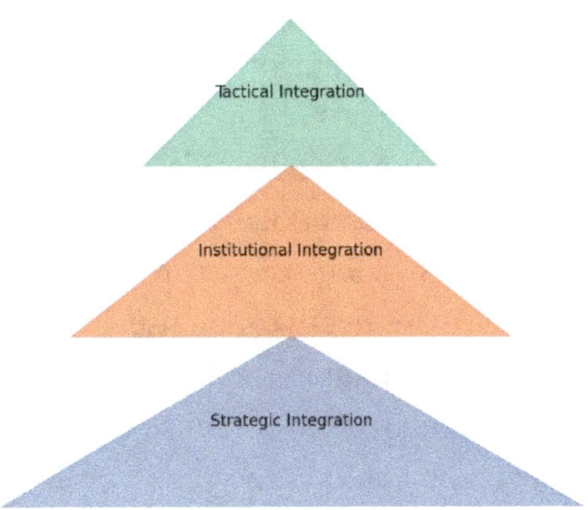

Figure 11: Pyramids of Integration with Allies and Partners in Cyberspace

Strategic Integration: Developing a Common Understanding and Prioritization

Strategic integration, representing the foundational layer and highest level of integration, poses significant challenges due to divergent strategic and policy perspectives among Allied and partner nations. It entails forging a collective comprehension and prioritization of threats while establishing a coordinated division of labor for countering these threats. Strategic integration necessitates the alignment of strategic visions and synchronized efforts in cyberspace between the DOD and its Allies and partners. By surmounting barriers and fostering a shared strategic approach, the United States and its Allied nations can effectively deter and respond to cyber threats from adversaries like China and Russia. We explore in the subsequent section a variety of pragmatic illustrations of strategic integration between the US and NATO Allies and partners.

NATO's Cyber Defence Policy

A quintessential example of the U.S. DOD working in tandem with European partners is NATO's evolving Cyber Defence Policy. According to the policy, NATO acknowledges the applicability of international law to cyberspace and underscores that cyber defense is an integral part of NATO's core responsibility of collective defense. As per the policy, Article 5 of the North Atlantic Treaty, pertaining to collective self-defense, can be invoked in response to a cyber attack that produces effects comparable to those of a conventional armed attack. Jamie Shea, Deputy Assistant Secretary General for Emerging Security Challenges at NATO Headquarters, clarified that the policy does not establish specific criteria for Article 5 activation, leaving such decisions to be made by the Allies on a case-by-case basis.

The Summit Declaration emphasized NATO's primary responsibility for defending its own systems, while member nations are expected to safeguard theirs. NATO commits to integrating cyber defense into its operations and planning, enhancing information sharing, and improving situational awareness. Active engagement on cyber issues with international organizations, particularly with the EU, is also outlined.

This policy is a testament to collaborative endeavors that amalgamate resources, expertise, and intelligence to bolster the defense mechanisms against cyber threats. The United States, alongside its European Allies, has been diligently working to create a cohesive framework to address and mitigate the vulnerabilities inherent in cyberspace.[xxix]

NATO Cyber Defence Pledge

The NATO Cyber Defence Pledge, signed in 2016, exemplifies the collective commitment to enhancing individual and collective cyber defenses. It lays the groundwork for shared understanding, prioritization of threats, and the allocation of resources, allowing member nations to pool knowledge and fortify their cyber defenses in a harmonious manner. This commitment is not merely an articulation of mutual cooperation but is an embodiment of the alignment of strategic visions and priorities in the cyber realm.[xxx]

The Allied Heads of State and Government acknowledge the evolving security threats in the cyber domain and commit to ensuring NATO's adaptability in this rapidly changing environment. They emphasize the importance of national capabilities to defend against cyber threats, aligning with their broader commitment to defense in air, land, and sea.

Reaffirming their national responsibility under Article 3 of the Washington Treaty, the leaders pledge to enhance cyber defenses for national infrastructures and networks. This commitment is consistent with the Enhanced NATO Policy on Cyber Defense adopted in Wales, highlighting the indivisibility of Allied security and collective defense. Emphasis is placed on the interconnectedness of nations, underscoring the need for strong and resilient cyber defenses to enable the Alliance to fulfill its core tasks.

The leaders express support for collaborative efforts between Allies and the EU in enhancing cybersecurity and reinforcing resilience in the Euro-Atlantic region. They endorse further NATO-EU cyber defense cooperation and recognize the applicability of international law in cyberspace. The value of NATO's partnerships with partner nations, industry, and academia, including the NATO Industry Cyber Partnership, is acknowledged, with a commitment to promoting responsible state behavior and confidence-building measures in cyberspace.

NATO's role in facilitating cooperation on cyber defense is emphasized, with commitments to multinational projects, education, training, exercises, and information exchange to support national cyber defense efforts. The leaders underscored the importance of ensuring that the Alliance is cyber-aware, cyber-trained, cyber-secure, and cyber-enabled to contribute to overall resilience.

The leaders pledge to prioritize strengthening and enhancing the cyber defenses of national networks and infrastructures. This includes developing a comprehensive range of capabilities, allocating adequate national resources, reinforcing interaction among national cyber defense stakeholders, improving understanding of cyber threats, enhancing skills and awareness at the national level, fostering cyber education, training, and exercises, and expediting the implementation of agreed cyber defense commitments, including those on which NATO relies.

Strategic Joint Cyber Exercises

Regular joint exercises such as "Cyber Coalition" involve extensive collaboration among NATO Allies at the strategic level, including the United States and European partners. These exercises serve as platforms for nations to share best practices, develop and refine strategies, and enhance interoperability in countering cyber and emerging threats. The collective insights and learnings gleaned from these exercises fortify the strategic vision and mutual understanding among Allies, thereby fostering strategic integration.

NATO Cyber Rapid Reaction Teams (CRRTs)

The creation of Cyber Rapid Reaction Teams (CRRTs) is another demonstration of the deepening cooperation between NATO Allies at the strategic level. NATO CRRTs are on standby 24 hours a day to assist Allies if and when requested and approved by the North Atlantic Council. These teams are developed to respond swiftly to cyber threats and attacks, ensuring a collective and synchronized response to emergent cyber threats.[xxxi]

In sum, the amalgamation of strategies, the deepening of ties, and the forging of common understandings and prioritizations transcend mere technical collaborations. They become intertwined with national security policies, global peace-keeping objectives, and strategic defense initiatives, thereby driving collective international security goals in cyberspace.

Enhancing Integrated Deterrence in Cyberspace

The multilevel and multi-aspect architecture proposed for integrated deterrence proves to be a powerful and flexible strategy. By holistically connecting varied deterrence capabilities and addressing diverse strategic contexts, this approach strengthens the overall integrated deterrence strategy.

Recognizing the crucial role of cyberspace in national security, the importance of deterrence in cyberspace becomes evident. Without effective deterrence in this domain, especially in gray zone contexts, the overall deterrence strategy remains incomplete. The proposed architecture enables the creation of novel deterrent capabilities at different levels and within various aspects, thereby elevating the role of deterrence in both national security and cyberspace.

This comprehensive approach offers national security decision-makers and strategists effective utilization of deterrent capabilities across different levels, maintaining a strategic advantage. Moreover, it seamlessly integrates deterrence in cyberspace into the broader framework of integrated deterrence. This integration empowers decision-makers to execute proportional and effective deterrence tailored to the requirements of specific strategic contexts, ultimately achieving national security goals successfully.

Institutional Integration: Building Trust and Cooperation

Institutional integration represents a deeper form of cooperation requiring higher trust and involvement. It involves incorporating Allies and partners into the decision-making processes of the DOD. Key areas of institutional integration include information sharing, research and development, and capability development, acquisition, and production. By fostering greater trust and collaboration in these areas, the United States and its Allies can enhance their collective cyber defense capabilities. Sharing information, conducting joint research and development initiatives, and coordinating capability development and acquisition processes will lead to greater interoperability and resilience in the face of cyber threats.

The Importance of Institutional Integration in Information Sharing

Institutional integration sets the stage for enhanced and consistent engagement, fortifying communication channels and encapsulating structured, sustained, and regularized interaction between the DOD and its Allied or partnered entities. This profound interweaving is pivotal in reinforcing mutual relations and embedding synergistic alliances in the everyday processes of both entities. Within this integration, a particular emphasis is laid on seamless and reciprocal information sharing, serving as the linchpin in weaving a dense fabric of shared intelligence, insights, and knowledge pertaining to cyber threats, vulnerabilities, and potential countermeasures. This integrated framework facilitates the seamless exchange of advanced threat intelligence, real-time alerts, incident reports, threat analyses, and strategic insights, enriching the collective knowledge pool and fostering a comprehensive understanding of the evolving cyber landscape.

The reciprocal flow of critical and enriched information enhances the anticipatory and reactive capabilities of Allied forces, enabling the orchestration of coordinated and informed responses to emerging threats and challenges, thus accelerating response times and enhancing situational awareness. By embedding such an extensive information-sharing network within institutional structures, the United States and its Allies foster a resilient and enduring alliance, enabling the development of robust and coordinated defense strategies that reflect deep-rooted strategic alignment and integration. This ensures the fortification of their collective defense posture in the ever-evolving global security landscape, addressing and neutralizing cyber threats and ensuring the security and integrity of national and collective digital infrastructures.

However, when it comes to information sharing, Allies and partners often encounter obstacles in deepening integration due to U.S. classification practices. The stringent classification protocols and information security measures can hamper the seamless flow of critical intelligence and operational information amongst partners. This limitation can inhibit collective situational awareness and timely decision-making, potentially affecting the efficacy of integrated deterrence strategies. It raises significant challenges, especially in the realm of cyber threats, where the rapid and unencumbered exchange of information is pivotal for identifying, understanding, and mitigating threats in real-time. The need for addressing and reconciling classification disparities is evident, as fostering a collaborative environment is paramount to advancing shared interests and ensuring mutual security.

The evolution of integrated deterrence strategies necessitates the development of mechanisms and protocols that facilitate secure, efficient, and inclusive information-sharing frameworks, balancing the need to protect sensitive information with the imperative to enhance collective defense capabilities. This delicate balance requires ongoing dialogue, trust-building, and the mutual understanding of each ally's legal, operational, and institutional constraints and capabilities, striving towards a coherent and effective international security paradigm. It is ideal for the DOD to maintain actionable cyber intelligence at the unclassified level, facilitating timely, relevant, and more effective information sharing with trusted

Allies and partners following the Five Eyes Alliance (FVEY) [xxxii] and NATO intelligence-sharing agreements.

For the U.S. DOD, institutional integration with European partners has been pivotal in aligning cyber strategies, advancing collective defenses, and addressing the myriad cyber threats that transcend national boundaries.

We explore in the subsequent section several tangible instances of institutional integration between the US and its strategic partners.

NATO Cooperative Cyber Defence Centre of Excellence (CCDCOE)

The U.S. DOD has been working closely with NATO, a pivotal European institution, to improve cyber defense capabilities. NATO and the U.S. have established Centres of Excellence (CoEs) focused on cyber defense, where member countries collectively engage in research, training, and development of cyber capabilities. The Cooperative Cyber Defence Centre of Excellence (CCDCOE) is one such example which underscores institutional integration by facilitating collaborative research and information sharing on cyber threats and defenses. [xxxiii]

The European Defence Agency (EDA)

The U.S. has been engaging with the European Defence Agency in areas of capability development, research, and technology. Through joint programs and projects, the EDA and the U.S. DOD are fostering institutional integration, which enables the alignment of cyber strategies and enhances mutual understanding of cyber threats, vulnerabilities, and resilience measures.

Information Sharing Platforms with US Allies & Partners

Information sharing is a cornerstone of institutional integration in cyberspace. The U.S. and its strategic partners have established various information-sharing platforms and arrangements to disseminate intelligence and cyber threat information promptly. The Malware Information Sharing Platform, also known as MISP, is an example where partnerships with NATO Allies and partners have been instrumental in sharing threat intelligence and enhancing situational awareness in cyberspace.

Bilateral Agreements

The U.S. has several bilateral agreements with European countries like the United Kingdom, Germany, and France. These agreements often encompass mutual commitments to share information, conduct joint research, and develop capabilities, thereby fostering institutional integration in the cyber domain.

Joint Exercises and Training

The U.S. and its European Allies regularly conduct joint exercises and training workshops focusing on cyber warfare and defense. These exercises, such as the US CYBERCOM Cyber Flag and USEUCOM Cyber Unity exercises[xxxiv], serve as platforms for testing and enhancing interoperability, sharing best practices, and strengthening the collective response to cyber threats.

Acquisition and Production Collaboration

Joint acquisition and collaborative production projects between the U.S. and its European partners, like the Multinational Capability Development Campaign (MCDC), emphasize the shared goal of developing advanced technologies and capabilities to address evolving cyber threats.

In sum, institutional integration between the U.S. DOD and European partners is integral to building a resilient and interoperable cyber defense architecture. By delving deep into the realms of information sharing, research and development, and capability acquisition and production, the United States and its Allies are crafting a robust alliance in cyberspace. This integration, whilst faced with the intricacies of classification and security protocols, remains pivotal to countering the ever-evolving landscape of cyber threats collectively. Lastly, the multitude of collaborations, agreements, and initiatives with European partners underscores the U.S. DOD's commitment to fostering institutional integration in cyberspace, building a foundation of trust, and enabling a collective approach to cybersecurity.

Tactical Integration: Promoting Technology Transfer, Interoperability, and Shared Tactics

Emphasizing the Importance of Cybersecurity for Developing Nations

Cybersecurity has become a critical aspect of modern military operations, and the United States Allies and Partners are increasingly finding themselves at the forefront of a digital battlefield. Access to cutting-edge cyber defense technologies and resources has become indispensable to protect their networks and sensitive data. The potential benefits of embracing advanced cybersecurity solutions are extensive. These advanced technologies, such as Machine Learning (ML), Intrusion Prevention Systems (IPS), Endpoint Detection and Response (EDR), and Security Orchestration, Automation, and Response (SOAR), offer a range of benefits, including improved threat detection capabilities, rapid incident response, and enhanced network visibility. By leveraging sophisticated cybersecurity solutions, developing nations can gain valuable insights into their network's vulnerabilities and potential threats, enabling them to proactively identify and neutralize malicious activities before they escalate.

Boosting Morale and Resilience

The significance of cyber defense for developing nations extends beyond technical concerns. The lack of access to state-of-the-art equipment and tools can leave their defense forces feeling demoralized and vulnerable when facing cyber-attacks. The knowledge that adversaries possess more advanced capabilities can dampen morale and confidence in their ability to withstand such threats. To address this challenge and bolster their resilience, support from the United States and its capable Allies is crucial. By providing developing partners with adequate resources, training, and technology transfer, these nations can gain the confidence and determination to effectively confront the ever-evolving cyber threat landscape. The United States' pivotal role in cyberspace security cooperation ensures that all nations, regardless of their current development stage, stand united against cyber threats, promoting a safer and more secure digital world for everyone.

Supporting Multinational Cyber Coalition Exercises

Currently, the planning and execution process for multinational cyber coalition exercises and operations pose significant challenges due to the diverse nature of participating forces and the lack of minimum requirements needed for standardization. These forces vary in terms of equipment types, capabilities, and levels of cyber proficiency. This dissimilarity complicates the planning process, requiring careful consideration of the branding of cyber defense equipment and tools. If a coalition's forces are truly interchangeable, planners theoretically do not need to worry about the branding of cyber defense tools and the proficiency of the operator. Instead, they can genuinely treat all forces who fulfill the minimum requirements as equal -all building blocks can be assembled in different ways to construct a larger whole. This level of interchangeability would enhance the coalition's defense posture and ability to concentrate cyber effects because commanders could employ the most proximate forces to the battlefield, ensuring faster response times and superior capabilities to outmatch adversaries.

Enabling Tactical Integration with Allies and Partners

To achieve deeper tactical integration, the U.S. DOD engages in a wide range of security cooperation activities. These activities aim to provide Allies and partners with cyber equipment, facilitate multinational cyber operations, and foster regular interactions among participating entities. One approach is through the sale of cyber defense equipment and tools to Allies and partners via Foreign Military Sales (FMS). By providing access to advanced cyber capabilities, the United States strengthens interoperability and enhances collective defense efforts. Additionally, international military education and training programs bring foreign officers to US military cyber schools. This exchange of knowledge and expertise further promotes interoperability and a shared understanding of cyber operations. Besides, participating in multilateral exercises serves as a valuable means to deepen tactical integration. These exercises provide opportunities for joint training on new cyber tools and equipment, coordination, and the development of standardized operating procedures, ultimately enhancing the effectiveness of multinational cyber operations.

Therefore, enabling tactical integration is paramount in forging cohesive and adaptive alliances, underpinning the collective capability to confront and neutralize cyber threats. By advancing technology transfers, interoperability, and the development and sharing of tactics, the United States and its Allies can present a unified front, melding disparate capabilities into a formidable, coherent defense. This integration necessitates a commitment to mutual learning and adjustment, accommodating varying levels of proficiency and technological disparities to formulate universally applicable strategies and responses. It also involves meticulous planning and coordination to execute multinational cyber coalition exercises, ensuring seamless interaction and enhanced collective response capabilities. The foundational ethos of such integration lies in fostering a shared sense of responsibility, resilience, and mutual support, enabling developing nations to uplift their cyber defense capabilities and morale. Through the comprehensive approach of equipping, training, and the constant exchange of knowledge and expertise, tactical integration serves as a linchpin, fortifying global cyber defenses and ensuring a more secure and resilient digital future for all nations involved. The robust collaboration and continuous refinement of shared tactics will enable nations to anticipate and counter emerging cyber threats, enhancing overall security and stability in an interconnected digital world.

Conclusion

In closing, integrated deterrence with Allies and partners in the realm of cyberspace is critical for effectively countering evolving threats. By implementing the strategic, institutional, and tactical integration framework, the United States can enhance collaboration, interoperability, and information sharing with its Allies and partners. This chapter highlights the importance of clarifying the concept of integrated deterrence, overcoming barriers to deeper cooperation, and aligning strategic visions to promote collective cyber defense. Through these efforts, the United States can fortify its cyber defense posture, deter aggression, and ensure the security of the digital realm for itself and its Allies and partners.

Chapter 5:

Applying Integrated Deterrence with Allies and Partners in Cyberspace Security Cooperation

Introduction

The United States has an essential responsibility to aid Allied and partner countries and organizations in enhancing their cyber capabilities. Policymakers reinforce U.S. national security and bolster it is cyber defense capabilities by supporting U.S. Allies and partners to prevent, manage, and recover from cyber-attacks. Moreover, some adversaries exploit U.S. partner countries as testing grounds for future cyber operations directed at the United States. Strengthening the cyber capacities of Allies and partners serves as a deterrent to such adversaries, hindering their attempts to experiment and refine cyber weaponry.

In the sphere of cyberspace, the concept of integrated deterrence with Allies and partners, as explained in the previous chapter, plays a vital role in countering evolving threats. Integrated deterrence is grounded in the understanding that adversaries employ comprehensive strategies, necessitating a holistic approach by the United States to safeguard its interests and pursue national objectives. This approach aims to optimize the utilization of all national power instruments.

Integrated deterrence requires collaboration at various levels, with strategic integration serving as the backbone of this approach. By developing a shared strategic vision and deepening institutional, tactical, and strategic integration, the United States and its Allies can enhance their collective deterrence capabilities in cyberspace. This chapter explores how integrated deterrence can be applied in the context of cyberspace security cooperation.

Strategic Integration: A Shared Vision

The first step towards achieving integrated deterrence in cybersecurity is the development of a shared strategic vision among the United States, its Allies, and partners globally. This collaborative effort must encompass both the public and private sectors, as the digital realm has blurred the traditional boundaries between state actors and corporations. A shared vision is imperative, as the threats in the cyber domain are not confined by borders or limited to specific regions. Nation-states, non-state actors, and cybercriminals operate globally, targeting infrastructures, stealing sensitive data, and seeking to disrupt critical services. Given the transnational nature of cyber threats, a fragmented or regionally isolated approach to defense will always fall short. The United States, with its technologically advanced cyber capabilities and expansive global reach, should take the lead in fostering a cohesive and unified strategy. This involves bringing its Allies, especially those in NATO, the Five Eyes, and key partners in Asia and the Middle East, onto a common platform. The objective would be to establish a consensus on threat assessments, identify vulnerabilities, set defense priorities, and streamline collective response mechanisms.

However, establishing a shared vision is not just about coordinating defense. It's also about overcoming barriers to deeper institutional and tactical integration by aligning priorities and understanding the prioritization of threats. To facilitate this, the U.S. Department of Defense (DOD) should work with its Allies and partners to assess strategic alignment and prioritize threats effectively. This assessment will lay the foundation for future integration plans that conform to shared priorities.

For instance, while all NATO parties may agree that Russia is their primary adversary, their specific concerns and focus areas can vary significantly. Albania might prioritize its conflict with Iran over the Mujahedin-e-Khalq Organization (MEK or MKO)[xxxv], Sweden may be focused on a potential Russian blockade of Gotland Island, the United States could be concerned about the prospect of a Moldova invasion[xxxvi] and the United Kingdom might be focused on its fishing fleet ban in the Barents Sea.[xxxvii] Geographical factors play a crucial role in determining the types of capabilities that would be most valuable and where they should be deployed. Additionally, it is vital for Allies and partners to align their timeframes. If some are preparing for near-term conflicts while others are developing plans for potential conflicts 10 or 15 years down the line, it can lead to confusion and disparate conclusions. Therefore, ensuring a shared understanding of geographical considerations and strategic timelines is essential for effective coordination and cooperation among Allies and partners.

Towards Cyber Unity: Fostering Strategic Alignment and Integration Among Allies

One of the immediate challenges to overcome in international security is the diverse range of threat perceptions among different nations in cyberspace. While some countries might be more concerned with cyber espionage and intellectual property theft, others might prioritize threats to critical infrastructure or disinformation campaigns. The sheer range of cyber threats, from ransomware attacks to state-sponsored intrusions, means that a one-size-fits-all approach is impractical. In light of this, a multilayered approach is required:

Threat Mapping and Analysis: The U.S. DOD should spearhead an initiative to collaboratively map out the entire spectrum of cyber threats. They can create a comprehensive threat matrix using advanced analytics and intelligence-sharing platforms. This matrix will classify threats based on factors like potential impact, likelihood, and the affected sectors.

Customized Response Strategies: Once the threat matrix is in place, customized response strategies can be devised for each threat category. Allies and partners can then choose which strategies align with their perceived threat landscape and prioritize their defenses accordingly.

Regular Dialogues and Workshops: Open channels of communication between nations are essential. Periodic meetings, seminars, and workshops can be platforms for nations to share their threat perceptions, discuss emerging trends, and brainstorm potential countermeasures.

Joint Task Forces: For threats deemed high-priority across the board, joint task forces can be established. These specialized teams would comprise experts from multiple countries and focus on developing cutting-edge defense mechanisms against specific threats.

Interoperability Testing: As nations work on aligning their defenses, ensuring that their systems and protocols are interoperable is crucial. Regular joint cybersecurity drills and simulations can assess the smooth functioning of integrated defense systems.

Similarly, acknowledging the significance of hybrid threats is essential. In today's interconnected world, cyber-attacks are often accompanied by other forms of aggression, such as disinformation campaigns, economic pressure, or conventional military actions. Recognizing the interplay of these hybrid tactics and developing a comprehensive response strategy is indispensable. Integrated deterrence should extend beyond just the cyber domain and encompass all aspects of hybrid warfare to ensure that Allies and partners are prepared to respond effectively to multifaceted threats.

Furthermore, the United States must specify its expectations from democratic European and Indo-Pacific Allies and partners, including a division of labor. Clearly defining roles and responsibilities allows each partner to contribute effectively to integrated deterrence efforts. This clarity will enable better coordination and cooperation in addressing cyber threats.

Institutional Integration: Sharing Information and Promoting Resiliency

In cyberspace security cooperation, institutional integration holds immense significance, particularly when enhancing information sharing among Allies and partners. To ensure effective integration, the U.S. Department of Defense (DOD) must prioritize improving information-sharing practices across its entire bureaucratic structure. By incentivizing and promoting a culture of collaboration and transparency, the DOD can encourage Allies and partners to actively share information. This proactive approach fosters a collective response to cyber threats, amplifying the overall effectiveness of cybersecurity efforts and enabling a more robust unified defense against evolving cyber risks.

To achieve this, various tools and platforms have emerged as valuable resources for information sharing among Allies and partners in cybersecurity. One notable example is the Malware Information Sharing Platform (MISP), renowned for enhancing collaboration and information exchange. As an open-source solution, MISP enables secure sharing of actionable threat intelligence, encompassing indicators of compromise, malware samples, and other pertinent data. By promoting real-time information sharing, MISP empowers Allies and partners to collectively identify, analyze, and respond to emerging cyber threats. Its adaptable data model and robust sharing capabilities foster interoperability and facilitate seamless integration within diverse cybersecurity ecosystems. Leveraging MISP, Allies, and partners can swiftly exchange vital insights, strengthen situational awareness, and collaboratively devise effective mitigation strategies. Through such collaborative efforts, the collective cyber defense posture is reinforced, fostering a proactive and unified approach to cybersecurity cooperation.

Information Sharing at the Institutional Level Through Hunt Forward Operations (HFOs)

Integrated deterrence is a concept that involves leveraging the entire spectrum of national and collective capabilities, both military and non-military, to dissuade adversaries from taking hostile actions. When applied to cyberspace, it signifies a comprehensive and collective approach to deterring malicious cyber activities.

Hunt Forward Operations (HFOs) are a prime example of integrated deterrence at the institutional level in cyberspace, in which defensive cyber operations are conducted by the U.S. Cyber Command (USCYBERCOM) at the request of partner nations (PNs). These operations are not only defensive but also proactive in nature, aimed at preemptively identifying vulnerabilities, malicious cyber activity, and adversary presence on the host nation's networks. The insights gained from these operations are shared with the Host Nation (HN), other government agencies, and the private industry, bolstering homeland and network defense while exposing adversary tactics, techniques, and procedures.

The significance of integrated deterrence in cyberspace is further underscored by the 'Defend Forward' policy of the Department of Defense. This policy emphasizes that defending the United States in cyberspace necessitates executing operations outside the U.S. military's networks, often in partnership with foreign governments that have formally requested such support. This strategy allows for the identification and understanding of adversaries' tradecrafts and tools, strengthening defenses not only for the United States and the requesting country but also for any entity that can access this information.

Tactical Integration: Strengthening Capabilities and Interoperability

Tactical integration is essential for effectively countering cyber threats. The U.S. DOD should collaborate with Congress, the National Security Council, and the State Department to reform the procurement process for cyber defense tools. This reform should expand the pool of implementing agencies and expedite the acquisition and provision of advanced cyber defense capabilities that can effectively deter cyber threats posed by Russia, China, or Iran. By streamlining the procurement process through Foreign Military Sales (FMS) to Allies and partners, the United States can ensure timely and efficient support to enhance its cybersecurity efforts. This collaborative reform effort will enable Allies and partners to acquire the necessary cyber defense tools promptly, strengthening their cyber defense postures and effectively mitigating cyber threats from adversarial nations.

From Tools to Tactics: Enhancing Cyber Defense Through Holistic Collaboration and Integration

Beyond the mere provision of tools, it is essential to ensure that the acquired capabilities are utilized optimally. To this end, the U.S. DOD should also invest in comprehensive training programs tailored for Allies and partners. These programs should focus on the technical aspects of the procured tools and the strategies for their deployment, maintenance, and upgrade.

Furthermore, joint cyber exercises should be organized regularly to foster a culture of cyber resilience. These exercises can provide real-world scenarios to test the newly acquired tools' capabilities and improve coordination between different nations. It's not just about having the best tools in the arsenal but also about knowing how to use them effectively in a synchronized manner.

In addition, the collaboration should not stop at just the top echelons of the defense hierarchy. Grassroots-level interactions with think tanks and academic partnerships can further the cause of cyber defense by generating new ideas, best practices, and innovative solutions. They can also facilitate a better understanding of the cyber terrain and the specific challenges each nation faces.

Lastly, a feedback mechanism should be established to ensure sustained progress and adaptation to the ever-evolving cyber landscape. Allies and partners should have a platform to communicate their experiences, challenges, and suggestions regarding the cyber tools they acquire. This feedback can then refine the procurement process, making it more responsive and dynamic.

In essence, tactical integration transcends mere procurement reforms. It encompasses the overarching need for deeper collaboration, information exchange, and joint readiness efforts among the U.S. and its Allies and partners. Embracing this holistic approach will pave the way for a more robust and unified cyber defense framework, safeguarding global digital infrastructure against increasingly sophisticated threats.

Moreover, adopting a multilateral exercise schedule that demonstrates interoperability and strengthens the capabilities of Allies and partners in high-end cyber conflicts is crucial.

Regular joint exercises provide an opportunity to test and enhance collective cyber defense capabilities. These exercises should focus on promoting tools standardization and interoperability, developing common operating procedures, and sharing best practices among participants.

In addition to multilateral exercises, the establishment of a rapid-response mechanism is vital for integrated deterrence in cybersecurity. This mechanism should enable swift information sharing, coordinated decision-making, and joint response actions in the event of a cyber incident or attack. By formalizing a protocol for cyber incident reporting and response, the United States and its Allies can ensure a rapid and effective reaction to emerging threats. This minimizes the potential damage and serves as a powerful deterrent, as adversaries know they will face a unified and immediate response from a coalition of nations. Such a mechanism strengthens the collective cybersecurity posture and reinforces the message that cyber aggression will not go unchecked.

Conclusion

In summary, applying the concept of integrated deterrence with Allies and partners in cyberspace involves a multi-faceted approach of cooperation, shared intelligence, and proactive defense. As cyber threats continue to evolve in complexity and scale, such an integrated approach will be crucial to ensuring cyberspace security.

Integrated deterrence with Allies and partners is an essential concept in cyberspace security cooperation. The United States and its Allies can effectively deter and counter cyber threats by deepening tactical, institutional, and strategic integration. Developing a shared strategic vision, enhanced information sharing, co-development of capabilities, and joint exercises are key components of integrated deterrence. Also, fostering public-private partnerships is another critical aspect of this approach. Collaborating with technology companies, critical infrastructure operators, and private sector entities can significantly enhance the cybersecurity posture of both the United States and its Allies. These partnerships can enable the sharing of threat intelligence, the development of innovative cyber defense solutions, and the swift response to emerging threats.

To realize the full potential of integrated deterrence in cybersecurity, the U.S. DOD must take immediate steps to implement the recommendations outlined in this chapter. By strengthening collaboration and cooperation, Allied and partner nations can collectively address emerging cyber challenges and maintain a secure cyberspace.

Chapter 6:

Developing A Combatant Command Campaign Plan (CCP) For Cyberspace Activities, Operations, And Investments (AOIs)

Introduction

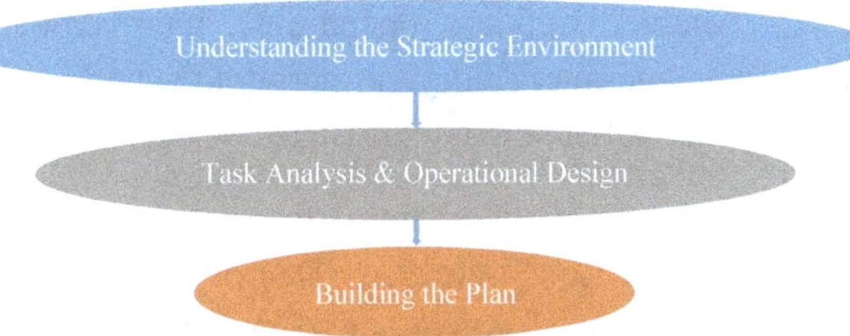

Figure 12: Development Phases of Combatant Command Campaign Plan (CCP)

Developing combatant command campaign plans (CCPs) is a core function of each geographic combatant command to integrate military operations, activities, and investments (AOIs) in its area of responsibility (AOR). The concepts behind and mechanics of developing CCPs are taught at service and joint professional military education programs. However, student planners rarely have sufficient time to create a CCP entirely. Furthermore, these programs often do not provide the context for a CCP's development. To better prepare future planners and country desk officers, the following is the author's perspective on the lessons learned developing a CCP at the US European Command (USEUCOM).

The purpose of Combatant Command Campaign Plans (CCPs)

To fully understand the purpose of a combatant command campaign plan (CCP), a planner must appreciate the purpose of the Geographic Combatant Command (GCC) in its specified area of responsibility (AOR). A GCC is directed to perform military operations, activities, and investments - or OAIs - in its AOR. A case in point is the mission of USEUCOM, which is to conduct military operations, international military partnering, and interagency partnering to enhance transatlantic security and defend the United States.

Most planners will examine the guidance provided in the National Defense Strategy (NDS) and National Military Strategy (NMS). However, new country desk officers and operational planning teams (OPTs) should also examine the following three critical documents: the National Security Strategy (NSS), the Unified Command Plan (UCP), and the Contingency Planning Guidance (CPG) to understand why every geographic combatant command needs to develop a CCP. [xxxviii, xxxix, xl, xli]

The following table highlights the differences between the National Security Strategy (NSS), National Defense Strategy (NDS), and National Military Strategy (NMS), showcasing their distinct roles within the U.S. strategic framework. It provides a comparative overview of each strategy's issuing authority, primary focus, scope, key components, intended audience, update frequency, example focus areas, relationship to other strategies, and level of detail. Each document serves a unique purpose, from broad national security goals in the NSS to specific defense objectives in the NDS and detailed military operational plans in the NMS. This structure ensures a coherent and coordinated approach to addressing current and emerging threats across all domains of national security.

Comparison of National Security Strategy (NSS), National Defense Strategy (NDS), and National Military Strategy (NMS):[xlii]

Attribute	National Security Strategy (NSS)	National Defense Strategy (NDS)	National Military Strategy (NMS)
Issuing Authority	President of the United States	Secretary of Defense	Chairman of the Joint Chiefs of Staff
Primary Focus	Broad national security priorities across multiple domains	Defense priorities and objectives for the Department of Defense	Operational and tactical plans for the military
Scope	Comprehensive, including defense, diplomacy, economy, energy, and more	Focused on defense and security priorities, military modernization, and resource allocation	Detailed military operations, force readiness, and campaign strategies

Key Components	Global threats and challenges, economic and diplomatic policies, alliances, defense	Strategic defense goals, force structure, partnerships, and innovation	Force employment plans, readiness, deterrence, and response measures
Audience	All U.S. government agencies, allies, and the public	Primarily the Department of Defense, U.S. military branches	Military leadership and the armed forces
Update Frequency	Typically, every 4 years	Typically, every 4 years, aligning with the NSS	As needed, based on changes in strategic or operational needs
Example Focus Areas	Cybersecurity, climate change, regional stability, trade security	Military alliances, deterrence, technological advancements	Operational tactics, readiness, specific adversary strategies
Relationship to Other Strategies	Highest level of guidance; shapes NDS and NMS	Informed by the NSS; guides the NMS	Implements the objectives of both NSS and NDS
Level of Detail	High-level vision and priorities	Mid-level, linking policy to resources and force structuring	Detailed, tactical, and operational plans

The NSS articulates the nation's broad national security objectives and encompasses the whole government. While student planners often learn strategy consists of ends, ways, and means, the NSS does not include that language. Rather, the NSS is an aspirational document specifying the nation's enduring and core regional interests.

For EUCOM, the core interests are broadly stated as requirements to:[xliii]

Fortify the Trans-Atlantic Alliance by increasing collaboration with European Allies and partners.

Ensure the region is not dominated by a hostile power, either from within the AOR or externally (e.g., Russia or China), and

Protect the homeland and counter security threats stemming from transnational organized crime and the illicit trafficking of narcotics, humans, and weapons, including weapons of mass destruction.

It is important to know that UCP is tied to the NSS - although this is not explicitly articulated in either document. The UCP defines the missions of the GCCs and the functional component commands such as the U.S. Special Operations Command (SOCOM). The UCP identifies each GCC's boundaries and broadly directs all GCCs to detect and counter functional threats to - and, if necessary, defend – the United States interests.

Functional threats refer to threats not tied to a specific geographic region but instead arise from certain functions or capabilities that adversaries possess. Here are a few examples:

Cyber Threats: This includes everything from cyber espionage and cyber warfare to cyber terrorism and cybercrime. The threat comes from the capability of adversaries to exploit vulnerabilities in information systems, networks, and cyberinfrastructure.

Space-Based Threats: This includes anti-satellite weapons and other capabilities that can disrupt or destroy space-based assets, such as satellites. These threats are functional because they are tied to the capabilities of these systems, not to a specific geographical area.

Information Warfare: This includes disinformation campaigns, propaganda, and other efforts to manipulate information to influence public opinion and decision-making. These threats are functional because they are tied to the capability to manipulate information, not a specific geographical area.

Economic Warfare: This includes economic sanctions, trade wars, and other economic actions taken to damage an adversary's economy. The threat is tied to the capability to disrupt or damage an economy, not a specific geographical area.

Weapons of Mass Destruction (WMD): The proliferation and potential use of chemical, biological, radiological, and nuclear (CBRN) weapons pose a major threat to national and global security. This threat is functional because it's tied to the capabilities of these weapons, not to a specific geographical area.

Terrorism: Terrorism is a global problem not confined to any geographical region. The threat is linked to the capability of terrorist groups to carry out attacks and spread fear.

Cumulatively, the OPT should learn the task and purpose of developing a CCP by reviewing those three documents: the National Security Strategy (NSS), the Unified Command Plan (UCP), and the Contingency Planning Guidance (CPG). Most CCP should be developed to become operational in a theater campaign order (TCO) that directs and assesses OAIs over a five-year timeline. The CCP and the TCO usually serve four key leaders:

the Commander, who owns every aspect of the plan and its execution,

the Chief of Staff, who integrates the entire staff in its implementation,

the Operations (J3) Directorate, which is responsible on behalf of the commander to prioritize resources and risk, and

the Component Commanders, who must execute the plan.

Since only the J3 has tasking authority, a TCO is a way to hold the staff and component commands accountable for the execution of the CCP. If done correctly, a synchronized CCP and TCO allow the Commander, the Chief of Staff, and J3 to manage the campaign in a resource- and risk-informed manner. The process is usually broken into two phases. Phase one consists of understanding the strategic environment, task analysis, and developing the operational approach. Phase two consists of developing the structure of the plan.

The unified command plan (UCP) and its associated combatant commands (COCOMs) exert a significant influence on the organization, training, and resourcing of the U.S. Armed Forces, areas that fall within the constitutional authority of Congress. The UCP, a classified executive branch document prepared by the Chairman of the Joint Chiefs of Staff (CJCS) and revised biennially, furnishes operational instructions, command, and control, as well as assigns missions, planning, training, and operational responsibilities to the COCOMs. These COCOMs, both functional and geographic, play crucial roles: functional COCOMs operate globally across boundaries, offering unique capabilities to both geographic combatant commands and the services, while geographic COCOMs concentrate on specific regions, delineating their areas of operation and maintaining a distinct regional military focus. There are currently nine COCOMs, as outlined below:[xliv]

- USSOCOM: U.S. Special Operations Command, MacDill Air Force Base, FL.

- USSTRATCOM: U.S. Strategic Command, Offutt Air Force Base, NE.

- USTRANSCOM: U.S. Transportation Command, Scott Air Force Base, IL.

- USAFRICOM: U.S. Africa Command, Kelley Barracks, Stuttgart, Germany.

- USCENTCOM: U.S. Central Command, MacDill Air Force Base, FL.

- USEUCOM: U.S. European Command, Patch Barracks, Stuttgart, Germany.

- USNORTHCOM: U.S. Northern Command, Peterson Air Force Base, CO.

- USPACOM: U.S. Pacific Command, Camp H.M. Smith, HI.

- USSOUTHCOM: U.S. Southern Command, Miami, FL.

Understanding the Strategic Environment

In phase one, we analyze the strategic environment by conducting an intelligence preparation of the battlefield (IPB). At the strategic and operational levels, this means examining the geography, history, economic drivers, and technological challenges and opportunities present in the AOR. A tabletop exercise should be conducted using the pieces from the board game Axis and Allies to lay out the AOR geography on a map to achieve understanding among the OPT. During that exercise, participants should lay out the configuration of the critical energy (oil, natural gas, and coal) sites, energy pipelines, rail and road infrastructure, digital infrastructure, maritime routes, and chokepoints. Then, we lay out where Russia, China, the United States, and regional powers such as Germany, the United Kingdom, and France are postured (both economically and militarily). Below is an example of a tabletop exercise that helps students understand the strategic environment in the European AOR.[xlv]

Tabletop Exercise: Axis and Allies - European Area of Responsibility (AOR)

Objective: To outline the geographical features and key elements of the European AOR in the Axis and Allies board game, emphasizing the geo-economic and geostrategic interests at play. Additionally, identify major US rivals and regional powers both economically and militarily and highlight three maritime chokepoints that could impact US joint operations.

Scenario: In this tabletop exercise scenario, the Map Configuration plays a crucial role in assessing the geopolitical landscape, as Geostrategic Interests intersect with US Rivals and Regional Powers near critical Maritime Chokepoints, creating a dynamic and complex strategic environment.

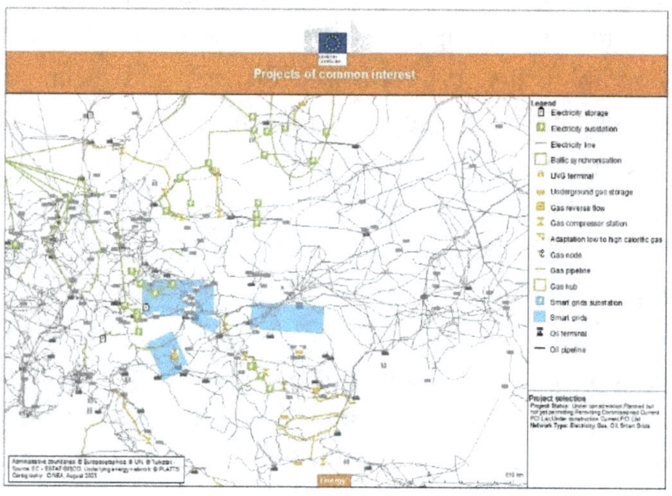

Figure 13: Electricity, Natural Gas, Smart Grids, and Oil Infrastructure in Europe

1. Map Configuration: Lay out the European AOR geography on the game map, including energy sites (oil, natural gas, electricity lines, and wind turbines), energy pipelines, rail and road infrastructure, digital infrastructure, and maritime routes.[xlvi]

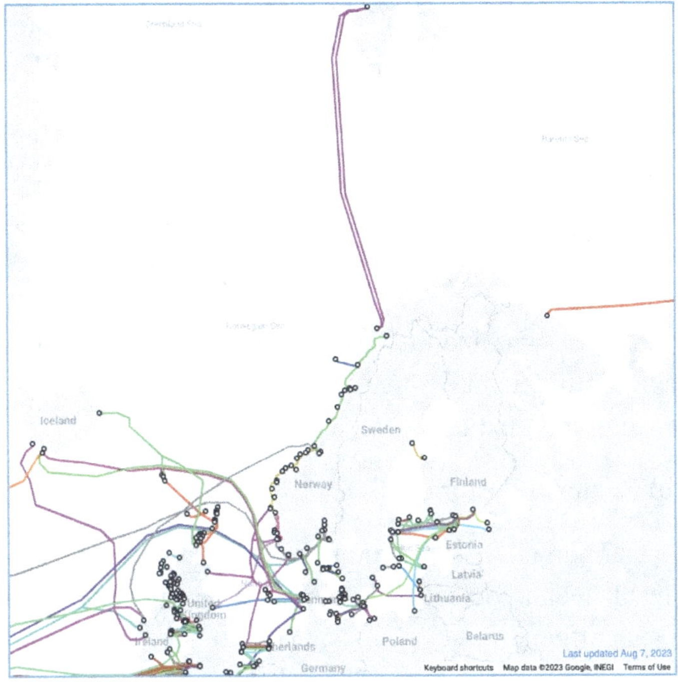

Figure 14: Submarine Cable Map in Europe

2. Geo-Economic Interests: Discuss the significant geo-economic interests within the European AOR, such as access to vital energy resources, control over transportation networks (pipelines, rail, and roads), and the influence exerted through digital infrastructure such as submarine cables.[xlvii]

3. Geostrategic Interests: Explore the key geostrategic interests of the AOR, including establishing regional dominance, maintaining the security of maritime routes, ensuring access to critical resources, and securing favorable trade agreements.

4. US Rivals and Regional Powers: Identify major US rivals and regional powers in the European AOR, both economically and militarily. These may include:

a) Rivals:

- Russia: A significant economic and military power with vast energy resources and a strong regional military presence.

- China: Expanding economic influence, particularly through infrastructure investments and a growing naval presence in the Mediterranean and Baltic seas

b) Regional Powers:

- Germany: An influential economic powerhouse with advanced technological capabilities and a key player in European affairs.

- United Kingdom: A major economic and military power with historical regional ties and a strong naval presence.

- France: A significant economic and military player interested in maintaining stability in the Mediterranean and its former colonies.

5. Maritime Chokepoints: Highlight three maritime chokepoints in the European AOR that could affect US joint operations. These chokepoints may include:

a) The Turkish Straits (Bosporus and Dardanelles): Essential for maritime access to the Black Sea and a critical transit point for goods and energy resources.

b) The English Channel: A narrow passage separating the UK from mainland Europe, controlling access to the North Sea and the Atlantic Ocean.

c) The Strait of Gibraltar: A crucial chokepoint between the Mediterranean Sea and the Atlantic Ocean, impacting access to the European AOR from the west.

Conclusion: The tabletop exercise provides an overview of the European AOR in Axis and Allies, highlighting the geography, key elements, and the geo-economic and geostrategic interests at play. Understanding the rivalries, regional powers, and maritime chokepoints is crucial for understanding the strategic environment.

When conducting such an exercise, the OPT should use operational terms such as key terrain and interior lines when discussing Russian and Chinese strategic and operational activities that could directly or indirectly control access to the AOR's key terrain. This analysis should expose EUCOM's posture against current and future threats and will help with the next part of the CCP development: task analysis.

Task Analysis and Operational Design Development

After a comprehensive understanding of the strategic environment, the OPT moves on to the task analysis. They review the tasks outlined in the NDS, NMS, global campaign plans (GCPs), and global integrated base plans. The team can manage the process more effectively by deconstructing these tasks into their essential elements. They focus on essential tasks that EUCOM needs to concentrate on to achieve its broad mission as outlined in the UCP. The tasks are then analyzed in relation to the NMS's five mission areas (Assure Allies and partners, Compete Below the Level of Armed Conflict, Deter Conventional Attack, Deter Strategic Attack, and Respond to Threats) and aligning them to the five threat areas (Russia, China, North Korea, Iran, and Non-state actors).

Next, we identify the military objectives because we understand the enduring nature of gaining and maintaining a position of advantage as articulated in Joint Doctrine Note 1-19: *Competition Continuum* and the *Joint Concept for Integrated Campaigning*.

Next, the OPT should inventory assets available in the theater (personnel, units, etc.) to establish a baseline. Additionally, the OPT should regularly conduct audits for plans and orders that are outdated or the ones that provide contradictory guidance. Furthermore, the OPT needs to properly account for how many tasks are assigned to the same component or unit or whether there are sufficient resources to accomplish those tasks.

The OPT's analysis and audit should allow the command to develop an operational design and a draft mission statement. Once the commander approves the mission statement and the operational design, the OPT transitions into phase two of campaign plan development.

Building the Command Campaign Plan (CCP)

Phase two consists of determining how to structure the campaign plan and how to tie it directly into the TCO. The aim is to create a concise yet comprehensive document that provides clear overarching guidance for the command to fulfill its intent. The plan is broken down into various lines of effort, each detailed in a separate appendix.

Using the National Military Strategy (NMS) mission areas, the OPT should develop intermediate military objectives (IMOs). IMOs are a series of objectives organized along a line of effort that are measurable and support the achievement of a military objective or end state. This will help identify critical IMOs that need to become tasks to be completed within the TCO's two-year timeline.

Creating a Joint Scheme of Maneuver for Coordinated Cyber Operations in Theater

To develop campaign synchronization, country desk officers and planners should create a joint scheme of maneuver to help the staff and components visualize and organize the IMO-task connection with proposed OAIs. The joint scheme of maneuver consisting of posture, security cooperation, and communications synchronization would directly influence the theater posture plan and security cooperation plan.

A joint scheme of maneuver is a military strategy that outlines how multiple branches of the armed forces (e.g., Army, Navy, Air Force, Marines, etc.) will coordinate and work together to achieve a common objective in a military operation. This scheme is typically developed during the planning phase of an operation and takes into account the unique capabilities and strengths of each military branch.

In the context of a combatant command campaign plan (CCP), a joint scheme of maneuver can help the staff and components visualize and organize how they will work together to achieve their objectives. This might involve outlining how the Army will secure a specific area, how the Air Force will provide air cover, and how the Navy will support with naval firepower, among other things. The joint scheme of maneuver can also help identify potential threats and opportunities and inform efforts to synchronize components' actions across the theater.

The goal of a joint scheme of maneuver is to maximize the effectiveness and efficiency of the operation by ensuring that all branches of the military are working together in a coordinated and cohesive way. It also helps reduce the risk of friendly fire and other potential issues arising when multiple branches operate in the same area.

In a hypothetical joint scheme of maneuver focused on defensive cyber operations, several branches of the U.S. military could collaborate to protect an ally's operational network against cyber threats. Here is a breakdown of the different phases:

1. Planning Phase: The U.S. Cyber Command (USCYBERCOM), in partnership with intelligence agencies such as the National Security Agency (NSA), conducts a comprehensive analysis of the ally's operational network to identify potential vulnerabilities and existing threats. This involves threat hunting, penetration testing, and vulnerability assessments. They also analyze the methods, tools, and tactics of potential adversaries who might threaten the network.

2. Preparation Phase: Marines Force in Europe (MARFOREUR) works on hardening and securing the ally's operational network. This could involve setting up firewalls, intrusion detection systems, and encryption protocols.

MARFOREUR could also implement network segmentation and least privilege policies to limit the potential damage of a successful attack.

3. Implementation Phase: USCYBERCOM sets up active cyber defense measures. This could involve setting up honeypots to trap and analyze attacks, deploying countermeasures against detected threats, and constantly monitoring the network for any signs of intrusion.

4. Coordination with Other Branches: The Air Force's Cyber Command could provide airborne cyber capabilities to help monitor and defend satellite networks against adversarial attacks. The Navy's Fleet Cyber Command could support securing communication and data transmission lines across naval platforms. The Army's Cyber Command could help secure ground-based infrastructure and provide mobile and tactical cyber defense capabilities.

5. Response to Incidents: In the event of a detected cyber attack, the joint forces would work together to mitigate the attack, analyze the attack vectors, and strengthen the network's defenses to prevent future attacks. They would also work with the ally's own cyber defense forces, sharing information and cooperating closely to respond effectively to the threat.

6. Ongoing Assessment and Adaptation: The joint scheme of maneuver would include an ongoing assessment of the Ally's networks' security and the effectiveness of the defense measures. As new threats are identified and the network grows, the defense measures would be adapted accordingly.

This example demonstrates a well-coordinated and comprehensive effort across multiple branches of the U.S.

military to defend an ally's operational network against cyber attacks. This sort of cooperation is a key part of the joint scheme of maneuver concept.

Using the joint scheme of maneuver described above, the OPT can develop the proposed plans for OAIs to guarantee consistency for the command's assessment model. By using this approach across different areas of focus, the OPT can spot potential threats and opportunities. For instance, pinpointing the necessities and weaknesses linked to contingency plans will inform endeavors with the contingency planning process (CCP) and future theater campaign plan (TCP), enabling the synchronization of components' actions throughout the theater. This process was designed to assist the command in forecasting and aligning its resource requirements.[xlviii]

Furthermore, integrating emerging joint warfighting concepts, such as the Army's multi-domain operations (e.g., cyberspace and electronic warfare (EW) capabilities), into the command's exercise program, especially when operating with Allies and partners, is crucial when building the plan.

Coordinating Components: The Impact of CCP and TCO on Force Management

The CCP's goal is to provide a clear framework for the components to visualize their requirements five years in the future with a level of fidelity to clearly articulate those requirements to their service headquarters as part of the program objective memoranda they submitted. This articulation is essential for posture-related adjustments since the theater posture plan covers a five-to-eight-year horizon.[xlix]

Similarly, the TCO synchronizes EUCOM's subordinate operations orders for named operations or exercises such as the Austere Challenge (AC)[1]. The TCO provides sufficient clarity that the components can plan and submit their global force management requirements to their service headquarters. As a result, both the campaign plan and the TCO provide a strategic and operational framework for the command and components to conduct OAIs, informed by annual assessments linked to the global force management and budgeting processes.

Conclusion

In summary, comprehending the intricacies of developing a Command Campaign Plan (CCP) is essential for future planners and country desk officers to effectively manage Operational Planning Teams (OPTs) and produce actionable plans. By delving deeper into the process beyond basic instruction, individuals can enhance their ability to navigate complexities and deliver valuable, executable products that align with strategic objectives, enabling planners to anticipate challenges, adapt strategies, and foster collaboration among diverse stakeholders, ultimately enhancing the efficiency and effectiveness of military operations and interagency efforts in complex operational environments.

Chapter 7:
Cyberspace Security Cooperation Platforms and Tools

Introduction

Theater security cooperation requirements for forces are currently managed and tracked in "Socium" (non-acronymous). "Socium" is an activity lifecycle management system that plans, executes, monitors, and evaluates security cooperation activities. This system is owned and maintained by the Defense Security Cooperation Agency (DSCA) and is intended to be used by SCOs, GCCs, MILDEPS, IAs, Regional Centers, and any other entities that seek to track the lifecycle of security cooperation activities. Its original premise was to replace the Global Theater Security Management Information System (G-TSCMIS). However, Socium's scope is substantially broader than the legacy system. It expands upon G-TSCMIS' event record management by (1) building and streamlining the approval process for Significant Security Cooperation Initiatives (SSCIs) or strategic alignment, (2) version control, collaboration, and development of the Training and Equipment Lists (TELs), (3) converting prose into structured data to enable business analytics, (4) archiving, uploading, and searching community documentation to aid knowledge transfer and records management, (5) centralizing an Assessment, Monitor, and Evaluation (AM&E) framework to house pertinent data points to improve execution, and (6) interfacing with other Authoritative Data Sources to increase knowledge and reduce data-entry.

Additionally, some commands have their own systems; for instance, the United States European Command (EUCOM) uses a process called Strategy for Active Security Plan (SASPLAN)[li] to track Theater Security Cooperation (TSC) requirements. There is also a Concept & Funding Request (CFR) system, a collaborative online database developed to capture all SC activities, engagements, and events happening in the theater with its funding source, authority, and approval status. CFR (Concept & Funding Request) is a GCC-specific platform used by the U.S. European Command (EUCOM), U.S. Africa Command (AFRICOM), and U.S. Central Command (CENTCOM). SASPLAN and Socium do share some compatibility and overlap in some functionalities. Below is a comparison of SC Platforms Based on GCC's Requirements:[lii]

Requirement	SAS-PLAN	CFR	Socium	G-TSCMIS
User-friendly	√	√	O	×
Consistently maintained	√	√	√	×
Program of record	√	√	√	√
Activity life-cycle management	O	O	O	×
Enforce policies related to mandatory use.	√	√	√	√
Data entry verification to ensure completeness (i.e., data standardization)	√	√	√	×
Provide the ability to pair activities with long-term planning and strategy.	√	√	O	×
Provide visibility over all activity types across all AORs	×	×	√	×
Support integrated analytic capabilities.	×	×	O	×
Single platform	×	×	O	×

NOTE: *Green (√) = requirements supported; Yellow (O) = requirements not completely supported or still in development; Red (✗) = requirements not supported.*

The Global Theater Security Cooperation Management Information System (G-TSCMIS) Program (Socium's predecessor) was initially an Office of the Secretary of Defense (OSD) initiative to develop and deploy a common web-based, centrally hosted Management Information System (MIS) that would serve as the information focal point for the Nation's Security Cooperation (SC) efforts by providing decision-makers, SC planners and other users with the ability to view, manage, assess, and report SC activities and events.[liii]

To meet the FY2017 NDAA requirements, DSCA developed Socium, a successor system to replace G-TSCMIS. Socium is an innovative platform capable of meeting the needs of the SC enterprise and developing enterprise-wide technology to facilitate and integrate planning, budgeting, collaboration, program design, assessment, monitoring, evaluation (AM&E), and reporting in support of all U.S. security cooperation activities.[liv]

Socium Functionality

The Socium portal's functionality is determined by the user's role within the application. Users can either view the data or edit the data. "Activity Planners" are tasked with creating and monitoring activities along with "Contributors" they choose to assist them along the way. "Reviewers" are charged with vetting activity data and determining its adequacy for progress along its lifecycle. Additionally, there are additional user roles that simply allow users to view all the data that is there. This falls in line with the notion that all users within Socium can view all of its data.

Socium Account Registration

To obtain access to Socium, prospective users must first submit a completed System Authorization Access Request (SAAR) form. An "Organization Information Owner" (OIO) signature is needed before the request can be sent to the help desk for account creation. There are OIOs embedded into each organization with data within the application. If there is not, that organization must submit a request to the Socium Program Team for authority to designate a member with the appropriate permissions to become an OIO.

Additional Cyberspace Security Cooperation Tools

In this section, we describe additional tools and platforms that support Cyberspace Security Cooperation in addition to those described above. These tools and platforms typically provide an important and targeted capability to stakeholders and the broader DOD community but are not tied to planning, requests for funding, or tracking activities and engagements.

All Partners Access Network (APAN)

APAN is an unclassified shared enterprise service dating back to 1997 that provides structured (via SharePoint) and unstructured (via Verint Telligent) collaboration capabilities with multinational partners, NGOs, and various U.S. federal and state agencies. APAN also makes use of ESRI ArcGIS analytic and visualization capabilities. APAN is not inherently responsible for any data; all data sets are imported via other activity tracking and managing systems. Although the number of users and communities continues to increase every year (to approximately 224,000 users in 2018), the user turnover rate is significant, with 30. percent of users returning in 2018.

Advana

Advana is an analytics platform for enterprise-wide authoritative data management and analytics for OSD. It houses a collection of enterprise data as a data warehouse and supports decision-making across DOD and business with support analytics, visualizations, and various support services. Developed as an authoritative source for audit and business data analytics, Advana hosts more than 15 billion transactions, with more than 7,000 users and 250-plus dashboards as of 2020. Advana has an automated data pipeline from more than 120 source systems from the broad DOD community and reconciles more than $1 trillion in financial transactions. It has the flexibility to support analytics in the areas of audit, financial operations, cost management, and performance management. Across OSD, Advana is used to improve data-sharing and transparency with a centralized repository of acquisition data.

Conclusion

In summary, security cooperation personnel have access to numerous automated systems. Access has transformed from direct links for a few specific users to worldwide access via the internet. Newer systems such as the EUCOM SASPLAN portal and CFR portal have been specifically designed with the needs of the end user in mind. The use of these systems has greatly enhanced communication between the Security Cooperation Offices (SCOs), Geographic Combatant Commands (GCCs),

Country Team, and Host Nation Team. The impact of the increased access to the systems has been profoundly beneficial, not only to security cooperation activities but, ultimately, to the international customer as well.

Chapter 8:

Country Plan, Cyber Line of Activity (LOA), and Cyber Engagement Plan

Introduction

When working with an ally or partner under Security Cooperation, Geographic Combatant Commands (GCC) must have a complete country plan. This country plan is essential for addressing emerging regional and ethnic alignments and emerging threats, including information operations (IO) and cyber warfare. The country plan is updated annually by the Country Team, led by the Office of Defense Cooperation (ODC), State Partnership Program (SPP), and country desk officers of these Allies and partners. Each country plan includes multiple Lines of Activities (LOAs) that define various engagement strategies and their implementation for each area of cooperation and support, such as IO or Cyber. Additionally, each LOA must have well-defined SMART objectives, outcomes, milestones, and tasks. In this chapter, we will explore the definition of the Cyber Line of Activity (LOA) and how it is implemented and executed at the GCC level.

Cyber LOA and Cyber Roadmap Explained

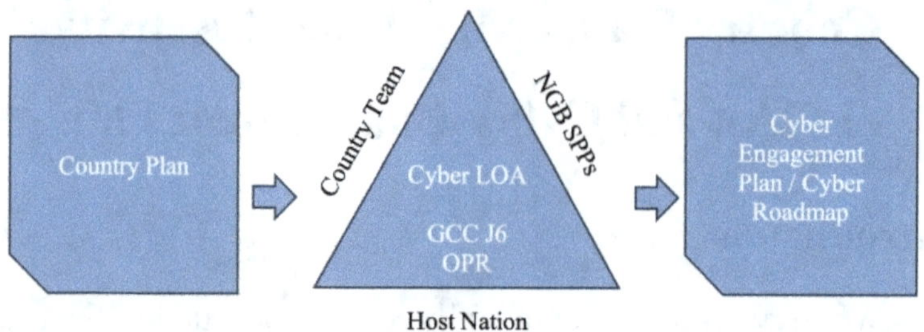

Figure 15: Cyber Roadmap

Before collaborating with an ally or partner under Cyberspace Security Cooperation, a Cyberspace Operations LOA must be defined, along with its end state and priorities. The Joint Staff (J6) typically serves as the Office of Primary Responsibility (OPR) for Cyberspace Operations LOA at the GCC level. The OPR is responsible for ensuring coordination among equity-holding components, including OSD Components, the General Counsel, the Joint Staff, Service Secretaries, and the Military Departments. Without a Cyber Engagement Plan (also known as a Cyber Roadmap), a Cyber LOA cannot exist. The Cyber Engagement Plan is a roadmap outlining the purpose and scope of cooperation, different Lines of Efforts (LOEs), long-term and short-term objectives, milestones, tasks, and the engagement map, listing all activities, meetings, and Key Leader Engagements (KLEs), also known as Concept and Funding Request (CFR) events, needed to achieve the calendar year objectives.

Cyberspace Operations LOA

The end state of the Cyber LOA is achieved when the GCC and its Allies and partners have synchronized cyber programs, skilled cyber professionals, formal sharing of cyber threat data and information, defense of Key Terrain-Cyber (KT-C) and infrastructure, and joint crisis planning actions. In the Army's Defense in Depth strategy, key cyber terrain includes "physical and logical infrastructure and mission data." Cyber LOA priorities should include cyber threat information sharing, conducting assessments to identify Cyberspace Security Cooperation focus areas, building Allies' and partners' cyberspace capacity and capabilities, synchronizing NGB/SPP and component efforts and activities, incorporating them into country plans/roadmaps, identifying available cyber training programs for foreign nationals, prioritizing 'Cyber Education' at the country level, and supporting Mil-cyber schools' training and education. Every Cyber LOA should support the following objectives:

1) Develop Network Operations and Defense Programs

2) Develop a Cyberspace Security Cooperation Roadmap

3) Establish and Maintain Policies and Practices

4) Maintain Visibility of the Cyberspace Program

5) Develop Cyberspace Professionals

6) Maintain Trusted Organizational Relationships

7) Shared Situational Awareness within Cyberspace

8) Identify Network Sharing Standards

9) Conduct Unclassified Information Sharing

10)   Conduct Classified Information Sharing

11)   Defend Key Terrain-Cyberspace

12)   Identify   KT-C   and   mission-relevant infrastructure

13)   Exercise Defense Employment

14)   Develop/Refine Defensive Tactics, Techniques and Procedures (TTPs)

15)   Deliver Warfighting Effects

16)   Identify   Required   Operational   Cyber Capabilities

17)   Practice Deliberate Planning and Crisis Action Planning

18)   Exercise Interoperability and Execution

19)   Prepare to Execute Joint Cyberspace Operations

The GCC J6 Role

As mentioned earlier, the GCC J6 serves as the Office of Primary Responsibility for the Cyber LOA. The LOA OPR is responsible for supporting the development and building of Allied and Partner Nation (PN)'s capability and capacity in cybersecurity and defensive cyber operations. This is achieved through a transparent and mutually beneficial partnership aimed at achieving agreed-upon goals and objectives. In collaboration with the Embassy/country team, NGB SPP, and Host Nation (HN) military-cyber representatives, the OPR collectively identifies cyberspace capabilities that align with the U.S. and its Allies' respective national and military cyber strategies. The OPR can leverage its expertise and resources, tasking components to achieve cyberspace security cooperation objectives within the geographical theater. They can use NGB SPP personnel with U.S.-based cyber expertise to support cyber capacity building for Allies and partners. They can also use Foreign Military Financing (FMF) and other dedicated Build Partner Capacity (BPC) programs to procure equipment, tools, and training while coordinating with additional partner nations (PNs) to support trilateral/multilateral efforts.

Cyber Roadmap Purpose

The Cyber Engagement Plan serves as a synchronized strategic direction and plan of action for partnership capacity with related capabilities to deter cyberspace aggression from threat actors based on coordinated priorities. It acts as a framework to identify specific tasks and track progress in coordination with all Cyberspace Security Cooperation stakeholders, including USCYBERCOM, USEUCOM Components, National Guard Bureau (NGB), State Partner to the Nation, U.S. Embassy Team, Ministry of Defense, and Military Defense Forces.

Cyber Roadmap Goals and Objectives

Strategic goals and objectives are unattainable without a unified approach among partners and other key friends and Allies abroad. Therefore, a Cyber Engagement Plan requires a long-term, focused approach to building the capacity and capability of mission-critical partnerships. It must be fully coordinated with all necessary players and stakeholders, including USCYBERCOM, GCC Components, NGB State Partner to the Nation, U.S. Embassy Team, Ministry of Defense, and Military Defense Forces.

Cyber Lines of Efforts

In the Cyber Engagement Plan, targeted efforts are meant to improve the cyberspace operations capabilities of partners, Allies, and friends. Cooperation between the OPR, GCC components, and the Ally and partner cyber units must be aligned under well-defined primary Lines of Efforts (LOEs). Some examples of these LOEs include:

Shared Situational Awareness: Supporting cyber threat and defense information exchange.

Cyberspace Operations: Supporting protection of critical information infrastructure and defensive cyber operations planning.

CFR Events (Activities/Meetings)

Planning and organizing CFR events to reach calendar year objectives are the responsibility of the OPR and their regional country desk officers. Applying the proper funding and fiscal authority for each of these events is crucial for approval. Proper classification of a proposed event as a Military-to-Military familiarization activity, as opposed to training or a multilateral exercise, is essential to use the respective fiscal authority for funding. According to Joint Publication 3-20 Security Cooperation, Military-to-Military engagement is not considered training. Activities in this category include military staff talks, Subject Matter Expert (SME) exchanges, conferences, planning workshops, and similar events. CFR events might include Key Leader Engagements (KLEs), SME Engagements, Action Officer Working Groups (WG), Technical Workshops, Cyber Exercises, Seminars, and Technical Exchanges.

Familiarization versus Training

The distinction between familiarization and training lies in whether the event is hands-on or involves substantial Partner Nation (PN) effort, certification, skill, or degree. If the event directly supports the development or sustainment of the operational readiness of the PN, it must be considered training. Familiarization, on the other hand, acquaints the country with U.S. DOD systems procedures or shapes their own long-term capabilities and strategy.

CFR Event Planning

To create a CFR event, a Request for Support (RFS) from the Partner Nation (PN) should be submitted to the GCC's OPR through the U.S. Embassy office or the Office of Defense Attaché or Cooperation office. The RFS should outline the requesting PN's organization and their Point of Contact (POC), the proposed event name, dates, and location, the event type (e.g., In-Country Event, Out of Country Event, Multi-Lateral Engagement, Senior Leader Visit, State Partnership Event, Exercise, Meeting, or other). The RFS should list the expected number of participants and the desired U.S. organizations' participation (e.g., USCYBERCOM, JFHQ, etc.). Additionally, the RFS should specify the event's purpose, desired outcome, draft agenda, content, and itinerary. Refer to Appendix A for the Cyber Engagement Form template.

CFR Event Management

When creating and managing CFR events, it is crucial to provide explicit and clear details on the 5 W's (Who, What, When, Where, and Why). Each CFR event must have a title indicating the authority for funding, an event type, a Line of Activity (e.g., Cyber LOA), a Partner Nation (PN) Objective, a Funding Request, and status flow, such as Draft, Submitted, Legal Review, Cleared Legal, Approved/Awaiting Funding, Funded, Executed, and Completed.

CFR status flow is usually processed in one of the following phases:

CFR Status	Phase Description
Draft	CFR has not yet been submitted, which means no action will be taken.
Submitted	CFR has been submitted by OPR and will be reviewed by country desk officers and the Office of Defense Cooperation (ODC) Chief before legal review.
Legal Review	CFR is in the COCOM's Judge Advocate queue for review or Pending Deputy Commander (DCOM) Approval (e.g., Section 321/TWFFCC).
Edit	CFR was found legally insufficient and needed updating or OPR requests to be able to edit.
Cleared Legal	CFR has made it through legal and policy checks. Awaiting upload of Cost Estimate Worksheet (CEW) and Fund Cite Memo (FCM).

Approved/ Awaiting Funding	CFR funding documents have been received, and Resources Managers will coordinate with the comptroller.
Funded	COCOM's comptroller completes funding.
Executed	OPR/Event's POC marks the event as "Executed," and the budget analyst updates the "Obligated" column while OPR uploads the event's After-Action Review (AAR).
Completed	After the Action Review (AAR) has been uploaded and accepted.

Conclusion

In summary, this chapter emphasizes the critical importance of comprehensive country plans in Security Cooperation efforts undertaken by Geographic Combatant Commands (GCC) when collaborating with allies or partners. These plans serve as essential roadmaps for addressing evolving regional dynamics and emerging threats, with a particular focus on areas like information operations (IO) and cyber warfare. Led by key stakeholders such as the Office of Defense Cooperation (ODC), State Partnership Program (SPP), and country desk officers, the annual updating of these plans ensures they remain relevant and effective. Central to these plans are the Lines of Activities (LOAs), which outline specific engagement strategies for different areas such as IO or Cyber. These LOAs are characterized by SMART objectives, ensuring clarity and accountability in their execution. Moving forward, understanding and implementing these principles will be crucial for enhancing Security Cooperation efforts at the GCC level.

Chapter 9:

Leveraging U.S. Fiscal Authorities and Investments for Enhanced Cyberspace Security Cooperation

Introduction

Cyberspace has become an essential domain in modern warfare and international security. The interconnectedness of nations through the internet and digital networks has brought about new challenges and opportunities for cooperation. To address these challenges, countries worldwide have recognized the importance of investing in cyberspace security cooperation funding. This chapter delves into the various fiscal authorities utilized to support such initiatives, with a particular focus on the United States' involvement in global cyberspace security.

The following table outlines the different fiscal authorities and funding methods available for use under Cyberspace Security Cooperation. In the following section, we will discuss them in detail:

Fiscal Authorities & Funding Initiatives Available for Cyberspace Security Cooperation								
Fiscal Authority	10 U.S. Code § 321 (Exercises – Developing Countries			10 U.S. Code § 312 (M2M Developing Countries)			NDAA FY16 §1251 (Training & Multilateral Exercises)	10 U.S. Code §16 (M2M)
Funding	TWFFC*	EDI*	WIF*	EDI*	TCA*	WIF*	EDI*	TCA*	TCA*	EDI*
Personnel Type	Payment of Partner Nation (PN) Personnel							Payment of U.S. Personnel

Funding:
*TWFFC   Training with Friendly Foreign Countries
*EDI   European Deterrence Initiative
*TCA   Traditional COCOM Activities
*WIF   Wales Initiative Funds
*USAI   Ukraine Security Assistance Initiative

U.S. Funding Initiatives

Training with Friendly Foreign Countries (TWFFC)

The Training with Friendly Foreign Countries (TWFFC) initiative finances various aspects of joint exercises led by the U.S., including travel expenses, personnel support, lodging, food (rations and meals), fuel, equipment transportation, training ammunition, and other reasonable incremental expenses incurred by partner nations as specified in Title 10 U.S. Code Section 321.

European Deterrence Initiative (EDI)

The Fiscal Year (FY) 2024 European Deterrence Initiative (EDI) budget request of $3.6 billion aims to enhance the capability and readiness of U.S. Forces, NATO Allies, and regional partners within the U.S. European Command (USEUCOM) to respond swiftly to aggression and transnational threats by regional adversaries, particularly Russia, against NATO sovereign territory. The EDI investments focus on strengthening deterrence against Russian aggression and bolstering the security and capacity of NATO Allies. The initiatives within the FY 2024 EDI request aim to enhance Joint Reception, Staging, Onward Movement, and Integration (JRSO&I), Air Force-European Contingency Air Operations Sets (ECAOS), and Army Prepositioned Stocks (APS) capabilities.

How EDI Supports Cyberspace Security Cooperation

1. Enhanced Cybersecurity Readiness: The EDI investments in enhancing the capability and readiness of U.S. forces, NATO Allies, and regional partners can extend to

strengthening their cybersecurity defenses. Cyberspace is a critical domain in modern warfare, and by supporting cyber training, exercises, and infrastructure improvements, EDI can contribute to the overall cybersecurity readiness of partner nations.

2. Information Sharing and Interoperability: As part of EDI's focus on improving theater Joint Reception, Staging, Onward Movement, and Integration (JRSO&I), NATO Allies can enhance their information-sharing capabilities and interoperability in cyberspace. Improved coordination and collaboration in the digital realm will contribute to more effective responses to cyber threats.

3. Building Partner Capacity in Cybersecurity: EDI's emphasis on building partner capacity can include efforts to strengthen partner nations' cybersecurity capabilities. This may involve providing training, resources, and expertise to enhance their ability to defend against cyber attacks and respond to incidents effectively.

4. Cyber Exercises and Training: The EDI initiatives include exercises and training to strengthen deterrence against Russian aggression. These exercises can also incorporate cyberspace scenarios, allowing participants to practice responding to cyber threats and building cooperation among U.S. forces, NATO Allies, and regional partners.

5. Improved Infrastructure for Cyber Defense: EDI's investments in infrastructure improvements can extend to enhancing the cybersecurity infrastructure of U.S. forces and NATO Allies. This can include upgrading and securing

communication networks, data centers, and other critical cyber assets.

6. Increased Cyber Presence: EDI's emphasis on increased presence can translate to enhanced cybersecurity engagement with partner nations. Cyber experts and resources can be deployed to work alongside partner nations, fostering information exchange and strengthening their cyber defense capabilities.

Overall, the FY 2024 EDI request plays a crucial role in enhancing the security posture in Europe and reinforcing deterrence against Russian aggression. By strategically incorporating cyber initiatives and investments, EDI can support cyberspace security cooperation, fostering collaboration and resilience among U.S. forces, NATO Allies, and regional partners in the face of evolving cyber threats.[lv]

Wales Initiative Fund (WIF)

The Wales Initiative Fund (WIF) operates as a bilateral U.S. security cooperation program funded by the NDS Implementation Account, aimed at supporting defense reform efforts and institutional capacity building. This program specifically targets Eastern European, African, and Central Asian countries, as well as all developing North Atlantic Treaty Organization (NATO) partners. The primary objectives of the WIF program are to achieve jointly developed NATO Partnership Goals for PfP (Partnership for Peace) nations, enhance capabilities for multinational operations, facilitate access for U.S. armed forces in both peacetime and contingency operations, and foster relationships that promote U.S. security interests.

Under the WIF/PfP program, activities are tailored to align with regional and country-specific priorities as established by the Office of the Under Secretary of Defense for Policy, applicable Geographic Combatant Commands (GCCs), and the NATO Individual Partnership Action Plan (IPAP) and Partnership Goals (PGs) agreed upon by the partner nations.[lvi]

Traditional Combatant Commander Activities (TCA)

Traditional Combatant Commander Activities (TCA) has emerged as a broader set of permissible pre-operational Operation and Maintenance (O&M) and military personnel-funded activities with friendly foreign countries' security forces. While initially laid out in a statutory authorization that lacked appropriations, the history of TCA has been somewhat convoluted. Currently, the TCA is primarily described in a series of orders from the Joint Chiefs of Staff (TCA Orders) and guidance published by the implementing geographic combatant commands. These activities fall within the combatant commanders' authority to execute necessary tasks assigned to their commands, including interaction with foreign militaries in their area of responsibility or area of interest to promote regional and national security goals.

Scope and Types of Traditional Combatant Commander Activities

The Joint Chiefs of Staff guidance outlines the scope of TCA, which includes various activities such as military liaison teams, traveling contact teams, state partnership programs, regional conferences and seminars, information exchanges, unit exchanges, staff assistance/assessment visits, training program review and assessments, ship rider programs, joint/combined exercise observers, limited humanitarian and civic assistance (HCA), bilateral staff talks, and medical and dental support planning. Some combatant commands have expanded on this list to include familiarization events. It's important to note that this list is non-exhaustive, and combatant commanders have some flexibility in determining appropriate activities to carry out their missions effectively.

Expenses of United States Forces Only

Under a statutory TCA authority, appropriated funds are intended for the expenses of United States forces. Generally, O&M appropriations are designated for the operation and maintenance of military departments and activities of the Department of Defense, which means they are not intended for the benefit of foreign forces. Therefore, the use of O&M funds for expenses related to foreign forces requires a separate, express statutory authority. In some cases, when TCA progresses beyond their initial scope, they may be executed, in whole or part, under other security cooperation authorities. This limitation ensures that TCA is executed efficiently without becoming a substitute for other security cooperation activities that might require higher approval levels or greater involvement from the Department of State (DoS).

Involvement of the Department of State

In the current implementation, combatant commanders are required to obtain the concurrence of the appropriate United States Embassy before conducting TCA. However, unlike most security cooperation authorities under Chapter 16, Title 10 of the United States Code, TCA does not necessarily require direct involvement from the Secretary of State. In order to maintain efficiency, the executing combatant command should always keep the responsible chief of mission "fully and currently informed" of all TCA activities in a given country. This allows for the DoS to play a role in the TCA process while ensuring the vital efficiency of TCA operations.[lvii]

Ukraine Security Assistance Initiative (USAI)

The Ukraine Security Assistance Initiative (USAI) was established to provide critical support to Ukraine in countering Russian aggression. It serves as a crucial component of the U.S. commitment to Ukraine's sovereignty and territorial integrity. The initiative encompasses financial, military, and strategic aid to bolster Ukraine's ability to defend against external threats, including cyber-attacks.[lviii]

The USAI has been utilized to provide vital assistance to Ukraine in its ongoing war with Russia. This assistance includes cybersecurity support aimed at protecting Ukrainian critical infrastructure from cyber threats. The U.S. has offered expertise, training, and resources to help Ukraine build robust cyber defenses and respond effectively to cyber incidents during this period of conflict.

The USAI remains committed to enhancing Ukraine's capacity to safeguard its sovereignty and territorial integrity and promote institutional transformation. Through this funding, vital assistance and support are extended to Ukraine's military and national security forces, including the replacement of any weapons or defensive articles previously provided to the Government of Ukraine from the United States inventory.

Working in close coordination with the Department of State, the USAI encompasses various security assistance activities. These activities encompass intelligence support, cybersecurity support, personnel training, equipment, and logistics assistance, as well as the provision of essential supplies and services. The primary goal of this initiative is to bolster Ukraine's defensive capabilities, act as a deterrent against further Russian aggression, and foster comprehensive defense reforms. By enhancing Ukraine's combat capability and promoting interoperability with NATO and Western forces, the USAI aims to strengthen Ukraine's ability to defend itself effectively.[lix]

U.S. Fiscal Authorities

10 U.S. Code § 321 - Training with Friendly Foreign Countries (TWICC): Payment of Training and Exercise Expenses

Section 10 U.S. Code § 321 facilitates funding for training and exercise expenses incurred during joint cyber training exercises with friendly foreign countries. This authority allows the U.S. to engage in bilateral or multilateral cyber exercises aimed at enhancing cyber incident response, information sharing, and coordination. By funding these initiatives, the U.S. can build robust cyber defenses and foster collaboration in the face of cyber threats.[lx]

Section 10 U.S. Code § 321 authorizes the training of U.S. armed forces with the military or security forces of friendly foreign countries, subject to the Secretary of Defense's determination that it is in the national security interest of the United States to do so. This provision imposes certain limitations and requirements to ensure the effectiveness and appropriateness of such training:

(a) Training Authorized

- U.S. armed forces may train with friendly foreign forces, with the Secretary's approval, as long as it serves the national security interests of the United States.

- General purpose forces of the U.S. armed forces are restricted to training only with the military forces of friendly foreign countries.

- The training conducted should align with the mission essential tasks of the U.S. armed forces unit participating in it.

- Training should include elements promoting respect for human rights, fundamental freedoms, and legitimate civilian authority in the foreign country concerned.

(b) Authority To Pay Training and Exercise Expenses:

- The Secretary of a military department or combatant command can pay or authorize payment for various expenses related to training and exercises with friendly foreign countries, subject to regulations prescribed under subsection (e).

- The expenses covered include training forces, deploying them for training, and covering the incremental expenses incurred by the foreign country due to its participation in the training or exercise.

- Small-scale construction directly related to the effective accomplishment of the training or exercise may also be funded.

(c) Purpose of Training and Exercises:

- The primary purpose of the training and exercises, for which payment may be made under subsection (b), is to train U.S. forces.

- Selection of foreign partners for training and exercises should align with applicable guidance relating to the security cooperation programs and activities of the Department of Defense.

(d) Availability of Funds for Activities That Cross Fiscal Years:

- Amounts available for paying expenses under subsection (b) for a fiscal year can be used to cover expenses for training and exercises that span across fiscal years.

(e) Quarterly Notice on Planned Training:

- The Secretary of Defense is required to submit quarterly notices to Congress outlining the schedule of planned training engagements with friendly foreign countries during the following calendar quarter.

(f) Regulations:

- The Secretary of Defense is responsible for prescribing regulations to administer this section effectively, which shall be submitted to the relevant committees of Congress.

- The regulations should include requirements for prior approval of training and exercise activities, appropriate accounting procedures for expenditures, and provisions to limit the payment of incremental expenses to developing countries, except under exceptional circumstances.[lxi]

10 U.S. Code § 312 - Payment of Personnel Expenses Necessary for Theater Security Cooperation

Title 10 U.S. Code § 312 empowers the Department of Defense to allocate funds for covering personnel expenses required for theater security cooperation. In the context of cyberspace security, this funding authority enables the U.S. to support the exchange of cyber expertise and knowledge-sharing with partner nations. Through this provision, the U.S. can deploy cybersecurity experts to collaborate with foreign counterparts and strengthen their cyber defense capabilities.[lxii]

NDAA FY16 §1251 - Training for Eastern European National Military Forces during Multilateral Exercises

The National Defense Authorization Act (NDAA) for Fiscal Year 2016, Section 1251, emphasizes the importance of training Eastern European national military forces through multilateral exercises. Although this provision primarily pertains to traditional military exercises, its principles can be applied to cyberspace security cooperation. By leveraging this authority, the U.S. can extend its support to Eastern European countries in the sphere of cyber defense, reinforcing regional resilience against cyber threats.[lxiii]

Section 1251 authorizes security assistance training of foreign military forces of post-1998 NATO Allies and non-NATO Partners for Peace (PfP) countries to increase:

- Interoperability and ability to participate in U.S. or NATO-led coalition efforts

- Capacity to respond to external threats

- Capacity to respond to hybrid warfare

- Capacity to respond to calls for collective action within NATO

The training must be in connection with a multinational exercise (Joint Exercise with three countries or more (USA, 1251 eligible country, third country, e.g., DEFENDER Europe). The 1251 training event can be incorporated into the joint exercise design. Additionally, Allied military forces receiving training must be Leahy vetted.

1251 authority – FY17 NDAA (Section 1233) expanded the provision of security assistance training to national security forces and vice-national military forces only. National military and national-level security forces must have functional responsibilities for operations or activities that contribute to an international coalition operation that is determined by the Secretary to be in the national interest of the United States (e.g., Military Intelligence Operations, Defensive Cyber Operations). Finally, 1251 - FY21 NDAA (Section 1243) expanded 1251 authority through the period ending on December 21, 2023.

10 U.S. Code §164 - Commanders of Combatant Commands: Assignment, Powers, and Duties

Title 10 U.S. Code § 164 defines the assignment, powers, and duties of commanders of combatant commands. Within the context of cyberspace security cooperation, combatant commanders play a vital role in coordinating and implementing joint cyber initiatives with partner nations. This fiscal authority enables commanders to access funds and allocate resources efficiently, thereby facilitating cyber capacity-building efforts.[lxiv]

Conclusion

In summary, cyberspace security cooperation funding is an essential aspect of modern international security efforts. The fiscal authorities discussed in this chapter empower the U.S. Department of Defense to allocate resources effectively, facilitate joint exercises, and enhance the cybersecurity capabilities of partner nations. Furthermore, the Ukraine Security Assistance Initiative showcases the application of such funding in supporting a nation under external threat, reinforcing the importance of international collaboration in addressing cyber threats. As the landscape of cyberspace continues to evolve, investment in security cooperation funding will remain a critical component of national and global security strategies.

Chapter 10:

From Policy to Practice: Exploring DOD's Title 10 and DOS's Title 22 in Cyberspace Security Cooperation

Introduction

Cyberspace security cooperation plays a crucial role in supporting U.S. national security and defense strategies. The Department of Defense (DOD) and the Department of State (DOS) are key players in this arena, operating under different legal authorities known as "Title 10" and "Title 22," respectively. This chapter provides an overview of the policies, objectives, roles, and responsibilities of DOD and DOS in cyberspace security cooperation, drawing information from the Congressional Research Service (CRS) report on Security Cooperation.

Security Cooperation Policy and Objectives

Security Cooperation activities have specific objectives aimed at advancing U.S. national security and defense strategies. The primary goals of security cooperation include promoting U.S. security interests, enhancing the military capabilities of U.S. Allies and partners, and gaining access to partner nations (PNs). These activities prioritize mutually beneficial partnerships, strengthening the ability to maintain internal security, contribute to regional security efforts, combat shared threats, and improve military interoperability with the United States.

Overview of Security Cooperation

The term security cooperation (SC) encompasses a wide range of interactions between the DOD and foreign security establishments. It involves the transfer of defense articles and services, military-to-military exercises, military education, training, and advising, and most importantly, in cyberspace security cooperation, capacity building of foreign security forces or Building Partnership Capacity (BPC) programs under the authority of Title 10 U.S. Code Section 333 (hereby referred to as "Section 333" or "333"). SC programs are designed to encourage partner nations (PNs) to collaborate with the United States in achieving strategic objectives. These programs are considered essential tools for advancing U.S. national security and foreign policy objectives. SC activities are executed through DOD-administered SC programs authorized under Title 10, U.S.C., as well as DOD-implemented State Department security assistance (SA) programs authorized under Title 22, U.S.C. In addition to grant-based programs, SC also includes the Foreign Military Sales program, which facilitates collaboration between the United States and partner nations (PNs) in the acquisition of defense articles.

Roles and Responsibilities in Security Cooperation

Coordinating security cooperation activities often requires close collaboration among various DOD components and other federal departments, with the Department of State being a primary partner. Within the DOD, the Undersecretary of Defense for Policy (USD(P)) holds the overall authority and control over security cooperation matters. The Defense Security Cooperation Agency (DSCA) represents the interests of the Secretary of Defense and USD(P) in SC matters. DSCA is responsible for directing, administering, and executing numerous SC programs, developing SC policy, and providing DOD-wide SC guidance. Additionally, DSCA serves as the main intermediary between partner nations (PNs), implementing agencies, and the defense industry. The Assistant Secretary of Defense for Special Operations and Low-Intensity Conflict (ASD-SO/LIC) oversees and approves certain SC training activities managed by DSCA. The U.S. Special Operations Command (SOCOM) coordinates SC activities executed by special operations forces (SOF). On the DOS side, the Bureau of Political-Military Affairs (PM) leads U.S. foreign aid efforts and serves as the principal link to the DOD. PM ensures that security assistance is integrated with other U.S. policies and activities at the country, regional, and global levels. Moreover, PM determines partner nation eligibility, appropriate security assistance programs, and the transfer of defense articles and equipment.[lxv]

Congressional Role in Security Cooperation

Congress plays a critical role in authorizing and funding security cooperation programs. Title 10 SC activities fall under the jurisdiction of the armed services committees, while Title 22 DOS security assistance activities are within the purview of the Senate Foreign Relations and House Foreign Affairs committees. Both sets of committees exercise oversight over SC activities and the management of SC policy, including the level of coordination between DOD and DOS. The funding for Title 10 SC programs and activities is provided through annual appropriations bills originating in the defense subcommittees of the appropriations committees. Congress, primarily through these six committees, is instrumental in designing and overseeing SC programs to ensure they align with U.S. national security and foreign policy objectives. By virtue of statutory authorities, the executive branch must regularly notify relevant committees about some SC activities. Congress exercises its oversight role in various ways, such as influencing decisions on the export of military items, using annual authorizing legislation to establish temporary authorities or modify the U.S. Code, reviewing proposed arms transfers and planned Security Cooperation/Security Assistance activities, mandating reports, and conducting hearings. Additionally, the Senate has the authority to advise and consent to the ratification of relevant treaties, which further impacts security cooperation efforts.[lxvi]

Conclusion

In closing, the Department of Defense and the Department of State operate under different legal authorities, namely "Title 10" and "Title 22" respectively. These authorities provide the framework for conducting security cooperation activities, which aim to advance U.S. national security and foreign policy objectives. With the involvement of various DOD components, DOS, and Congress, security cooperation efforts seek to build defense relationships, enhance the military capabilities of partner nations (PNs), and promote mutual interests while addressing shared threats in the cyberspace domain.

Chapter 11:

Security Cooperation Funding Options Under Title 22: Foreign Military Sales (FMS) and Foreign Military Financing (FMF)

Introduction

Foreign Military Sales and Foreign Military Financing Programs: The FMS program is the United States government's primary vehicle for selling weapons-associated equipment, including software and hardware, and training to friendly foreign governments. Through the FMF element of the program, the U.S. government may extend grants or loans to countries facing difficulty paying for needed weapons, military equipment, and related items, or it may forgive payments altogether. The State Department is primarily responsible for determining which nations receive military assistance from this program, with DOD's DSCA bearing primary responsibility for program implementation. FMS is authorized by Sections 1-4 of the Arms Export Control Act (AECA, P.L. 90-629; 22 U.S.C. 2751 - 2754), as amended, while FMF is authorized by Section 23 of the AECA (22 U.S.C. 2763).

As discussed earlier, Foreign Military Sales (FMS) are predominantly funded by the purchasing country's national funds, supplemented by U.S. Security Assistance, such as the Foreign Military Financing (FMF) program. The Department of State plays a key role in determining which countries are eligible to acquire defense articles through the FMS program. Subsequently, the Department of Defense executes these arms transfers following established guidelines and regulations.

Foreign Military Financing (FMF) assistance, which includes the Countering Russian Influence Fund (CRIF) and the Counter China Influence Funds (CCIF), is primarily managed by the State Department and the U.S. Agency for International Development (USAID). FMF provides grants for acquiring U.S. defense equipment, services, and training, contributing to U.S. national security by enhancing regional and global stability.

Countering Russian Influence Fund (CRIF)

The Countering Russian Influence Fund (CRIF) is a specific funding mechanism established by the United States to address the challenges of Russian influence and aggression. CRIF is a dedicated fund within the broader framework of Foreign Military Sales, focusing on countering Russian activities and enhancing security cooperation in regions affected by Russian influence.

CRIF funding supports a range of initiatives aimed at countering Russian aggression, strengthening democratic institutions, and enhancing the defense capabilities of partner nations (PNs). The funds are allocated to various programs and projects that directly address Russian malign influence, including cybersecurity, intelligence sharing, military exercises, strategic communications, and support for defense sector reforms.

CRIF funding empowers partner nations (PNs) to better detect, deter, and defend against Russian aggression in their respective regions. It provides resources for critical capabilities, training, equipment, and technical assistance to strengthen security and resilience against Russian threats.

Refer to Appendix B for an example of Bandoria (a fictitious country) CRIF proposal supporting Cyberspace Security Cooperation.

Counter China Influence Funds (CCIF)

In addition to CRIF, the United States has established Counter China Influence Funds (CCIF) to address the challenges of Chinese influence and assertiveness. CCIF serves as a specific funding mechanism within the broader framework of SSCI, dedicated to countering Chinese influence and enhancing security cooperation in regions affected by Chinese activities.

CCIF funding supports initiatives aimed at countering Chinese influence, promoting transparency, strengthening democratic institutions, and enhancing the defense capabilities of partner nations (PNs). These initiatives may include capacity building, military modernization, cybersecurity, infrastructure development, regional security cooperation, and countering disinformation campaigns.

CCIF funds are allocated to projects and programs that directly address challenges posed by Chinese influence, aiming to enhance partner nations (PNs)' ability to mitigate risks, protect their sovereignty, and maintain a free and open regional order.

In summary, SSCI planning should be coordinated with expected security sector assistance initiatives overseen by the

Department of State and various interagency programs, including but not limited to Counter Russian Influence Funds, Counter China Influence Funds (CCIF), and Ukraine Security Assistance Initiative (USAI). Each fund allocates resources to initiatives and projects tailored to address challenges posed by Russian and Chinese activities, strengthening partner nations (PNs) security capabilities and promoting regional stability.

Case Study: Strengthening Cyberspace Security Cooperation through FMS and FMF in Montenegro

As one of NATO's newest members, Montenegro has recognized the importance of bolstering its cybersecurity capabilities to counter emerging threats. In this case study, we highlight how the United States Office of Defense Cooperation (ODC) in Montenegro leveraged the Foreign Military Sales (FMS) program and the Countering Russian Influence Fund (CRIF) funding in conjunction with the Defense Security Cooperation Agency's (DSCA) mission, to enhance cyberspace security cooperation and support Montenegro's ability to respond to cyber threats.[lxvii]

1. DSCA's Mission and Security Cooperation:

The Defense Security Cooperation Agency (DSCA) is crucial in advancing U.S. national security and foreign policy interests. Its mission involves building the capacity of foreign security forces to respond to shared challenges and promoting interoperability with the United States. Through implementing various programs and initiatives, including CRIF, DSCA facilitates security cooperation and supports partner nations (PNs) in strengthening their defense capabilities.

2. Engagement of Cybersecurity Consultants:

In close collaboration with the Montenegrin Ministry of Defense, the ODC deployed two full-time cybersecurity consultants to the Montenegrin Ministry of Defense using CRIF funding. These consultants brought on board for 20 months, have worked tirelessly to assess Montenegro's existing cybersecurity frameworks, identify vulnerabilities, and propose tailored solutions. Their expertise and guidance have been invaluable in strengthening Montenegro's cyber defenses and shaping robust policies aligned with international best practices.

3. Enhancing Cyber Software and Hardware:

Recognizing the evolving cyber landscape, the ODC in Montenegro allocated a significant portion of CRIF funds, amounting to $8 million, to strengthen cyber software and hardware. These investments enabled the acquisition of state-of-the-art technologies for detecting, mitigating, and responding to cyber threats. By strengthening Montenegro's cyber software and hardware capabilities, the country became better equipped to protect critical infrastructure and respond effectively to evolving cyber challenges.

4. Capacity Building and Training:

Capacity building and training initiatives were prioritized by the ODC in Montenegro, consistent with DSCA's mission to build the capacity of foreign security forces. These initiatives, supported by CRIF, focused on equipping Montenegrin forces with the necessary knowledge, skills, and tools to detect, prevent, and respond effectively to cyber attacks. These programs covered incident response, network security, threat intelligence analysis, and secure coding practices. By investing in the training and development of Montenegrin cybersecurity personnel, the ODC enhanced the country's ability to address cyber threats independently. Additionally, the collaboration between the ODC and Montenegro's Ministry of Defense ensured these training efforts aligned with the country's cybersecurity needs.

5. State Partnership Program and Maine National Guard:

One of the notable partnerships for the Montenegrin Armed Forces is with the State Partnership Program and the Maine National Guard. Since 2006, this partnership has contributed to enhancing bilateral relations. Despite COVID-19 restrictions, the ODC and the Maine National Guard virtually continued mil-to-mil training and relationship building. The presence of a Maine Air National Guard Bilateral Affairs Officer (BAO) within the ODC facilitated planning for future in-person events focusing on various lines of effort, including cybersecurity, C4I (Command, Control, Communications, Computers, and Intelligence), medical, and engineering.

6. Cybersecurity Exercises and Information Sharing:

The ODC in Montenegro facilitated joint cyber exercises and information-sharing activities to enhance operational readiness and foster interoperability. These exercises allowed Montenegrin cybersecurity personnel to train alongside their U.S. counterparts, share best practices, and simulate realistic cyberattack scenarios. The collaborative nature of these exercises enhanced the understanding of cyber threats and improved response capabilities for both Montenegro and the

United States. This aligns with DSCA's mission of promoting interoperability and strengthening defense capabilities among partner nations (PNs).

7. Continuous Assessment and Improvement:

The ODC has adopted a proactive approach to continuous assessment and improvement to ensure the sustainability of cyberspace security cooperation efforts. By regularly evaluating Montenegro's cybersecurity landscape and identifying emerging challenges, the ODC can effectively adapt its strategies and initiatives to address evolving threats. This iterative process ensures Montenegro remains resilient and adaptive in dynamic cybersecurity environments.

Conclusion

Ultimately, the utilization of the Countering Russian Influence Fund (CRIF) by the United States Office of Defense Cooperation in Montenegro has played a pivotal role in strengthening cyberspace security cooperation with a NATO Ally. The ODC. has bolstered Montenegro's cyber defense capabilities by deploying cybersecurity consultants, investing in software and hardware upgrades, knowledge transfer, and establishing resilient partnerships. Collaboration with SPP and the facilitation of joint exercises further enhanced information sharing and interoperability. This case study exemplifies how the strategic utilization of CRIF funding and the implementation of DSCA's mission can advance U.S. national security and foreign policy interests by building the capacity of foreign security forces to respond to shared challenges and promote regional cooperation in countering cyber threats.

Chapter 12:

Strengthening Cyberspace Security Cooperation through Foreign Military Sales (FMS)

Introduction

In a world marked by escalating interconnectedness, cyber threats have become a significant concern for nations across the globe. To effectively combat these threats and ensure the protection of critical infrastructure, governments recognize the need for enhanced cyberspace security cooperation with partner nations (PNs). One avenue through which this cooperation can be achieved is the Foreign Military Sales (FMS) program. This chapter explores the role of FMS in strengthening cyberspace security cooperation with partner nations (PNs) and highlights its benefits and challenges.

The Foreign Military Sales (FMS) Program

The Foreign Military Sales program is a vital tool the United States and other countries employ to enhance defense cooperation with partner nations (PNs). Through FMS, countries can procure defense articles, services, and training from the United States, promoting interoperability and strengthening military capabilities. Traditionally, FMS has focused on conventional defense equipment, but in recent years, its scope has expanded to include cybersecurity capabilities. FMS is financed primarily by national funds and additional U.S. Security Assistance (e.g., through Foreign

Military Financing (FMF)). Under the FMS program, the Department of State determines which countries may purchase defense articles, and the Department of Defense executes these arms transfers.

The Role of FMS in Cyberspace Security Cooperation

Cybersecurity has emerged as a critical domain in modern warfare, potentially disrupting military operations and compromising national security. Recognizing this, the United States and its partner nations (PNs) have begun utilizing the FMS program to enhance cyberspace security cooperation. The FMS program facilitates the transfer of cyber technologies, equipment, and training, enabling partner nations (PNs) to develop their capabilities and effectively respond to cyber threats.

Benefits of FMS in Strengthening Cyberspace Security Cooperation

Enhanced Information Sharing:

Through the FMS program, partner nations (PNs) can access cutting-edge cybersecurity technologies and solutions developed by the United States. This fosters information sharing and enables partner nations (PNs) to learn from the experiences and best practices of the United States, thereby strengthening their own cyber defense capabilities.

Capacity Building:

Cybersecurity requires skilled personnel and robust infrastructure. FMS provides partner nations (PNs) training programs, workshops, and technical assistance to develop their cybersecurity workforce. This capacity building enhances partner nations' (PNs) ability to effectively detect, prevent, and respond to cyber threats.

Interoperability:

In the cyber domain, interoperability is crucial for effective defense against cyber attacks. FMS promotes the standardization of cybersecurity protocols, procedures, and technologies between the United States and partner nations (PNs). This interoperability enables seamless information sharing, joint cyber exercises, and coordinated responses to cyber incidents.

Challenges and Security Concerns:

While FMS offers numerous benefits for strengthening cyberspace security cooperation, transferring cybersecurity technologies and capabilities through FMS raises some security concerns, as sensitive national security information could be compromised. Stringent export control measures and information-sharing protocols must be implemented to mitigate this risk. Partner nations (PNs) must demonstrate their commitment to safeguarding sensitive technologies and information.

Technological Maturity:

Partner nations (PNs) may have varying levels of technological maturity in cybersecurity. FMS programs must account for these differences by offering tailored training and capacity-building initiatives to ensure that partner nations

(PNs) can effectively utilize and integrate the transferred cybersecurity technologies.

Cultural and Legal Differences:

Cultural and legal differences between the United States and partner nations (PNs) can challenge effective cyberspace security cooperation. FMS programs must incorporate comprehensive legal frameworks and cultural sensitivity to overcome these challenges and foster effective collaboration.

FMS' Cybersecurity-Focused Use Cases

To illustrate the effectiveness of FMS in strengthening cyberspace security cooperation, this section presents three use cases:

Use Case 1: FMS Cybersecurity Assistance Framework

The FMS Cybersecurity Assistance (FCA) framework represents a strategic initiative leveraging MITRE's extensive cybersecurity expertise to support partner nations (PNs) in enhancing their cyber defense capabilities. This initiative is particularly crucial in the context of integrating PN command and control (C2) networks with U.S. bilateral warfighting networks, a move that, while beneficial for interoperability, also escalates cybersecurity risks for both parties involved.

The U.S. government, recognizing these elevated risks, advocates for the application of its Risk Management Framework (RMF) to identify and mitigate potential cyber threats. The RMF offers a holistic approach, encompassing a wide spectrum of best practices applicable at all organizational levels, from strategic to operational. This framework moves beyond mere compliance-driven checklists, advocating for a more nuanced and tailored application of security protocols.

MITRE's role in this framework is instrumental. With its profound expertise in cybersecurity, MITRE aids PNs in strategically implementing industry best practices and the RMF. A testament to MITRE's effectiveness is its contribution to a USAFRICOM cyber program, which not only enhanced the organization's cyber maturity but also led to the adoption of an innovative risk management strategy.

The structure of the FMS Cybersecurity Assistance framework, developed in collaboration with the U.S. Defense Security Cooperation Agency (DSCU) and Geographic Combatant Commands (GCC), is designed to be highly adaptable, catering to the unique cybersecurity needs of each partner nation. The framework primarily focuses on three areas:

1. Cybersecurity Maturity Assessments: Evaluating and enhancing the current state of a PN's cybersecurity readiness.

2. Cybersecurity Capability Development/Enhancement: Building or improving upon existing cybersecurity infrastructures.

3. Bilateral Cyber Risk Assessments: Joint US-PN evaluations aimed at ensuring secure and effective capability integration.

While the initial phase might be driven by the requirements of Bilateral Risk Cyber Assessment (BCRA), it often reveals various policy, procedural, or technical deficiencies that, although outside the direct scope of FMS programs, require attention.

The FCA framework is structured to allow for flexible tasking and resource allocation, ensuring that a wide array of PN needs can be addressed effectively at various organizational levels. This approach is segmented into three tiers of engagement:

Tier 1: National or Ministry of Defense/Organization Level, focusing on the development of cyber strategies, policies, workforce, implementation roadmaps, and resource planning.

Tier 2: Mission/Business Process Level, where PNs assess existing cybersecurity capabilities, personnel, facilities, and resources.

Tier 3: Platforms/Information System Level, involving the identification of mission-critical data, necessary data exchanges, and the technologies and environments these exchanges will occur in.

In summary, the FMS Cybersecurity Assistance framework, through its multi-tiered and flexible approach, provides a comprehensive solution for PNs to bolster their cybersecurity posture, ensuring safer integration into global defense networks.[lxviii]

Use Case 2: FMS Cybersecurity Training Program

In this use case, the United States collaborated with a partner nation (PN) to develop a comprehensive cybersecurity training program. Through FMS, the partner nation received specialized training courses, equipment, and simulation tools to enhance its cyber defense capabilities. The program facilitated knowledge transfer and enabled the PN to develop its cybersecurity workforce.

Use Case 2: FMS Cyber Incident Response Center

In this use case, the United States assisted a partner nation (PN) in establishing a Cyber Incident Response Center (CIRC) through the FMS program. The CIRC offered advanced cyber defense technologies, threat intelligence-sharing tools, and self-paced training programs. The FMS program enabled the PN to establish a robust cyber defense infrastructure and effectively enhanced its ability to respond to cyber incidents.

Conclusion

In closing, the Foreign Military Sales program offers a valuable avenue for strengthening cyberspace security cooperation with partner nations (PNs). By leveraging FMS, countries can enhance information sharing, capacity building, and interoperability in the cyber domain. While challenges exist, they can be mitigated through robust security measures and tailored programs. The FMS program can contribute significantly to bolstering global cybersecurity efforts and promoting a secure and resilient digital environment through sustained collaboration.

Chapter 13:

Foreign Military Sales Process and Case Development for Acquiring Cyber Capabilities for partner nations (PNs)

Introduction

In a progressively interconnected and digitized world, robust cyber defenses have become paramount for nations seeking to safeguard their interests. As part of this endeavor, the Foreign Military Sales (FMS) program has emerged as a strategic avenue for Allies and partners to acquire cutting-edge defensive cyber capabilities from more advanced and capable nations like the United States.

The process of Foreign Military Sales (FMS) is crucial for the United States Department of Defense to provide foreign partners with the necessary military capabilities. While the delivery of cyber tools and equipment, aircraft, missiles, and weapon systems may catch people's attention, a significant amount of work goes on behind the scenes to develop FMS cases. This chapter delves into the comprehensive process of FMS case development for acquiring defensive cyber capabilities, outlining the distinct phases involved in this intricate endeavor. And how various stakeholders collaborate to acquire cyber capabilities that address partner nations (PNs) national security concerns while supporting the U.S. National Defense Strategy (NDS).

Initiation and Assessment

The FMS case development journey commences with recognizing the need for enhanced cyber defense capabilities within a recipient nation's armed forces. This may arise from various factors, such as the evolving threat landscape, recent cyber incidents, or the desire to modernize existing cybersecurity infrastructure. In close collaboration with foreign partners, the recipient nation's defense authorities outline their requirements, articulating the defensive cyber capabilities needed to strengthen their national security posture with the help of U.S. country teams and international programs offices like the Program Executive Office (PEO) Command, Control, Communications, Computers, and Intelligence (C4I), or Allied Information Technology (AIT).

PEO C4I allows partner nations (PNs) to develop an enterprise-wide approach to cybersecurity using the Foreign Military Sales process. In contrast, PEO AIT. Specializes in providing customized, non-standard, commercial-off-the-shelf (COTS) IT and Cyber Defense solutions to build resilient and resistant capable forces for Partner Nations through the Foreign Military Sales (FMS) process.

Partner Engagement and Capability Identification

Upon defining the desired cyber capabilities, the recipient nation initiates engagement with the Program Executive Office (PEO) through the U.S. country team within the respective COCOM, possessing the requisite technological expertise to advise and assist in the FMS process. Bilateral discussions, site surveys, and technical evaluations ensue to determine the compatibility of the offered cyber solutions with the recipient nation's defense architecture.

FMS Case Development and Agreement

With a potential capability identified, both nations formulate an FMS case agreement. This entails detailed negotiations regarding the scope of the defensive cyber capabilities, cost considerations, delivery timelines, and associated training and support services. Legal and diplomatic aspects are meticulously addressed during this phase to ensure the alignment of interests and responsibilities between the participating nations.

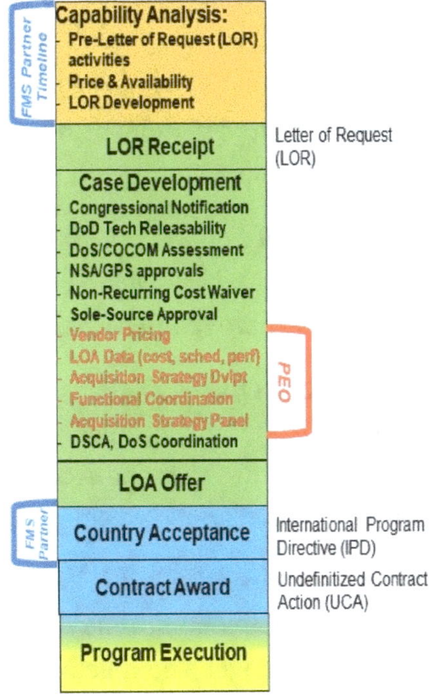

Figure 16: FMS Process Overview

In the FMS case development phase, different entities come together to facilitate the process. When authorized personnel of the U.S. Government (USG) receive a complete and actionable Letter of Request (LOR) from an authorized representative of a partner nation, it marks the beginning of the FMS case development process.

Several key tasks are involved in the FMS case development. Still, it is important to know that collaboration among various stakeholders ensures that requests meet the required criteria and align with national security objectives.

1. *Congressional Notification:* If the request meets specific budget and scope thresholds, the U.S. Congress is notified to approve or disapprove the potential sale.

2. *U.S. Department of Defense (DOD) Tech Releasability:* The DOD is consulted to determine if the requested capability can be authorized for release to foreign partners.

3. *U.S. Department of State (DOS) Combatant Command (COCOM) Assessment:* The DOS evaluates whether the requesting country is approved to participate in USG FMS.

4. *DOD Program Offices (POs):* Collaboration with the POs is necessary to gather the technical capability data needed to draft a formal Letter of Offer and Acceptance (LOA) to the partner nation.

Once an LOA is developed, it is presented to the partner nation, marking the completion of the FMS case development process. The LOA can cover a completely new capability or an amendment or modification to an existing one.

Technical Assessment and Customization

Once the FMS case agreement is formalized, the recipient nation's cybersecurity experts work closely with their foreign counterparts to conduct an in-depth technical assessment. This assessment entails tailoring the acquired cyber capabilities to align with the recipient nation's specific requirements, existing infrastructure, and operational procedures. Customization may encompass software modifications, hardware integration, and interoperability testing.

Training and Capacity Building

Acquiring defensive cyber capabilities is not solely about technology; it also necessitates developing human expertise to effectively operate and manage these tools. In this phase, comprehensive training programs are developed to impart the necessary skills to the recipient nation's cybersecurity personnel. Training sessions may cover threat analysis, incident response, vulnerability assessment, and other crucial aspects of cyber defense.

Integration and Deployment

As the recipient nation's cybersecurity personnel undergo training, the acquired defensive cyber capabilities are prepared for integration into the existing defense infrastructure. This phase entails rigorous testing and validation to ensure the seamless functioning of the new tools alongside the recipient nation's existing systems. Once the integration process is complete, the cyber capabilities are deployed and operational, bolstering the nation's cyber resilience.

Monitoring and Continuous Improvement

Following the deployment of defensive cyber capabilities, an ongoing monitoring and evaluation process is crucial to identify emerging threats or evolving requirements. Collaborative efforts between the recipient nation and its foreign partner continue as they jointly assess the effectiveness of the acquired tools, implement necessary updates, and refine cybersecurity strategies to counter the ever-changing threat landscape.

Conclusion

In summary, the journey of FMS case development for acquiring defensive cyber capabilities underscores the importance of international collaboration in addressing the shared challenges posed by cyber threats. Through a meticulous and multi-phased approach, developing nations can enhance their cyber defenses, leveraging the expertise of the United States military organizations and forging strong alliances within the dynamic landscape of cyber operations. As technology evolves and threats become increasingly sophisticated, the FMS program remains a cornerstone of global efforts to safeguard national security in the digital age.

Chapter 14:

Security Cooperation Funding Options Under Title 10: Significant Security Cooperation Initiatives (SSCIs)

Introduction

Significant Security Cooperation Initiatives (SSCIs) is a comprehensive security cooperation program initiated by the United States to enhance defense partnerships and strengthen national security capabilities with partner nations (PNs). SSCIs encompass various initiatives designed to address shared security challenges, promote regional stability, and foster interoperability between the United States and its Allies and partners.

SSCIs involve utilizing various security cooperation tools and programs over an extended period to achieve specific country- or region-focused objectives. These initiatives, known as SSCIs, are comprehensive plans that span multiple years, authorities, and recipients. They establish a connection between security cooperation activities and the strategic objectives outlined in the National Defense Strategy (NDS) by employing Specific, Measurable, Achievable, Relevant, and Time-Bound (SMART) objectives.

Significant Security Cooperation Initiatives (SSCIs)

The purpose of SSCIs is to encompass all DOD efforts planned over a five-year timeframe to accomplish these objectives. These initiatives should adopt a comprehensive approach, considering all relevant factors, and be subject to DOD's review and prioritization. Whenever feasible, SSCI planning should align with anticipated security sector assistance initiatives led by the Department of State and other interagency programs, like Counter Russian Influence Funds, Counter China Influence Funds (CCIF), and Ukraine Security Assistance Initiative (USAI) funds, for example.

Finally, approval by Combatant Commanders (CCMDs) is mandatory for all SSCIs, followed by reviews from DSCA (Office of Strategy, Plans, and Policy, Regional Planning and Program Design Directorate (SPP/RPPD)) and DSCA (Office of International Operations, Regional Execution Directorate, Global Capability Development Division (IOPS/REX/GCD)) before the creation of a Building Partnership Capacity (BPC) proposal.

Utilizing Significant Security Cooperation Initiatives (SSCI) for funding partner nations (PNs) capability needs involves specific requirements and considerations. Here are the key factors to consider:

Eligibility: To be eligible for Significant Security Cooperation Initiatives (SSCI) funding, the capability needs must fall within the national security forces, military, or civilian personnel of one or more foreign countries to build their capacity to conduct Cyberspace security and defensive cyberspace operations. This requirement ensures that SSCI funding is specifically targeted toward enhancing the cyber capabilities of partner nations (PNs) and strengthening their ability to address cyber threats and challenges. Partner nations (PNs) seeking SSCI funding must meet the eligibility criteria based on the strategic importance of the partnership, mutual security interests, alignment with U.S. foreign policy objectives, and the specific focus on building cyber capacity. The determination of eligibility is made through close coordination between the U.S. Department of Defense (DOD) and the U.S. Department of State (DOS). It's important to emphasize that the SSCI funding supports initiatives that enhance regional stability, promote cyber resilience, counter shared threats in the cyber domain, and foster interoperability with U.S. forces. The eligibility requirement ensures that partner nations (PNs) with a genuine need to enhance their cyberspace security capabilities can access the necessary funding and support from the United States. The formal request, interagency coordination, congressional approval, case development, and execution and oversight processes mentioned earlier also apply to using SSCI funding for building partner nations (PNs) cyber capabilities. The close collaboration among relevant U.S. government agencies and partner nation representatives remains crucial throughout the entire process to ensure effective and targeted utilization of SSCI funding for enhancing partner nations (PNs)' ability to conduct cyberspace security and defensive cyberspace operations.

Partner nations (PNs) must meet certain criteria for SSCI funding eligibility. These criteria are typically based on the strategic importance of the partnership, mutual security interests, and alignment with U.S. foreign policy objectives. The eligibility determination is made through close coordination between the U.S. Department of Defense (DOD) and the U.S. Department of State (DOS).

National Security Objectives: The partner nation's capability needs must align with U.S. national security objectives. SSCI funding is intended to support initiatives that enhance regional stability, build partner nation capacity, counter shared threats, and promote interoperability with U.S. forces.

Formal Request: The partner nation must submit a formal request for assistance, typically in a Letter of Request (LOR) or similar document. This request should outline the specific capability needs, the desired outcomes, and how the proposed assistance aligns with the partner nation's national security strategy.

Interagency Coordination: Utilizing SSCI funding involves close coordination among various U.S. government agencies, including the DOD, DOS, DSCA, and other relevant departments or agencies. These agencies work together to assess the partner nation's request, evaluate the feasibility and cost of the proposed assistance, and determine the appropriate funding mechanisms.

Congressional Approval: SSCI funding requires congressional approval, as it involves allocating resources and funding from the U.S. government. The partner nation's request and the proposed funding amount must go through the congressional appropriations process and receive the necessary authorizations and appropriations.

Case Development: The case development process begins once the SSCI funding is approved. This process may involve DSCA or other relevant entities responsible for managing foreign military sales. The case development process includes defining requirements, drafting formal agreements (such as Letters of Offer and Acceptance - LOAs), and ensuring compliance with legal, regulatory, and policy requirements.

Execution and Oversight: After the funding and agreements are in place, the execution phase begins. The implementation of the capability assistance is closely monitored to ensure effective use of funds, adherence to agreed-upon timelines, and achievement of desired outcomes. Regular reporting and oversight mechanisms are established to assess progress and provide accountability.

It's important to note that the specific requirements and processes may vary based on the nature of the assistance, the partner nation involved, and any specific agreements or regulations governing SSCI funding. Close coordination among the relevant U.S. government agencies and partner nation representatives is essential throughout the entire process to ensure the successful utilization of SSCI funding for addressing partner nations (PNs) capability needs.

Conclusion

Ultimately, Significant Security Cooperation Initiatives (SSCI) play a vital role in advancing U.S. national security and foreign policy interests by fostering collaboration and building the capacity of foreign security forces to address shared challenges.

SSCI initiatives are tailored to each partner nation's needs and priorities, focusing on capacity building, military modernization, counterterrorism, cybersecurity, maritime security, and humanitarian assistance. These initiatives involve a comprehensive approach that combines training, equipment transfers, technical assistance, institutional capacity building, and information sharing.

The overarching goal of SSCI is to deepen security cooperation, strengthen partner nations (PNs) self-defense capabilities, and promote regional stability. These initiatives reflect a long-term commitment to building enduring partnerships and promoting shared security interests.

Chapter 15:

Assessment, Monitoring, and Evaluation (AM&E) in Cyberspace Security Cooperation

Introduction

The Assessment, Monitoring, and Evaluation (AM&E) framework commences with capability-based assessments, outlining the desired roles and outcomes for partner nations (PNs) to attain strategic effects. As per guidance from the Under Secretary of Defense for Policy (USD(P)), these assessments are crucial for evaluating a partner's capability needs, identifying potential programmatic risks, establishing baseline information, and determining effectiveness indicators. This information is essential for planning, monitoring, and evaluating DOD's security cooperation programs and activities in cyberspace.

Per DOD Instruction 5132.14, "Assessment, Monitoring, and Evaluation Policy for the Security Cooperation Enterprise," CCMDs with geographic areas of responsibility lead initial assessment efforts, facilitate the participation of relevant subject matter experts and other appropriate participants as they assess the development of an initiative design document (IDD) and monitor implementation.[lxix]

DOD AM&E officials are encouraged to coordinate AM&E activities to include initial assessment and ongoing cyberspace security cooperation events with host nation representatives, country teams, and implementing partners like State Partnership Program (SPP) coordinators and country desk officers to ensure the efficiency of data-collection efforts.

Figure 17: AM&E Framework

According to DOD, the general process and standards for the AM&E framework include the following:[lxx, lxxi]

Initial Assessments (e.g., analysis of foreign country's willingness to implement and sustain security cooperation initiatives);

Initiative Design Documents (IDDs) (e.g., identification of specific security cooperation activities to be conducted, authorities to be utilized, how they will be synchronized, measurable and time-bound objectives, theory of change, and performance management plans);

Performance management and monitoring (e.g., output monitoring, outcome monitoring, site visits, and data collection and organization); and

Evaluations that comply with specific standards (e.g., usefulness, independence, methodological and analytical rigor, cost-effectiveness, and adherence to international and U.S. government-recognized ethical standards).

In the upcoming section, we will provide a detailed description of each phase of the AM&E framework:

Initial Assessment

Initial assessments are required before all SSCIs are developed.[lxxii] For each capability considered, the initial assessment will include an analysis of the following elements:

Political, Military, Economy, Society, Information, Infrastructure, Physical Environment, and Time (PMESII-PT)

Doctrine, Organization, Training, Materiel, Leadership (and Education), Personnel, Facilities and Policy (DOTMLPF-P)

Strengths, Weaknesses, Opportunities, and Threats (SWOT)

The extent to which an Allied or Partner Nation (BENEFITTING COUNTRY) shares relevant strategic objectives with the United States, as well as a partner's current ability to contribute to missions to address such shared objectives, based on a detailed holistic analysis of relevant partner capabilities, including institutional capabilities, at the strategic as well as operational and unit levels.

Analysis of potential risks, including assumptions documented in the logic tree model and possible consequences of implementing and not implementing the initiative, program, or activity.

Information to inform initiative design, including available contextual data, baselines, suggested objectives, indicators, milestones, and recommendations on what can be achieved within a given timeframe with anticipated resources.

The feasibility of achieving successful outcomes based on a partner's political willingness to pursue the desired outcome; its absorptive capacity, including the extent to which a partner can support, employ, and sustain assistance independently; its political stability; and its respect for the rule of law and human rights (HR).

Analysis of the partner's ability and willingness to provide oversight and accountability to ensure effective and responsible employment of its forces and the capabilities to be supported by the initiative, program, or activity, including observance of and respect for the law of armed conflict, human rights, and fundamental freedoms, the rule of law, and civilian control of the military.

Other relevant information, assessments, completed evaluations, and related documents provide context for the initial assessment process.

Initiative Design Document

An Initiative Design Document (IDD) is required for all SSCIs. The IDD will be developed through a deliberate and inclusive process to create a comprehensive document informed by the opportunities and risks identified in the initial assessment. IDDs will provide an overview of the activities and authorities to be synchronized to achieve the planned security cooperation outcome. Specifically, IDDs will include:

Clear linkage to goals or objectives in the theater campaign plan or other higher-level guidance.

The problem statement, derived from the initial assessment, clearly describes the issue or challenge the initiative seeks to address. Also known as the rationale, the problem statement provides the basis and reasons for implementing a security cooperation initiative.

A comprehensive performance management section that includes:

a. A logic framework for the initiative that maps goals and specific, measurable, achievable, relevant/results-oriented, and time-bound objectives to the activities necessary to achieve desired changes. The logic framework visually describes activities and the planned process of contributing to initiative goals and achieving objectives.

b. Indicators and milestones, ideally with baselines and targets, tied to the specific, measurable, achievable, relevant/results-oriented, and time-bound objectives that quantitatively or qualitatively measure the outputs and outcomes of the security cooperation initiative toward achieving stated objectives.

c. A theory of change intended to make implicit assumptions more explicit, which describes why certain actions will produce a desired change in a given context and clearly states the initiative's intended outcome and how it will be achieved.

Guidance to relevant stakeholders on how their security cooperation tools and activities should contribute to the security cooperation initiative and expectations regarding their role in supporting Assessment, Monitoring, and Evaluation (AM&E) efforts. It should also include data-collection details, parameters, frequency, and responsibility; how results will be used and communicated; and recommendations on when to evaluate the program.

The IDD document, accompanied by the Train and Equipment List (TEL), the primary document linking desired capabilities to specific acquisition requirements, will constitute a comprehensive BPC Proposal. DSCA will utilize this proposal to develop a program, seek Congress approval when necessary, and execute the program. The BPC Proposal encompasses essential elements such as program description, role analysis, material, and non-material solutions, integration with other initiatives, mandatory human rights training, and supporting documentation. All BPC Proposals must receive approval from CCMDs, DSCA (SPP/RPPD), DSCA (Defense Security Cooperation University, Institutional Capacity Building and Program Design (DSCU/ICBPD)), and DSCA (IOPS/REX/GCD).

Performance Management and Monitoring

Performance management and monitoring play a crucial role in ensuring the effectiveness of security cooperation programs. This includes output monitoring, outcome monitoring, site visits, and data collection and organization.

Output monitoring involves tracking and evaluating the deliverables and activities of the programs to assess whether they are meeting the intended objectives.

Outcome monitoring measures the programs' broader impact and results, such as partner nation capabilities or regional security improvements.

Site visits allow for firsthand observations and assessments of program implementation, providing valuable insights into progress and challenges.

Data collection and organization involve gathering relevant data, analyzing it, and organizing it systematically to inform decision-making and evaluate program performance.

By employing these performance management and monitoring measures, security cooperation programs can be continuously assessed and adjusted to maximize their effectiveness and achieve desired outcomes.

Standards-based Evaluations in Security Cooperation Programs

Conducting evaluations that adhere to specific standards is crucial in ensuring the credibility and validity of security cooperation programs. These standards encompass various aspects, including usefulness, independence, methodological and analytical rigor, cost-effectiveness, and adherence to international and U.S. government-recognized ethical standards.

Evaluations should be designed to provide meaningful and relevant insights into the program's impact, effectiveness, and efficiency. Independence ensures impartiality and minimizes potential biases in the evaluation process.

Methodological and analytical rigor entails employing robust research methods and data analysis techniques to ensure the reliability and validity of the evaluation findings.

Cost-effectiveness considerations ensure that evaluations are conducted efficiently and with optimal resource allocation.

Adherence to recognized ethical standards guarantees that evaluations are conducted ethically, respecting program participants' and stakeholders' rights and privacy.

By upholding these standards, evaluations can generate reliable evidence to inform decision-making, enhance program effectiveness, and promote accountability in security cooperation initiatives.

Refer to Appendix C for a template of a performance-based site survey designed to evaluate the deliverables and activities of the different SC programs and assess whether they are meeting the intended objectives. The site visit with force providers like the State Partners (SPP) is recommended to ensure all cyber requirements and existing and proposed solutions are captured properly.

Conclusion

In summary, the Assessment, Monitoring, and Evaluation (AM&E) framework is a vital component of strategic planning for security cooperation programs in cyberspace. It begins with capability-based assessments that define the desired roles and outcomes for partner nations (PNs) to achieve strategic effects. Guided by directives from the Under Secretary of Defense for

Policy (USD(P)), these assessments serve multiple crucial purposes: evaluating partner capability needs, identifying programmatic risks, establishing baseline information, and determining effectiveness indicators. This comprehensive approach provides essential insights for planning, monitoring, and evaluating the Department of Defense's security cooperation efforts in the realm of cyberspace, ensuring effective collaboration and strategic alignment with partner nations.

Chapter 16:

Leveraging Cyberspace Security Cooperation Maturity Model and Cybersecurity Focus Area Maturity Model in Capacity Building

Introduction

The Joint Staff Cyberspace Security Cooperation Maturity Model (CSCM) was developed by IAW CJCSI 5215.01B and the White House International Strategy for Cyberspace, which outlines the U.S. vision for the future of cyberspace and sets the agenda for partnering with other nations and peoples to realize it. As described in the International Strategy, the United States seeks a cyberspace environment that rewards innovation, empowers individuals, strengthens communities, builds better governments, expands accountability, safeguards fundamental freedoms, enhances personal privacy, and strengthens national and international security. In the following section, we will divulge the different CSCM levels and how each level supports security cooperation (SC) activities and partner end states according to the U.S. National Institute of Standards and Technology (NIST) core functions.

We will also discuss a new exploratory model called the Cybersecurity Focus Area Maturity (CYSFAM) model.[lxxiii] This comprehensive framework is designed to enable an insightful evaluation of a nation's cybersecurity stance, breaking it down into distinct focus areas. Such a structured approach aids stakeholders and policymakers in making well-informed decisions about their cybersecurity strategies and investments. Furthermore, CYSFAM is a valuable tool for planners, country desk officers, and partner nations (PNs). It helps in assessing their current security posture, identifying any existing gaps, and fine-tuning their investments in security cooperation. This model is crucial for a nuanced understanding of national cybersecurity readiness and for strategizing improvements in this vital area.

Joint Staff Cyberspace Security Cooperation Maturity Model (CSCM)

Table 1: Joint Staff Cyberspace Security Cooperation Maturity Model (CSCM)

Maturity Level / Lead DOD Partner	SC Activities	Demonstrated NIST Core Functions	Partner End State
Level 4: Cyberspace Operations (USCYBERCOM) Capable of conducting cyberspace operation planning & execution and providing advanced capabilities toward common cyberspace objectives. Partnering regionally to robust others' cyber maturity	Classified intelligence sharing, liaison exchanges, RDT&E agreements, combined operations training, and 8 multinational exercises. Cyber education.	Identify Protect Respond Recover	Routinely participates in activities that contribute towards both the U.S. & the partner's strategic cyberspace objectives.
Level 3: Common Defense (GCC/USCYBERCOM) Proactive network defense. Possess the ability to share threat information & cooperation across internal & external partners towards improving the common defense.	Classified intelligence & threat sharing, liaison exchanges DCO-IDM, multinational exercises, technical exchanges, advanced training. Institutional Capacity Building. Cyber education.	Identify Protect Respond Recover	Regularly partners with the U.S. towards common cyber defense objectives. Mature organizations. Policy and workforce.
Level 2: Risk-Driven Cybersecurity (GCC) Cybersecurity principles are well established, including national and military cyber strategies/policies/laws, resilient critical infrastructure, and the ability to identify risks.	Classified intelligence & threat sharing. Training, workshops & multinational exercises on advanced cybersecurity principles. Institutional Capacity Building. Cyber education.	Identify Protect Respond	Demonstrated ability to identify risk within cyber terrain & react to risk accordingly: Willingness to share threats & best practices.
Level 1: Compliance-Driven Cybersecurity (GCC) Basic cybersecurity knowledge & technology established. Building cybersecurity principles into organizations, workforce, & technologies	Tailored unclassified briefs, training, workshops, & exercises on cybersecurity principles, policy, & doctrine. Commercial training. Institutional Capacity Building. Cyber education	None	Demonstrated ability to identify sovereign cyber terrain & org/policy and provide compliance-driven cybersecurity.
Level 0: Foundational Awareness (GCC) Basic technical knowledge & technology. An acknowledgment that cybersecurity is important to collective defense	Unclassified briefs, training, & workshops on basic cybersecurity principles, policy, & doctrine. Commercial training, Institutional Capacity Building	None	Commitment to invest in cyberspace & adhere to international norms.

CJCSI 5215.01: Implementing instructions to focus cyber international engagements IAW POTUS International Strategy for Cyberspace (2011), DOD Strategy for Operating in Cyberspace (2011), GEF (2012) and DOD Cyberspace Security Cooperation Guidance (2013)
*GCC: Geographical Combatant Command
*RDT&E: Research, Development, Test, and Evaluation.
*DCO-IDM: Defensive Cyberspace Operations-Internal Defensive Measures.

CSCM is a crucial framework developed by the Office of the Secretary of Defense and Joint Staff (OSD/JS) for understanding and improving the cybersecurity posture of Partner Nations (PNs) military organizations, particularly within the context of the Department of Defense (DOD). This model serves as a roadmap, outlining the key security cooperation activities that must be accomplished at each stage of maturity. It provides a clear path for progression and offers insights into the desired end state of a partner at each level. The model is strategically designed to align with the National Institute of Standards and Technology (NIST) Core Functions: Identify, Protect, Detect, Respond, and Recover.

The CSCM comprises five distinct levels, each with its unique focus and its respective lead DOD partner. These levels are:

Level 0: Foundational Awareness

The first level of the CSCM is Foundational Awareness. At this stage, the focus is on building a basic understanding and appreciation of the importance and implications of cybersecurity. This foundational level is led by the Geographic Combatant Command (GCC), the primary DOD partner at this stage. Here, the GCC fosters an initial awareness of cyberspace's potential risks and vulnerabilities.

At this level, the desired Partner End State is an awareness of the need for cybersecurity and the basic concepts underpinning it. The partner should understand what cyberspace is, what the key threats are, and why it is essential to secure it. This foundational awareness is crucial as it sets the stage for further development and growth in the subsequent stages of the model.

Level 1: Compliance-Driven Cybersecurity

Once the foundational awareness has been established, the next level is Compliance-Driven Cybersecurity. Again, the GCC is the lead DOD partner at this level, but now the focus shifts from simply building awareness to implementing fundamental cybersecurity measures. These measures are driven by compliance requirements, as laid out by regulatory bodies and industry standards.

The desired Partner End State at this level is a partner that is not only aware of cybersecurity but also complies with basic cybersecurity norms. This includes adhering to established cybersecurity policies and regulations, implementing standard security measures, and focusing on cybersecurity in their operations.

Level 2: Risk-Driven Cybersecurity

After compliance is achieved, the CSCM model progresses to Risk-Driven Cybersecurity. At this level, the GCC continues to lead the DOD partnership, but the focus shifts towards a more proactive approach to cybersecurity. This involves identifying, assessing, and managing risks in cyberspace and tailoring cybersecurity measures to the organization's specific risk profile.

The desired Partner End State at this level is a partner that is compliant with cybersecurity norms and actively manages cybersecurity risks. This entails a thorough understanding of the potential threats in cyberspace, a robust system for risk assessment and management, and a proactive approach to implementing and updating cybersecurity measures.

Level 3: Common Defense

At the Common Defense level, the role of the lead DOD partner is shared between the GCC and the U.S. Cyber Command. The focus at this stage shifts from individual cybersecurity efforts to a collective defense strategy. This involves close collaboration and coordination with other organizations, sharing information and resources, and working together to defend against common threats in cyberspace.

The desired Partner End State at this level is a partner that manages its own cybersecurity and contributes to a common defense. This means actively participating in collective defense efforts, sharing threat intelligence, and coordinating responses to cyber incidents with other organizations.

Level 4: Cyberspace Operations

The final level of the CSCM is Full Spectrum Cyberspace Operations, with the U.S. Cyber Command taking the lead as the DOD partner. At this stage, the focus is on advanced cyberspace operations, which include active defense measures, offensive operations, and the use of cyberspace for military and strategic purposes.

At this level, the desired Partner End State is a partner that is not just a participant in cyberspace defense but also an active contributor to cyberspace operations. This requires a high level of cybersecurity maturity, with advanced capabilities in threat intelligence, incident response, and cyberspace operations.

In summary, the Cyberspace Security Cooperation Maturity Model (CSCM) provides a comprehensive framework for building and improving cybersecurity capabilities. By aligning with the NIST Core Functions and outlining clear progression steps and end states, the CSCM offers a strategic and systematic approach to enhancing cybersecurity posture and cooperation.

Cybersecurity Focus Area Maturity (CYSFAM) Model

CYSFAM Focus Area	Maturity Level												
	0	1	2	3	4	5	6	7	8	9	10	11	12
Technical													
Server Protection					A					C	D		
End-user Controls					A		B		C			D	
Network Security				A		B		C			D		
Application Security					A		B		C			D	
Cryptography						A	B		C			D	
Mobile Security					A	B		C			D		
Vulnerability Management					A	B		C			D		
Organizational													
Social Engineering Controls				A		B		C			D		
Cybersecurity Incident Management				A			B		C			D	
Cybersecurity Awareness				A		B		C			D		E
Cybersecurity Governance		A	B						C	D			

Figure 18: Focus areas and capabilities of CYSFAM. The letters (A–E) represent the capabilities; shaded areas show the maximum capability in the corresponding focus area.

The Cybersecurity Focus Area Maturity (CYSFAM) model is a comprehensive framework designed to provide an insightful evaluation of a nation's cybersecurity posture broken down by focus areas, enabling stakeholders and policymakers to make informed decisions about cybersecurity strategies and investments. This model serves as a tool to assist planners, country desk officers, and partner nations (PNs) in understanding their current security posture, identifying gaps, and optimizing their security cooperation investments.

The Need for Cybersecurity Focus Area Maturity Model

A comprehensive cybersecurity maturity model is crucial for several reasons. First, it offers a way for PNs to understand their cybersecurity posture and capabilities. This understanding is vital in identifying gaps in cybersecurity infrastructure and capabilities, informing strategies for improvement. By offering a clear snapshot of cybersecurity's current state, the model empowers PNs to communicate these gaps and areas of needed improvement to decision-makers.

Second, the CYSFAM aids in the optimization of security cooperation investments. The model highlights where resources and efforts need to be channeled to bolster cybersecurity capabilities by illuminating the current cybersecurity posture. This strategic allocation of resources ensures that investments in cybersecurity yield the maximum possible benefit.

Third, the CYSFAM provides a roadmap for the creation of cybersecurity strategies. The model highlights the current state of cybersecurity and provides a clear pathway toward improvement. This roadmap is crucial in helping PNs set clear, achievable goals for their cybersecurity efforts.

Finally, the CYSFAM allows PNs to benchmark their cybersecurity capabilities against other PNs. This benchmarking is crucial in understanding where a PN stands relative to others and helps plan and strategize to improve their cybersecurity capabilities.

Furthermore, a comprehensive cybersecurity maturity model, such as the CYSFAM, plays a pivotal role in fostering international collaboration. By providing partner nations (PNs) with a standardized framework, the model facilitates communication and cooperation among nations striving to enhance their cybersecurity capabilities. The shared understanding of cybersecurity maturity levels allows PNs to engage in meaningful dialogues, exchange best practices, and collectively address common challenges. This collaborative approach not only strengthens individual nations but also contributes to global resilience against evolving cyber threats. As cybersecurity is inherently interconnected, fostering a community of nations aligned on a common framework is essential for mitigating the increasingly sophisticated and cross-border nature of cyber threats. The CYSFAM, in this context, becomes a tool for building a united front against cyber adversaries, promoting information sharing, and ultimately creating a more secure cyberspace for all nations involved.

The CYSFAM and Computer Incident Response Teams (CIRTs)

In tandem with its broader applications, the CYSFAM also plays a critical role in evaluating and improving the capabilities of Computer Incident Response Teams (CIRTs). In the face of cyber threats of varying magnitudes, the capacity of CIRTs to respond effectively and efficiently is crucial. The CSCMM comprehensively evaluates CIRT's capabilities, highlighting areas of strength and areas needing improvement. This evaluation can then be used to train and equip CIRTs better to respond to cyber threats.

Additionally, the CYSFAM enables benchmarking of CIRTs' capacity across PNs. This benchmarking allows for comparative analysis and learning from other nations' experiences and best practices. It also fosters collaboration among PNs in strengthening their collective cybersecurity capabilities.

Assessing Cybersecurity Capabilities using CYSFAM

This section explores cybersecurity capabilities assessment using the Cybersecurity Focus Area Maturity (CYSFAM) model. This model offers a unique way of evaluating and improving cybersecurity capabilities, leveraging focus areas as the primary unit of assessment and improvement. Developed through an extensive review of numerous cybersecurity standards, CYSFAM encompasses 11 focus areas and uses a comprehensive assessment instrument of 144 questions.

Conceptual Foundations of CYSFAM

The CYSFAM is based on focus area maturity models, demonstrated in previous scientific work to offer significant advantages as improvement frameworks. They allow for a more granular and detailed understanding of an organization's cybersecurity capabilities and provide a clear path for improvement within each focus area.

To elucidate further, the focus areas embedded in CYSFAM encompass critical dimensions of cybersecurity, including but not limited to threat intelligence, incident response, network security, and personnel training. These focus area maturity models are not solely tailored to military organizations but also integrate insights gleaned from diverse sectors, ensuring a comprehensive and adaptable framework. Beyond the foundational conference paper, CYSFAM incorporates iterative refinement mechanisms informed by ongoing cybersecurity research and real-world incidents. This dynamic approach ensures the continued relevance and responsiveness of the maturity models to the ever-evolving landscape of cyber threats and rapid technological advancements.

The primary research question driving the development of the CYSFAM was: "How can cybersecurity capabilities for military organizations be modeled in a focus area maturity model?" Considering this question, the model was developed based on the method presented in a conference paper titled "The Design of Focus Area Maturity Models."

Distinctive Characteristics of CYSFAM

Amongst the numerous existing cybersecurity maturity models, CYSFAM distinguishes itself with several unique characteristics:

Foundation on International Standards: The CYSFAM is based on international standards and frameworks, as seen in Table 1, ensuring its relevance and applicability across various contexts and organizations.

Applicability to Generic and Military Organizations: While it is designed to apply to various generic organizations, CYSFAM is particularly suited to military organizations, addressing the unique cybersecurity challenges that such organizations often face.

Structure as a Focus Area Maturity Model: The CYSFAM is the only cybersecurity maturity model structured as a focus area maturity model. This structure allows for a more detailed and nuanced assessment and improvement of cybersecurity capabilities.

Utilizing the CYSFAM model in Security Cooperation (SC) Activities

The CYSFAM is designed to be used by Security Cooperation (SC) auditors and practitioners to assess and improve the cybersecurity capabilities of a partner nation (PN). The model provides 144 assessment questions, or capabilities, categorized into the 11 identified focus areas divided into technical and organizational. The technical ones are Server Protection, End-User Controls, Network Security, Application Security, Cryptography, Mobile Security, and Vulnerability Management. In contrast, the organizational ones are Social Engineering Controls, Cybersecurity Incident Management, Cybersecurity Awareness, and Cybersecurity Governance. The assessment questions provide a comprehensive picture of an organization's cybersecurity capabilities and facilitate targeted improvements within each focus area.

CYSFAM Artifact Development

This section presents the development steps of CYSFAM in any given organization:

Identifying the Initial Set of Focus Areas and Relevant Standards & Frameworks

Table 2: The initial set of focus areas of CYSFAM

Focus Area	Reference
Server protection (elaborated upon in ISO/IEC 27032)	[lxxiv]
End-user controls (elaborated upon in ISO/IEC 27032)	[lxxv]

Controls against Social Engineering (elaborated upon in ISO/IEC 27032)	[lxxvi]
Network security (the main focus of ISO/IEC 27033)	[lxxvii]
Application security (the main focus of ISO/IEC 27034)	[lxxviii]
Cyber/Information Security Incident Management (the main focus of ISO/IEC 27035)	[lxxix]

Table 3: International standards and frameworks CYSFAM is founded on: ITU, International Telecommunication Union; ISA, International Society of Automation; NIST, National Institute of Standards and Technology; NERC, North American Electric Reliability Corporation.

Standard / Framework	Reference
ITU-T ICT Security Standards Roadmap	[lxxx]
Guidebook on National Cyber Security Strategies	[lxxxi]
ISA/IEC-62443	[lxxxii]
NIST 800-12 and NIST 800-14	[lxxxiii], [lxxxiv]
NERC Critical Infrastructure Protection (CIP) Standards	[lxxxv]
NERC Security Guidelines	[lxxxvi]

In this step, we identify the focus areas using international standards that characterize the cybersecurity domain. Due to their high level of usage and acceptance, the standards published by the International Organization for Standardization (ISO) were used to compose the initial list of cybersecurity focus areas, as shown in Table 3. Additional standards and frameworks identified in this step are given in Table 4.

Defining the Cybersecurity Focus Areas and Capabilities

Table 4: Focus areas of CYSFAM and reference standards, models, and frameworks

#	Focus Area	# of Capability Assessment Questions	Standard / Framework
1	Server protection	16	ISO/IEC 27032 [lxxxvii], The ISF Standard of Good Practice for Information Security [lxxxviii][lxxxix]
2	End-user controls	15	ISO/IEC 27032[xc]
3	Controls against Social Engineering	7	ISO/IEC 27032 [xci]
4	Network security	12	ISO/IEC 27033 [xcii]
5	Application security	8	ISO/IEC 27033 [xciii]

6	Cybersecurity Incident Management	16	ISO/IEC 27034 [xciv]
7	Cybersecurity awareness	16	ISO/IEC 27035 [xcv]
8	Cryptography	16	Security Awareness Roadmap [xcvi], ISO/IEC 27001 [xcvii]
9	Cybersecurity governance	14	Cyber Security Self-Assessment Guidance [xcviii
10	Mobile security	16	Guidelines for Managing the Security of Mobile Devices in the Enterprise [xcix]
11	Vulnerability management	8	Critical Security Controls for Effective Cyber Defense [c]

In this step, we determine the capabilities under each focus area by analyzing the resources that led the authors to the focus areas. The number of capability statements identified for each focus area and related standards, models, and frameworks are given in Table 4 above. The total number of capability statements was 144.

Identifying the Dependencies and Positioning the Capabilities in the Maturity Matrix

Table 5: Dependencies of the capabilities in CYSFAM

#	Prerequisite Capability	Dependent Capability
1	Cybersecurity Governance A	Cybersecurity Governance B
2	Cybersecurity Governance B	Network Security A
3	Cybersecurity Governance B	Social Engineering Controls A
4	Cybersecurity Governance B	Incident Management A
5	Cybersecurity Governance B	Cybersecurity Awareness A
6	Network Security A	Server Protection A
7	Network Security A	End-user Controls A
8	Network Security A	Application Security A
9	Network Security A	Cryptography A
10	Network Security A	Mobile Security A
11	Network Security A	Vulnerability Management A
12	Incident Management B	Cybersecurity Governance C
13	Vulnerability Management B	Incident Management B
14	Server Protection A	Vulnerability Management B
15	Cybersecurity Awareness A	Mobile Security A
16	Cybersecurity Awareness B	Social Engineering Controls C

17	Server Protection A	End-user Controls B
18	Application Security A	Cryptography A
19	Cybersecurity Awareness A	Application Security B
20	Cybersecurity Awareness B	Incident Management C
21	Cybersecurity Governance D	Social Engineering Controls D
22	Incident Management B	Server Protection D

CYSFAM Focus Area	Maturity Level												
	0	1	2	3	4	5	6	7	8	9	10	11	12
Technical													
Server Protection					A					C	D		
End-user Controls					A		B		C			D	
Network Security				A		B		C			D		
Application Security					A		B		C			D	
Cryptography						A	B		C			D	
Mobile Security					A	B		C			D		
Vulnerability Management					A	B		C			D		
Organizational													
Social Engineering Controls				A		B		C			D		
Cybersecurity Incident Management				A			B		C			D	
Cybersecurity Awareness				A		B		C			D		E
Cybersecurity Governance		A	B					C	D				

Figure 19: CYSFAM maturity matrix and dependencies of the capabilities: The letters (A–E) represent the capabilities; arrows (in blue) depict the dependencies.

The thirteen columns in the CYSFAM Maturity matrix of Figure 19 define progressive overall maturity scales, with scale 0 being the lowest and scale 12 being the highest scale achievable. An organization is said to be at the maturity scale represented by the rightmost column for which it has achieved all focus area capabilities positioned in that column and all columns to its left.

All the focus areas and 144 capability statements/assessment questions for the capabilities included in the model can be found in Appendix D.

Focus Area Example: Server Protection

This subsection describes the process for determining the capabilities of the "Server Protection" focus area. According to ISO/IEC 27032, server protection entails the protection of servers against unauthorized access and hosting of malicious content. Capabilities for the "Server Protection" focus area are listed in Table 6 below.

Table 6: Initial set of capabilities for server protection focus area.

Capability	Reference
Configuration according to a baseline security configuration	ISO/IEC 27032 [ci]
Testing and deployment of updates for the server operating system and the applications	[cii]
Implementing security incident event monitoring (SIEM)	[ciii]
Implementing technical state compliance monitoring (TSCM)	[civ]

As shown in Table 5, the "Server Protection" focus area has 16 capability statements within these capabilities. These capabilities were represented in maturity levels (A–D), as shown in Table 7 below.

Table 7: The final set of capabilities for the Server Protection focus area.

Capability Statements	Capability
■ The organization's baseline security configuration is described. ■ Patch management is tool-supported (patch-management suites). ■ A SIEM solution is in place. ■ A technical compliance checking solution is in place.	A
■ The baseline security configuration is based on an open standard. ■ The deployment of patches is tested and approved at least once before deployment in the production environment. ■ The SIEM implementation is based on a baseline set of events. ■ Technical compliance checking is performed manually (supported by appropriate tools).	B
■ The baseline security configuration is reviewed at least once a year. ■ A process is in place that assures the organization learns about patch releases as soon as possible. ■ The SIEM implementation includes events that were identified during a risk assessment. ■ Technical compliance checking is performed with the assistance of automated tools (with a reporting functionality).	C

- The baseline security configuration is updated after every significant configuration change or demonstrated vulnerability. **D**
- The prioritization of patches is risk-based; the business's cruciality is taken into account.
- The SIEM solution is connected to a security operations center (SOC) for a correlation of events and is connected to the organization's incident management system.
- The technical compliance checking solution is connected to the organization's incident management system.

CYSFAM Assessment Results

CYSFAM Focus Area	Maturity Level												
	0	1	2	3	4	5	6	7	8	9	10	11	12
Technical													
Server Protection					A					C	D		
End-user Controls					A		B		C			D	
Network Security				A		B		C			D		
Application Security					A		B		C			D	
Cryptography						A	B		C			D	
Mobile Security					A	B		C			D		
Vulnerability Management					A	B		C			D		
Organizational													
Social Engineering Controls				A		B		C			D		
Cybersecurity Incident Management				A			B		C			D	
Cybersecurity Awareness				A		B		C			D		E
Cybersecurity Governance		A	B					C	D				

Figure 20: An example of the outcome of the CYSFAM assessment within a given organization. The letters (A–E) represent the capabilities; shaded areas show the maximum capability achieved for the corresponding focus area.

The organization depicted in Figure 20 has already implemented some capabilities, as indicated by the colored cells. It shows an unbalance, however, in that some focus areas, like Server Protection, are quite advanced, while others, like Vulnerability Management and Social Engineering Controls, are not fully developed yet. Thus, despite the development of some of the focus areas, the organization as a whole is still only at scale 4, as shown in Figure 20. To achieve a more mature cybersecurity function, its first step should be to develop the focus area of Vulnerability Management to its second capability (the B in column 5), followed by the second capability of Social Engineering Controls (the B in column 5 under Organizational). By implementing these capabilities, the organization will progress from maturity scale 4 to scale 5.

The CYSFAM presents an overarching approach to cybersecurity, offering a broad view of the cybersecurity domain. It enables organizations to understand their cybersecurity capabilities comprehensively and provides a clear roadmap for improvement.

Moreover, the CYSFAM analyzes the dependencies between the different capabilities, presented visually to facilitate understanding and planning. This visual presentation helps organizations see the connections and interdependencies between different capabilities and assists in planning capability improvement initiatives.

Furthermore, the CYSFAM not only serves as an assessment tool but also plays a pivotal role in aligning cybersecurity strategies with organizational objectives. By identifying the interdependencies among various capabilities, organizations can strategically prioritize their efforts to address critical areas first. This alignment ensures that cybersecurity initiatives are in harmony with overall organization goals, enhancing the effectiveness of the cybersecurity function.

Additionally, the CYSFAM's visual representation aids in communicating the cybersecurity status and improvement plans to stakeholders, fostering a transparent and collaborative approach to cybersecurity governance. As organizations work towards advancing their cybersecurity maturity, utilizing the CYSFAM as a guiding framework can lead to a more resilient and adaptive security posture, ultimately safeguarding valuable assets and maintaining the trust of stakeholders.

Future Improvements

While the novel scoring metric used in the CYSFAM has been proven to be adequate, there is room for further improvement. Future work on the model could focus on refining this scoring metric to provide an even more accurate and meaningful assessment of cybersecurity capabilities.

Conclusion

In conclusion, the Cybersecurity Focus Area Maturity model offers a unique and powerful tool for assessing and improving cybersecurity capabilities. By focusing on specific areas of cybersecurity and leveraging a comprehensive set of assessment questions, the CYSFAM enables organizations to gain a detailed understanding of their cybersecurity capabilities and provides a clear path for improvement.

The CYSFAM is an indispensable tool for enhanced cybersecurity in military organizations. Providing a comprehensive evaluation of a nation's cybersecurity posture allows for identifying gaps, strategically allocating resources, and creating robust cybersecurity strategies. Additionally, it fosters collaboration and learning among PNs by enabling benchmarking of cybersecurity capabilities. The CYSFAM is, therefore, a crucial instrument in ensuring a secure cyberspace for all nations.

Finally, extensive research was conducted to explore the security-related features and controls of cloud computing. The findings indicated that due to the broad scope of this subject, a dedicated cloud security maturity model could be developed, given its complexity. A recent study filled this gap in the literature by proposing a cloud computing security maturity model.[cv] Consequently, cloud security was not encompassed as a focus area in CYSFAM since it was considered more appropriate to be treated as a separate and self-contained maturity model.

Chapter 17:

State Partnership Program (SPP)

Introduction

In the realm of cyberspace security cooperation, the State Partnership Program (SPP) plays a vital role in fostering international relations and facilitating collaboration. With a history spanning 30 years, the SPP has grown to encompass 88 partnerships with 100 nations worldwide. The SPP operates by working side-by-side with willing partners around the Globe, administered by the National Guard Bureau, in close consultation with Defense Department officials and the State Department. The aim is to build trust, confidence, and capabilities with partner nations (PNs). The SPP is authorized by law (Section 341 of Title 10, United States Code) and governed by DOD Instruction 5111.20. This chapter explores how the SPP serves as a critical component of cyberspace security cooperation, leveraging military-to-military engagements and whole-of-society relationships to enhance international collaboration in the cyber domain.[cvi]

Origins and Evolution of the State Partnership Program (SPP)

The State Partnership Program (SPP) has its roots in a significant decision made by the U.S. European Command in 1991. At that time, the U.S. military recognized the need for greater engagement and collaboration with nations in the Baltic Region, particularly those emerging from the former Soviet Bloc. In response to this need, the U.S. European Command established the Joint Contact Team Program, an initiative that involved Reserve component Soldiers and Airmen.

The success and value of this initial program became evident over time. Recognizing the positive outcomes and the potential for expanding these partnerships, the National Guard Bureau proposed an innovative idea – to pair U.S. states with nations in the Baltic Region and other countries emerging from the former Soviet Bloc. This visionary proposal laid the foundation for the establishment of the State Partnership Program as we know it today.

As the SPP developed and matured, it evolved into a vital tool for U.S. security cooperation on the global stage. It not only facilitates military-to-military collaboration but also plays a crucial role in fostering international civil-military affairs. The program serves as a bridge between U.S. states and partner nations, enabling them to work together on a wide range of initiatives, including disaster response, peacekeeping, cybersecurity, and defense sector reform.

One of the unique aspects of State Partnerships is their emphasis on people-to-people ties at the state level. These partnerships go beyond military engagements, promoting cultural exchanges, educational programs, and community outreach. They strengthen international relations and enhance mutual understanding between nations by connecting people from different backgrounds and cultures.

In summary, State Partnerships are designed to achieve multiple objectives simultaneously. They bolster international relations and security, promote cooperation and collaboration, and facilitate knowledge sharing and capacity building. These partnerships have proven to be effective tools in advancing U.S. foreign policy goals, enhancing global security, and fostering lasting relationships between the United States and its partner nations.

Establishing State Partnerships: A Strategic Framework

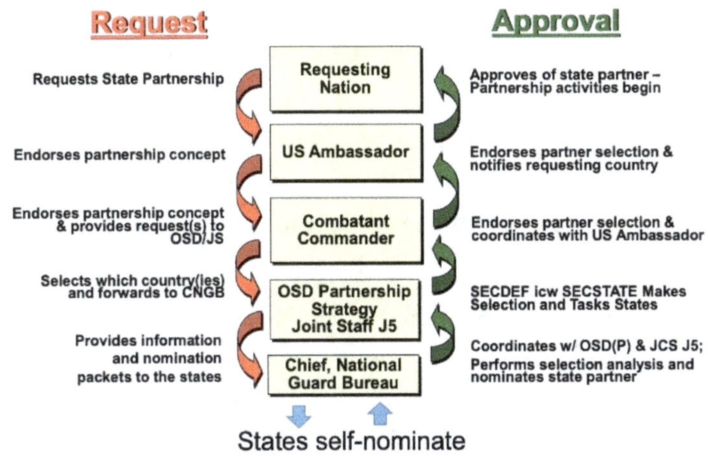

Figure 21: How Partnerships are Developed

The development of State Partnerships is a meticulously structured process aimed at fostering meaningful relationships between U.S. states and foreign nations for strategic purposes. It commences with a Requesting Nation expressing interest in establishing a partnership, followed by crucial endorsements from key stakeholders. The U.S. Ambassador in the requesting nation plays a pivotal role by endorsing the partnership concept and recognizing its strategic significance. The endorsement is further strengthened when the Combatant Commander endorses the partnership concept, providing formal requests to the Office of the Secretary of Defense (OSD) and the Joint Staff (JS). The OSD, particularly the Joint Staff J5, then selects the appropriate country or countries for partnership, forwarding these recommendations to the Chief National Guard Bureau (CNGB).

The strategic benefits of these partnerships are manifold. They facilitate military-to-military and civil-military cooperation, allowing for the exchange of knowledge, expertise, and best practices. This collaboration can enhance the capabilities of partner nations in areas such as disaster response, peacekeeping, and regional security. Additionally, these partnerships promote diplomacy and strengthen international relationships by leveraging the soft power of states and their National Guard forces. Moreover, they contribute to building regional stability and security, which, in turn, supports broader U.S. national security objectives. The process ensures a comprehensive and coordinated approach to partnership development, aligning the interests of various stakeholders, including the U.S. Department of Defense, the Department of State, and U.S. Combatant Commands, to achieve strategic goals effectively. Ultimately, State Partnerships serve as valuable tools for advancing U.S. foreign policy and security interests while fostering international collaboration and goodwill.

Below is an overview of how State Partnerships are typically developed:

1. **Requesting Nation Requests State Partnership:** The process begins when a foreign nation expresses interest in establishing a partnership with a U.S. state.

2. **US Ambassador Endorses Partnership Concept:** The U.S. Ambassador in the requesting nation endorses the partnership concept, recognizing its potential benefits.

3. **Combatant Commander Endorses Partnership Concept:** The Combatant Commander also endorses the partnership concept and provides formal requests to the Office of the Secretary of Defense (OSD) and the Joint Staff (JS).

4. **OSD Partnership Strategy:** The OSD, specifically the Joint Staff J5, selects which country or countries are suitable for partnership and forwards these recommendations to the Chief, National Guard Bureau (CNGB).

5. **Chief, National Guard Bureau:** The CNGB provides information and nomination packets to the U.S. states and coordinates with OSD (P) and JCS J5. They perform a selection analysis and nominate a state partner.

6. **SECDEF ICW SECSTATE:** The Secretary of Defense (SECDEF), in coordination with the Secretary of State (SECSTATE), makes the final selection and tasks the selected U.S. states to establish the partnership.

7. **Combatant Commander Coordinates:** The Combatant Commander further endorses the partner selection and coordinates with the U.S. Ambassador in the partner nation.

8. **U.S. Ambassador Notifies Requesting Country:** The U.S. Ambassador informs the requesting country about the selection of the state partner.

9. **Approval of State Partner:** Once all parties are in agreement, the state partner is approved, and partnership activities begin with the partner nation (PN).

This structured process ensures that State Partnerships are developed in a coordinated and strategic manner, promoting international cooperation and mutual security objectives.

Program Administration and Objectives

The SPP is administered by the National Guard Bureau (NGB) and guided by the foreign policy goals of the U.S. Department of State. It is executed by the state adjutants general, who work in alignment with the Geographic Combatant Commander (GCC) and U.S. Chief of Mission security cooperation objectives, as well as Department of Defense policy goals. This multi-level coordination ensures that the SPP aligns with broader national security and foreign policy objectives.

Military-to-Military Engagements and Defense Security Goals

One of the primary functions of the SPP is to conduct military-to-military engagements in support of defense security goals. Through these engagements, the National Guard builds relationships and exchanges knowledge and best practices with partner nations (PNs) in the cyber domain. This includes capacity-building efforts, joint exercises, training programs, and information sharing. By enhancing the capabilities of partner nations (PNs) cyber defense forces, the SPP contributes to a more secure and resilient global cyber environment. SPP's tailored approach per country is developed with Geographic

Combatant Command (GCC) and Embassy input and includes Key Leader Engagement with Presidents, Prime Ministers, Minister of Defense, Chief of Defense, subject matter experts (SMEs) exchanges, familiarization visits, training, exercises, and co-deployments. Historic focus areas include cyber defense & communications security, aviation operations, maintenance & safety, disaster response/emergency response, counterterrorism, and infantry tactics.

Leveraging Whole-of-Society Relationships and Capabilities

The SPP extends beyond military engagements, utilizing whole-of-society (Diplomatic, Informational, Military, and Economic) relationships and capabilities to facilitate broader interagency and corollary engagements. Recognizing that cybersecurity is not solely a military concern, the SPP engages various stakeholders in the military, government, economic, and social spheres. Unlike National Cyber Mission Forces (CMNF), which operate under Title 22 and focus solely on military organizations, SPP goes beyond defense organizations and engages with civic institutions (Governance, Economics, Law Enforcement) and academia. This comprehensive approach allows for the exchange of expertise, coordination of efforts, and collaboration in addressing cyber threats holistically. By fostering relationships and leveraging the expertise of non-military entities, the SPP contributes to a more comprehensive and effective approach to cyberspace security cooperation.

Enduring Relationships

One unique aspect of the SPP is its ability to forge enduring relationships between individuals over an extended period. For active component personnel, a duty assignment that includes regular contact with the military of a foreign nation typically lasts about two to three years. At the end of the tour of duty, the U.S. servicemember is usually reassigned as part of their career progression. In contrast, National Guard personnel participating in the SPP may engage with partner nation military personnel repeatedly throughout their career. This is due to both the duration of the state National Guard and foreign nation partnership - some of which have been in existence for nearly two decades - and the frequency with which National Guard personnel serve their entire reserve careers within one state National Guard.

Statutory Authorities

The SPP lacks dedicated statutory authority; rather, SPP activities are presently carried out under Title 10 (Armed Forces), Title 32 (National Guard), and National Defense Authorization Act authorities related to the types of missions conducted. However, any activity carried out by a state National Guard and its partner nation under a Title 22 authority is, by definition, not an SPP event.

In Section 341 of Title 10, United States Code, Congress authorized the Secretary of Defense to establish a program of activities "to support the Security Cooperation objectives of the United States, between members of the National Guard of a State or territory and any of the following: a) the military forces of a foreign country, b) the security forces of a foreign country,

c) governmental organizations of a foreign country whose primary functions include disaster response or emergency response."

Cost-Effectiveness and Value of the State Partnership Program

The SPP is recognized for its cost-effectiveness and value as a security cooperation program. Current funding for SPP activities is less than 1% of the $6B Security Cooperation budget. Despite its relatively small budget, 20-30% of all COCOM engagements are SPP-organized and managed events. By leveraging the existing National Guard infrastructure and expertise, the program optimizes resources and achieves significant outcomes with limited funding. The long-standing relationships developed through the SPP foster trust and cooperation, allowing for sustained and impactful cyberspace security cooperation efforts with U.S. Allies and partners.[cvii]

Here are some examples of the State Partnership Program (SPP) collaborations between U.S. states and European nations: [cviii]

1. Alabama and Romania, established in 1993

2. California and Ukraine, established in 1993

3. Colorado and Slovenia, established in 1993

4. Georgia (U.S.) and Georgia (Europe), established in 1994

5. Illinois and Poland, established in 1993

6. Indiana and Slovakia, established in 1994

7. Iowa and Kosovo, established in 2011

8. Maine and Montenegro, established in 2006

9. Maryland and Estonia, established in 1993

10. Maryland and Bosnia and Herzegovina, established in 2003

11. Michigan and Latvia, established in 1993

12. Minnesota and Croatia, established in 1996

13. Minnesota and Norway, established in 2023

14. New Jersey and Albania, established in 2001

15. New Jersey and Cyprus, established in 2022

16. North Carolina and Moldova, established in 1996

17. Ohio and Hungary, established in 1993

18. Ohio and Serbia, established in 2006

19. Oklahoma and Azerbaijan, established in 2003

20. Pennsylvania and Lithuania, established in 1993

21. Tennessee and Bulgaria, established in 1993

22. Texas, Nebraska, and the Czech Republic, established in 1993

23. Vermont and North Macedonia, established in 1993

24. Vermont and Austria, established in 2021.

See Appendix E for the full SPP partnership map outlining current collaborations between U.S. states and nations around the world.

Conclusion

The State Partnership Program (SPP) serves as a critical component of cyberspace security cooperation, leveraging military-to-military engagements, cross-sector collaboration, and cost effective approaches to foster trust, share best practices, and enhance the defensive capabilities of partner nations. With its 30-year history and partnerships with 100 nations worldwide, the SPP contributes to the enhancement of international collaboration in the cyber domain. By exchanging knowledge, building capacity, and fostering relationships, the SPP strengthens cyber defense capabilities globally and promotes a secure and resilient cyber environment for all stakeholders involved.

The SPP is a joint initiative of the United States Department of Defense (DOD) and individual states, territories, and the District of Columbia. This program links National Guard units of U.S. States with partner countries worldwide to support the security cooperation objectives of the geographic Combatant Commands. It involves various activities, including joint training exercises, crisis relief, and humanitarian efforts. The SPP is particularly effective as it allows a state's National Guard unit to maintain its state identity while conducting joint exercises with a partner nation.

The SPP directly supports Department of Defense objectives and theater campaign plans by building relationships that enhance global security, understanding, and cooperation.

The program fosters long-term relationships across all levels of society and encourages the development of economic, political, and military ties between the states and partner nations (PNs).

Established in 1993 as a simplified form of the previously established Joint Contact Team Program (JCTP), the State Partnership Program (SPP) is a joint initiative of the United States Department of Defense (DOD) and individual states, territories, and the District of Columbia. The primary goal of the SPP was to assist the former Warsaw Pact and Soviet Union Republics, now independent, in forming democracies and their defense forces.

The program links National Guard units of U.S. States with partner countries worldwide to support the security cooperation objectives of the geographic Combatant Commands (CCMDs). This cooperation extends beyond pure security, involving a significant number of crisis relief and humanitarian activities. The State Partnership constitutes an agreement between the United States and a foreign government to conduct joint security operations with the United States National Guard. These operations mainly involve training exercises, which may (or may not) lead to the partner's membership in regional defense organizations.

In terms of management, the SPP is a collaboration between the state (or territory, etc.) and the DOD in deploying the unit, which maintains its state identity. The National Guard Bureau manages it, but the states execute it. Collaboration between the state Adjutant General and the commander in the field occurs during this process.

Regarding its relevance to U.S. cybersecurity cooperation, the State Partnership Program facilitates cooperation across all aspects of international civil-military affairs, including cybersecurity. It encourages people-to-people ties at the state level, directly supports Department of Defense objectives, and builds relationships that enhance global security, understanding, and cooperation. The program fosters long-term relationships across all levels of society and encourages the development of economic, political, and military ties between the states and partner nations (PNs).

Chapter 18:

The State Partnership Program (SPP): A Critical Component of Cyberspace Security Cooperation

Introduction

In the realm of cyberspace security cooperation, the State Partnership Program (SPP) plays a vital role in fostering international relations and facilitating collaboration. With a history spanning 30 years, the SPP has grown to encompass 88 partnerships with 100 nations worldwide. This chapter explores how the SPP serves as a critical component of cyberspace security cooperation, leveraging military-to-military engagements and whole-of-society relationships to enhance international collaboration in the cyber domain. In this section, we will delve into real-world cases where the SPP has been leveraged to support cybersecurity and rapid cyber incident responses for partner nations (PNs).

Special Capabilities of the SPP

One distinctive aspect of the State Partnership Program (SPP) lies in the unique capabilities offered by the National Guard, setting it apart from similar engagements by active component forces. The National Guard serves a dual status as both a state and federal organization. In its federal status, it operates as a reserve component of the Army and Air Force, trained and equipped for a broad range of military activities. Simultaneously, the National Guard functions as the organized militia of each state, primarily assisting in disaster response, cyber attacks, and civil disorder situations under the control of state governors.

One area where the National Guard brings exceptional value is in the sphere of real-world cyber operations. Many National Guard personnel possess specialized cyber expertise acquired from working in the private sector. This unique skill set, combined with their military training, positions the National Guard as a valuable resource in addressing cyber threats and vulnerabilities. The integration of cyber expertise allows the National Guard to contribute significantly to cyber defense efforts, including supporting partner nations in enhancing their cybersecurity capabilities and resilience.

For example, the National Guard has been actively engaged in cyber operations, providing vital support in response to major cyber attacks. Its significant role includes sharing technical knowledge, conducting joint cyber exercises, and providing incident response support. The National Guard's expertise has proven invaluable in mitigating the impact of cyber incidents and enhancing the cyber defenses of partner nations.

While active component forces also possess cyber capabilities, the National Guard's unique combination of private sector cyber expertise, military training, and its ability to operate under state control makes it a valuable asset in cybersecurity engagements. The National Guard's frequent engagement in cyber defense activities further enhances their practical experience and effectiveness in addressing emerging cyber threats.

In conclusion, the National Guard's special capabilities extend beyond traditional military activities. With their private sector cyber expertise and involvement in cyber engagements, the National Guard brings valuable skills and knowledge to the table. This expertise, combined with their military training and state-controlled operations, makes the National Guard a valuable partner in enhancing cybersecurity and addressing cyber threats within the framework of the State Partnership Program.

Case 1: Cyber Defense Capacity Building in Ukraine

Ukraine has been a partner nation under the SPP since 1991. In recent years, the SPP has played a significant role in supporting Ukraine's cyber defense capabilities. The National Guard, through the SPP, has conducted joint exercises, training programs, and knowledge exchanges with Ukrainian cyber defense forces. These engagements have focused on enhancing incident response capabilities, improving information-sharing mechanisms, and developing cyber defense strategies. In 2017, during the "NotPetya" ransomware attack that severely impacted Ukraine, the SPP facilitated rapid incident response support, leveraging its established relationships and expertise to assist in mitigating the cyber-attack and restoring critical systems.

Case 2: Enhancing Cyber Resilience in the Baltic States

The SPP partnerships with the Baltic states, including Estonia, Latvia, and Lithuania, have been instrumental in enhancing their cyber resilience and incident response capabilities. Through the SPP, the National Guard has conducted joint cyber exercises, workshops, and knowledge-sharing sessions with partner nations (PNs). These engagements have focused on developing cyber incident response plans, improving information sharing and collaboration between military and civilian entities, and enhancing technical capabilities. The SPP has played a crucial role in strengthening the cyber defense posture of the Baltic states, particularly in response to the growing cyber threats in the region.

Case 3: Strengthening Cyber Defense Capabilities in Albania

Albania has been a partner nation under the State Partnership Program (SPP) since 1993. The SPP has played a crucial role in supporting Albania's efforts to strengthen its cyber defense capabilities. Through the partnership, the National Guard has conducted joint training exercises, workshops, and knowledge exchanges focused on cyber defense strategies, incident response, and information sharing. These initiatives have helped Albania enhance its cyber defense posture and develop a robust framework for rapid cyber incident response. In a real-world case, when Albania faced a significant cyber-attack targeting its critical infrastructure, the SPP facilitated rapid incident response support by leveraging its established relationships and expertise, assisting Albania in mitigating the attack and restoring affected systems.

Case 4: Promoting Cybersecurity Cooperation in Poland

Poland has been a longstanding partner nation under the SPP, fostering cybersecurity cooperation and collaboration with the United States. The SPP has played an essential role in promoting information sharing, joint exercises, and capacity-building initiatives in the cyber domain. The National Guard, through the SPP, has conducted cybersecurity workshops, training programs, and tabletop exercises with Polish cyber defense forces. These engagements have focused on enhancing incident response capabilities, strengthening cybersecurity frameworks, and fostering collaboration between military and civilian entities. By leveraging the SPP, Poland has been able to enhance its cyber defense capabilities and strengthen its ability to respond to cyber threats effectively.

Case 5: Building Cyber Defense Partnerships in Romania

Romania has been an active partner nation under the State Partnership Program (SPP) for many years, focusing on strengthening its cyber defense capabilities. The SPP has played a significant role in building cyber defense partnerships between the United States and Romania. Through joint exercises, workshops, and knowledge sharing, the National Guard, in collaboration with Romanian cyber defense forces, has worked to enhance incident response capabilities, develop cyber defense strategies, and improve information-sharing mechanisms. The SPP has facilitated the exchange of best practices, technical expertise, and training opportunities, enabling Romania to bolster its cyber defense posture and respond effectively to cyber threats. In a real-world case, when Romania faced a sophisticated cyber-attack on its critical infrastructure, the SPP provided rapid incident response support, leveraging its established relationships and expertise to assist Romania in mitigating the attack and restoring affected systems.

Case 6: Strengthening Cyber Resilience in Bulgaria

Bulgaria, as a partner nation under the State Partnership Program (SPP), has benefited from the program's support in strengthening its cyber resilience. The SPP has played a critical role in fostering cybersecurity cooperation between the United States and Bulgaria. Through joint training exercises, capacity-building programs, and information-sharing initiatives, the SPP has helped Bulgaria enhance its cyber defense capabilities and incident response readiness. The National Guard, working closely with Bulgarian cyber defense forces, has conducted tabletop exercises and workshops focused on cyber incident management, threat intelligence sharing, and technical skills development. These efforts have contributed to improving Bulgaria's ability to detect, respond to, and recover from cyber incidents. Additionally, the SPP has facilitated the exchange of expertise and best practices between military and civilian entities, enabling a comprehensive and coordinated approach to cybersecurity in Bulgaria.

Case 7: Advancing Cybersecurity Cooperation in Montenegro

Montenegro, as a partner nation under the State Partnership Program (SPP), has benefited from the program's support in advancing cybersecurity cooperation. The SPP has played a crucial role in fostering collaboration between the United States and Montenegro in the cyber domain. Through joint training exercises, knowledge-sharing sessions, and capacity-building initiatives, the National Guard, in collaboration with Montenegrin cyber defense forces, has worked to enhance cyber defense capabilities, develop incident response strategies, and improve information-sharing mechanisms. The SPP has facilitated the exchange of best practices, technical expertise, and training opportunities, enabling Montenegro to strengthen its cyber defense posture and respond effectively to cyber threats. In a real-world case, when Montenegro faced a significant cyber-attack targeting its critical infrastructure, the SPP provided rapid incident response support, leveraging its established relationships and expertise to assist Montenegro in mitigating the attack and restoring affected systems.

Case 8: Strengthening Cyber Resilience in North Macedonia

North Macedonia, a partner nation under the State Partnership Program (SPP), has leveraged the program's support to strengthen its cyber resilience. The SPP has played a pivotal role in promoting cybersecurity cooperation between the United States and North Macedonia. Through joint exercises, workshops, and knowledge-sharing initiatives, the

National Guard, in collaboration with North Macedonian cyber defense forces, has focused on enhancing incident response capabilities, developing cyber defense strategies, and fostering information-sharing mechanisms. The SPP has facilitated the exchange of expertise, best practices, and technical training opportunities, enabling North Macedonia to improve its cyber defense capabilities and respond effectively to cyber threats. By leveraging the SPP, North Macedonia has enhanced its ability to detect, respond to, and recover from cyber incidents. Additionally, the SPP has fostered collaboration between military and civilian entities, promoting a comprehensive and coordinated approach to cybersecurity in North Macedonia.

Case 9: Strengthening Cyber Defense Capabilities in Bosnia and Herzegovina

Bosnia and Herzegovina, as a partner nation under the State Partnership Program (SPP), has benefited from the program's support in strengthening its cyber defense capabilities. The SPP has played a vital role in building cyber defense partnerships between the United States and Bosnia and Herzegovina. Through joint training exercises, workshops, and knowledge exchanges, the National Guard, in collaboration with Bosnian cyber defense forces, has worked to enhance incident response capabilities, develop cyber defense strategies, and improve information-sharing mechanisms. These initiatives have helped Bosnia and Herzegovina enhance its cyber defense posture and develop a robust framework for rapid cyber incident response. In a real-world case, when Bosnia and Herzegovina faced a significant cyber-attack targeting its critical infrastructure, the SPP facilitated rapid incident response support by leveraging its established relationships and expertise, assisting in mitigating the attack and restoring affected systems.

Case 10: Fostering Cybersecurity Cooperation in Kosovo

Kosovo, a partner nation under the State Partnership Program (SPP), has leveraged the program's support to foster cybersecurity cooperation. The SPP has played a significant role in promoting collaboration between the United States and Kosovo in the cyber domain. Through joint exercises, workshops, and knowledge-sharing initiatives, the National Guard, in collaboration with Kosovar cyber defense forces, has focused on enhancing incident response capabilities, developing cyber defense strategies, and improving information-sharing mechanisms. The SPP has facilitated the exchange of best practices, technical expertise, and training opportunities, enabling Kosovo to bolster its cyber defense posture and respond effectively to cyber threats. By leveraging the SPP, Kosovo has enhanced its ability to detect, respond to, and recover from cyber incidents. Additionally, the SPP has fostered collaboration between military and civilian entities, promoting a comprehensive and coordinated approach to cybersecurity in Kosovo.

Conclusion

In conclusion, the State Partnership Program (SPP) stands as a cornerstone in the realm of cyberspace security cooperation, demonstrating its significance in fostering international relations and facilitating collaboration. With a rich history spanning three decades, the SPP has evolved into a robust network comprising 88 partnerships with 100 nations globally. Throughout this chapter, we've explored the pivotal role of the SPP in enhancing international collaboration in cyberspace security.

By leveraging military-to-military engagements and whole-of-society relationships, the SPP serves as a linchpin in bolstering cybersecurity efforts across partner nations (PNs). Real-world cases have underscored the program's effectiveness in supporting rapid cyber incident responses and fortifying cyber defenses for PNs. From joint exercises to information-sharing initiatives, the SPP has demonstrated its adaptability and effectiveness in addressing the evolving cyber threats facing nations worldwide.

As we navigate the complex landscape of cyberspace security, the SPP remains a vital mechanism for promoting cooperation, resilience, and collective defense in the digital domain. Through continued investment and collaboration, the program will undoubtedly play a pivotal role in safeguarding the interconnected world of cyberspace for years to come.

Chapter 19:

The SPP in Focus: Examining Concerns and Strategies for Successful Cyberspace Security Cooperation

Introduction

The State Partnership Program (SPP) has raised three primary concerns among stakeholders in cyberspace security cooperation. Firstly, questions have been raised regarding the effectiveness of aligning SPP activities with the priorities of combatant commanders and U.S. ambassadors. Secondly, there has been criticism of certain SPP events for providing funding for engagements involving U.S. civilians and foreign civilians that may exceed the legal limits. Lastly, concerns have been expressed about the potential "militarization of foreign policy" resulting from the overlap between Department of Defense (DOD) security cooperation activities, including SPP events, and the roles of the Department of State and the U.S. Agency for International Development (USAID).[cix]

Integration with Priorities of Combatant Commanders and Ambassadors

One of the primary concerns surrounding the State Partnership Program (SPP) is the effectiveness of integrating its activities with the priorities of combatant commanders and U.S. ambassadors. Some observers argue that certain SPP activities in specific countries have not been well-coordinated with the combatant command and the U.S. embassy, resulting in a lack of alignment with their priorities. This concern underscores the need for improved event coordination procedures to ensure that the activities of the SPP are consistently linked to the priorities of combatant commanders and ambassadors.

Civilian Engagements

Another concern related to the SPP pertains to civilian engagements. The program operates within a range of statutory authorities, some of which permit civilian involvement to varying degrees. However, questions have been raised about the funding of engagements involving U.S. civilians and foreign civilians beyond the scope of authorized statutes. The extent to which these engagements complied with statutory requirements remains unclear. Efforts have been made to ensure that foreign civilians participating in SPP activities are requested by the partner nation's Ministry of Defense and contribute to their mission. It is also notable that funding for exchanges with foreign civilian personnel is authorized, but only if they are part of the defense ministry of a foreign government.

Encroachment on DOS and USAID Responsibilities

The SPP's alignment with authorities has raised concerns about the potential "militarization" of U.S. foreign assistance. Critics argue that these activities, traditionally conducted under State Department authority, should be carried out by military personnel under the supervision and funding of the State Department or USAID. The inclusion of the National Guard in these activities further fuels the debate surrounding militarization. While National Guard personnel are subject to U.S. military law when deployed abroad, they also possess civilian skills, experiences, and perspectives that may help address concerns when engaged in missions overseas.

In conclusion, concerns have been raised regarding the integration of SPP activities with the priorities of combatant commanders and ambassadors. Additionally, questions have been raised about civilian engagements and the potential encroachment on the responsibilities of the Department of State and USAID. These concerns highlight the need for improved coordination procedures and clear alignment with strategic priorities to ensure the effectiveness and appropriateness of SPP activities.

Future Strategies with the SPP

Understanding the above concerns should give policymakers and country desk officers some directions on how to effectively leverage the National Guard's special cyber expertise within the State Partnership Program (SPP) to enhance cyberspace security cooperation and support partner nations in strengthening their cyber defense capabilities. By harnessing the National Guard's dual status as a state and federal organization, we can tap into their unique combination of private-sector cyber expertise, military training, and state-controlled operations to address emerging cyber threats and vulnerabilities.

One potential direction is to leverage specialized cyber units within the National Guard to focus on cybersecurity capacity building and support for partner nations. These units can be composed of highly skilled cyber professionals with diverse backgrounds and experiences in both the private and military sectors. Through targeted training programs and knowledge sharing, these units can help partner nations develop robust cyber defense strategies, enhance their incident response capabilities, and establish effective cyber governance frameworks.

Furthermore, the National Guard's involvement in cyber engagements should be expanded to include joint cyber exercises, information-sharing initiatives, and collaborative cybersecurity research and development projects. These activities can facilitate the exchange of best practices, foster innovation, and strengthen the partnership between the National Guard and partner nations in the cyber domain. By leveraging their practical experience and expertise, the National Guard can actively contribute to enhancing the cyber resilience and capabilities of partner nations.

To ensure effective integration of the National Guard's cyber expertise within the SPP, it is crucial to establish clear coordination mechanisms with combatant commanders, U.S. embassies, and partner nation stakeholders. This coordination should include regular communication, joint planning, and shared situational awareness to align cyber activities with the priorities of combatant commanders and ambassadors. Additionally, close collaboration with other U.S. government agencies, such as the Department of State and the U.S. Agency for International Development, can help mitigate concerns of potential "militarization of foreign policy" and ensure a balanced approach to cybersecurity cooperation.

Conclusion

In summary, by capitalizing on the National Guard's special cyber expertise and incorporating it into the State Partnership Program, we can strengthen cybersecurity cooperation and support partner nations in their cyber defense efforts. Establishing specialized cyber units, expanding involvement in cyber engagements, and ensuring effective coordination with relevant stakeholders will be essential in maximizing the value and impact of the National Guard's capabilities within the SPP.

Chapter 20:

Supporting Cyberspace Security Cooperation: PEO EIS's Defensive Cyber Operations (DCO) and the Allied Information Technology (AIT) Product Office

Introduction

In the realm of cyberspace security cooperation, the Program Executive Office Enterprise Information Systems (PEO EIS) plays a vital role in supporting defensive cyber operations (DCO) and fostering collaboration through the Allied Information Technology (AIT) product office. With a focus on tailored security cooperation projects, AIT aims to meet the capacity-building requirements of partner nations (PNs) in command, control, communications, computers, cyber, and intelligence. This chapter explores how PEO EIS's DCO, specifically the AIT product office, supports efforts in cyberspace security cooperation.

PEO EIS Mission and AIT Areas of Support

PEO EIS's mission is to enhance U.S. and Partner Nation security and interoperability by delivering non-standard Command, Control, Communications, Computers, Cyber, and Intelligence (C5I) capabilities under Defense Security Cooperation and Assistance programs, primarily utilizing the Foreign Military Sales (FMS) process. Tasked with executing this mission, the Allied Information Technology (AIT) product office supports various areas under Security Cooperation, including project management, capability gap decomposition, Combatant Command coordination, drafting letters of request, concept development, pricing in letters of offer and acceptance, contract requirements and management, training, initial logistics support, testing, and transfer of ownership.

Establishment and Reputation Building

Established in October 2017 within PEO EIS's Installation Information Infrastructure Communications and Capabilities portfolio, AIT (formerly known as the International Programs Division) has quietly built a reputation for providing IT systems and services to Allies and foreign partners globally. As the demand for network modernization and cyber projects continues to grow, the approximately 30-member strong AIT team is actively expanding its workforce to meet the increasing needs of smaller countries across diverse geographic regions.

Comprehensive Service Delivery

AIT shoulders the responsibility of delivering comprehensive services to its customers, with a specific focus on network modernization and cyber projects. The office manages diverse tasks, including infrastructure evaluations, requirements gathering, project management, procurement of commercial off-the-shelf (COTS) hardware and software, implementation, training, and testing. By offering end-to-end support, AIT ensures that partner nations (PNs) receive the necessary assistance to enhance their cyber defense capabilities.

Collaboration with Stakeholders

AIT maintains close collaboration with key stakeholders, including the Deputy Assistant Secretary of the Army for Defense Exports and Cooperation, the Defense Security Cooperation Agency, and other entities linked to combatant commands. This collaboration enables AIT to align its efforts with broader defense cooperation initiatives and leverage existing networks and relationships to enhance cyberspace security cooperation.

Data Utilization and Dashboard Development

Recognizing the importance of effective data utilization, AIT has recently developed a dashboard for the U.S. Central Command, aiming to provide valuable insights and metrics. With plans to expand the usage of the dashboard across other geographical combatant commands, AIT demonstrates its commitment to leveraging data-driven approaches to enhance situational awareness and decision-making processes.

Exploring Alternative Acquisition Strategies

AIT proactively explores alternative acquisition strategies aligned with the Army's evolution toward Agile methodologies. Embracing flexibility and adaptability in the acquisition process allows AIT to respond efficiently to the dynamic cyber landscape and deliver tailored solutions to partner nations (PNs).

Strategic Process and Mission Accomplishment

Ultimately, AIT strives to embed a strategic process that enhances its mission accomplishment. By adopting a task-organized approach, AIT aims to support host nations in improving their capabilities, enabling them to effectively assist U.S. warfighters and other Allies. The office's focus on strategic alignment, collaboration, and customized solutions reinforces its commitment to advancing cyberspace security cooperation.

Conclusion

Through PEO EIS's DCO efforts, particularly the AIT product office, significant support is provided for cyberspace security cooperation. AIT's focus on tailored security cooperation projects, comprehensive service delivery, collaboration with stakeholders, data utilization, and exploration of alternative acquisition strategies demonstrates its commitment to enhancing partner nations (P.Ns.) cyber defense capabilities. By fostering collaboration and leveraging expertise, PEO EIS's DCO and the AIT product office contribute to a more secure and resilient cyber environment, benefiting both the United States and its Allies in their collective defense efforts.

Chapter 21:

Leveraging Defensive Cyber Operations (DCO) Capabilities and Platforms for Cyber Capacity Building

Introduction

In the domain of cyberspace security cooperation, Defensive Cyber Operations (DCO) play a pivotal role in countering and mitigating cyber threats. The establishment of robust DCO capabilities and platforms is crucial to supporting the cyber capacity building of U.S. Allies and partners. These capabilities are designed to achieve various objectives, including deterring, neutralizing, and defeating cyber threats, gaining time, ensuring an economy of force, controlling key terrain, protecting critical assets and infrastructure, and developing intelligence. This chapter explores the type of DCO capabilities and platforms required to bolster cyberspace security cooperation efforts.

Emerging Capabilities Platforms

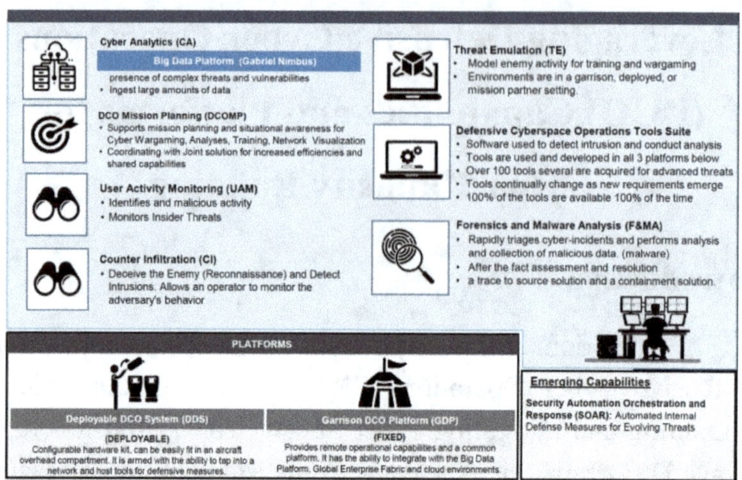

Figure 22: U.S. Army Defensive Cyber Operations (DCO) Operational Overview

Understanding Deployable and Garrison DCO Solutions in Cyber Defense

To bolster the cyber capacity building of partner nations, two key platforms take the forefront: the Deployable DCO System and the Garrison DCO Platform. The Deployable DCO System is a compact and configurable hardware kit designed for easy transport, even fitting into an aircraft overhead compartment. It enables tapping into networks and hosting defensive tools for rapid response and support in remote or deployed environments, such as mission partner settings.[cx] The Deployable DCO System facilitates counter-reconnaissance activities, vulnerability discovery, and the implementation of defensive measures. On the other hand, the Garrison DCO System provides a fixed platform for continuous cyber surveillance, in-depth data analysis, and robust defense mechanisms against persistent threats, ensuring a stable and secure cyber infrastructure within military installations. Integrated with a Big Data Platform, the Garrison DCO System ensures seamless information sharing and coordination.

Deployable DCO System (DDS) in Focus: A Comprehensive Overview

Deployable Defense Cyber Operations (DCO) platforms are indispensable for defense cyber institutions and military organizations in modern warfare due to their versatility, mobility, and capacity to enhance operational security, provide real-time threat intelligence, and ensure robust communication networks in rapidly evolving threat environments. These platforms play a vital role in strengthening the cybersecurity capabilities of nations and bolstering their cyber resilience. Here's why they are an essential cyber capability for every military organization:

1. Rapid Response and Support:

In today's dynamic cyber threat landscape, the ability to respond swiftly to emerging threats is crucial. Deployable DCO Systems are designed for easy transport and deployment, making them invaluable for rapid response situations. These platforms can be swiftly deployed to forward operating bases (FOBs) or mission partner settings, enabling military organizations in the garrison to provide immediate support in the event of a cyber incident. This rapid response capability is essential for mitigating threats and minimizing potential damage.

Moreover, the real-time connectivity and communication capabilities of Deployable DCO Systems enable seamless collaboration during cyber crises. These platforms serve as a linchpin in fostering information sharing and joint efforts to counter cyber threats, enhancing the collective cyber defense posture. The collaborative nature of these responses not only ensures a more robust defense but also strengthens national cyber alliances, reinforcing partner nations' resilience against cyber adversaries. As the interconnected nature of cyberspace continues to pose challenges, the collaborative and rapid response features of Deployable DCO Systems are becoming increasingly critical components of effective cybersecurity strategies for military organizations worldwide.

2. Enhanced Remote Capabilities:

In an era where military operations often extend beyond traditional borders, having a stable and secure cyber platform in remote locations is essential. This platform allows military organizations to maintain a continuous cyber presence, monitor networks, and respond to threats in real time, regardless of their geographic location.

Furthermore, the Deployable DCO Platform's enhanced remote capabilities go beyond immediate cyber response. It acts as a hub for sustained operations, facilitating ongoing monitoring and analysis of cyber activities over extended periods. Integrated with advanced analytics and threat intelligence, this platform provides military organizations with the capability to anticipate and proactively address emerging threats before they escalate. The ability to establish and maintain a robust cyber defense infrastructure is crucial for ensuring the security of military networks and communication systems.

3. Counter-Reconnaissance Activities:

Deployable DCO Systems are equipped to conduct counter-reconnaissance activities, which are essential for identifying and thwarting potential cyber threats. These platforms can actively monitor and analyze network traffic to detect suspicious or unauthorized activities. By identifying reconnaissance efforts early, military organizations can take proactive measures to protect their networks and assets.

4. Vulnerability Discovery:

Vulnerability discovery is a critical aspect of cybersecurity. Deployable DCO Systems are equipped with tools and capabilities to identify vulnerabilities within networks and systems. By proactively identifying weaknesses, military organizations can patch or mitigate them before they can be exploited by adversaries, reducing the risk of successful cyber attacks.

5. Defensive Measures Implementation:

One of the primary functions of Deployable DCO Systems is the implementation of defensive measures. These platforms can deploy defensive tools and techniques to safeguard military networks and critical infrastructure. This capability is vital for actively defending against cyber threats and maintaining the integrity and availability of military systems.

Additionally, the deployment of defensive measures is not limited to reactionary responses; these platforms also contribute to proactive cybersecurity strategies. By continuously monitoring network activities and employing preemptive defensive measures, military organizations can create a resilient cyber environment that anticipates and mitigates potential threats before they manifest. The ability to implement dynamic and adaptive defensive measures is particularly crucial in the face of evolving cyber threats, ensuring that military networks remain secure and operational even in the midst of sophisticated and persistent attacks.

6. Information Sharing and Coordination:

The Deployable DCO System can also be integrated with Big Data Platforms to ensure seamless information sharing and coordination among military organizations. These platforms facilitate the sharing of threat intelligence, best practices, and real-time situational awareness, enhancing the collective defense posture.

The deployable DCO platform's mobility, rapid response capabilities, and ability to conduct counter-reconnaissance, vulnerability discovery, and defensive measures implementation are crucial in today's interconnected and rapidly evolving digital battlefield. These platforms play a pivotal role in safeguarding national security interests and ensuring the resilience of critical military infrastructure on the battlefield.

Defensive Cyberspace Operations Tools Suite

The Defensive Cyberspace Operations tools suite encompasses a diverse range of software tools crucial for detecting intrusions, conducting forensics analysis, and responding to cyber threats. These tools undergo continuous updates and development to address emerging threats and meet evolving cyber defense requirements. They play a critical role in monitoring, analyzing, and responding to cyber incidents effectively. Here's an overview of some of these tools:

Security Automation Orchestration and Response (SOAR): Automated Internal Defense Measures for Evolving Threats

Security Automation Orchestration and Response (SOAR) stands out as a critical capability supporting the automation and coordination of internal defense measures in response to evolving threats. It enables organizations to automate routine tasks, streamline incident response processes, and enhance overall cyber defense capabilities. SOAR platforms provide the necessary automation and orchestration capabilities to detect, respond to, and mitigate cyber threats effectively.

Cyber Analytics (CA): Enhancing Situational Awareness and Threat Detection

Cyber Analytics (CA) emerged as a critical capability facilitating counter-reconnaissance activities and aiding in the discovery of complex threats and vulnerabilities. CA platforms excel in ingesting large amounts of data, allowing for comprehensive analysis and the detection of potential threats. Leveraging advanced analytics and machine learning techniques, CA platforms enhance situational awareness, enabling proactive threat detection and timely responses to cyber incidents.

Threat Emulation (TE): Modeling Adversary Activity for Training and Wargaming

Threat Emulation (TE) capabilities serve the purpose of modeling enemy activity for training and wargaming scenarios.

These platforms simulate adversary behavior in various environments, including garrison, deployed, or mission partner settings. By creating realistic cyber threat scenarios, TE platforms contribute to improving readiness, developing effective defensive strategies, and enhancing the overall capabilities of cybersecurity forces. Realistic threat scenario replication allows cybersecurity practitioners to enhance their skills, test defensive strategies, and improve incident response capabilities.

TE platforms play an essential role in identifying and addressing vulnerabilities within military networks. When emulating sophisticated cyber threats, these platforms help assess the resilience of existing security measures and identify potential weaknesses. The data gathered from threat emulation exercises can then be used to fine-tune defensive strategies, implement targeted improvements, and ensure that military organizations are well-prepared to face diverse and evolving cyber threats. The integration of Threat Emulation capabilities into cybersecurity training and wargaming not only enhances the realism of exercises but also provides valuable insights that contribute to the continuous improvement of military cyber defenses.

Counter Infiltration (CI): Enhancing Surveillance and Threat Detection

Counter Infiltration (CI) is a strategic security approach designed to counteract hostile infiltrations effectively. A pivotal aspect of CI involves "Enhancing Surveillance and Threat Detection," enabling cyber operators to actively monitor and assess the behavior of adversaries. This entails comprehensive reconnaissance efforts, gathering critical intelligence on adversary tactics and procedures to enhance preparedness against potential infiltrations.

User Activity Monitoring (UAM): Detecting and Monitoring Insider Threats

User Activity Monitoring (UAM) capabilities play a vital role in identifying and monitoring malicious activity within a network. UAM platforms enable the detection of insider threats and provide continuous monitoring to identify suspicious behavior. Through the analysis of user activities and network traffic, UAM platforms contribute significantly to early threat detection and incident response.

Big Data Platform: Processing and Analyzing Large Data Sets

The Big Data Platform assumes a pivotal role in handling and analyzing large data sets generated from various DCO capabilities. This platform ensures efficient storage, processing, and analysis of data to derive actionable insights. Leveraging advanced data analytics and visualization techniques, the Big Data Platform enhances the effectiveness of DCO operations.

DCO Mission Planning (DCOMP): Enabling Mission Planning and Situational Awareness

DCO Mission Planning (DCOMP) platforms provide support for mission planning, situational awareness, cyber wargaming, analysis, and network visualization. These tools facilitate coordination and collaboration among cybersecurity teams, fostering increased efficiencies and shared capabilities both within the organization and through joint solutions.

Offering a comprehensive view of the cyber landscape, DCOMP platforms contribute to effective decision-making and response to cyber threats.

Forensics and Malware Analysis (F&MA): Investigating and Resolving Cyber Incidents

Forensics and Malware Analysis (F&MA) capabilities are essential for rapidly triaging cyber incidents, conducting in-depth analysis, and collecting malicious data, including malware. F&MA platforms empower cybersecurity analysts to trace incidents back to their source, contain threats, and resolve security breaches. These capabilities are crucial for conducting post-incident assessments and implementing necessary remediation measures.

In addition to resolving immediate cyber incidents, F&MA platforms play a pivotal role in proactive cybersecurity measures. By analyzing malware and understanding its behavior, cybersecurity professionals can anticipate potential future threats and strengthen preventive measures. The insights gained from forensics and malware analysis contribute to the continuous improvement of security protocols, allowing military organizations to stay ahead of emerging cyber threats.

Deployable DCO Solutions in the Modern Market

As cyber threats continue to intensify, deployable DCO solutions have become essential tools for bolstering the defense capabilities of military organizations. Two notable solutions in the modern market are HII's SABERHUNT and Booz Allen's Cyber Precog.

Huntington Ingalls Industries (HII)'s SABERHUNT

Developed by HII's Mission Technologies division, SABERHUNT is a cutting-edge prototype kit designed for cyber threat hunting. This solution is tailored to safeguard U.S. federal networks and those of partner nations. What sets SABERHUNT apart is its adaptability to various operational environments, including traditional, cloud, and hybrid networks. Its modular design allows for scalability in computing and storage, enabling the provision of customized solutions for specific mission requirements. This versatility is a testament to the kit's design philosophy, focusing on the evolving needs of cyber protection.

SABERHUNT is also characterized by its portability, conveniently fitting into airline-approved carry-on cases. This feature, coupled with its 24/7 global support network – inclusive of remote troubleshooting and expedited hardware delivery – underlines its readiness for diverse operational scenarios. The development, provisioning, and deployment of SABERHUNT kits are a collaborative effort involving HII and partners like Dell Technologies and VMware, ensuring a robust and comprehensive solution.[cxi]

Booz Allen Hamilton (BAH)'s Cyber Precog

In response to the challenges posed by increasingly sophisticated cyber actors and the limitations of current field-deployable hardware, Booz Allen, in partnership with NVIDIA, has developed the Cyber Precog kit. This next-generation flyaway kit is a testament to the synergy between GPU-accelerated computing and advanced cyber operations.

Cyber Precog is built on the NVIDIA Morpheus framework, integrating advanced cyber tools, AI models, and modular pipelines for swift deployment. Its GPU-enablement allows for a level of data analysis and processing speed previously unattainable in field operations. This rapid processing capability is crucial for incident response teams, especially when operating in time-sensitive and data-intensive scenarios.

Notably, Cyber Precog is not just a tool for accelerated data processing; it's an adaptable platform. Its open architecture facilitates the integration and customization of tools and data flows, allowing cyber operators to adapt to various mission requirements rapidly. This flexibility is further enhanced by the platform's ability to support the development of new GPU-accelerated analytics, making it an invaluable asset for proactive and reactive cyber operations. Tailorable to any GPU-enabled hardware, Cyber Precog is optimized to meet the unique needs of individual organizations. It's currently available for pilot projects, testing, evaluation, and integration, marking a significant advancement in the capabilities of incident response teams. [cxii]

These solutions, SABERHUNT and Cyber Precog represent the forefront of deployable DCO technology. They offer unparalleled adaptability, processing power, and tool customization, catering to the diverse and dynamic needs of modern cyber defense operations.

Conclusion

In conclusion, Defensive Cyber Operations (DCO) capabilities and platforms stand as indispensable pillars supporting cyberspace security cooperation efforts. Platforms such as the fixed Garrison DCO Platform and Deployable DCO System provide the necessary infrastructure for collaborative defensive measures. Additionally, capabilities like Cyber Analytics, Threat Emulation, Counter Infiltration, DCO Mission Planning, User Activity Monitoring, Forensics and Malware Analysis, and the Big Data Platform contribute to enhancing situational awareness, enabling proactive threat detection, and supporting effective decision-making. By leveraging these capabilities and platforms, Allied nations and partners can elevate their collective defensive cyber capabilities, deter cyber threats, and ensure the security and resilience of cyberspace.

Chapter 22:

Revolutionizing Defense Cyber Institutions Through Cybersecurity Skills and Training (CS&T) Platforms

Introduction

Within the domain of cybersecurity, the traditional landscape of training and skill development has long been dominated by two primary avenues: costly, exam-focused certification courses and vendor-specific training programs. These methods, while providing a foundational entry into the cybersecurity world, often fall short of equipping practitioners with the necessary skills to combat the latest cyber threats, exploit vulnerabilities, and understand the nuances of complex security landscapes. To safeguard their national interests, partner nations (PNs) recognize the critical need to build robust cyber defense capabilities. One of the essential components of bolstering these capabilities is investing in cybersecurity skills and training (CS&T) platforms. In the following section, we delve into cybersecurity skills and training (CS&T) platforms and how they can help build cyber capacity and develop cyber talents for military organizations.

In recent years, a paradigm shift has emerged in the cybersecurity training landscape with the rise of gamified learning platforms. These platforms leverage interactive and immersive approaches, incorporating realistic scenarios and simulations to enhance practical skills and decision-making abilities. Gamification not only makes cybersecurity training more engaging but also fosters a dynamic learning environment where professionals can hone their skills by responding to simulated cyber threats. This innovative approach enables practitioners to stay ahead of the rapidly evolving threat landscape, ensuring they are well-equipped to face sophisticated cyber adversaries. As military organizations increasingly embrace gamified cybersecurity training, they not only strengthen their cyber defense capabilities but also cultivate a workforce that is adept at handling the complexities of modern digital warfare.

The Transformative Power of CS&T Platforms

CS&T platforms have emerged as powerful tools for military organizations worldwide. They offer an innovative approach to cybersecurity skill development, which is essential for reducing the reliance on traditional cybersecurity certifications. These platforms not only expedite the cultivation of a new generation of cybersecurity talent but also adapt to the rapidly evolving threat landscape. The emergence of Cybersecurity Skills and Training platforms marks a pivotal shift in how defense cyber institutions for partner nations (PNs) develop their cybersecurity capabilities. These platforms offer a comprehensive approach, focusing not just on certifications but on practical, hands-on experiences and real-world applications.[cxiii]

As these platforms continue to evolve, their transformative power extends beyond individual skill development to shaping a cybersecurity ecosystem that emphasizes continuous learning and adaptability. They facilitate the creation of a dynamic learning environment where professionals are not just consumers of information but active participants in their ongoing development. Furthermore, the data-driven insights generated by CS&T platforms provide valuable metrics for organizations to measure the effectiveness of their training programs, enabling informed decisions on resource allocation and strategic planning. In essence, these platforms represent a fundamental shift towards a more resilient and responsive cybersecurity posture for military institutions globally.

Skill Demonstration and Potential Assessment

The fundamental strength of CS&T platforms lies in their ability to assess and validate an individual's skills, experience, and potential. Instead of relying solely on formal certifications, military organizations can now gauge a candidate's abilities through practical assessments and simulations. This approach ensures that individuals with true cybersecurity skills and the potential to excel in the field are identified and nurtured.

Furthermore, CS&T platforms provide an ever-evolving environment for skill demonstration, allowing individuals to showcase their capabilities in real-world scenarios. This not only enhances the credibility of the assessment process but also empowers military organizations to tailor their training programs based on the specific strengths and areas of improvement identified during these assessments. By embracing this holistic approach to talent identification and development, military entities can build a highly skilled and adaptable cybersecurity workforce capable of effectively safeguarding national security interests in the present digital landscape.

Comprehensive Skills and Gap Analysis

CS&T platforms empower military organizations to gain a comprehensive understanding of the skills, strengths, and gaps within their cyber defense teams. These platforms provide detailed insights into an individual's capabilities, allowing for precise placement and team assembly. By knowing the strengths and weaknesses of their workforce, PNs can allocate resources more effectively and enhance their overall cyber defense posture.

Customized Development Paths

Once a clear assessment of skills and potential is established, CS&T platforms enable the creation of customized development paths for individuals and teams. These paths are designed to challenge, engage, and retain top cybersecurity talent. Whether it's providing advanced training modules, assigning mentorship opportunities, or offering specialized projects, CS&T platforms facilitate targeted skill development to address specific gaps within the organization. Moreover, these platforms leverage data analytics and machine learning algorithms to continuously adapt and refine the development paths based on the evolving threat landscape and individual performance metrics. This adaptive approach ensures that cybersecurity professionals receive ongoing, relevant training, allowing them to stay at the forefront of emerging technologies and tactics employed by cyber adversaries.

Leveraging CS&T Platforms for Partner Nations

Partner nations seeking to enhance their cyber defense capabilities can benefit immensely from adopting CS&T platforms. Here are some key considerations for effectively utilizing these platforms:

1. Identifying Top Talent: CS&T platforms can help PNs identify individuals with exceptional cybersecurity skills and potential. By focusing on these promising talents, PNs can allocate resources more efficiently and groom a cadre of elite cyber defenders.

2. Bridging Skill Gaps: Understanding the skills and gaps within cyber defense teams is crucial. With the insights provided by CS&T platforms, PNs can develop targeted training programs to address specific shortcomings, ensuring a well-rounded and capable workforce.

3. Encouraging Home-Grown Talent: CS&T platforms facilitate the cultivation of home-grown cyber talent. PNs can identify individuals with potential early in their careers and provide them with opportunities to grow within the organization, reducing dependence on external hires.

4. Cyber Resilience Development: By leveraging CS&T platforms, PNs can enhance their overall cyber resilience. These platforms enable the creation of well-balanced teams with diverse skill sets, prepared to defend against a wide range of cyber threats effectively.

5. Continuous Improvement: Cyber threats are constantly evolving, and so should cyber defense strategies. CS&T platforms empower PNs to keep their teams up-to-date with the

latest threats and technologies, ensuring their cyber defense capabilities remain robust and agile.

Key Advantages of CS&T Platforms

1. Reduced Reliance on Certifications: CS&T platforms enable organizations to prioritize demonstrable skills, experience, and potential over traditional certification paths.

2. Personalized Skill Development: By assessing individual and team strengths and gaps, these platforms facilitate tailored development paths, ensuring relevant and effective skill enhancement.

3. Real-Time Content Relevance: Given the dynamic nature of cybersecurity threats, CS&T platforms provide up-to-date training content, staying ahead of emerging threats and technological advancements.

4. Expansive Skill Coverage: Moving beyond basic Security Operations Center (SOC) skills, these platforms offer training in areas such as governance, risk, compliance (GRC), application security, DevOps, and more, promoting a well-rounded cybersecurity skill set.

5. Collaboration and Simulation-Based Learning: CS&T platforms foster collaborative learning environments through simulation exercises and interactive scenarios. These features allow cybersecurity professionals to work together in simulated real-world situations, enhancing teamwork and communication skills crucial for effective incident response. The immersive nature of simulation-based learning ensures that individuals can apply theoretical knowledge in practical settings, preparing them for the complexities of cybersecurity operations.

Implementing CS&T Platforms in Defense Cyber Institutions

For defense cyber institutions, the implementation of CS&T platforms involves several critical considerations:

1. Content Relevance and Timeliness: Institutions should seek platforms offering hands-on, current training content, especially in the context of zero-day vulnerabilities and the increasing use of generative AI in cyber attacks and defenses.

2. Comprehensive Skill Development: A robust platform should cover a broad spectrum of cybersecurity domains, including offensive and defensive strategies, digital forensics, incident response, and cross-functional skills.

3. Actionable Feedback and Assessment: Platforms must provide valuable insights into skill development, readiness for incident response, and detailed recommendations for improvement based on comprehensive evaluations.

Case Study: Leading CS&T Platforms[cxiv]

The following is a list of CS&T platform providers that were highlighted by a 2023 Q4 Forrester Wave evaluation report:

SimSpace: a US organization founded in 2015 by experts from the U.S. Cyber Command and MIT's Lincoln Laboratory, SimSpace is renowned for its highly realistic simulations. SimSpace is particularly favored by large financial institutions, governments, and critical infrastructure providers. The platform's strength lies in its ability to simulate almost any cyber environment, offering granular training and curriculum management. While it lacks elements like gamification to drive learner adoption, its attack simulation exercises use bots to mimic advanced persistent threat (APT) tactics, adding a layer of realism. SimSpace is well-suited for organizations with mature cybersecurity practices looking to enhance attack simulation and optimize their security tech stacks.

Hack The Box: a US-based organization founded in 2017 that stands out for its community-driven approach, offering gamified content and a skills-based talent search, ideal for organizations seeking cost-effective solutions.

Immersive Labs: a UK-based organization founded in 2017 that offers a comprehensive approach to organizational incident readiness and resilience, with a focus on engaging, gamified learning experiences.

Cyberbit: an Israel-based organization founded in 2015 and is known for its cross-sector, realistic upskilling experiences and deep focus on innovation. It provides customized live-fire exercises and superior reporting mechanisms. Cyberbit offers superior reporting and multilevel dashboards with intuitive heatmaps to track and demonstrate skill proficiency across frameworks like MITRE ATT&CK and NIST NICE.

Conclusion

In closing, cybersecurity skills and training platforms offer partner nations a transformative approach to building their cyberdefense capacity. By focusing on skills, experience, and potential rather than traditional certifications, PNs can identify, nurture, and retain top talent in the field of cybersecurity. Leveraging these platforms allows PNs to develop a strong and agile cyber defense force capable of defending their national interests in an ever-changing digital landscape. As the cyber threat landscape continues to evolve, PNs must invest in these platforms to stay ahead and secure their digital future.

The transformation of defense cyber institutions through the integration of Cybersecurity Skills and Training platforms is not just a trend but a necessity in the rapidly evolving cyber landscape. These platforms represent a holistic approach to cybersecurity training, emphasizing real-world skills, continuous content updating, and a broad coverage of cybersecurity domains. As cyber threats continue to evolve, the adoption of such platforms will be crucial in building resilient, skilled, and well-prepared cyber defense forces for partner nations.

Chapter 23:

Hunt Forward Operations and U.S. Cyberspace Security Cooperation

Introduction

As the 21st century unfolds, the surge in cyber threats has compelled the United States to rethink its approach to national defense. Embracing the global nature of these threats, the U.S. has enacted International Cyberspace Security Cooperation, employing a spectrum of operations and partnerships. The U.S. Cyber Command (USCYBERCOM)'s Hunt Forward Operations (HFOs) is at the heart of this strategy. This chapter delves into HFOs as a pivotal element of U.S. cybersecurity strategy and their profound impact on the United States Cyberspace Security Cooperation initiative.

HFOs' Defensive Nature

HFOs, conducted by USCYBERCOM, are strictly defensive cyber operations carried out at the request of U.S. Allies and partners. Upon formal request, USCYBERCOM Hunt Forward Teams are dispatched to the host nation to actively observe and detect malicious cyber activities on their military networks. These forward-deployed operations are designed to yield insights that fortify homeland defense and enhance shared information networks' resilience against cyber threats.[cxv]

The HFOs' strategy revolves around persistent engagement and defending forward. In a scenario where U.S. networks are consistently under assault from adversary nations and malicious cyber actors, persistent engagement becomes imperative. This involves actively countering adversaries, disrupting cyber threats, degrading adversary capabilities and networks, and continuously fortifying the Department of Defense Information Network (DODIN).

On the other hand, the "defend forward" strategy aims to disrupt cyber threats, degrade the capabilities and networks of adversaries, and continuously harden DODIN and Allies networks. This strategy involves operating as close to the origin of adversary activity as possible in what the U.S. military calls "red space" (adversary cyberspace) and "gray space" (everywhere else), thus increasing the reach of U.S. cyber operators and neutralizing the threat at its source.[cxvi]

The 2018 Defend Forward policy, acknowledged as the "cornerstone" of the Department of Defense's cyber strategy, underscores the indispensability of HFOs. This policy recognizes that defending the United States in cyberspace necessitates operations beyond U.S. military networks, aka "blue space" (U.S. domestic cyberspace). HFOs, therefore, play a pivotal role, operating based on requests for support (RFS) from foreign military forces of U.S. Allies and partners to proactively identify adversaries, understand their tradecraft, and unveil their tools.

These operations are executed by the Cyber National Mission Force (CNMF), an integral component of USCYBERCOM consisting of specially trained cyber operators. The CNMF is entrusted with securing and defending the Department of Defense Information Network (DODIN) against cyber threats. Collaborating with cyber forces of foreign partners, CNMF operators pinpoint vulnerabilities, track malware, and investigate adversary presence on host nation networks. The insights garnered from joint HFOs are disseminated to the host nation and U.S. government agencies, such as the FBI or Cybersecurity and Infrastructure Security Agency (CISA), within the Department of Homeland Security (DHS). In each instance, these partner-enabled operations have led to the public release of malware samples for analysis by the cybersecurity community. [cxvii]

U.S. Cyber Forces and Command Authorities

In the following section, we will discuss the history of USCYBERCOM and the origin of CNMF teams.[cxviii]

The United States Cyber Command (USCYBERCOM), established in 2009, is a sub-unified command to the United States Strategic Command (USSTRATCOM). A significant turning point for CYBERCOM, one of the world's first and most prominent cyber commands, occurred with the Fiscal Year 2017 National Defense Authorization Act, elevating it to a combatant command (COCOM). It became responsible for planning, coordinating, integrating, and conducting activities to operate and defend the DOD's Information Networks (DODIN) and to prepare for and respond to cyber threats and attacks. It became one of the eleven unified combatant commands of the United States military, playing a crucial role in ensuring the security and resilience of U.S. military cyberspace operations.

Service Components

USCYBERCOM's service elements include Army Cyber Command/2d Army (ARCYBER), U.S. Fleet Cyber Command/10th Fleet (FCC/C10F or FLTCYBER), Air Forces Cyber/24th Air Force (AFCYBER), and Marine Corps Cyberspace Command (MARFORCYBER). U.S. Coast Guard Cyber (CGCYBER), though subordinate to the Department of Homeland Security, maintains a direct support relationship with USCYBERCOM. Each service is responsible for safeguarding its service-specific cyber network, ensuring the capability to detect, mitigate, and overcome advanced persistent threats capable of compromising the network and the DODIN itself. Service components collaborate with parent services, USCYBERCOM, JFHQ-DODIN (described below), the Defense Information Systems Agency (DISA), and the National Security Agency (NSA) to prevent malicious actors from gaining access to service-specific networks. "The service components function at the operational and tactical levels, relying on JFHQ-DODIN to ensure lateral coordination, information sharing, and synchronization -ensuring the unity of effort for the operation and defense of the entire DOD information environment."

The Cyber Mission Force (CMF)

In 2012, the Joint Staff and USCYBERCOM directed the services to collectively build a Cyber Mission Force of 133 Cyber Mission teams. These teams, described below, constitute four Joint Force Headquarters (JFHQs) and one Cyber National Mission Force (CNMF). USCYBERCOM has delegated operational-level cyber missions to these components. Each component of the Cyber Mission Force consists of teams or "maneuver elements" that break down into four separate categories based on their respective responsibilities: National Mission Teams (NMTs) defend the United States and its interests against cyberattacks of significant consequence. Cyber Protection Teams (CPTs) defend priority DOD networks and systems against priority threats. Combat Mission Teams (CMTs) support combatant commands by generating integrated cyberspace effects supporting operational plans and contingency operations. Cyber Support Teams (CSTs) provide analytic and planning support to National Mission and Combat Mission teams.

Cyber National Mission Force

The Cyber National Mission Force (CNMF) consists of National Mission Teams (NMTs), National-level Cyber Protection Teams (N-CPTs) and Cyber Support Teams (CSTs). USCYBERCOM controls these forces and "helps defend America's critical infrastructure against malicious cyber activity of significant consequence." According to a recent USCYBERCOM article, the CNMF is a joint force of military and civilian members from the Army, Marine Corps, Navy, Air Force, Coast Guard, and Intelligence Community. It comprises 39 teams and nearly 2,000 personnel spread over four locations. N-CPTs are defensive elements working within DOD networks and, when authorized, outside DOD networks, identifying and mitigating vulnerabilities, assessing threat presence and activities, and responding to adversary actions. NMTs are maneuver elements conducting on-network operations in neutral and adversary territory, looking for indications and warnings of adversary cyber activities, and enabling cyber effects when authorized and directed. National CSTs are analytic elements providing planning, development, and technical support to National CPTs and Mission Teams.

Cyber Combat Mission Force

The Cyber Combat Mission Force focuses on providing support to the Combatant Commands. That support comes from designated CMTs, CPTs, and CSTs. These teams fall under one of three Joint Force Headquarters – Cyber (JFHQ-C). USCYBERCOM has designated responsibility for each JFHQ-C to one of its service components.

DODIN Operations and Defense

The final Joint Force Headquarters is JFHQ-DODIN, responsible for the overall operation and defense of DOD information systems. While each service maintains some responsibility for protecting and operating its networks, JFHQ-DODIN provides overall unity of effort and command for sustained efforts at scale. Generally, this means identifying and imposing standards for application across the DODIN. JFHQ-DODIN serves as a "functional component command" of USCYBERCOM, and its commander is dual-hatted as Director of the Defense Information Systems Agency (DISA).

The Value of HFOs

In 2022, a cyber attack occurred in Ukraine involving new malware named "AcidRain." The attack targeted Viasat, a satellite communications company, resulting in the inoperability of Viasat KA-SAT modems in Ukraine and several downstream effects, such as the malfunction of 5,800 Enercon wind turbines in Germany and disruptions to thousands of organizations across Europe.

This attack highlighted the need for international cooperation in cybersecurity. The investigation into the cyber attack involved multiple agencies worldwide, and the results were shared with the global cybersecurity community. This form of cooperation and information sharing is at the heart of the U.S. strategy of Cyberspace Security Cooperation.

The success of an HFO is primarily measured by the value of the insights gained and shared, both with the host nation and other partners. In the case of the HFOs in Ukraine, for example, the sheer scale and scope of Russian cyber activity were revealed, providing valuable knowledge for both the United States and Ukraine.

Hunt Forward Operations have been conducted in more than a dozen countries, including Ukraine, Estonia, and Lithuania, to name a few. The insights generated from these operations have proven invaluable in defending the United States and its Allies from outside aggression and malicious behavior in cyberspace.

From 2018 to 2022, the CNMF has conducted numerous HFOs with partner nations (PNs) worldwide. These partner-enabled operations have led to the public release of numerous malware samples for analysis by the cybersecurity community, demonstrating the value of these operations in enhancing cyber threat intelligence.

The information gathered during an HFO is widely shared, extending beyond the partner nation. It's sanitized and disseminated among U.S. government partners, broader U.S. government entities, and Allies and partners worldwide. This approach emphasizes the collaborative nature of cybersecurity and the shared goal of protecting against malicious cyber actors.

The ultimate goal of an HFO is threefold: to improve the cybersecurity posture of the partner nation, to help them better understand the threat landscape, and to share information so that all involved parties can learn and adapt. It's not just about the immediate operation but also about fostering a culture of shared knowledge and resilience in the face of persistent cyber threats.

In conclusion, HFOs have proven invaluable in defending the United States from outside aggression and malicious behavior in cyberspace. For instance, in 2020, USCYBERCOM conducted eleven HFOs in nine different nations, contributing to the successful defense of the 2020 elections from foreign influence and interference. In 2021, USCYBERCOM conducted a joint HFO with the Cybersecurity and Infrastructure Security Agency (CISA) in response to the SolarWinds supply chain attack that yielded eight files attributed to the Russian Intelligence Service (SVR) APT 29. These operations yielded information about adversary tactics, techniques, procedures (TTPs), and intentions.

Future HFOs and Expansion

Looking ahead, the U.S. Cyber Command anticipates the expansion of cyber forces' activities, considering it a growth industry for the United States and aligned with the preferences of its partners for collaboration. Conducting forward-deployed cyber missions enables the U.S. to enhance protections against adversaries, notably China, Russia, North Korea, and Iran, operating with unprecedented scope, scale, and sophistication. Broadcasting information about an adversary's cyber weapons serves as a crucial inoculation, benefiting the requesting country and everyone accessing this information. As it was proven in numerous cases, the widespread dissemination of adversary tradecraft details is a powerful global cyber defense strategy tool.

USCYBERCOM is dedicated to persistently engaging adversaries posing harm to the United States. It will continue to conduct HFOs at the request of Allied and partner nations (PNs) to contribute to building a safer, more secure world in cyberspace. The innovative and collaborative approach demonstrated by Hunt Forward Operations underscores the pivotal role of international cooperation in the dynamic landscape of cybersecurity.

An intriguing aspect of Hunt Forward Operations is the meticulous consideration of where to conduct such operations. This decision depends not only on the partner nation's request but also on the specific mission set of the national mission force. This reflects the necessity of responding to the distinct needs and threat landscapes of different nations while aligning with the strategic aims of the U.S. Cyber Command.

Teams deployed for HFOs must comprehend the unique aspects of the cyber landscape in the host country. For example, when USCYBERCOM teams were deployed to Ukraine, understanding the country's unique cyber landscape was a prerequisite before initiating the hunt for the activity of the Russian nation-state threat group. This initial stage is crucial as it lays the foundation for the entire operation.

A significant challenge in conducting HFOs is operating in complex and dynamic environments. Each host nation presents unique conditions and challenges, demanding adaptability and a deep understanding of potential threats landscapes.

Case Study: Unmasking Adversaries: HFOs as a Tool for Cyberspace Security Cooperation with Albania

Hunt Forward Operations (HFOs) play a pivotal role in U.S. Cyberspace Security Cooperation, enabling proactive engagement with partner nations (PNs) to detect and respond to malicious cyber activity. This case study delves into a specific instance where HFOs were deployed to Albania following cyber attacks attributed to Iran. These HFOs aimed to support Albania in recovering from the attacks, gather intelligence on the tactics, techniques, and procedures (TTPs) of malicious cyber actors, and enhance the cybersecurity posture of the United States and its strategic ally.

Background

In July and September of 2022, Albania experienced cyber attacks targeting government websites and disrupting essential government services for Albanian citizens. The Albanian government attributed these attacks to Iran, leading to the expulsion of Iranian officials from the country. Subsequently, a U.S. Cyber National Mission Force (CNMF) team was deployed to Albania to assist with recovery efforts and conduct HFOs to gather valuable insights.

Insights and Information Sharing

The HFOs conducted in Albania yielded significant results, providing valuable insights into the tools, techniques, and procedures used by malicious cyber actors attempting to disrupt government networks and systems. Major Katrina Cheesman of the Cyber National Mission Force highlighted the importance of these operations in enhancing the cybersecurity defenses of the United States and its partner nations. The information obtained was shared with the Albanian government and critical private companies involved in the digital infrastructure of both countries.

Imposing Costs on Adversaries

Major General William Hartman, the U.S. Cyber National Mission Force (CNMF) commander, emphasized the significance of HFOs in imposing costs on adversaries by exposing their tools, tactics, and procedures. Actively hunting on partner nations' networks allows U.S. cyber teams to identify adversary activities and defend against them effectively. The insights gained from these operations contribute to the cybersecurity posture of the United States and its Allies and strengthen the defenses of partner nations like Albania.

Cooperation and Attribution

Albania's claims regarding Iranian responsibility for the cyber attacks were backed by the United States, condemning the actions of Iranian state cyber actors as counter to international norms. The collaboration between U.S. Cyber Command and Albania's National Agency for Information Society was highly effective. Albanian officials wanted to continue working with U.S. cyber teams to strengthen their defenses.

Synthesis

This case study underscores the value of Hunt Forward Operations in achieving U.S. Cyberspace Security Cooperation objectives. By actively engaging with partner nations like Albania, the United States can detect and respond to cyber threats, gather intelligence on adversary tactics, and enhance the cybersecurity posture of both the United States and its Allies. The insights obtained through HFOs contribute to a better understanding of cyber threats and enable joint efforts to counter malicious cyber actors. The continued cooperation between the United States and Albania is a testament to the effectiveness of HFOs in achieving cybersecurity cooperation goals and building stronger cyber defenses.

Case Study: Defending Democracy: The Role of HFOs in Enhancing Cyberspace Security Cooperation with Montenegro

Hunt Forward Operations (HFOs), executed by the Cyber National Mission Force (CNMF) team of experts, are crucial in achieving U.S. Cyberspace Security Cooperation objectives. This case study delves into deploying CNMF experts to Montenegro, a small Balkan nation, to address potential Russian and other cyber threats leading up to the Montenegrin elections. It accentuates the importance of HFOs in bolstering cyber defense capabilities and fostering cooperation between the United States and its partners.

Background

As a recent NATO member, Montenegro has become a strategic ally where Russia aims to reinstate its influence. The country faced targeted cyber attacks and a Moscow-backed coup attempt in 2016, prompting the deployment of CNMF experts to counter potential cyber threats. Montenegro's commitment to Euro-Atlantic integration and its role as a key Western ally among post-Soviet Balkan states make it a prime target for cyber disruptions.

Enhancing Cyber Defense

CNMF experts in Montenegro engaged in strategic planning and operations within the communist-era army command headquarters. They aim to defend against potential cyber-attacks and disinformation campaigns, especially those linked to Russia. Leveraging their expertise and advanced cyber capabilities, CNMF experts contributed to fortifying

Montenegro's cyber defense capabilities and safeguarding the integrity of the Montenegrin elections.

Lessons Learned from Past Attacks

The 2016 U.S. election, facing hybrid and cyber attacks, provided valuable lessons for both nations. Having experienced a comprehensive attack before its NATO accession and subsequent elections, Montenegro offered insights to the United States regarding potential threats to their systems and networks. The collaborative approach between CNMF experts and Montenegrin authorities allowed for knowledge exchange and the development of effective strategies to counter existing and emerging cyber threats.

Building Resilience and Countering Influence

Russia's tactics in undermining Euro-Atlantic integration and spreading anti-Western propaganda pose a significant challenge to stability in the Balkan region. CNMF experts' operations in Montenegro, part of U.S. Cyberspace Security Cooperation efforts, focus on protecting critical infrastructure and countering adversarial cyber threats. Working alongside valued partners and Allies like Montenegro, CNMF experts aim to build resilience against cyber intrusions and minimize the influence of malign actors.

Cooperation and Preparedness

The partnership between the United States and Montenegro, facilitated by CNMF experts, has yielded fruitful results in countering Russian cyber threats and enhancing cybersecurity measures. CNMF experts' engagement in Montenegro is a testament to U.S. Cyberspace Security

Cooperation efforts, emphasizing the importance of joint operations, information sharing, and preparedness for upcoming elections. Their collaboration establishes a robust cyber defense posture and fosters trust and cooperation between the two nations.

Synthesis

The case study on HFOs conducted by CNMF experts in Montenegro underscores the value of these operations in achieving U.S. Cyberspace Security Cooperation objectives. By assisting Montenegro in countering cyber threats, CNMF experts strengthen the partnership between the United States and a key Western ally, enhance cyber defense capabilities, and promote stability in the Balkan region. The collaboration is a proactive measure to mitigate potential cyber disruptions during the American and Montenegrin elections while building resilience against adversarial cyber activities. The continuous cooperation between CNMF experts and Montenegro exemplifies the significance of HFOs in achieving Cyberspace Security Cooperation objectives and fortifying the cyber defenses of partner nations (PNs).

Case Study: Uniting Forces: The Birth of Cyber Command's Under Advisement Program for Enhanced Hunt Forward Operations (HFOs)

In an era marked by escalating cyber threats and an imperative for heightened collaboration between government and private sector entities, U.S. Cyber Command has taken a significant stride by inaugurating the "Under Advisement" program in 2022. This initiative aims to cultivate cooperation and information sharing between the Cyber National Mission

Force (CNMF), responsible for global Hunt Forward Operations (HFOs), and the private sector, ultimately fortifying national and regional cybersecurity.[cxix]

The Imperative for Enhanced Collaboration

The establishment of the Under Advisement program was a response to the escalating complexity and interconnectedness of the cyber landscape. Historically, the Department of Defense encountered challenges in harnessing its cyber force to shield the nation from relentless cyber intrusions and breaches. The distinctive nature of cyber threats necessitated a collaborative approach to fortify the nation's cybersecurity, given that most networks were privately owned.

The Role of the Cyber National Mission Force

The Cyber National Mission Force (CNMF) lies at the Under Advisement program's core. Comprising technical experts responsible for tracking and disrupting nation-state adversaries, the CNMF plays a pivotal role in defending critical infrastructure and identifying foreign cyber threats in the U.S. and abroad. These individuals possess profound cybersecurity expertise and real-time knowledge about emerging threats.

Cybersecurity Dialogues and Initiatives

The Under Advisement program adopts an innovative approach to information sharing. Members of the CNMF actively engage in chat rooms with private sector representatives, participating in discussions and exchanging threat information. Military personnel use their real names to ensure transparency and accountability, fostering trust and collaboration.

Elite Forums and Transparent Attribution

These discussions occur on reputable cybersecurity forums such as Signal and exclusive, invite-only industry platforms. Major General William Hartman, the commander of the CNMF, emphasizes that these engagements occur with full names and transparent attribution. This commitment to openness and accountability fosters effective communication and information exchange between the public and private sectors.

Enriching Data and Strengthening Defense

The mutual sharing of threat information between the CNMF and the private sector yields substantial benefits. When the CNMF identifies a foreign threat, sharing this information with industry partners empowers them to bolster their defenses. Simultaneously, private-sector cybersecurity experts can enhance the data the CNMF provides with their own expertise. This bidirectional sharing enhances the effectiveness of operations against foreign cyber actors and fortifies homeland network defense.

A Symbiotic Relationship

Cybersecurity is often called the ultimate team sport, as threats affecting one entity can have far-reaching consequences for others. Major General Hartman underscores the importance of information sharing, stating that threats to one network are threats to all networks. By sharing information and collaborating, vulnerabilities can be reduced, and preemptive actions can be taken to prevent attacks. The partnership between Cyber Command and industry partners benefits the

Department of Defense and enables industry partners to leverage the expertise and information provided by the CNMF.

Synthesis

The creation of the Under Advisement program by the U.S. Cyber Command represents a significant milestone in strengthening national cybersecurity. By establishing a collaborative platform for information sharing, Cyber Command aims to leverage the expertise of the Cyber National Mission Force and industry partners to mitigate cyber threats. The program's emphasis on transparency, accountability, and bidirectional sharing sets the stage for enhanced cooperation during cyber crises. As the program continues to evolve and expand, it is poised to play a vital role in safeguarding national security in the face of evolving cyber threats.

Conclusion

In this chapter, we explored the evolving landscape of cyber threats in the 21st century, which has necessitated a fundamental reassessment of the United States' national defense approach. Recognizing the global nature of these threats, the U.S. has adopted a strategy of International Cyberspace Security Cooperation, leveraging a range of operations and partnerships.

Central to this strategy is the role of the U.S. Cyber Command (USCYBERCOM) and its Hunt Forward Operations (HFOs). These operations serve as a cornerstone of U.S. cybersecurity efforts, allowing for proactive engagement with adversaries and the mitigation of potential threats before they escalate. Through HFOs, the United States not only defends its own cyberspace but also contributes to broader international efforts to secure cyberspace.

Throughout this chapter, we have delved into the intricacies of HFOs and their significant impact on the United States Cyberspace Security Cooperation initiative. By embracing this proactive and collaborative approach, the U.S. aims to effectively confront the challenges posed by cyber threats in the modern era, safeguarding not only its own interests but also those of its allies and partners around the world.

Chapter 24:

Advise & Assist (A&A) versus Hunt Forward Operations (HFOs) in Cyberspace Security Cooperation Activities

Introduction

In the domain of Cyberspace Security Cooperation, the strategies of "Advise & Assist" and "Hunt Forward Operations" stand out as distinct approaches with unique objectives and methodologies. This chapter provides a detailed breakdown of each concept.

1. Advise & Assist:

Advise & Assist represents a collaborative approach wherein an entity imparts guidance, expertise, and support to another entity to enhance its cybersecurity capabilities. Typically, this involves experienced organizations or individuals providing advice, best practices, and technical assistance to counterparts with less experience.

The objective of Advise & Assist is to boost the cyber defense capabilities of the assisted entity through knowledge sharing, recommending security measures, conducting assessments, and providing guidance on incident response and mitigation strategies. This approach is often directed at organizations or nations with limited resources, expertise, or maturity in cybersecurity, aiding them in fortifying defenses and establishing sustainable cybersecurity programs.

Advise & Assist engagements prioritize capacity building, knowledge transfer, and fostering self-reliance. The emphasis lies in empowering the assisted entity to independently manage and respond to cyber threats effectively. Assistance may involve conducting training programs, performing vulnerability assessments, or establishing incident response frameworks. Additionally, Advise & Assist engagements prioritize the thorough examination and enhancement of existing cybersecurity policies and procedures. Cybersecurity policies serve as the foundation for a robust defense posture, guiding organizations in their approach to risk management, data protection, and incident response. Advisors work closely with the assisted entity to evaluate the effectiveness of current policies, identifying potential gaps or areas for improvement. This process may involve aligning policies with international standards, ensuring compliance with legal frameworks, and incorporating industry best practices.

2. Hunt Forward Operations:

Hunt Forward Operations, also known as Active Defense, encompass actively seeking out and countering cyber threats beyond one's own network or jurisdiction. This involves proactive cyber operations beyond defense to disrupt, deter, or gather intelligence on potential adversaries.

These operations typically involve cybersecurity teams or organizations with advanced capabilities and expertise in offensive and defensive cyber activities. They engage in intelligence gathering, threat hunting, and targeted operations to identify and neutralize threats in their early stages, even if originating from foreign jurisdictions.

Hunt Forward Operations aims to anticipate and preemptively respond to cyber threats by actively engaging with potential attackers or threat actors. This approach necessitates close collaboration with intelligence agencies, law enforcement, and international partners to collect and share information, attribute attacks, and take appropriate actions to mitigate risks.

Executing Hunt Forward Operations demands careful coordination, adherence to legal frameworks, and compliance with established norms and rules of engagement to avoid potential escalation or violation of international laws. Specialized teams typically conduct these operations, possessing the required technical capabilities, intelligence analysis skills, and in-depth knowledge of threat landscapes.

Synergies and Trade-offs

Advise & Assist and Hunt Forward Operations share the goal of enhancing the cyber defense of Allies and partners. However, they often diverge in their focus and methodology. Advise & Assist centers on capacity building, knowledge sharing, and support to improve cyber defense capabilities. In contrast, Hunt Forward Operations involve proactive, defensive operations targeting potential threats outside one's network, aiming for early detection, disruption, and deterrence.

While Advise & Assist and Hunt Forward Operations serve distinct purposes, there exist potential synergies and trade-offs when combining these approaches. Collaborative efforts can benefit from a holistic strategy that combines the knowledge-sharing aspect of Advise & Assist with the proactive threat-hunting nature of HFOs. This synergy can create a comprehensive cybersecurity framework that not only strengthens defensive capabilities but also actively identifies and mitigates potential threats.

However, it's crucial to recognize the inherent trade-offs involved in balancing these two approaches. The proactive nature of HFOs may, at times, overshadow the capacity-building efforts of Advise & Assist, potentially straining diplomatic relations or creating unintended consequences. Striking the right balance between these approaches requires careful consideration of the specific cybersecurity needs, geopolitical context, and maturity level of the entities involved. Ultimately, successful security cooperation in cyberspace demands a nuanced and adaptive approach that leverages the strengths of both Advise & Assist and Hunt Forward Operations.

Scope, Objectives, Engagement, and Collaboration

Advise & Assist and Hunt Forward Operations differ significantly in terms of authority and mission objectives as two distinct approaches to Cyberspace Security Cooperation. Here are the key differences between the two:

Criteria	Advise & Assist	Hunt Forward Operations
Scope	This model provides guidance, expertise, and support to the host nation or organization. Decision-making and action authority primarily reside with the host entity.	This model grants broader authority to actively conduct defensive cyber operations within the host nation or organization's networks. The cooperating entity is empowered to identify, track, and neutralize cyber threats within the host's infrastructure.
Mission Objectives	The primary mission is to enhance the host's cyber defense capabilities, focusing on knowledge transfer, skill development, and supporting the establishment of effective	The primary mission is to proactively identify and neutralize cyber threats in real-time, often in collaboration with the host entity. Emphasis is on active

	cybersecurity practices.	cyber defense, threat hunting, and disrupting malicious actors within the host nation's networks.
Engagement Approach	This approach is consultative, involving close collaboration with the host nation's military organization to assess their cybersecurity posture, provide recommendations, and assist in implementing best practices.	This approach is more hands-on and operationally driven. It actively hunts for threats, conducts cyber operations, and shares threat intelligence and analysis with the host nation's entity to proactively identify and respond to threats, potentially including neutralizing actions against threat actors.

| Degree of Collaboration | Collaboration in the Advise & Assist model is rooted in cooperative partnerships. The cooperating entity closely collaborates with the host nation's defense cyber forces, sharing expertise, providing training, and assisting in developing policies and procedures. The goal is to empower the host entity to independently manage its cybersecurity. | Collaboration is a fundamental aspect of Hunt Forward Operations as well, with the cooperating entity assuming a more proactive role in executing operations in conjunction with the host entity. This entails a close and synchronized effort characterized by joint analysis and coordinated responses aimed at countering identified threats. |

NOTE: It is significant to mention that these approaches' specific implementation and terms can vary based on agreements, legal frameworks, and policies established between cooperating entities. The nature of cooperation may also differ based on each situation's unique requirements and priorities.

Authority Titles

Different authority titles can be associated with Advice & Assist and Hunt Forward Operations in Cyberspace Security Cooperation. The titles may vary depending on the context, organization, or framework used. Here are some commonly used authority titles associated with each approach:

Authority Titles in Advice & Assist

Advisors: Individuals or teams providing expert advice, guidance, and support to the host entity. Titles may include Cybersecurity Advisors, Technical Advisors, or Subject Matter Experts (SMEs).

Consultants: Individuals with specialized knowledge and experience designated as Consultants. They offer recommendations, conduct assessments, and assist the host entity in improving its cybersecurity posture.

Mentors: Guide and coach the host entity in developing its cyber defense capabilities. They provide ongoing support training and help implement best practices.

Instructors: Deliver training programs and workshops to enhance the host entity's cybersecurity skills and knowledge. Titles may include Cybersecurity Instructors, Training Specialists, or Educators.

Authority Titles in Hunt Forward Operations

Operators: Personnel responsible for actively conducting defensive cyber operations within the host nation's network. Titles may include Cyber Operators, Threat Hunters, or Cyber Warfare Specialists.

Analysts: Play a critical role in gathering, analyzing, and interpreting cyber threat intelligence. Titles may include Cyber Threat Analysts, Intelligence Analysts, or Security Analysts.

Incident Responders: Experts investigating and responding to cyber incidents within the host entity's infrastructure. Titles may include Incident Response Specialists, Incident Handlers, or Cybersecurity Incident Responders.

Coordinators: Facilitate collaboration and coordination between the cooperating and host entities. They help manage information-sharing joint operations and ensure effective communication. Titles may include Cybersecurity Coordinators or Operational Coordinators.

NOTE: It is significant to mention that these titles are not exhaustive and may vary depending on the specific operational context, organizational structures, or the terminology used by different entities engaged in Cyberspace Security Cooperation.

Response Time During Cyber Crises

Hunt Forward Operations tend to be more rapid and deployable during cyber attacks compared to the Advise & Assist approach. Here's why:

Hunt Forward Operations

Rapid Response: Characterized by a proactive and agile response to cyber threats, Hunt Forward Operations enables the cooperating entity to quickly mobilize resources, deploy specialized teams, and actively hunt for threats within the host entity's networks. This rapid response is crucial in minimizing the impact of the attack and identifying and neutralizing the threat actors swiftly.

Direct Action: In Hunt Forward Operations, the cooperating entity often has greater authority and autonomy to act directly against identified threats. This may include conducting disruption operations to neutralize threat actors, actively hunting for indicators of compromise, or conducting real-time incident response activities. The ability to take immediate action enhances the effectiveness and speed of the response during cyber attacks.

On-the-Ground Expertise: Hunt Forward Operations often involve deploying highly skilled personnel with specialized expertise in cyber threat hunting, intelligence analysis, and offensive/defensive operations. These experts work alongside the host entity's teams, leveraging their knowledge and experience to rapidly identify and respond to the evolving threat landscape.

Advise & Assist

Consultative Approach: The Advise & Assist approach focuses more on providing guidance, expertise, and support to the host entity rather than directly responding to cyber attacks. While the cooperating entity can offer advice and assistance during an ongoing attack, it focuses on helping the host entity improve its cyber defense capabilities, incident response planning, and overall cyber resilience.

Capacity Building: The Advise & Assist approach often involves longer-term initiatives for capacity building and knowledge transfer. While this is essential for strengthening the host entity's cybersecurity posture in the long run, it may not provide an immediate and rapid response during active cyber attacks. To further augment the rapid response capabilities of the Advise & Assist strategy, there is a strategic integration of simulation exercises focused on real-time incident response scenarios. These exercises immerse cybersecurity teams from the host entity in simulated cyber attack situations, providing them with hands-on experience in making quick decisions and executing swift responses. By replicating the intensity and urgency of actual cyber incidents, these simulations bridge the gap between traditional capacity-building efforts and the need for immediate responsiveness.

Collaborative Decision-Making: In Advise & Assist, decision-making authority largely rests with the host entity, which may involve a more collaborative decision-making process. While valuable for fostering partnerships and building trust, this collaborative approach can sometimes slow down the response time during urgent and time-sensitive cyber attacks. These adaptive protocols would establish predefined thresholds for various cyber incident scenarios, allowing the host entity and cooperating organization to make rapid decisions within agreed-upon parameters. While Hunt Forward Operations provides a more rapid and deployable response during cyber attacks, it is crucial to acknowledge that each approach's specific implementation and effectiveness depend on the cooperation agreements, legal frameworks, and policies established between the cooperating entities. The suitability of each approach may vary based on the nature of the threat, the host entity's capabilities, and the overall goals of the cooperation.

Conclusion

In summary, within the domain of Cyberspace Security Cooperation, the strategies of "Advise & Assist" and "Hunt Forward Operations" offer distinct yet complementary approaches. These strategies represent innovative approaches aimed at enhancing cybersecurity capabilities for partner nations and mitigating digital threats.

"Advise & Assist" entails providing guidance, expertise, and resources to bolster the cybersecurity posture of partner entities. It focuses on capacity building, knowledge transfer, and collaborative efforts to fortify defenses against cyber attacks. Through this approach, organizations can leverage shared expertise and resources to address evolving cyber threats effectively.

On the other hand, "Hunt Forward Operations" involves proactive measures to detect and disrupt malicious cyber activities at their source. This strategy emphasizes early threat detection, attribution, and preemptive action to mitigate potential cyber threats before they escalate. By actively pursuing threat actors and their infrastructure, organizations can minimize the impact of cyber-attacks and safeguard critical systems and data.

While both strategies aim to enhance cybersecurity resilience, they differ in their emphasis and execution. "Advise

& Assist" focuses on empowerment and collaboration, fostering long-term partnerships and capacity building. In contrast, "Hunt Forward Operations" prioritizes proactive threat mitigation, leveraging intelligence and defensive cyber tools and capabilities to preemptively neutralize cyber threats.

Ultimately, the adoption of these distinct strategies reflects the evolving nature of cyber threats and the need for flexible and multifaceted approaches to cyberspace security cooperation. By leveraging the strengths of both "Advise & Assist" and "Hunt Forward Operations," U.S. Allies and partners' military and government organizations can enhance their cybersecurity capabilities and effectively navigate the complex landscape of cyberspace security.

Chapter 25:

The Bureau of Cyberspace and Digital Policy: Supporting Cyberspace Security Cooperation Objectives

Introduction

The creation of the Bureau of Cyberspace and Digital Policy (CDP) is a pivotal moment in the U.S. State Department's modernization initiatives. Launched in April 2022, the CDP is geared to navigate the intricate landscape of cyberspace, digital technologies, and digital policy. Under Secretary Blinken's guidance, the CDP takes on the responsibility of addressing crucial national security challenges while exploring the economic potential of the digital realm. Furthermore, the bureau examines the implications of cyberspace and digital technologies on U.S. values. Comprising three policy units - International Cyberspace Security, International Information and Communications Policy, and Digital Freedom - the CDP is strategically positioned to navigate the diverse dimensions of the digital age and formulate policies in harmony with U.S. interests and values. This chapter delves into the bureau's mission, key objectives, and endeavors to promote Cyberspace Security Cooperation through international engagement.[cxx]

The mission of the Bureau

The Bureau of Cyberspace and Digital Policy within the U.S. State Department plays a pivotal role in promoting responsible state behavior in cyberspace and advancing policies that safeguard the integrity and security of internet infrastructure. With a mission encompassing national security challenges, economic opportunities, and value considerations arising from cyberspace, digital technologies, and digital policy, the bureau promotes stability and security in cyberspace through international cooperation.

Collaborating with colleagues across the federal government, the Bureau of Cyberspace and Digital Policy develops recommendations and strategies to protect America's cyber interests through international engagement. These efforts aim to deter adversaries, better protect the American people from cyber threats, and ensure the internet and connected technologies remain valuable and viable tools for future generations.

Challenges in an Evolving Cyberspace Environment

The United States contends with numerous threats in cyberspace, both domestically and internationally. Poor cybersecurity practices pose a significant risk, especially to critical infrastructure relying on interconnected global systems. Countries with weak governance or rule of law can be safe havens for cybercriminals and malicious actors. Moreover, nations developing cyber capabilities for their domestic and foreign policy goals, which may not align with U.S. interests, add to the complexity. Malicious state and non-state actors increasingly use cyber operations to support military and political objectives, conduct disruptive attacks, steal sensitive information, and prepare for future operations. These challenges underscore the imperative for international cooperation and collaboration to effectively address the evolving cyberspace environment.

Bureau of Cyberspace and Digital Policy (BCDP)'s Objectives

International Stability in Cyberspace

A key objective of the Bureau of Cyberspace and Digital Policy is to enhance international stability and reduce the risk of conflict in cyberspace. This goal is realized by promoting international commitments to responsible state behavior in cyberspace, developing cyber confidence-building measures, and establishing a cooperative framework for cyber deterrence. The bureau aims to foster a safer and more secure cyberspace environment for all nations through these actions.

Another crucial objective is to identify, detect, disrupt, and deter malicious cyber actors while protecting critical infrastructure and enhancing the resilience of the global cyber ecosystem. This involves enhancing information sharing, managing cyber crises, improving cooperation to manage systemic cyber risks, promoting cybersecurity education and workforce development, prioritizing law enforcement cooperation, advancing military cyber cooperation, and fostering cooperation on sensitive cyber intelligence issues with partners and Allies.

Open, Secure, and Interoperable Internet

A critical objective is to uphold an open and interoperable Internet, where human rights are protected and cross-border data flows are preserved. The bureau defends access to an open internet and supports the multistakeholder approach to internet governance. It also engages in diplomatic coordination with like-minded countries to advance internet freedom. It supports global programs that fund civil society organizations involved in technology development, digital safety training, policy advocacy, and applied research.

Ensuring the security and openness of the internet presents both diplomatic and technical challenges. To create an internet that prioritizes information confidentiality, integrity, and availability for all users, it is crucial to collectively adopt secure protocols and standards. The U.S. technical community, spearheaded by the National Institute of Standards and Technology (NIST), actively participates in standards-setting bodies and contributes to global best practices. Through collaboration with state and non-state entities, this united effort acts as a defense against those seeking to exploit the internet for surveillance and fragmentation.

To reinforce this goal, the focus is strengthening norms and employing non-military tools of state power. The Bureau of Cyberspace and Digital Policy within the U.S. Department of State will lead in enhancing various tools, including cyber capacity building, international cyber law enforcement, sanctions and trade enforcement, attribution capability, and confidence-building measures. Utilizing these tools in coordination with Allies and partners, the United States can impose consequences on adversaries, promote responsible state behavior, and foster a stable and secure cyberspace.

Cyberspace Governance

The Bureau of Cyberspace and Digital Policy recognizes the indispensable role of non-governmental stakeholders in governing cyberspace. It actively supports the existing multistakeholder internet governance system, characterized by transparent, consensus-driven processes with equal participation from governments, the private sector, civil society, academia, and the technical community. The bureau also advocates for developing, adopting, and using voluntary, consensus-based, industry-driven technical standards.

Another key objective is advancing an international regulatory environment conducive to innovation and respecting cyberspace's global nature. This involves maintaining a flexible, risk-management approach to cybersecurity, opposing unwarranted market access restrictions, championing a fair and competitive global market, fostering private sector innovation, and upholding a robust intellectual property protection system while encouraging innovation.

The Bureau of Cyberspace and Digital Policy engages in various forms of international collaboration to realize these objectives. These include direct diplomatic actions, foreign assistance programs, participation in policy and technical standard-setting bodies, joint military exercises, and collaboration with non-governmental stakeholders. The bureau maximizes the effectiveness of its efforts by adopting a comprehensive and strategic approach, acknowledging the complexity and comprehensiveness of cyberspace issues.

Cyber Capacity Building

Aligned with broader initiatives such as Advancing the Digital Economy, Advancing Digital Freedom, and Building Digital Connectivity and Global Cyber Capacity, the bureau focuses on fostering a connected, innovative, and secure digital economy, safeguarding democratic principles and human rights in cyberspace, and utilizing foreign assistance funding to bolster international partnerships and promote rights-respecting best practices.

The capacity-building programs led by the Bureau of Cyberspace and Digital Policy play a crucial role in strengthening international partnerships and promoting responsible state behavior in cyberspace. These programs encompass training on cyber attribution, advocating for the adoption of norms of responsible state behavior, and developing practical confidence-building measures. Collaborating with regional security organizations and global partners, the bureau actively shapes the international agenda for cyber capacity building, enhancing national cybersecurity efforts. The CDP's efforts assist partners in establishing and fortifying their Cybersecurity Incident Response Teams (CSIRTs), formulating comprehensive national cyber strategies and policies, and fostering cybersecurity awareness within their jurisdictions.

Through its multifaceted approach and collaboration with partners and stakeholders, the Bureau of Cyberspace and Digital Policy significantly contributes to achieving Cyberspace Security Cooperation objectives. By championing responsible state behavior, promoting stability and security, and advancing an open, secure, and resilient cyberspace, the bureau plays a pivotal role in safeguarding U.S. interests, the global economy, and democratic values in the digital age.

Conclusion

In summary, the Bureau of Cyberspace and Digital Policy is vital in promoting cybersecurity through international engagement. By advocating for responsible state behavior, promoting stability and security, upholding an open and interoperable internet, maintaining the involvement of non-governmental stakeholders, and advancing an international regulatory environment that supports innovation, the bureau strives to protect U.S. interests, uphold democratic values, and ensure the competitiveness of the digital ecosystem. Through its multifaceted approach and collaboration with partners and stakeholders, the bureau's work contributes to a safer and more secure cyberspace.

Chapter 26:

Empowering Global Defense: The Role of Senior Cyber Advisors in Supporting Cyberspace Security Cooperation under the Global Defense Reform Program

Introduction

Amidst the deepening interdependence of nations, cybersecurity has become a critical component of national security for countries across the globe. Recognizing the importance of cyber defense in bolstering international security, the United States State Department has taken proactive measures to support partner nations in their pursuit of defense reform and civil-military institutional capacity building. At the forefront of these efforts is the role of the Senior Cyber Advisor, playing a pivotal role in assisting partner nations with their cybersecurity initiatives under the Global Defense Reform Program (GDPR). This chapter explores the significance of the Senior Cyber Advisor role and its contributions to cybersecurity capacity-building efforts and defense reform programs.

GDPR in Focus

Understanding the Global Defense Reform Program

The Global Defense Reform Program (GDRP) is a State Department-funded initiative managed by the Bureau of Political-Military Affairs. Its objective is to assist partner nations in enhancing their defense capabilities, strengthening civil-military institutional capacity, and building the resilience of their security institutions. One essential aspect of the program focuses on cybersecurity, acknowledging the increasingly pervasive cyber threats faced by nations.

Through the GDRP, the United States Department of State provides technical expertise, resources, and guidance to partner nations to improve their cybersecurity posture and establish robust defense reforms. This advisory assistance also emphasizes good governance principles and addresses the needs and challenges of the partner nation and its citizens, thereby strengthening key bilateral relationships. Additionally, the GDRP aids in modernizing and improving national security policies, strategies, and organizational frameworks, contributing to the advancement of the overall missions of our alliances and partnerships.

Supporting Cyberspace Security Cooperation through GDPR

The Global Defense Reform Program (GDPR) plays a crucial role in promoting cyberspace security cooperation among partner nations. By focusing on cybersecurity as an integral part of defense reform and civil-military institutional capacity building, the GDPR facilitates collaboration and information sharing in the cyber domain. The program recognizes that cyber threats transcend national borders and require collective efforts to address them effectively.

Under the GDPR, partner nations receive support in developing and implementing cybersecurity strategies, enhancing their technical capabilities, and fostering cooperation with other nations. The Senior Cyber Advisor, as a key facilitator, works closely with partner nations to identify common challenges, establish networks of trust, and promote joint exercises and training programs. By fostering cyberspace security cooperation, the GDPR strengthens the collective defense posture against cyber threats and facilitates a more coordinated response in the event of a cyber incident.

Advancing NATO's Collective Defense Mission

NATO's Collective Defense is a fundamental principle of the North Atlantic Treaty Organization (NATO), enshrined in Article 5 of the NATO treaty. It states that an attack against one member of the Alliance is considered an attack against all members. Therefore, if any NATO member faces aggression, the other member states are obligated to come to their defense and provide assistance, including the use of armed force if necessary. This principle is at the core of NATO's mission to ensure the security and protection of all its members.

In Europe, the GDRP plays an essential role in furthering NATO's Collective Defense Mission. GDRP advisors work closely with NATO Allies to align their national strategies with the defense and security commitments and objectives of the Alliance. By doing so, these advisors empower NATO Allies to be better prepared for NATO missions and operations, ultimately strengthening the overall capability and readiness of the Alliance.

Albania and North Macedonia, as NATO Allies, actively collaborate with GDRP advisors to develop, implement, and operationalize new National Security Strategies (NSS) and National Defense Strategies (NDS) for their countries. These strategic documents serve as important tools in articulating each nation's security aspirations and NATO defense goals. For North Macedonia, in particular, their first NSS since becoming a NATO member in 2020 is of particular significance, as it helps synchronize their initiatives in support of their obligations to NATO and informs their planning and resource allocation over the long term.

Through this process, the updated NSS and NDS for both Albania and North Macedonia will not only reflect the current security environment but also contribute to aligning resources and priorities with NATO's Collective Defense Mission. By enhancing the national security and defense capabilities of NATO Allies, the GDRP's efforts complement and reinforce the broader mission of the Alliance, ensuring the readiness and unity of NATO in facing potential threats and challenges.

Funding for the GDPR

The Global Defense Reform Program (GDPR) is funded by the United States State Department. As part of the broader U.S. foreign assistance framework, the GDPR receives financial resources to support its initiatives and activities. The funding for the program is allocated through the State Department's budgetary process, which considers the strategic priorities and objectives of U.S. foreign policy.

The financial resources provided by the State Department enable the GDPR to allocate funds for various purposes, including technical assistance, training programs, capacity-building efforts, policy development, and knowledge exchange activities. The funding supports the deployment of Senior Cyber Advisors to partner nations and facilitates collaboration between U.S. government agencies, international organizations, and partner nation stakeholders.

Moreover, the GDPR also leverages partnerships and collaborations with other entities and organizations to maximize the impact of its funding. This may include cooperation with other U.S. government agencies, such as the Department of Defense or the U.S. Agency for International Development, as well as international organizations and non-governmental entities that share similar objectives in promoting defense reform and cybersecurity capacity building.

The Role of Senior Cyber Advisor

The Senior Cyber Advisor is a pivotal figure within the GDPR, tasked with guiding and supporting partner nations in their cybersecurity endeavors. This multifaceted role combines technical expertise, policy knowledge, and diplomatic skills to facilitate effective collaboration and capacity building. Typically embedded within the Ministry of Defense (MoD), the Senior Advisor commits to a full-time, twelve-month role, focusing on cyber defense and coordinating with all necessary partners to enhance cybersecurity capabilities. Working closely with the MoD and other government entities, the Senior Advisor assists in building the capacity of their Cybersecurity Units, improving cybersecurity within the MoD, and fostering joint cyber defense coordination across service branches and interagency efforts. The Senior Advisor provides expert guidance, training, advice, and technical assistance necessary to develop and implement cyber reforms and policies at the Joint Staff. During cyber crises, the Senior Advisor advises the Ministry of Defense and supports effective interagency coordination on cybersecurity within the MoD and beyond.

Assessing Partner Nations' Cybersecurity Capabilities

A primary responsibility of the Senior Cyber Advisor is to conduct comprehensive assessments of partner nations' cybersecurity capabilities. These evaluations aim to identify strengths, weaknesses, and areas requiring improvement. Through this assessment, the Senior Cyber Advisor gains a deeper understanding of the partner nation's cyber landscape, enabling the tailoring of capacity-building efforts accordingly.

Developing Tailored Capacity-Building Programs

Building on the assessment findings, the Senior Cyber Advisor designs and implements tailored capacity-building programs for partner nations. These programs encompass a broad spectrum of activities, including training, knowledge sharing, policy development, and technical assistance. Collaborating closely with the partner nation's defense and civilian institutions, the Senior Cyber Advisor focuses on developing sustainable cybersecurity strategies that align with specific needs and challenges.

Facilitating Knowledge Exchange and Collaboration

As a facilitator, the Senior Cyber Advisor fosters knowledge exchange and collaboration between partner nations and relevant U.S. government agencies, cybersecurity experts, and international organizations. This involves organizing workshops, conferences, and training sessions that bring together stakeholders from various sectors to share best practices, discuss emerging cyber threats, and develop cooperative strategies.

Monitoring Progress and Providing Ongoing Support

The Senior Cyber Advisor plays a critical role in monitoring the progress of partner nations' cybersecurity initiatives and providing ongoing support. This includes regular evaluations, technical assistance visits, and continuous engagement to ensure that capacity-building efforts remain effective and aligned with the evolving cybersecurity landscape. Serving as a trusted advisor, the Senior Cyber Advisor offers guidance and expertise to overcome challenges and adapt to emerging threats.

Conclusion

The Global Defense Reform Program (GDPR) actively promotes cyberspace security cooperation by integrating cybersecurity into defense reform and capacity-building efforts. Through the GDPR, partner nations receive essential support to enhance their cyber defense capabilities, foster collaboration, and strengthen their collective ability to counter cyber threats. Funding for the GDPR is provided by the United States State Department, acknowledging the importance of cybersecurity in international security and supporting initiatives aimed at promoting defense reform and civil-military institutional capacity building. The financial resources allocated to the GDPR enable the program to implement tailored cybersecurity programs, facilitate knowledge exchange, and support the deployment of Senior Cyber Advisors to partner nations.

The role of the Senior Cyber Advisor in supporting the Global Defense Reform Program initiatives and assisting partner nations with defense reform and civil-military institutional capacity-building efforts focused on cybersecurity is vital. Through their technical expertise, policy knowledge, and diplomatic skills, Senior Cyber Advisors significantly contribute to enhancing partner nations' cyber defense capabilities. Their role in developing tailored capacity-building programs, fostering collaboration, and providing ongoing support is instrumental in strengthening international cybersecurity cooperation and ensuring a safer and more secure global digital environment.

Chapter 27:

U.S. Cyberspace Security Cooperation and the Role of Multinational Cyber Exercises in the U.S. National Defense Strategy

Introduction

In the modern era, cybersecurity has become a critical aspect of national defense due to the increasing reliance on digital systems and networks. The United States recognizes the significance of cybersecurity as a fundamental pillar in its defense strategy. Cyberspace security cooperation, supported by exercises such as Cyber Flag and Cyber Unity, plays a crucial role in deterring, detecting, and countering cyber threats. This chapter explores the dimensional benefits that multinational exercises bring in support of the U.S. Cyberspace Security Cooperation mission.

Benefits of Multinational Cyber Exercises

The history of U.S. cyberspace security cooperation spans several decades and has evolved to address the growing recognition of the importance of cybersecurity in national and international security. The United States actively fosters cyberspace security cooperation through various initiatives, partnerships, and multinational cyber exercises, such as Cyber Flag and Cyber Unity.

Multinational cyber exercises provide several benefits to the U.S. mission of ensuring cyberspace security. Firstly, these exercises allow participants to share best practices, exchange knowledge, and enhance their technical skills in countering cyber threats. By working alongside Allies and partners, the United States can leverage the expertise and capabilities of other nations, thereby strengthening its own cyber defense capabilities.

Secondly, multinational cyber exercises foster interoperability among participating nations. Collaboration is essential for effectively responding to and mitigating cyber threats that transcend national borders. Through joint exercises, the United States can improve information sharing, develop common standards and procedures, and establish trusted relationships with partner nations, enabling more effective coordination during crises.

Furthermore, multinational cyber exercises provide an opportunity for the United States to build and strengthen diplomatic and military relationships with its Allies and partners. Actively engaging in cybersecurity cooperation enhances trust and cooperation, bolstering influence and creating a network of trusted partners who can collaborate to address emerging cyber challenges.

The history of U.S. cyberspace security cooperation is characterized by a growing recognition of the importance of collaboration and multinational efforts to counter cyber threats. Multinational cyber exercises play a crucial role in advancing the U.S. mission by facilitating knowledge sharing, promoting interoperability, and fostering strong relationships with partner nations. Through these exercises, the United States enhances its own cyber defense capabilities while working collectively to safeguard cyberspace for the benefit of all.

NATO Cyber Defence Pledge and its Impact on U.S. National Defense Strategy

NATO (North Atlantic Treaty Organization), formed in 1949, is a military alliance aimed at ensuring the collective defense and security of its member states. Over time, NATO has adapted to address contemporary security challenges, including those in the cyber domain. A crucial development in NATO's approach to cybersecurity is the Cyber Defence Pledge, adopted in 2016.

The Cyber Defence Pledge underscores cyberspace as a domain of operations and commits NATO members to enhance individual and collective cyber defense capabilities. For the United States, this pledge aligns with its National Defense Strategy (NDS), emphasizing the need to prioritize the development of advanced cyber capabilities and partnerships to protect U.S. interests.

The Cyber Defence Pledge complements the U.S. National Defense Strategy by promoting cooperation and information sharing among NATO members. It facilitates joint training and exercises and fosters collaboration in cyber defense research and development. Through this pledge, the United States strengthens its collective defense capabilities, ensuring a more resilient posture against cyber threats and enhancing its ability to deter and respond to malicious cyber activities.

In summary, NATO's Cyber Defence Pledge reinforces the commitment of member states, including the United States, to strengthen their cyber defense capabilities. Aligned with the U.S. National Defense Strategy, the pledge contributes to the overall security and resilience of NATO's member states.

Overview of Current Multinational DOD's Cyber Military Exercises

Multinational cyber exercises like "Cyber Flag" and "Cyber Unity" aim to provide hands-on experience, exercising specific cyberspace objectives, including technical and non-technical coordination aspects, decision-making advisory processes, and collaboration among participants. These exercises offer valuable insights to improve the U.S. and Alliance's cyber deterrence and defense posture. The knowledge gained enhances the cybersecurity posture of participating nations, contributing to the continuous evolution of their cyber defense capabilities.

Cyber Unity Exercise

Cyber Unity, sponsored by EUCOM, is a cyber seminar and exercise designed to create a dedicated environment for Military Computer Incident Response Teams (MilCIRTs) from NATO countries. In its inaugural year in 2023, the exercise focuses on Balkan and Black Sea Allies. The primary objective is to bolster cyber defense skills through training and simulated live-fire events. By delving into the NATO Cyber Defence Pledge, Cyber Unity engages in strategic political-military dialogue to ensure strong and resilient cyber defenses within the Alliance. Emphasizing NATO's unity principle, the exercise aims to strengthen the weakest link. Allied MilCIRTs participating in Cyber Unity are expected to enhance their network protection, contributing to the success of Allied operations. The exercise covers a spectrum of training objectives, including cyberspace situational awareness, procedural incident handling, and collaboration within the NATO Enterprise Cyber Force Structure.

Cyber Flag Exercise

Cyber Flag, initiated in 2010 and led by U.S. Cyber Command (CYBERCOM), is a multinational cybersecurity exercise integral to the U.S. defense strategy. It brings together cyber defense professionals from various nations to simulate and respond to sophisticated cyber threats in a controlled environment. The exercise serves as a platform for cyber defense forces from the U.S. and partner nations to train collaboratively, improving their collective response capabilities. Conducted annually, Cyber Flag is a significant component of CYBERCOM's multinational cyber exercises. Valuable insights gained from these exercises contribute to defending against cyber threats and refining the nation's cyber defense strategy. Notably, the 2020 Cyber Flag exercise played a role in safeguarding the U.S. elections from foreign influence, highlighting the practical impact of these exercises on national security.

Building Multinational Cyber Exercises for Cyberspace Security Cooperation

Recognizing the importance of multinational cybersecurity cooperation, exercises like Cyber Flag and Cyber Unity align with the U.S. Defense Strategy. The 'Defend Forward' policy, introduced in 2018, emphasizes proactive engagement in cyberspace, making these exercises crucial for policy implementation.

When constructing multinational cyber exercises for Cyberspace Security Cooperation, organizations must ensure conditions are set for developing and testing technical and operational tools and procedures for a collective response to cyber threats. The exercises should align with the following aims and objectives:

Exercises Aim: Multinational exercises should bring together a cyber coalition of U.S. Allies and Partners to strengthen the Alliance's ability to deter, defend, and counter threats in and through cyberspace in support of NATO's Cyber Defence Pledge.

Exercises Objectives:

Exercise existing mechanisms for interaction between NATO Allies to improve collaboration in the cyberspace domain.

Enable dialogue among Allies to collectively identify future NATO standards and requirements within the cyberspace domain, drawing on the NATO Cyber Defence Pledge.

Provide an open environment for Allied Nations to test, validate, and verify interoperability tools such as the Malware Information Sharing Platform or MISP.

Build a NATO-centric military-focused cyberspace exercise for collaboration among Allied MiCIRTs to exchange highly technical information on threats, vulnerabilities, and defensive cyber tools.

Introduce Defensive Cyber Operations (DCO) tools standardization, like the Open-Source Security stack tools that are available to all Allies and partners from the open-source community and can provide an opportunity for nations to exercise both static and deployable Defensive Cyber Operations (DCO) capabilities.

Incorporate realistic cyber-attack scenarios affecting military warfighting functions (command and control), Fires, or Intelligence to evaluate collective defense measures and information sharing among Allies.

Incorporate reporting tools used in Allies' daily cyber operations like cyber incident reports, cyber incident trackers, cyber situational reports, and cyber prioritized assets list.

Conclusion

In essence, cyberspace security cooperation and exercises such as Cyber Flag and Cyber Unity are integral to the U.S. defense strategy. These exercises provide a platform for the U.S. and its partner nations to enhance their cyber defense capabilities, share valuable insights, and work collectively towards a more secure cyberspace.

Chapter 28:

Harnessing Cyber Defense and CSIRT Assistance Programs for Cyberspace Security Cooperation with US Allies and Partners

Introduction

In the digital age, characterized by constantly evolving cyber threats, the imperative for robust cybersecurity measures and international cooperation has reached unprecedented levels. This chapter delves into the significance of Computer Security Incident Response Team (CSIRT) Assistance Programs, exemplified by initiatives like Team Cymru and CSIRT Global. These programs play a pivotal role in empowering nations with less-developed digital infrastructures to defend against increasingly sophisticated cyber threats. By fostering a global community and instilling a shared commitment to solving security problems, CSIRT assistance programs aim to enhance global cybersecurity and expedite the achievement of cyberspace security cooperation goals.

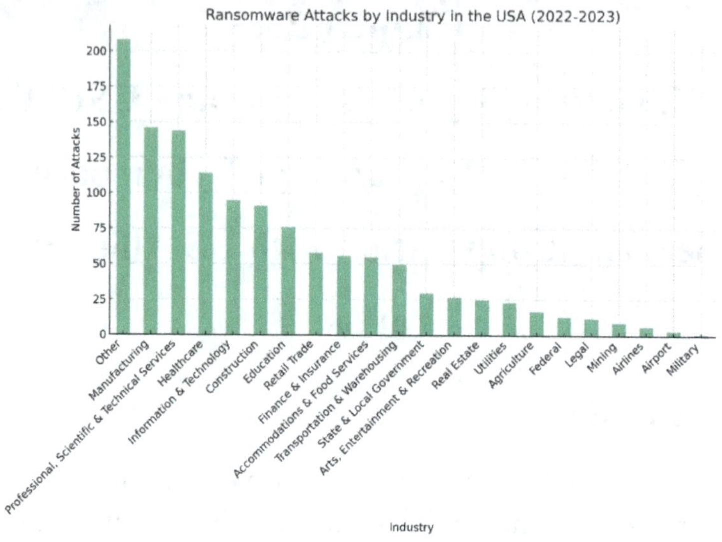

Figure 23: The bar chart above showcases the distribution of ransomware attacks across different industries from 2022 to 2023.

The graph above illustrates the pervasive nature of ransomware attacks across diverse sectors in 2022-2023, including Healthcare, Education, and State and Local Government.[cxxi] Responding to this escalating challenge underscores the paramount role of Computer Security Incident Response Team (CSIRT) Assistance Programs and global CSIRT efforts. These specialized teams possess the expertise to detect, respond to, and mitigate ransomware attacks, offering a crucial line of defense for targeted industries. Collaborative efforts across CSIRTs on a global scale are instrumental in sharing threat intelligence, best practices, and coordinated response strategies. Such a unified approach is vital for protecting the integrity and resilience of essential services and infrastructure, particularly in industries like healthcare, where the impact of a ransomware attack can be life-threatening. By leveraging CSIRT Assistance Programs and fostering international cooperation, industries can fortify their cybersecurity posture and defend against the evolving landscape of sophisticated ransomware attacks.

CSIRT Assistance Program (CAP) offered by Team Cymru

For U.S. Allies and partners facing resource limitations in defending against cyber attacks, Team Cymru, a prominent U.S. cybersecurity organization, offers a distinctive non-commercial CSIRT Assistance Program (CAP). This program provides an opportunity to enhance cyber defense capabilities, exchange threat intelligence, and collaborate toward creating a safer digital environment.

Benefits for U.S. Allies and Partners

The CAP offers several benefits to Allies and partners' Computer Emergency Response Teams (CERTs):

Access to High-Quality Threat Intelligence

Participation in the CAP grants Allies and partners access to Team Cymru's world-class threat intelligence resources, known as Pure Signal™. This intelligence provides insights into emerging cyber threats, adversary tactics, and global trends. Leveraging this intelligence strengthens situational awareness, enhances risk understanding, and improves the ability to detect and respond to cyber threats.

Strengthened Collaboration and Information Sharing

The CAP serves as a platform for fostering collaboration and information sharing among CSIRTs. Participating countries can establish trusted relationships, exchange best practices, and share threat intelligence in real-time. This collaborative approach creates a unified front against cyber threats, facilitating proactive and coordinated responses to shared challenges.

Capacity Building and Skill Development

The CAP offers opportunities for capacity building and skill development, empowering Allies and partners to enhance their cyber defense capabilities. Team Cymru provides guidance, recommendations, and knowledge transfer initiatives, supporting the development of a skilled cyber workforce. This contributes to building sustainable cyber defense capabilities and cultivating a culture of cyber resilience.

Strengthened Partnerships with the United States

Engaging in the CAP allows Allies and partners to forge closer ties with the United States in the realm of cyberspace security. Collaboration through this program enhances interoperability, aligns strategies, and builds mutual trust. Partnerships formed through the CAP serve as a foundation for broader cyberspace security cooperation initiatives, allowing for more effective joint responses to cyber incidents and shared threats.

Expanding Opportunities with Team Cymru

Team Cymru extends its support beyond the CAP, offering additional opportunities for national and international CSIRT organizations to strengthen their cybersecurity efforts. The company introduced the Nimbus Threat Monitor, leveraging leading Internet Protocol (IP) reputation data to deliver no-cost threat intelligence monitoring to network operators worldwide. This tool aids in identifying and mitigating potential threats by providing insights into the reputation of IP addresses.

Moreover, Team Cymru provides a no-cost Distributed Denial of Service (DDoS) solution, enabling organizations to enhance their resilience against DDoS attacks. This solution empowers U.S. Allies and partners to protect critical networks and maintain operational continuity even under intense DDoS attack scenarios.

Together with the CAP, these offerings from Team Cymru provide U.S. Allies and partners with a comprehensive suite of tools to strengthen their cybersecurity posture and facilitate greater cooperation in countering cyber threats.

Leveraging the CAP and Additional Offerings: Practical Steps

Establish Collaboration Frameworks: U.S. Allies and partners should initiate collaboration frameworks with Team Cymru to participate in the CAP and leverage additional offerings. Formalize agreements, sign Memorandums of Understanding (MoUs), and define the scope of cooperation to ensure a structured and mutually beneficial engagement.

Participate in Threat Intelligence Exchange: Actively engage in the threat intelligence exchange facilitated by Team Cymru through the CAP. Share and receive real-time threat information, contribute to threat analysis, and utilize the Nimbus Threat Monitor to gain insights into IP reputation data. This exchange ensures staying ahead of emerging threats and adopting proactive defense measures.

Strengthen Cyber Resilience: Leverage Team Cymru's no-cost DDoS solution to fortify network resilience against DDoS attacks. Collaborate with Team Cymru to understand the capabilities and implementation process for this solution, enabling U.S. Allies and partners to mitigate the disruptive effects of DDoS incidents and maintain critical operations.

Integrate Intelligence into Workflows: CSIRT organizations of Allies and partners should integrate acquired threat intelligence into their existing workflows and security operations. This may involve integrating Team Cymru's intelligence feeds into security information and event management (SIEM) systems, leveraging APIs for automated threat data ingestion, or incorporating intelligence into incident response playbooks.

Foster Collaboration and Knowledge Sharing: Actively participate in collaboration with Team Cymru and other CSIRTs to share best practices and enhance collective knowledge. Encourage cross-national information sharing, take part in joint exercises and training initiatives, and contribute to the broader community of cybersecurity professionals.

CSIRT Assistance Program offered by CSIRT Global

CSIRT Global is a not-for-profit, volunteer-led global organization dedicated to enhancing global cybersecurity by addressing often overlooked vulnerabilities. As a sister organization to the Dutch Institute for Vulnerability Disclosure (DIVD), CSIRT Global focuses on coordinating international CSIRT activities and building a network of like-minded individuals. Despite being separate legal entities, CSIRT Global and DIVD share a common vision. Volunteers at CSIRT

Global adhere to a comprehensive code of conduct outlining their principles and responsibilities.

CSIRT Global's Mission

At the heart of CSIRT Global's mission is the objective to build a global community united by a shared commitment to solving security issues, including vulnerabilities. By identifying owners of vulnerable systems and disclosing their findings, CSIRT Global strives to prevent incidents and create a more secure digital environment. The organization operates in a non-partisan, apolitical, inclusive, and open manner, emphasizing realism, the protection of sensitive data, and acknowledgment of its impact.

CSIRT Global's Code of Conduct

The code of conduct serves as the ethical foundation guiding the work of CSIRT Global volunteers. Their commitment to making the digital world safer is underscored by adherence to principles prioritizing societal need, proportionality, and subsidiarity. CSIRT Global operates within legally permissible boundaries, ensuring alignment with these principles. They rely on third-party findings, validating them when necessary, to avoid reporting false positives or missing critical vulnerabilities. To protect the confidentiality of sensitive data, CSIRT Global takes every precaution necessary. The organization discloses vulnerabilities to vendors first, seeking CVE numbers and negotiating disclosure timeframes while collaborating with trusted partners to extend their reach.

CSIRT Assistance and Security Cooperation

CSIRT Global's assistance program plays a crucial role in fostering security cooperation among nations. By providing vulnerability disclosures and remediation recommendations, CSIRT Global supports organizations and individuals in fortifying their digital infrastructure. Their work extends beyond individual systems, benefiting the broader security community and the public. Recognizing geographical differences, CSIRT Global offers escalation paths to address conflicts arising from variations in culture, law, and customs. The organization promotes a learning and teaching environment, encouraging diversity and open dialogue among its members. The chapter emphasizes CSIRT Global's commitment to personal and collective growth, encouraging members to challenge inappropriate behavior and providing escalation paths for conflict resolution.

The Cyber Defense Assistance Imperative (CDA)

The invasion of Ukraine by Russia in February 2022 marked a turning point in the world's understanding of the significance of cyber warfare. With major nation-states engaging in coordinated digital and physical attacks to conquer a neighboring country, the importance of effective and adaptable cyber defense capabilities became evident. This chapter delves into the concept of cyber defense assistance (CDA) and explores how partners delivered support to Ukraine during the conflict, offering crucial insights into conducting similar operations in future geopolitical conflicts.

Defining Cyber Defense Assistance (CDA) and its Benefits

Cyber defense assistance refers to cyber support activities provided to friendly or Allied nation-states under threat or actual attack from hostile nation-states. Unlike traditional cyber capacity building, CDA is specifically geared toward achieving national security objectives in response to discrete geopolitical risks. It encompasses a range of activities, including intelligence sharing, vulnerability management, distributed denial of service (DDoS) mitigation, threat intelligence access, and more. CDA serves multiple purposes, from deterring aggression and mitigating attacks during conflict to assisting with post-conflict stability and resiliency.

Challenges in Establishing Cyber Defense Assistance

The success of CDA efforts depends on early connections and trust between assistance recipients and capability providers. Developing personal relationships between key players and understanding the culture and management approaches of recipients are critical to success. Identifying, assembling, and organizing capability providers is vital to ensure a critical mass of support. CDA initiatives must align activities and establish priorities to avoid duplication of efforts and maximize impact. Collaboration among like-minded governments can enhance the efficacy of assistance.

The Cyber Defense Assistance Collaborative (CDAC) for Ukraine

CDAC is a volunteer group of cybersecurity and technology organizations that provided intelligence, technology, training, advisory, and other services to Ukrainian institutions during the conflict. CDAC played a vital role in coordinating and delivering cyber defense assistance, benefiting from pre-existing relationships with Ukraine's national security leadership. By bridging requests and capability providers, CDAC facilitated effective communication and assistance delivery.

The Future of Cyber Defense Assistance

As cyber conflicts become more prevalent, the ability to provide organized, effective cyber defense assistance will be crucial for safeguarding global stability. The lessons learned from the ad hoc conduct of assistance in Ukraine should be institutionalized and scaled to provide new approaches and tools for preventing and managing cyber conflicts. Strengthening capabilities to deter and respond to cyber aggression is imperative for the U.S. and its Allies to uphold the post-war order and counter potential aggressors effectively.

In summary, cyber defense assistance proved to be a vital component of Ukraine's response to Russian aggression. The lessons learned from this conflict underscore the need for coordinated, adaptable, and well-organized CDA efforts in future geopolitical conflicts. By harnessing the power of collaboration between governments, private sector companies, and non-profit organizations, the international community can enhance its collective ability to confront and defend against cyber threats on a global scale. The future of cybersecurity depends on embracing these lessons and evolving to meet the ever-changing cyber threat landscape.

Conclusion

By capitalizing on CSIRT Assistance Programs, like Team Cymru's and CSIRT Global, U.S. Allies and partners can strengthen their cybersecurity posture. These initiatives provide access to high-quality threat intelligence, foster collaboration and information sharing, and enhance cyber resilience against DDoS attacks. By offering their expertise, promoting vulnerability disclosure, and advocating for a safer digital environment, these programs empower nations with less developed digital infrastructures to effectively combat cyber threats. Engaging in close partnership with cybersecurity practitioners, Allies, and partners can bolster their cyber defense capabilities, promote collective security, and contribute to a safer and more secure cyberspace.

Overall, the experience of cyber defense assistance in Ukraine has demonstrated its effectiveness in improving national cyber resiliency. As the global landscape faces continued geopolitical challenges, the ability to deliver well-coordinated and effective cyber defense assistance will remain essential in safeguarding the post-war order from potential cyber aggression. Drawing upon the lessons from Ukraine, this knowledge emphasizes the need to institutionalize and scale these efforts, providing new approaches and tools for preventing and managing cyber conflicts in the future.

Chapter 29:

U.S. Cyberspace Security Cooperation and the Role of Multinational Cyber Exercises in the U.S. National Defense Strategy

Introduction

In the modern era, cybersecurity has become a critical aspect of national defense due to the increasing reliance on digital systems and networks. The United States recognizes the significance of cybersecurity as a fundamental pillar in its defense strategy. Cyberspace security cooperation, supported by exercises such as Cyber Flag and Cyber Unity, plays a crucial role in deterring, detecting, and countering cyber threats. This chapter explores the dimensional benefits that multinational exercises bring in support of the U.S. Cyberspace Security Cooperation mission.

Benefits of Multinational Cyber Exercises

The history of U.S. cyberspace security cooperation spans several decades and has evolved to address the growing recognition of the importance of cybersecurity in national and international security. The United States actively fosters cyberspace security cooperation through various initiatives, partnerships, and multinational cyber exercises, such as Cyber Flag and Cyber Unity.

Multinational cyber exercises provide several benefits to the U.S. mission of ensuring cyberspace security. Firstly, these exercises allow participants to share best practices, exchange knowledge, and enhance their technical skills in countering cyber threats. By working alongside Allies and partners, the United States can leverage the expertise and capabilities of other nations, thereby strengthening its own cyber defense capabilities.

Secondly, multinational cyber exercises foster interoperability among participating nations. Collaboration is essential for effectively responding to and mitigating cyber threats that transcend national borders. Through joint exercises, the United States can improve information sharing, develop common standards and procedures, and establish trusted relationships with partner nations, enabling more effective coordination during crises.

Furthermore, multinational cyber exercises provide an opportunity for the United States to build and strengthen diplomatic and military relationships with its Allies and partners. Actively engaging in cybersecurity cooperation enhances trust and cooperation, bolstering influence and creating a network of trusted partners who can collaborate to address emerging cyber challenges.

In conclusion, the history of U.S. cyberspace security cooperation is characterized by a growing recognition of the importance of collaboration and multinational efforts to counter cyber threats. Multinational cyber exercises play a crucial role in advancing the U.S. mission by facilitating knowledge sharing, promoting interoperability, and fostering strong relationships with partner nations. Through these exercises, the United States enhances its own cyber defense capabilities while working collectively to safeguard cyberspace for the benefit of all.

NATO Cyber Defence Pledge and its Impact on U.S. National Defense Strategy

NATO, formed in 1949, is a military alliance aimed at ensuring the collective defense and security of its member states. Over time, NATO has adapted to address contemporary security challenges, including those in the cyber domain. At present, NATO has 32 member countries. These countries called NATO Allies, are sovereign states that come together through NATO to discuss political and military issues and make collective decisions by consensus.[cxxii] A crucial development in NATO's approach to cybersecurity is the Cyber Defence Pledge, adopted in 2016.

The Cyber Defence Pledge underscores cyberspace as a domain of operations and commits NATO members to enhance individual and collective cyber defense capabilities. For the United States, this pledge aligns with its National Defense Strategy (NDS), emphasizing the need to prioritize the development of advanced cyber capabilities and partnerships to protect U.S. interests.

The Cyber Defence Pledge complements the U.S. National Defense Strategy by promoting cooperation and information sharing among NATO members. It facilitates joint training and exercises and fosters collaboration in cyber defense research and development. Through this pledge, the United States strengthens its collective defense capabilities, ensuring a more resilient posture against cyber threats and enhancing its ability to deter and respond to malicious cyber activities.

In summary, NATO's Cyber Defence Pledge reinforces the commitment of member states, including the United States, to strengthen their cyber defense capabilities. Aligned with the U.S. National Defense Strategy, the pledge contributes to the overall security and resilience of NATO's member states.

Overview of Current Multinational DOD's Cyber Exercises

Multinational cyber exercises like "Cyber Flag" and "Cyber Unity" aim to provide hands-on experience, exercising specific cyberspace objectives, including technical and non-technical coordination aspects, decision-making advisory processes, and collaboration among participants. These exercises offer valuable insights to improve the U.S. and Alliance's cyber deterrence and defense posture. The knowledge gained enhances the cybersecurity posture of participating nations, contributing to the continuous evolution of their cyber defense capabilities.

Cyber Unity

Cyber Unity, sponsored by EUCOM, is a cyber seminar and exercise designed to create a dedicated environment for Military Computer Incident Response Teams (MilCIRTs) from NATO countries. In its inaugural year in 2023, the exercise focuses on Balkan and Black Sea Allies. The primary objective is to bolster cyber defense skills through training and simulated live-fire events. By delving into the NATO Cyber Defence Pledge, Cyber Unity engages in strategic political-military dialogue to ensure strong and resilient cyber defenses within the Alliance. Emphasizing NATO's unity principle, the exercise aims to strengthen the weakest link. Allied MilCIRTs participating in Cyber Unity are expected to enhance their network protection, contributing to the success of Allied operations. The exercise covers a spectrum of training objectives, including cyberspace situational awareness, procedural incident handling, and collaboration within the NATO Enterprise Cyber Force Structure.

Cyber Flag

Cyber Flag, initiated in 2010 and led by U.S. Cyber Command, is a multinational cybersecurity exercise integral to the U.S. defense strategy. It brings together cyber defense professionals from various nations to simulate and respond to sophisticated cyber threats in a controlled environment. The exercise serves as a platform for cyber defense forces from the U.S. and partner nations to train collaboratively, improving their collective response capabilities. Conducted annually, Cyber Flag is a significant component of the U.S. Cyber Command's multinational cyber exercises. Valuable insights gained from these exercises contribute to defending against cyber threats and refining the nation's cyber defense strategy. Notably, the 2020 Cyber Flag exercise played a role in safeguarding the U.S. elections from foreign influence, highlighting the practical impact of these exercises on national security.

Building Multinational Cyber Exercises for Cyberspace Security Cooperation

Recognizing the importance of multinational cybersecurity cooperation, exercises like Cyber Flag and Cyber Unity align with the U.S. Defense Strategy. The 'Defend Forward' policy, introduced in 2018, emphasizes proactive engagement in cyberspace, making these exercises crucial for policy implementation.

When constructing multinational cyber exercises for Cyberspace Security Cooperation, organizations must ensure conditions are set for developing and testing technical and operational tools and procedures for a collective response to cyber threats. The exercises should align with the following aims and objectives:

Exercises Aim: Multinational exercises should bring together a cyber coalition of U.S. Allies and partners to strengthen the Alliance's ability to deter, defend, and counter threats in and through cyberspace in support of NATO's Cyber Defence Pledge.

Exercises Objectives:

Exercise existing mechanisms for interaction between NATO Allies to improve collaboration in the cyberspace domain.

Enable dialogue among Allies to collectively identify future NATO standards and requirements within the cyberspace domain, drawing on the NATO Cyber Defence Pledge.

Provide an open environment for Allied Nations to test, validate, and verify interoperability tools.

Build a NATO-centric military-focused cyberspace exercise for collaboration among Allied MiCIRTs.

Introduce Defensive Cyber Operations (DCO) tools standardization, like the Open-Source Security stack tools that are available to all Allies and partners from the open-source community and can provide an opportunity for nations to exercise both static and deployable Defensive Cyber Operations (DCO) capabilities.

Incorporate realistic cyber-attack scenarios affecting military warfighting functions (command and control), Fires, or Intelligence to evaluate collective defense measures and information sharing among Allies.

Incorporate reporting tools used in Allies' daily cyber operations like cyber incident reports, cyber incident trackers, cyber situational reports, and cyber prioritized assets list.

Conclusion

In essence, cyberspace security cooperation and exercises such as Cyber Flag and Cyber Unity are integral to the U.S. defense strategy. These exercises provide a platform for the U.S. and its partner nations to enhance their cyber defense capabilities, share valuable insights, and work collectively towards a safer and more secure cyberspace.

Chapter 30:

Rapid Response and International Cooperation: How the FBI's Cyber Action Team Assists U.S. Allies During Cyber Attacks

Introduction

Amidst the burgeoning interconnectivity of nations and societies, cyber attacks pose a significant threat to governments, organizations, and individuals. To combat these threats and provide rapid response capabilities, the FBI established the Cyber Action Team (CAT) in 2006. Comprising cyber experts with advanced training in computer languages, forensic investigations, and malware analysis, CAT can be deployed globally within 48 hours to support investigations into major computer intrusions and cyber-related emergencies. This chapter explores how the CAT can assist U.S. Allies and partners during cyber attacks, with specific examples from Albania and Montenegro.

The FBI's Cyber Action Team in Focus

The CAT's Mission and Expertise

The primary mission of the Cyber Action Team is to respond swiftly to cyber intrusions and provide investigative support. With approximately 50 members stationed across various field offices, the team includes both special agents and computer scientists. These experts possess specialized skills in analyzing cyber threats, identifying hacker signatures, and understanding the evolving language of cybercrime.

Immediate Response and Implications of Cyber Attacks

Cyber intrusions can have severe consequences, compromising military secrets, confidential information, and critical national security data. The CAT recognizes the urgency of addressing such incidents, as evidence may vanish quickly, leaving a cold trail, hindering attribution, and obstructing the ability to implement effective countermeasures or legal repercussions against the perpetrators. The team's objective is to swiftly gather actionable information, enabling immediate response measures and preventing further system compromises, data breaches, or escalation of the cyber attack's impact.

Overseas Deployments and International Cooperation

The CAT's expertise extends beyond U.S. borders, as some cyber-attacks affect U.S. interests abroad. In such cases, the team collaborates with the FBI's legal attaché (LEGAT) offices and international partners to provide assistance. This collaboration enhances the global fight against cybercrime and ensures efficient information sharing and joint investigations.

Case Study 1: Iranian-sponsored Cyber Attack against Albania

In July 2022, Albania experienced a significant cyber attack that targeted the country's institutions, causing disruptions in major government websites belonging to the Albanian Prime Minister's Office, the Parliament, and the e-Albania portal used to access public services. Recognizing the severity of the incident, the FBI deployed a cyber action team (CAT) to Tirana to support the investigation. The Deputy Prime Minister and Minister of Infrastructure, Belinda Balluku, emphasized the importance of this deep investigation conducted by the FBI and other law enforcement agencies. The collaboration aimed to uncover the attack's origin and techniques employed and enhance defenses to guard against future incidents.[cxxiii, cxxiv]

Case Study 2: Russian-linked Cyber Attack against Montenegro

In August 2022, Montenegro faced a massive, coordinated cyber attack that targeted its government servers, rendering key web services of public utilities, transportation (including border crossings and airports), and telecommunication sectors inaccessible. In response to this unprecedented cyber attack, Montenegro's Ministry of Internal Affairs announced the deployment of a rapid deployment team consisting of FBI cyber experts, aka Cyber Action Team (CAT). Following the incident, Montenegro's National Security Agency (ANB) announced that the disruption was likely caused by Russian actors using a mix of ransomware and distributed denial of service (DDoS) attacks. The collaboration between the FBI and

Montenegro during this crisis highlighted the robust partnership and mutual support between the two countries in combating cyber threats. The FBI's involvement not only demonstrated the excellent cooperation between the United States and Montenegro but also provided valuable expertise for investigating the attack, aiding in identifying the perpetrators, and ensuring the rapid restoration of the country's ICT services. cxxv

Conclusion

The FBI's Cyber Action Team (CAT) plays a crucial role in combating cyber threats and assisting U.S. Allies and partners during cyber attacks. With its rapid deployment capabilities, advanced expertise, and commitment to international cooperation, the CAT provides valuable support to investigations, information sharing, and preventive measures. The cases in Albania and Montenegro exemplify the CAT's global reach and its commitment to safeguarding cybersecurity and countering cybercriminal activities. As cyber threats continue to evolve, the CAT's role will remain essential in protecting critical infrastructure, defending against cyber attacks, and fostering international collaboration to address this shared challenge.

Chapter 31:

Beyond Security: Cyber Capacity's Impact on Global Development

Introduction

Militaries, governments, international organizations, and the private sector increasingly acknowledge the significance of capacity building in cyberspace. Amidst mounting pressure to demonstrate results, it's essential not to lose sight of the overarching goal: establishing a resilient ICT domain that fosters economic and social progress.

Efforts in cyber capacity building should be viewed as a sequential process, wherein small-scale initiatives contribute to larger, more comprehensive projects. This sequential approach should inform ongoing assessments and future planning to ensure effectiveness and scalability.

Establishing a Common Language for Cyber Capacity Building

As society becomes increasingly reliant on ICT across various sectors, integrating cyber issues into broader policy debates is essential. However, discussions often suffer from misconceptions regarding cybersecurity, cybercrime, and cyber defense, hindering implementation. Demystifying cybersecurity is crucial, emphasizing its role in combating crime, building resilience, and fostering a safe environment for development.[cxxvi]

Cyber capacity building extends beyond security concerns, impacting social and economic development globally. With many countries relying on the internet and ICT for governance and service delivery, security improvements must be considered within the broader context of governance transparency, human rights, and economic freedom. Linking these efforts to overarching development goals offers unique opportunities for progress.

Addressing Diverse Challenges in Capacity Building

Challenges in cyber capacity building vary among stakeholders and stem from the diverse nature of their roles and contexts. For security cooperation organizations, one of the primary hurdles lies in developing scalable models and strategic frameworks that can effectively engage leaders at all levels. This task demands a comprehensive understanding of the intricate dynamics of cyberspace and the ability to tailor capacity-building initiatives to meet the evolving needs of different stakeholders. Additionally, coordinating with appropriate partners, both nationally and globally, is crucial to ensure the success and sustainability of these efforts. This requires forging strategic partnerships with governmental agencies, international organizations, private sector entities, and civil society groups to leverage their expertise, resources, and networks effectively.

Moreover, strategies for sustainability must be integrated into capacity-building initiatives from the outset to ensure their long-term effectiveness. This entails not only building technical capabilities but also fostering a culture of cybersecurity awareness, establishing robust legal frameworks, and promoting continuous learning and adaptation. By embedding sustainability principles into the planning and implementation process, security cooperation organizations can help foster lasting improvements in cyberspace resilience and security.

For the beneficiaries of cyber capacity-building initiatives, navigating the challenges posed by their unique contexts is paramount. These challenges may include navigating regional complexities, such as differing legal and regulatory frameworks, cultural norms, and geopolitical dynamics. Harmonizing efforts amidst diverse regional landscapes requires careful coordination and collaboration among various stakeholders to avoid duplication of efforts and ensure coherence in approach.

Additionally, activating leaders to recognize the realities of cybercrime and the importance of cybersecurity is essential for fostering a proactive response to emerging threats. This involves raising awareness about the potential impact of cyber attacks on national security, economic stability, and public safety and mobilizing political will and resources to address these challenges effectively.

Furthermore, beneficiaries must navigate the transition from the planning stages to the effective implementation of cyber capacity-building initiatives. This requires setting clear priorities amidst competing demands, such as addressing immediate threats like organized crime or war, while also investing in long-term measures to build cyber resilience and capabilities. By adopting a structured approach that emphasizes collaboration, clear communication, and strategic planning, stakeholders can overcome these challenges and achieve sustainable progress in cyberspace.

Divergent Priorities in Cyber Capacity Building

Within the sphere of enhancing cyber capabilities, there exists a complex interplay of priorities between security cooperation organizations and the security forces of the countries they aim to assist. This dynamic is shaped by the unique perspectives and objectives of each party involved.

Security cooperation organizations, which could include multinational alliances, intergovernmental bodies, or non-governmental organizations (NGOs), typically approach cyber capacity building with a broad lens focused on fostering an open and secure internet environment. This overarching goal reflects their commitment to promoting global cybersecurity standards, facilitating information sharing, and bolstering collaborative efforts to combat cyber threats on a large scale. Their priorities often revolve around initiatives aimed at enhancing cybersecurity frameworks, promoting international norms and standards, and facilitating cooperation among nations to address cyber challenges collectively. Such organizations may emphasize the importance of developing robust legal frameworks, enhancing incident response capabilities, and promoting cybersecurity awareness and education programs.

On the other hand, the security forces of the countries receiving assistance prioritize tailored capacity-building programs that address their specific needs and challenges. These needs can vary widely depending on factors such as the country's level of technological development, the nature and sophistication of cyber threats they face, and the capacity of their security institutions to respond effectively. As a result, their priorities often center around practical measures such as training and skills development for cybersecurity personnel, strengthening capabilities for cybercrime investigation and prosecution, and acquiring the necessary tools and equipment to defend against cyber attacks.

In essence, while security cooperation organizations focus on broader goals of promoting secure cyberspace at the global level, the benefitting countries prioritize more localized efforts to build their own cyber resilience and capabilities. This divergence in priorities underscores the importance of a nuanced and context-specific approach to cyber capacity building, one that takes into account the distinct perspectives and objectives of all stakeholders involved. By aligning these priorities and fostering collaboration between security organizations and beneficiary countries, more effective and sustainable cybersecurity outcomes can be achieved in the long run.

Tailoring Solutions: One Size Does Not Fit All

Crafting robust frameworks for capacity building in cybersecurity necessitates a deep comprehension of the distinct cultural, political, and social landscapes characterizing each country or region. Recognizing the intricacies of these contexts is imperative as it enables tailored approaches that resonate with local stakeholders and address specific challenges effectively. While certain components of capacity-building initiatives may demand customization to suit the idiosyncrasies of individual environments, overarching strategies and goals can often be replicated across diverse contexts. This balance between customization and replication ensures both relevance and efficiency in capacity-building efforts.

Despite the diversity of responsibilities and priorities across different regions, the fundamental principles underpinning capacity-building frameworks remain consistent. These frameworks prioritize local ownership, acknowledging the importance of empowering communities and institutions to drive sustainable change from within. By fostering a sense of ownership, capacity-building initiatives are more likely to gain traction and endure beyond the lifespan of external support. Additionally, adaptability emerges as a key feature of effective frameworks, enabling stakeholders to respond agilely to evolving threats and challenges in the cybersecurity landscape.

At their core, capacity-building frameworks are designed to enhance the resilience and capabilities of local actors in addressing cyber threats and vulnerabilities. This may involve strengthening technical expertise, improving institutional capacity, or promoting cybersecurity awareness and best practices. Regardless of the specific focus areas, the overarching goal remains consistent: to build a robust and sustainable cybersecurity ecosystem that can withstand emerging threats and safeguard the interests of individuals, organizations, and nations alike. Through a nuanced understanding of local contexts and a commitment to core principles of ownership and adaptability, effective capacity-building frameworks can lay the groundwork for a safer and more secure cyberspace for all.

The Role of National Cybersecurity Strategies

National cybersecurity strategies serve as vital components of capacity-building efforts, albeit with varying levels of implementation. Clarity in objectives, such as promoting economic and social development or combating cybercrime, is crucial, as is defining mandates for each organization involved. Stakeholders, including the state, industry, and various interest groups, must collaboratively design policies and legislation, ensuring accountability and effective enforcement.

Addressing the diverse needs and motivations of stakeholders requires flexible strategies that accommodate varying incentives. Whether technical, managerial, or political, each stakeholder group responds differently to messaging and incentives. Therefore, strategies must be adaptable to ensure effective implementation models that align with these differing motivations, ultimately enhancing the success of capacity-building efforts.

International Coordination in Cyber Capacity Building

Efficient international coordination is essential in addressing cyber threats due to their borderless nature and the extensive investment required to fully leverage ICT opportunities. Both donor and beneficiary communities must focus on identifying and sharing best practices while coordinating resources effectively. However, effective exchange of promising practices requires peers to be at similar stages of implementation, ensuring relevance and applicability.

Sharing information among various actors, including governments and international organizations, is fundamental for identifying needs, successes, and failures. Improved exchange between regional and international organizations, such as the World Bank and United Nations agencies, can enhance capacity-building efforts. While competition for resources is inevitable, monitoring resource allocation can ensure efficient utilization. Regional organizations like the Organization of American States, the African Union Commission, ASEAN, and the Council of Europe can serve as effective channels for capacity-building efforts, although their effectiveness may be influenced by cultural, linguistic, and legal differences.

Stakeholders' Cooperation in Cyber Capacity Building

Collaboration among stakeholders is essential for driving effective cyber capacity-building initiatives and achieving comprehensive outcomes that are widely accepted and supported. Embracing a multistakeholder approach involves setting clear objectives and engaging a diverse range of actors, including government entities, industry representatives, community organizations, local councils, and state governments.

The private sector plays a pivotal role in this cooperative effort by raising awareness of cybersecurity issues and establishing constructive partnerships with governments. By sharing insights, resources, and expertise, private sector entities can contribute significantly to the development and implementation of effective cybersecurity strategies. Furthermore, enhancing communication channels and transparency regarding decision-making processes is crucial for fostering trust and cooperation between public and private stakeholders.

Civil society organizations, encompassing NGOs, think tanks, and trade unions, also play a vital role in advancing cyber capacity-building efforts. These organizations often serve as watchdogs, advocating for the protection of individual rights and freedoms in cyberspace. They contribute by identifying the specific needs and implications of capacity-building initiatives, particularly in terms of the social and economic impacts of internet proliferation and the potential abuses that may arise in cyberspace. By representing diverse perspectives and interests, civil society organizations help ensure that capacity-building efforts are inclusive, responsive to community needs, and aligned with broader societal goals.

In essence, stakeholder cooperation forms the bedrock of successful cyber capacity-building endeavors. By leveraging the expertise, resources, and perspectives of various actors, including government, industry, and civil society, stakeholders can work together to address the multifaceted challenges posed by cybersecurity and promote a safer, more resilient cyberspace for all.

Addressing Challenges in Incident Reporting

Addressing challenges in incident reporting is a critical aspect of cyber capacity building, yet it presents formidable obstacles that demand nuanced solutions. In certain countries, like Kenya, there is deliberation over imposing affirmative obligations on the private sector to report cyber incidents. While this approach aims to enhance cybersecurity by ensuring timely detection and response to threats, it also raises concerns about potential repercussions, particularly regarding reputational damage for affected entities.

To mitigate these concerns and encourage more effective incident reporting, the development of non-attributive reporting mechanisms is essential. These mechanisms offer a way for organizations to report incidents without fear of immediate attribution or adverse consequences. One such approach involves reporting incidents to a trusted third party, such as a government agency or industry-specific organization, which can act as an intermediary and safeguard the anonymity of the reporting entity.

However, implementing non-attributive reporting mechanisms is not without its challenges. A fundamental issue is the lack of trust between the various actors involved in incident response, including government agencies, private sector organizations, and other stakeholders. Building trust requires transparent communication, collaboration, and a shared commitment to cybersecurity objectives. Additionally, the absence of clear and standardized reporting mechanisms complicates the process, as organizations may struggle to understand their reporting obligations and navigate the complexities of incident response.

Addressing these challenges requires a multi-faceted approach that combines legal and regulatory frameworks, technical solutions, and stakeholder engagement efforts. Establishing clear guidelines and incentives for incident reporting, along with robust protections for the confidentiality of reporting entities, can help overcome barriers to participation. Moreover, fostering collaboration and information-sharing initiatives among public and private sector organizations can enhance trust and facilitate more effective incident response efforts.

Overall, addressing challenges in incident reporting requires a balanced approach that recognizes the need for both accountability and anonymity. By developing non-attributive reporting mechanisms and fostering a culture of trust and collaboration, countries can strengthen their cyber resilience and enhance their ability to respond to cyber threats effectively.

Essential Elements for Success

Achieving success in cyber capacity building demands the integration of several crucial elements, each playing a vital role in shaping the outcome of these efforts. These essential elements encompass both practical and strategic considerations, contributing to the effectiveness and sustainability of capacity-building initiatives.

1. Effective Leadership: Leadership serves as the cornerstone of successful cyber capacity building. Effective leaders provide vision, direction, and guidance, rallying stakeholders around common objectives. They foster collaboration, inspire innovation, and navigate challenges adeptly, driving progress toward established goals. Leadership in this context extends beyond individual figures to include organizational leadership structures and coordination mechanisms that facilitate decision-making and implementation.

2. Inclusive Process: An inclusive approach is essential for ensuring that the diverse perspectives and expertise of all stakeholders are taken into account. By engaging a wide range

of actors, including government agencies, private sector entities, civil society organizations, and technical experts, capacity-building initiatives can benefit from a broader pool of knowledge, resources, and experiences. Inclusivity fosters buy-in, promotes ownership, and enhances the relevance and legitimacy of interventions within the communities they aim to serve.

3. Diversity in Approach: Cyber capacity building is not a one-size-fits-all endeavor. It requires a diverse range of strategies, tools, and methodologies tailored to the specific needs and contexts of different stakeholders. This diversity in approach enables flexibility and adaptability, allowing interventions to be customized to address evolving challenges and priorities effectively. Whether through training programs, technical assistance, policy development, or public awareness campaigns, leveraging a variety of approaches maximizes the likelihood of success.

4. Alignment Towards Common Goals: Success hinges on the alignment of efforts towards shared objectives and outcomes. Establishing clear, measurable goals and fostering alignment among stakeholders ensures that resources are directed towards priority areas and that activities are coordinated for maximum impact. Alignment promotes synergy, minimizes duplication of efforts, and enhances the overall effectiveness and efficiency of capacity-building initiatives.

5. Recognition of Tangible and Intangible Benefits: Beyond tangible outcomes such as improved technical capabilities or strengthened legal frameworks, success in cyber capacity building also entails recognizing and valuing

intangible benefits. These may include enhanced trust and cooperation among stakeholders, increased resilience to cyber threats, and improved awareness and understanding of cybersecurity issues within society. Acknowledging both the tangible and intangible benefits reinforces the value proposition of capacity-building efforts and underscores their broader impact on national security, economic prosperity, and social well-being.

Incorporating these essential elements into the design, implementation, and evaluation of cyber capacity-building initiatives lays the foundation for sustained success and resilience in the face of evolving cyber threats and challenges. By prioritizing effective leadership, inclusivity, diversity in approach, alignment towards common goals, and recognition of both tangible and intangible benefits, stakeholders can maximize the impact and sustainability of their efforts to strengthen cybersecurity capabilities at local, national, and global levels.

Elevating the Priority of Cyber Capacity Building

In the realm of contemporary governance, cybersecurity often struggles to secure a prominent position on the political agenda. This isn't due to a lack of importance but rather the presence of pressing, tangible concerns that demand immediate attention. Issues such as food security, sanitation, and crime are often at the forefront of policymakers' minds, overshadowing the less visible but equally critical domain of cybersecurity.

Despite its invisibility in comparison to more tangible threats, the risks posed by cybersecurity breaches are undeniable. The interconnected nature of our modern world means that vulnerabilities in digital systems can have far-reaching consequences, impacting everything from national security to individual privacy. However, the intangible nature of these risks can make them easier to overlook, especially when governments and policymakers are grappling with more immediate challenges.

The significance of cybersecurity tends to become more apparent in contexts where technology plays a central role in the functioning of the public sector. As governments increasingly rely on digital infrastructure to deliver services and manage essential functions, the importance of safeguarding these systems against cyber threats becomes increasingly evident. Similarly, in societies where scientific and technological advancements are highly valued, cybersecurity gains greater recognition as an essential component of maintaining progress and stability.

Despite the growing importance of cybersecurity in these contexts, governments often fail to adequately appreciate the risks or allocate sufficient resources to address them. This neglect can stem from a variety of factors, including a lack of understanding of the evolving cyber threat landscape, competing budgetary priorities, or a failure to recognize the long-term implications of insufficient investment in cybersecurity.

As a result, initiatives aimed at strengthening IT infrastructure and building cybersecurity capacity may languish due to a lack of political will or resources. This neglect can leave governments and societies vulnerable to cyber attacks, undermining public trust and impeding progress in an increasingly digitized world.

Transitioning from Needs to Delivery

As capacity-building programs in cybersecurity progress, it becomes imperative for them to transition effectively from identifying needs to delivering tangible outcomes. This evolution requires a dynamic approach that can adapt to changing contexts, emerging needs, and the maturation of cyber policy frameworks. While defining outcomes at the outset can provide direction, rigidly adhering to predetermined goals risks stifling innovation and failing to address evolving challenges adequately. Therefore, it is essential to incorporate learning mechanisms throughout the process, allowing for flexibility and continuous improvement based on feedback and lessons learned.

Political leaders hold a pivotal role in ensuring the success of capacity-building efforts by empowering decision-makers and providing the necessary support and resources. Their commitment to cybersecurity initiatives can set the tone for prioritizing cybersecurity within national agendas and allocating resources accordingly. Moreover, political leadership can facilitate collaboration between different stakeholders, including government agencies, private sector entities, academia, and civil society, fostering a more holistic and effective approach to cybersecurity capacity building.

Key success conditions for capacity-building programs include having a well-defined strategy that aligns with national cybersecurity objectives, a team of qualified staff with the necessary expertise and skills, flexibility to adapt to evolving threats and technologies, adequate resources to support implementation, and the establishment of networks for information sharing and collaboration. Furthermore, leveraging international cooperation and experience sharing can enhance the effectiveness of capacity-building initiatives by drawing on best practices and lessons learned from other countries and organizations.

In essence, transitioning from identifying needs to delivering outcomes in cybersecurity capacity building requires a comprehensive approach that emphasizes flexibility, collaboration, political commitment, and continuous learning. By adhering to these principles and success conditions, capacity-building programs can effectively enhance cyber resilience and capabilities, ultimately contributing to a more secure and resilient cyberspace.

Conclusion

At the close of this chapter and the book as a whole, it becomes evident that stakeholders across various sectors are recognizing the critical importance of capacity building in cyberspace. From militaries and governments to international organizations and the private sector, there is a growing acknowledgment of the need to bolster capabilities in the digital realm.

In delving deeper into the realm of cyber capacity building, it becomes apparent that this endeavor transcends mere technical upgrades or security enhancements. It requires a comprehensive strategy that encompasses various facets of society and governance. Here are key considerations that underscore the complexity and importance of cyber capacity-building efforts:

Cyber capacity building is not a short-term endeavor but rather a sustained effort over time. Similar to a marathon, it requires dedication, perseverance, and a focus on long-term goals rather than quick fixes.

Effective communication is essential in cyber capacity-building efforts. A common language ensures that stakeholders can understand and collaborate effectively, facilitating smoother coordination and implementation of initiatives.

Recognizing that cyber capacity building extends beyond security concerns is crucial. It plays a significant role in shaping social and economic development globally, underscoring its importance beyond mere cybersecurity measures.

Challenges in cyber capacity building vary depending on the context, including regional, cultural, and political factors. Understanding these differences is essential for addressing challenges effectively and tailoring solutions to specific needs.

Given the diverse priorities among stakeholders, flexibility in approach is necessary. Acknowledging that priorities differ allows for customized strategies that cater to the unique needs and objectives of various stakeholders.

While there is no one-size-fits-all solution, many aspects of cyber capacity building can be universally applied. Recognizing this diversity in approaches ensures that initiatives can be tailored to specific contexts while still adhering to overarching objectives.

Given the transnational nature of cyber threats, international coordination is imperative. Collaborative efforts among nations and organizations are necessary to effectively address cyber challenges and leverage resources efficiently.

Engaging stakeholders from diverse sectors, including government, industry, civil society, and academia, is essential for success. Cooperation and collaboration among these stakeholders enhance the legitimacy and effectiveness of cyber capacity-building initiatives.

Although cybersecurity may not always be prioritized by governments and organizations, its importance cannot be understated. Elevating cyber capacity building as a priority ensures that resources are allocated effectively to address evolving threats and challenges.

Moving from identifying needs to delivering tangible outcomes is essential. Action-oriented approaches that focus on implementation and delivery are necessary to drive meaningful progress in cyber capacity-building initiatives.

APPENDIX A: Sample Cyber Engagement Form

Mil to Mil Engagement Request Form
Request No 1

Submit Completed Requests to:
EUCOM J67 – Ms. Jane Doe
U.S. Embassy, Bandaria – MAJ J. Doe

Requesting Organization:	CYBER DEFENSE UNIT / BANDARIA CYBER COMMAND	Date of Request:	JAN 11, 2024
Bandarian (BND) POC Contact Information			
Rank / Name	COL Richard Smith	Organization	Cyber Cooperation Division
Position	Cyber Analyst – Cooperation Division	Email:	Richard.Smith@bandaria.mil
Telephone:	+12345678910	Website:	Bandaria.mil
Event or Engagement Information			
Event Title:	CYBER DEFENSE WORKSHOP		
Event Location – City or Training Area:	Bandarian Capital	Event Dates:	NLT MAR, 2024

Event Type – Select All That Apply (X)		Purpose of Event	
X	In-Country Event (ICE)	Information and lessons learned exchange	
	Out of Country Event (OCE)	USA	
	Exercise (EXE)		
	Multi-Lateral Engagement (MLE)		
	Senior Leader Visit (SLV)		
X	State Partnership Event (SPP)	Hawaii State	**Desired Outcome**
	Meeting (MTG)		Technical information exchange
	Other		

Expected Number of Participants			
BND:	2	US:	3

Select US Organizations Requested to Participate (X)			
USCYBERCOM		AFCYBER	
JFHQ - Cyber		ARCYBER	X
USAREUR J6		MARFOR	
OTHER: Specify			

Content / Agenda / Itinerary / Description

APPENDIX B: Sample CRIF Proposal

COUNTERING RUSSIAN INFLUENCE FUND –

FOREIGN MILITARY FINANCING PROGRAM

PROPOSAL FY 23

SECTION 1 – BASIC INFORMATION	
Country Recipient	Bandaria (BND)
Project Name	BND MoD Cyber Defense and Digital Infrastructure Upgrade
Project Originator	Mr. John Doe, FMS, FMF Program Manager, ODC Bandaria, john.doe.civ@mail.mil; JohnDoe@state.gov; +12345678910
Coordination with the Embassy, DoD, and SPP	US Embassy: LTC Richard Roe, SDO/DATT, US Embassy Bandaria, RichardRoe@state.gov CDR Jane Roe, ODC Chief, US Embassy Bandaria, JaneRoe@state.gov John Doe, Econ Chief, US Embassy Bandaria, JohnDoe@state.gov CCMD: John Smith, ECJ67, EUCOM, john.smith.civ@mail.mil SPP: LTC Jane Smith, State National Guard G-6 Cyber Defense Chief, jane.smith.mil@mail.mil
SECTION 2 – STRATEGIC CONTENT	
ICS Objective	**(U) Mission Objective 4.1:** More capable, stronger Bandarian government institutions improve regional security and border control, thereby enhancing shared responsibilities in promoting regional and global security. **(U) Mission Objective 4.2:** Strengthen Bandarian capacity to actively participate in NATO, EU, and UN exercises and operations; Bandaria plays a significant role in supporting NATO's goals.
SECTION 3 – PARTNER NATION CAPABILITY AND CAPACITY	
Intended Recipient Unit or Organization	J-6 General Staff of the Armed Forces of Bandaria, Ministry of Defense, MoD Military CSIRT
Threat / Capability Gap	Bandarian Armed Forces are currently in the process of identifying and replacing legacy computer systems across all military branches, as such, support is needed to replace these technologies that reached end of life, procure, and install new hardware/software. The Bandarian Armed Forces need to establish a state-of-the-art Security Operations Center (SOC) to protect their military networks from Advanced Persistent Threats (APT) and cybercrime Actors. NATO Light Infantry Battalion Group (INF-L-BNG) is a capability target that requires certain equipment and technologies to achieve, like a Mobile CSIRT and Command, Control, and Information Systems (C2IS), which currently does not exist or offered through degraded Yugoslav (legacy) C4I systems and equipment. BND continues to be a potential target of sophisticated cyber attacks against defense and government information technology (IT) networks, systems, and assets, of which many malicious anomalies have been found embedded within the MoD systems. While the MoD has been able to handle many of these anomalies utilizing open-source software, it is imperative to establish a defense in-depth approach using state-of-the-art technology software and hardware to counter sophisticated cyber threats.

SMART Objective	Fully funding this proposal will support national, regional, and NATO cyber defense capabilities and assist BND MoD in meeting its NATO capability targets to be a capable and ready force that supports the U.S., NATO Allies, and partners.	
SECTION 4 – PROJECT SPEND PLAN		
Training	Information Technology (IT) training with subject matter experts (SMEs) from a U.S. vendor can assist with establishing a sustainable cyber range program local to military establishments for continued cyber education and knowledge exchange. Recommend the training requirement to be tied together under one vendor who can provide both, training and logistical support. Also, recommend the State Partner to be involved in all phases of implementation.	$50,000
Advisers and Contracted Logistical Support	Contractor for cyber ($100K USD) and for SOC infrastructure upgrade ($50K)	$150,000
Equipment	Deployable /Field-ready C4I Capability o One (1) Fully trained signal unit operating Mobile CIRT to support operations in accordance with the NATO Federated Military Network (FMN). o One (1) Mobile CSIRT system with cyber range hardware and software Additional SOC Capabilities o Upgrade SOC equipment through technology replacement and installation of new hardware. o Upgrade SOC software through procurement and installation of Endpoint Detection Response (EDR) for improved visibility, security, and vulnerability management.	$100,00
Sustainment	Spare parts and sustainment services (24 months)	$20,000
Other	Misc. components in support of system upgrades	$10,000
Total		$330,000
SECTION 5 – ROLE OF THE PARTNER NATION		
Political Will	BND continues to commit national funds toward land forces and cyber security modernization. The BND government and the BND military are working towards establishing knowledge sharing and continuing development of military and civil institutions. The BND Military is striving to meet NATO capability targets and participate as a security contributor to the Alliance in the next 5 years. They continue to support efforts to combat corruption and organized crime and strengthen their cohesiveness as an organization through institutional capacity-building efforts. The new Prime Minister has emphasized the Bandoria government's goals in strengthening ties with NATO and Euro-Atlantic relations.	
Status of Engagement with Partner Nation	The ODC office is co-located in the BND MoD, and DoD enjoys an open, continuous, and healthy relationship due to this setup. BND MoD and General Staff representatives, as well as cyber team members have been closely involved in developing this CRIF proposal, including identifying existing gaps and requirements as it pertains to BND military and NATO requirements. This proposal, if approved, will enable BND to continue to move forward in reaching their Armed Forces' modernization plans as coordinated through previous CRIF, FMF, and SPP mil-mil exchange engagements and initiatives.	

Expected Timeline for LOR Submission	An LOR submission can be expected within 120 days of funding approval.
Sustainment Planning	BND continues to maintain a good track record of sustaining equipment. BND has a self-funded modernization budget barrier, and this proposal would provide them with additional means of overcoming internal and external budgetary obstacles in support of the U.S. and NATO strategies.
SECTION 6 – RISKS AND CHALLENGES	
Political	In early 2020, the BND government received a vote of no confidence in Parliament which led to a change of ministerial leadership. The new government has replaced the PM and MINDEF offices to support the country to shift more towards EU membership and NATO participation, including 4% GDP defense spending goals by 2025.
Institutional	BND's long-term strategic planning remains stable but still presents an institutional issue. The BND MoD does not have enough personnel to sustain multiple major acquisition projects or strategic defense reviews. This proposal will strive to synchronize with ODC's Bandaria to ensure organic capacity-building efforts within the MoD. The ODC will help the BND MoD to examine the defense and security landscape, identify current and emerging threats, and then decide how best to organize and equip the Armed Forces with future capabilities.
Conduct and Appearances	Leahy law compliance and vetting will be conducted as necessary to ensure the U.S. Government funds are not used for assistance to units of foreign security forces where there is credible information implicating that unit in the commission of gross violations of human rights. Bandoria seeks to be a provider of security and stability in the region. The US Embassy in Bandoria supports this proposal and its efforts.
Absorptive Capacity	**Human Resources:** BND is expanding the size of its armed forces with a focus on staffing the recipient units of this project. **Operations and Maintenance:** BND has a good track record of sustaining end-of-life/legacy equipment. This proposal, if approved, would support the replacement of outdated software and hardware. ODC assesses the equipment and training provided through this proposal would be well maintained. **Long-Term Sustainment:** BND understands the long-term sustainment requirements associated with the equipment that would be provided. **Integration:** BND can integrate the capability on its own. However, it will be important to involve the State Partner in this integration and have the appropriate training with US-sourced Methods, Techniques, and Tools (MTT) to ensure successful and complete integration.
Other	The newly established Bandorian government is temporary with a one-year term. If the BND government is voted out in the coming year's elections, we could see a slowdown or change in interaction rates with the MoD, although this is not anticipated.
SECTION 7 – INTEGRATION WITH OTHER EFFORTS	
Available Resources	Previous FMF grants have been fully consumed and the only remaining uncommitted funds are minor (less than $5K total).
Past Related Assistance	The U.S. has provided FMF in the past to support Cyber Experts.
Coinciding Partner Efforts	BND has a modernization program for its entire land force. However, limited resources have been received from their modernization budget due to slower-than-expected GDP.

Third Country Donations	Canada has offered to support to BND MoD with cybersecurity training, which might overlap with this proposal in the cyber domain.

SECTION 8 – OTHER	
Remarks	Bandorian MoD and their Cyber Defense Team have the workforce and capability, along with doctrine that is currently being modernized, to develop, train, test, implement, and exercise Tactics, Techniques, Procedures, and laws that mitigate the threat of malign cyber activities. What they need more of is training and tools to expand and modernize their capabilities and workforce for better cyber defense and partner knowledge sharing through NATO CERT-CERT cooperation and engagement.

APPENDIX C: Performance-based Site Survey Assessment Template

MILESTONE	INDICATOR	YES	NO	PROPOSED CYBER CAPACITY BUILDING ACTIVITY
SECURITY OPERATIONS CENTER	PN has developed, implemented, and exercised the Tactics, Techniques, and Procedures (TTPs) to perform core defensive cyberspace operations functions.	PN has developed TTPs, standard / tailored playbooks for proactive threat hunting and Incident response and can demonstrate TTP proficiency in cyber exercises.	☐ Y	☐ N	If YES, help PN exercise incident response TTPs in a bi-lateral or multi-lateral cyber drill to hone PN skills and ability to conduct Defensive Cyber Operations. If NO, help PN develop standard and tailored playbooks for incident response and threat hunting in a workshop-like event with force providers, like the SPP.

SECURITY OPERATIONS MATURITY				
PN can both detect, respond, and prevent cyber intrusions.	Mean Time to Detect (MTTD): Threat present on the network for less than 30 days before detection.	☐ Y	☐ N	If YES, help PN achieve an industry standard for Mean Time to Detect (MTTD) from weeks to days, Mean Time to Respond (MTTR) from days to hours, and Mean Time to Prevent (MTTP) by developing better security analytics and training personnel on assessing threats to determine acceptable risks. If NO, help PN decrease the time to detect (MTTD) an incident from months to weeks by having the right means to collect, discover, and assess threats. Also, helps PN to decrease the time to patch vulnerabilities
	Mean Time to Respond (MTTR): Recover or Resolving an incident is less than 15 days.	☐ Y	☐ N	
	Mean Time to Prevent (MTTP): Patch vulnerabilities once discovered.	☐ Y	☐ N	

		Y	N	
				(MTTP) and respond (MTTR) by investigating, neutralizing, and recovering after an incident.
CSIRT CAPABILITY	PN has a 24/7 Computer Security Incident Response Team (CSIRT) in FOC to support the cyber incident response function with a cyber Common Operating Picture (COP) across all military networks.	PN has a fully functional cyber operations center with 24/7 manning to support indications and warning (I&W), incident response, threat hunting, and forensics.	☐	☐	If YES, enhance PN training capability with access to video training courses for IT professionals. If NO, help PN with recruitment efforts and business case development to convert to a 24/7 schedule. Help PN with funding requests to provide a Security Orchestration, Automation, and Response (SOAR) solution to automate incident investigation and response to

SIEM CAPABILITY	PN has employed cyber tools/solutions, like Security Information Event Management (SIEM), to detect intrusions and defend its military networks.	PN has operational SIEM aggregating logs from all cyber assets across the networks.	☐ Y	☐ N	If YES, coordinate workshops for PN to enhance threat hunting capability with threat intel-based searches and feeds using advanced analytics. If NO, help PN with funding requests and proposals to upgrade their infrastructure with an operational SIEM capability, preferably with SOAR capability.
					augment the 24/7 CSIRT support. A 7-day SOC requires at least 4 crews, which requires a major cultural, organizational, and operational change.

NIDS CAPABILITY	PN has employed cyber tools/solutions, like a Network Intrusion Detection System (NIDS), to mitigate intrusions and defend its military networks.	PN has operational NIDS to monitor and analyze network traffic across all segments.	☐ Y ☐ N	If YES, coordinate workshops for PN to enhance NIDS placement, deployment, and management. If NO, help PN with funding requests and proposals to upgrade their infrastructure with an operational NIDS capability.
HIDS CAPABILITY	PN has employed cyber tools/solutions, like a Host-based Intrusion Detection System (HIDS), to mitigate intrusions and defend its military networks.	PN has operational HIDS to monitor and analyze traffic on individual hosts across all networks.	☐ Y ☐ N	If YES, coordinate workshops for PN to enhance threat-hunting capability using open-source HIDS to hone skills and improve proficiency. If NO, help PN with funding requests and proposals for an operational HIDS capability.

CYBER RANGE (VTE)	PN can utilize a Virtual Training Environment (VTE) to simulate cybersecurity/ response actions.	PN uses VTE to exercise simulation, cybersecurity education, testing network changes, or patch deployment.	☐ Y	☐ N	If YES, coordinate with PN to host cyber exercises to improve teamwork and team capabilities. Coordinate workshops for PN to help utilize the VTE efficiently for hands-on and specialized training. If NO, help PN with funding requests and proposals for operating and maintaining a VTE. Help PN with the VTE questionnaire and checklist to determine features and options if funding is already approved.

CERT ACCREDITATION	PN's CSIRT meets all qualifications to become a full member of FIRST (Forum of Incident Response and Security Teams).	PN has technically qualified and certified CSIRT members to support their Security Operations Center (SOC).	☐ Y ☐ N	If YES, enhance PN training capability with access to video training courses for IT professionals. If NO, coordinate a Subject Matter Experts Engagement (SME) with NATO-affiliated operational CERTs to share best practices and TTPs supporting this objective.
NATIONAL COLLABORATION	PN has a cyber-focused inter-agency information exchange and cooperation with public and private industry sectors.	PN has established a joint regularly occurring cyber board to enhance cyber defense capabilities across the different military organizations.	☐ Y ☐ N	If YES, ask PN to share lessons learned and benefits gained from establishing a cyber board to ensure national laws are aligned with international standards and NATO directives. If NO, help PN engage with their inter-agency

				directorates and private / public sectors to unite cyber stakeholders to adequately secure infrastructure and conduct DCO.
DEPLOYABLE CSIRT	PN has mobile cyber support and incident response kits for tactical military units' deployment in the field.	PN has an operational mobile cyber incident response kit dedicated to mobilizing the NATO-Light Infantry Battalion and meets NATO's combat readiness evaluation standards.	☐ ☐ Y N	If YES, ask PN to share lessons learned and benefits gained from operating and maintaining a mobile CSIRT. If NO, help PN with funding requests and proposals for obtaining such capability.
COOP	PN has a continuity of operations and disaster recovery plan with practiced drills.	PN has an established disaster recovery plan for multiple sites in case of a cyber attack, natural disaster, or installation service failure.	☐ ☐ Y N	If YES, help PN exercise disaster recovery plans with Allies and partners. If NO, recommend SME disaster recovery workshops with the PN.

INTEROPERABILITY	PN has cyber assets and institutional knowledge that are interoperable with US / NATO systems.	PN's cyber tools are standardized among U.S. and NATO Allies and are interoperable during bilateral and multi-lateral engagements.	☐ Y ☐ N	If YES, facilitate PN exchange of various cyber defense-related information and assistance to improve cyber incident prevention, resilience and response capability among NATO Allies and partners. If NO, recommend CND tools standardization to the PN for interoperability and cohesion purposes.
SUPPLY CHAIN	PN has established Risk Management policies for new and existing IT software and hardware assets.	PN conducts risk assessments for supply chain compromise, procurement practices, security baselines, and vulnerability management.	☐ Y ☐ N	If YES, ask PN to share lessons learned and best practices in conducting this assessment. If NO, include the topic for SME Engagement.

RED TEAM SUPPORT	PN conducts red teaming exercises to include activating defensive measures, assessing the effectiveness of people, processes, and technology, and implementing post-exercise enhancements in these areas.	PN can regularly conduct penetration testing of the network boundary, DMZ (Demilitarized), and internal networks to identify security control gaps.	☐ ☐ Y N	If YES, help PN exercise penetration testing TTPs in a bi-lateral or multi-lateral cyber drill to hone PN skills and ability to conduct DCO. If NO, help PN develop standard/tailored playbooks for red teaming in a workshop-like event, preferably with force providers, e.g., MARFOREUR.
HUNT FORWARD OPERATIONS	PN is willing to accept. Hunt Forward team deployment to conduct DCO on their national defense networks or Foreign Military Networks.	Previous HFO engagements have helped PN bolster homeland defense and increase the resiliency of critical networks to shared cyber threats.	☐ ☐ Y N	If YES, request additional HFOs support and coordinate the visit with the country team. If NO, offer PN SME Engagement instead to share TTPs and best practices on how

				CNMF teams conduct HFO support missions. Hunt Forward Operations are defensive cyber operations that are intel-driven and partner-requested. As of May 2022, CNMF has conducted 28 HFOs globally in 16 countries, including Lithuania, Montenegro, North Macedonia, and Ukraine.
INFORMATION EXCHANGE	PN has unclassified and classified cyber threat information exchange mechanisms in place.	PN has an information sharing policy or SOP, access to the BICES network and MISP tool on unclassified and restricted networks.	☐ Y ☐ N	If YES, enhance Information Exchange bi-lateral by ensuring the PN Indications and Warning mission is adequately supported using publicly available cyber tools and methods.

			Y	N	
		PN can take action on information shared for DCO purposes.			If NO, coordinate an Information Exchange visit with the PN to explain various mechanisms to exchange classified and unclassified information in bilateral and multilateral formats. PN agrees to the SOP that will be outlined during the visit.
RECRUITMENT & RETENTION	PN has established retention management and recruiting of cyber professionals.	PN Recruiting Command engages in marketing efforts to promote cyber forces recruitment and brand awareness to generate interest among youth.	☐	☐	If YES, help PN establish competitive in-person Capture The Flag (CTF) and eSports events to increase cyber capabilities within the military to generate the cyber forces needed to bolster the PN's military cyber workforce.

				If NO, coordinate an SME Engagement with U.S. military recruitment organizations to share best practices and TTPs supporting this objective.

APPENDIX D – CYSFAM Model
Assessment Questions

Cybersecurity Focus Area Maturity Model (CYSFAM)					
Focus Areas	**Capabilities**				
	A	B	C	D	E
Organizational and Technical					
Server Protection					
End-user Controls					
Social Engineering Controls					
Network Security					
Application Security					
Cryptography					
Mobile Security					
Vulnerability Management					
Organizational					
Cybersecurity Incident Management					
Cybersecurity Awareness					
Cybersecurity Governance					

Source: Department of Information and Computing Sciences at Utrecht University

The following 144 yes/no questions cover 11 focus areas and constitute the Cybersecurity Focus Area Maturity (CYSFAM) model, version 1.0. Please refer to the main journal publication," CYSFAM: The Cybersecurity Focus Area Maturity Model," for further information.

i. *Server Protection*

Area	Capability Maturity	Capability
	A	The organization's baseline security configuration is described.
	A	Patch management is tool-supported (patch-management suites).
	A	A SIEM solution is in place.
	A	A technical compliance checking solution is in place.
	B	The baseline security configuration is based on an open standard.
	B	The deployment of patches is tested and approved at least once before deployment in the production environment.
	B	The SIEM implementation is based on a baseline set of events.
	B	Technical compliance checking is performed manually (supported by appropriate tools).
	C	The baseline security configuration is reviewed at least once a year.
	C	A process is in place that assures the organization learns about patch releases as soon as possible.
	C	The SIEM implementation includes events that were identified during a risk assessment.
	C	Technical compliance checking is performed with the assistance of automated tools (with a reporting functionality).

D		The baseline security configuration is updated after every significant configuration change or demonstrated vulnerability.
D		The prioritization of patches is risk-based; the business's cruciality is taken into account.
D		The SIEM solution is connected to a managed SOC for a correlation of events, and is connected to the organizations' incident management system.
D		The technical compliance checking solution is connected to the organization's incident management system.

ii. *End-user Controls*

Area	Capability Maturity	Capability
	A	The organization has a policy on user authentication.
	A	The organization employs an enterprise-wide, standardized anti-malware protection solution.
	A	The organization employs an automated patch management solution.
	A	The organization makes a distinction between normal end-users and privileged end-users (local administrators).
	B	The organization employs one-factor authentication for all relevant assets.
	B	The organization employs multiple anti-malware protection solutions in an enterprise-wide manner.
	B	The organization employs a standardized, enterprise-wide automated patch management solution.
	B	Using local administrator rights is an auditable event.
	C	The organization has the (in-house) capabilities to provide two- or three-factor authentication for relevant assets.
	C	The organization employs application control whitelisting.
	C	The organization has defined a Patch and Vulnerability Group (PVG) that is

		formally responsible for the organization's patch management.
	C	The organizations' decision to provide local-administrator rights is taken risk-based, and provided by a formal end-user management committee.
	D	The organization employs a number of factors in the authentication process in a risk-based manner, based on their authentication policy.
	D	The organization has an anti-malware policy that describes the handling and escalation channels of a malware infection, AND the organization tests the effectiveness of the anti-malware protection solution on a periodic basis.
	D	The organization evaluates the effectiveness of the patch management solution on aperiodic basis, in a consistent manner AND a risk assessment of every patch is a common practice.

iii. *Social Engineering*

Area	Capability Maturity	Capability
	A	The organization has implemented automated tools to circumvent poor, human-originated decisions.
	A	The organization has implemented social engineering defenses within the information security policies.
	B	The organization embraces management practices to foster a productive work environment (e.g., decreasing stress and increasing self-care).
	B	The organization undertakes risk management assessments in the context of Social Engineering.
	C	The organization has a training/awareness program in which employees are trained in both cognitive biases and historical accidents.
	C	The organization has developed a security management framework.
	D	The defense against Social Engineering threats is an integral part of the organizations' Security Management process.

iv. Network Security

Area	Capability Maturity	Capability
	A	The organization uses relevant security documentation in configuring network components.
	A	By automated means, the organization ensures that only ports, protocols, and services with validated business needs are running on each system.
	A	The organization designs its network using a minimum of a three-tier architecture (DMZ, middleware, private network).
	B	The organization uses a configuration management system to record and document the configuration files of network devices.
	B	The organization operates all critical infrastructural services (DNS, file, mail, web, database) on a separate physical or virtual machine.
	B	The organization has an (operational) method to quickly alter ACLs, rules, signatures, blocks, and so forth in case of an attack.
	C	The organization manages the network infrastructure by using a separate VLAN for which the routing access is controlled.

	C	The organization has placed application firewalls in front of any critical servers.
	C	The organization segments the enterprise network into multiple separate trust zones.
	D	The organization manages the network infrastructure on an entirely different physical stream of connectivity.
	D	The organizations' firewalls that protect critical components have functionality that automatically blocks unauthorized traffic, which in turn alerts about it.
	D	The organization assures that entering and leaving a trust zone is an audited event.

v. *Web Application Security*

Area	Capability Maturity	Capability
	A	The organization has implemented Version Control in its Application Change Management process.
	A	The organization employs Secure Development Lifecycle activities on a manual, ad-hoc basis.
	B	The organizations employ Source Code or Web Scanning tools.
	B	The organization trains its staff specifically on Application Security (awareness-training, followed by technical training).
	C	The organization employs both Source Code and Web scanning Tools, and its results are adopted in a Defect Management System.
	C	The organization has assigned internal "Red Teams."
	D	The organization automates all testing (not only security testing but also other test-disciplines, such as regression testing)
	D	The organization integrates its Application Security vulnerability-assessment process with relevant governing parties (such as IRM and Compliance).

vi. *Cyber Security Incident Management*

Area	Capabiliy Maturity	Capability
	A	The CIRT is mandated by upper management.
	A	There is a skillset description available describing the required skills to operate in the CIRT.
	A	The CIRT is able to get access to the complete IT resources list, but there is a process in place that regulates this access.
	A	The organization has a policy describing the security incident prevention, detection, and resolution processes.
	B	The authority and responsibility of the CIRT are described in an official service description.
	B	The organization provides internal CIRT training (of any kind), AND the CIRT staffing pays attention to personal resilience (staffing during holidays, weekends, et cetera).
	B	The CIRT receives its vulnerability/trend/scanning information from reliable sources.
	B	The CIRT has a way of handling "common mailbox names" (security@; cert@; abuse@) AND has a reporting process in place.

	C	The levels of service the CIRT offers are described in a service level description.
	C	The organization offers its CIRT members external technical and communication training.
	C	On a regular basis, the CIRT receives the outcome of prevention, detection, and resolution toolsets.
	C	The organization documented the CIRT emergency reachability process, which is also communicated and tested frequently.
	D	The organization has a security incident whistleblowers program in place, which is mandated by upper management.
	D	External networking with other CIRTs or related knowledge-sharing platforms is a CIRT habit.
	D	The CIRT has a robust and resilient (fail-safe) setup of all communication methods. (Internet/email/phone) AND the CIRT incident management system is isolated from other incident management systems.
	D	The CIRT has a process in place that describes the different escalation scenarios (governance level, press function, legal function, et cetera).

vii. Cyber Security Awareness

Area	Capability Maturity	Capability
	A	The compliance or audit standards that the organization needs to adhere to are identified.
	A	The security awareness requirements for these standards are known – possibly coordinated by a compliance or audit officer.
	A	The organization possesses the security awareness training material to meet the compliance and audit demands.
	A	There is a process that tracks security awareness training participation.
	B	The security awareness program is actively promoted by stakeholders in the organization.
	B	The organization has conducted a security awareness level baseline measurement.
	B	The security awareness program is managed by a project charter – which in turn is governed by a steering committee.
	B	The security awareness training is tailored towards the needs of specific roles.
	C	The security awareness program is reviewed for effectiveness on a periodic basis.
	C	The organization actively surveys staff that has participated in the program for

		feedback.
	C	The security awareness program is updated when changes in the technology, threat-landscape, business processes, or compliance standards occur.
	C	(Optional – provided that the data is available) The organization compares its current security awareness measurements to earlier baselines.
	D	The organization has identified metrics that relate to the business goals of the security awareness training.
	D	The organization documents how (and when) these metrics are measured.
	D	The organization has identified to whom the results are communicated and in which manner.
	E	The organization executes its security awareness training metrics measurement.

viii. Cryptography

Area	Capability Maturity	Capability
	A	Key generation is consistent within applications, AND recipients are authenticated before the key is handed out.
	A	The access to key storage is defined in the application's individual processes, AND key backup is consistent within applications.
	A	Updating and renewing keys is dealt with and is consistent throughout applications AND recovery processes are implemented per application.
	A	Key revocation is consistent within applications, AND key disposal processes are implemented.
	B	Key generation follows a standard that has attention to symmetric and asymmetric standards AND the symmetric and asymmetric key distribution is always mutually authenticated and secured.
	B	Key storage containers ensure assuring authentication of the recipient, AND key backup containers ensure assuring authentication of the recipient.
	B	Key updating is dealt with by automated capabilities AND recovery processes per application are implemented.

	B	Key revocation is driven by a number of processes, namely key notification, key-generation, and key distribution, AND encrypted material is removed during the key disposal process.
	C	Key generation standards are managed at the organizational level, AND all applications in the enterprise comply with these standards.
	C	Key storage standards are managed at the organizational level, AND key backup standards are managed at the organizational level.
	C	Key update standards are managed at the organizational level, AND key recovery processes are consistent with standards.
	C	Key revocation standards are managed at the organizational level, AND key disposal standards are managed at the organizational level.
	D	Key generation endures continuous testing to ensure compliance, AND there is a process in place to evaluate (new) standards for key generation.
	D	Key storage endures continuous testing to ensure compliance, AND there is a process in place to evaluate (new) standards for key backup.
	D	Key updating and the technology it supports are continuously evaluated AND there is a process in place for evaluating

		additions to the key recovery process.
	D	Key revocation and the technology it supports are continuously evaluated AND there is a process in place to evaluate (new) standards for key disposal.

ix.   Governance

Area	Capability Maturity	Capability
	A	The organization has defined an organization-wide cyber security policy.
	A	The organizations' second line of defense addresses Root Cause Analyses for cyber security risk and mitigating controls.
	A	The organizations' internal audit capability is organized in a way that it can audit a broad range of cyber security domains.
	A	The organization has adequate funding to support the implementation of cyber security.
	B	The organization's cyber security policy contains the roles and responsibilities of the three lines of defense.
	B	The organization's second line of defense assesses cyber security risk within the organization's change management process.
	B	The organizations' internal audit capability determines the frequency of audit risk- based AND the organizations' internal audit capability carries out both a ToD (Test of Design) and a ToE (Test of Effectiveness).

	B	The organization has established a Senior Management committee that takes an active interest in cybersecurity matters.
	C	The cyber security policy is mandated in all of the organizations' groups and entities –including subsidiaries.
	C	The organizations' second line of defense challenges the cyber security risk assessments of the first line of defense on a periodic basis.
	C	The organization has defined processes for escalating serious breaches/cyber security incidents.
	C	The organization has conducted an external review of its cyber security policies.
	D	The organization has aligned its cyber security strategy with its business strategy, AND key cyber security initiatives and timelines are defined.
	D	The organization's second line of defense actively monitors the identification and remediation of findings dealt with by the first line of defense AND the organization's second line of defense incorporates cyber security risk in the operational risk appetite.

x. *Mobile Security*

Area	Capability Maturity	Capability
	A	The organization has a repeatable process in place to identify smartphone systems and data owners.
	A	The organization has a repeatable process in place regarding smartphone information (at least elaborating upon the management of authentication, removable media, ownership, restoration and continuity, and backup policies/schemes).
	A	The organization has a repeatable process in place regarding infrastructural affairs (at least elaborating on configuration policies, communication policies, physical threats, infrastructural system ownership, and supplier/service delivery management).
	A	The organization has a repeatable process in place regarding people matters (at least elaborating on user awareness programs, control frameworks, rights and privileges, and governance reporting).
	B	The organization has a defined process in place to identify smartphone systems and data owners.
	B	The organization has a defined process in place regarding smartphone information (at least elaborating upon the management of authentication, removable media,

		ownership, restoration and continuity, and backup policies/schemes).
	B	The organization has a defined process in place regarding infrastructural affairs (at least elaborating on configuration policies, communication policies, physical threats, infrastructural system ownership, and supplier/service delivery management).
	B	The organization has a defined process in place regarding people matters (at least elaborating on user awareness programs, control frameworks, rights and privileges, and governance reporting).
	C	The organization has a managed process in place to identify smartphone systems and data owners, in which metrics are defined.
	C	The organization has a managed process in place regarding smartphone information (at least elaborating upon the management of authentication, removable media, ownership, restoration and continuity, and backup policies/schemes), in which metrics are defined.
	C	The organization has a managed process in place regarding infrastructural affairs (at least elaborating on configuration policies, communication policies, physical threats, infrastructural system ownership, and supplier/service delivery management), in which metrics are defined.

	C	The organization has a managed process in place regarding people matters (at least elaborating on user awareness programs, control frameworks, rights and privileges, and governance reporting), in which metrics are defined.
	D	The organization has a fully optimized process in place to identify smartphone systems and data owners, in which metrics are defined and respected.
	D	The organization has a fully optimized process in place regarding smartphone information (at least elaborating upon the management of authentication, removable media, ownership, restoration and continuity, and backup policies/schemes), in which metrics are defined and respected.
	D	The organization has a fully optimized process in place regarding infrastructural affairs (at least elaborating on configuration policies, communication policies, physical threats, infrastructural system ownership, and supplier/service delivery management), in which metrics are defined and respected.
	D	The organization has a fully optimized process in place regarding people matters (at least elaborating on user awareness programs, control frameworks, rights and privileges, and governance reporting), in which metrics are defined and respected.

xi.   *Vulnerability Management*

Area	Capability Maturity	Capability
	A	The organization runs scheduled vulnerability scans on all production machines on their network.
	A	The organization has subscribed itself to vulnerability intelligence services, and this information is incorporated into the vulnerability management process.
	B	The organization runs scheduled vulnerability scans on all DTAP machines on their network.
	B	The organization measures the delay in the patching of vulnerabilities.
	C	The organization feeds a Vulnerability Management System (VMS) with the outcomes of the periodic machine scans.
	C	The organization has a process in which vulnerabilities are risk-rated based on the assets' characteristics.
	D	The VMS compares systems to configuration baselines automatically.
	D	There is a Role Based Access Control (RBAC) solution to regulate who has access to the vulnerability management platform.

APPENDIX E: National Guard State Partnership Program Map

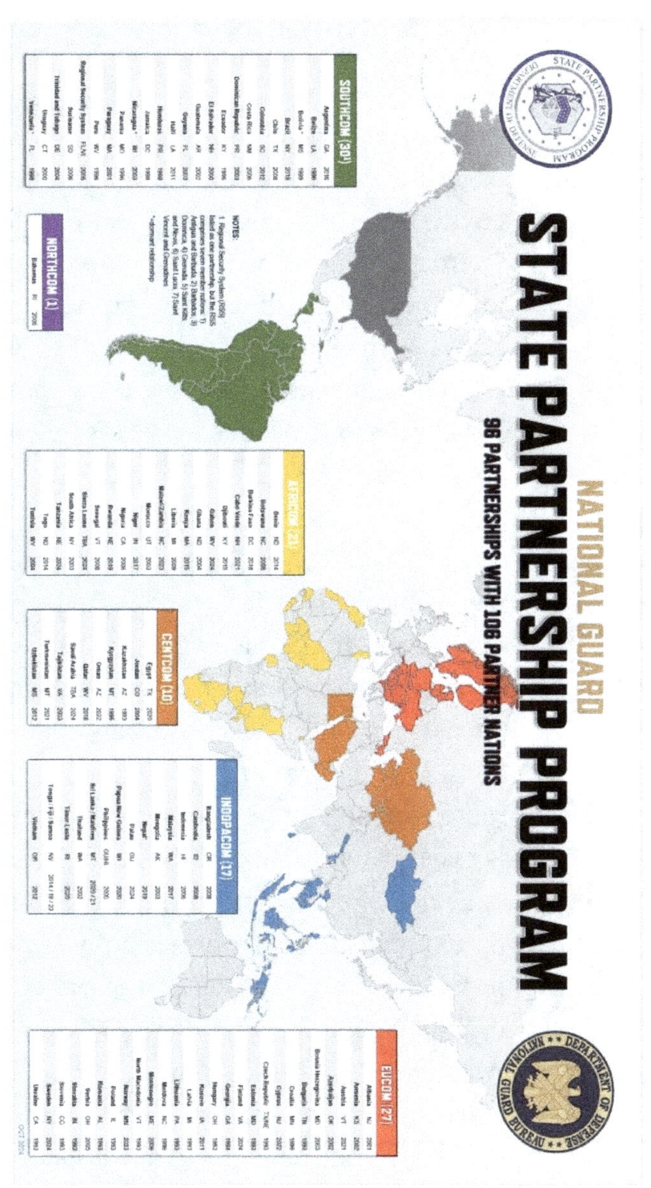

APPENDIX F: Lexicon Of Cyberspace Security Cooperation Terms and Related Definitions

Acronym	Definition
Cyberspace	A global domain within the information environment consists of the interdependent networks of information technology infrastructures and resident data, including the Internet, telecommunications networks, computer systems, and embedded processors and controllers. (JP 3-12).
Cyberspace Attack or Cyber Attack	Actions taken in cyberspace that create noticeable denial effects (i.e., degradation, disruption, or destruction) in cyberspace or manipulation that leads to denial that appears in a physical domain and is considered a form of fire. (JP 3-12). The more commonly referenced industry term is cyber network attack (CNA).
Cyberspace Capability	A device or computer program, including any combination of software, firmware, or hardware, designed to create an effect in or through cyberspace. (JP 3-12)
Cyber Capacity	Activities designed to educate, train and equip partner nations to protect themselves and assist the United States in

Building (CB)	addressing cyber threats that target our mutual interests. CB initiatives are activities that build strategic partnerships that promote cybersecurity best practices. The capacity building allowed for the opportunity to share cyber threat information and enabled the US and our partners to better defend domestic critical infrastructure and global supply chains, as well as focus the whole of government cyber engagements.
Cyberspace Defense	Actions taken within protected cyberspace to defeat specific threats that have breached or are threatening to breach cyberspace security measures include actions to detect, characterize, counter, and mitigate threats, including malware or the unauthorized activities of users, and to restore the system to a secure configuration. (JP 3-12).
Cyberspace Exploitation	Actions taken in cyberspace to gain intelligence, maneuver, collect information, or perform other enabling actions required to prepare for future military operations. (JP 3-12) This term is more commonly referenced industry term is cyber network exploitation (CNE).
Cyberspace Operations	The employment of cyberspace capabilities where the primary purpose is to achieve objectives in or through cyberspace. Also called CO. (JP 3-0).

Cyberspace Security Operations	Actions taken within protected cyberspace to prevent unauthorized access to, exploitation of, or damage to computers, electronic communications systems, and other information technology, including platform information technology, as well as the information contained therein, to ensure its availability, integrity, authentication, confidentiality, and nonrepudiation. (JP 3-12).
Cyberspace Superiority	The degree of dominance in cyberspace by one force that permits the secure, reliable conduct of operations by that force and its related land, air, maritime, and space forces at a given time and place without prohibitive interference. (JP 3-12).
Blue Cyberspace	The term "blue cyberspace" denotes areas in cyberspace protected by the US, its mission partners, and other areas DOD may be ordered to protect. Although DOD has standing orders to protect only the Department of Defense information network (DODIN), cyberspace forces prepare, on order, and when requested by other authorities, to defend or secure other United States Government (US) or other cyberspace, as well as cyberspace related to critical infrastructure and key resources (CIKR) of the US and PNs (JP 3-12).

Red Cyberspace	The term "red cyberspace" refers to those portions of cyberspace owned or controlled by an adversary or enemy. In this case, "controlled" means more than simply "having a presence on" since threats may have clandestine access to elements of global cyberspace where their presence is undetected and without apparent impact on the operation of the system. Here, controlled means the ability to direct the operations of a link or node of cyberspace to the exclusion of others. (JP 3-12).
Gray Cyberspace	All cyberspace that does not meet the description of either "blue" or "red" is referred to as "gray." Cyberspace-controlled PN requesting Cyber ICB may transition from "gray" to "blue" as PN cyber capacity increases in maturity and effectiveness.
Security Cooperation	Security cooperation (SC) encompasses all Department of Defense (DOD) interactions, programs, and activities with foreign security forces (FS) and their institutions to build relationships that help promote US interests and enable partner nations (Ps) to provide the US access to territory, infrastructure, information, and resources; and/or to build and apply their capacity and capabilities consistent with US defense objectives. It includes but is

	not limited to military engagements with foreign defense and security establishments (including those governmental organizations that primarily perform disaster or emergency response functions), DOD-administered security assistance (SA) programs, combined exercises, international armaments cooperation, and information sharing and collaboration. (JP 3-20).
Theater-wide SC Planning	SC planning is required for each PN where the GCC intends to apply resources, and SCOs prioritize their PN's requirements identified for SC activities/ investments. Once coordination with the Office of the Secretary of Defense (OSD) and DOS authorizes and funds SC activities, SC planning for each PN takes the form of mission planning among the geographic CCMD, DSCA, the applicable SCO and country team, the Service and special operations component(s), and the PN representatives.
SC Assessment	Similar to functional evaluation, operation assessment is a continuous process that evaluates changes in the O and measures the progress of executing tasks, creating effects, and achieving objectives toward attaining the desired end state of a particular military operation. Operation assessment informs planning; decision-

	makers continuously analyze the OE and the progress of operations, compared to their initial assessment, understanding, visualization, and intent; and operation assessment helps them adjust planning and operations to make efficient use of limited resources. Assessment informs decision-making by helping to establish information about the conditions present within a PN that are relevant to planning a successful SC initiative. Assessments serve at least two critical functions: providing relevant information to inform the design of SC activities, programs, or initiatives and providing baseline information to enable accurate measurement of progress as an activity, program, or initiative progresses.
SC Monitoring	Monitoring enables planners to understand changes in the operational environment (OE) based on the implementation of SC initiatives, and it further informs a commander's intent guidance for planning, prioritization, and execution. This includes monitoring individual tasks, normally using measures of performance and measures of effectiveness, and functional evaluation at the strategic level. Task monitoring includes tracking whether tasks are completed as planned, whether tasks are

	completed according to the planned timeline, whether costs are as projected, and other indicators used to determine whether planned activities are being executed successfully, and it informs leaders and decision-makers at all levels.

APPENDIX G: U.S. Security Cooperation Organizations Guide

ORGANIZATION	DESCRIPTION OF CYBER PROCESS FOR MISSION/SERVICES IN SUPPORT OF PN COORDINATING SUPPORT CB EFFORTS	PROCESS FOR COORDINATING SUPPORT	ORGANIZATION CONTACT INFORMATION
OUSDP/CYBER POLICY	Establishes and oversees the work collaboratively with policy implementation of DoD cyberspace Policy functional and policy and strategy; integrates national and regional desks, the Joint cyberspace policy and guidance with Staff, the U.S. interagency, DoD cyberspace policy; and provides other stakeholders with guidance and oversight on DoD meet Departmental cyberspace activities as they relate to objectives in cyberspace. foreign cyberspace threats, international cooperation, engagement with foreign partners and international organizations, and implementation of DoD cyberspace strategy and plans, including those related to cyberspace forces, capabilities, and their employment.	Work collaboratively with Policy functional and regional desks, the Joint Staff, the U.S. interagency, and other stakeholders to meet Departmental objectives in cyberspace.	OUSDP/Cyber Policy/Strategy, Defense, & Capabilities Div. International Team; Email: osd.pentagon.ousd-policy.mbx.cyber-security-cooperation@mail.mil
ODASD-Security Cooperation	ODASD(SC) oversees security cooperation strategic resource prioritization, implements congressional reforms to the broader SC enterprise, and drives assessment, monitoring, and evaluation (AM&E) efforts of security cooperation programs.	Reach out regarding any questions on cyber-related SSCIs or AM&E questions	https://open.defense.gov/Transparency/Security-Cooperation/

DSCA Institute for Security Governance (ISG)	As a DSCA schoolhouse, institutional capacity building provider, and DoD ICB Center of Excellence, ISG is one of the implementers of cyberspace capacity bulling and educational engagements. ISG: 1) assists in the integration of PN cyber-related requirements into ICB planning and design; 2) supports GCCs in assessing partner cyber capability gaps; 3) conducts educational and advisor programs in cybersecurity; and, 4) provides support to the cyber capacity-building community of interest.	Partner-related activities are generally coordinated directly between the relevant Country Team, combatant Command, and the ISG Functional Lead. For other matters, such as requesting ISG support (in general or not focused on a particular partner) or to suggest Ideas in support of the community of interest. Contact the ISG Functional Lead.	Email: isgcyber@nps.edu
Navy: PEO C4I/PMW740	PMW 740 of the Program Executive Office, Command, Control, Communications, Computers and Intelligence (PEO C41) provides integrated C4l solutions for international customers in support of US National Security and foreign policy objectives. We offer partner nations the ability to develop an enterprise-wide approach to cybersecurity using the Foreign Military Sales process.	Building cybersecurity capacity for partner nations includes efforts to strengthen their cyber capacity, resilience, and interoperability. Assisting partners in building cyber-secure infrastructures, protecting networks, developing their cyber workforce, and supporting institutional reform to promote the secure and open use of cyberspace.	PMW.740_Ops_Team.fct@navy.mil
Army: PEO EIS/AIT	Allied Information Technology (AIT) is the international programs office that supports SC for the Program Executive Office - Enterprise Information Systems (PEO EIS). AIT specializes in providing customized, non-standard, commercial-off-the-shelf (COTS) IT,	AIT recognizes that Country Teams would benefit from subject matter assistance to develop both technical and programmatic requirements for IT. INFOSYS and Cyber Defense projects. AIT engages early and throughout the	usarmy.belvoir.peo-eis.mbx.ait@mail.mil

	INFOSYS and Cyber Defense solutions to build resilient and resistant capable forces for our Partner Nations through the Foreign Military Sales (FMS) process.	FMF/FMS acquisition and execution process to assist Country Teams in developing accurate requirements for Letters of Request (LORs).	
USAF: AFLCMC (Air Force Life Cycle Management Center)/HNAI	HAI is the International Programs branch supporting SC Capacity Building for AFLCMC and specializes in assisting foreign partners with all aspects of integration in support of interoperability. HAI has long understood cybersecurity to be a key interoperability enabler. Over the past 10 years, we have worked with multiple Partner Nations in every Global Combatant Command to promote adoption or standards-based. Cybersecurity best practices in support of bilateral cyber risk assessments to enable secure interoperability. We also work with Partners seeking to develop organic cybersecurity capabilities in their own right.	Please contact the HNAI Cyber Lead with any questions regarding cybersecurity support or assistance with FMS Weapon System fielding or Cyber Capability Development requests.	https://www.aflcmc.af.mil/
FUNCTIONAL COMMAND			
US Cyber Command	CYBERCOM conducts cyberspace Command capacity-building activities aligned to U.S. and DoD objectives for cyberspace operations, synchronized with appropriate geographic CCMDs. CYBERCOM defers the vast majority of capacity building for cyberspace security and	Reach out to the geographic CCMD Security Cooperation Office for initial assistance.	NIPR: USCCJ54Ldrship@nsa.gov JWICS: USCC_J54_Leadership@nsa.ic.gov

	cyberspace defense to the geographic CCMDs while retaining responsibility for advanced operational training, exercises, and combined capability development with mature partners as directed by DoD International Cyberspace Security Cooperation Guidance (May 2019).		
GEOGRAPHIC COMBATANT COMMANDS			
INDOPACOM-Cyber Staff/Division	The Cyber Security Capacity Building Program (CCBP) focuses specifically on building and enhancing cyber security with allies & partners in the AOR. Works in conjunction with the Command & Control Interoperability Board (CCIBs) Country Desk Officers by having established Cyber Working Groups (CWGs). The CWGs establish the Terms of Reference & Charters to aid, guide & implement the CWGs with Partner Nations. The CWG Charters list requirements and publish a POA&M, which guides and manages the Partner Nation objectives, milestones, tasks, and training. The CWGs are hosted and facilitated with the help of our identified Lead Service Component State Partners. The CCBP has published the Cybersecurity Interoperability Playbook and the Cybersecurity Capabilities Framework (CSCF) to assist partners & allies with cybersecurity assessments.	The CCBP works in conjunction with Lead Service Components, DSCA INDOPACOM J54, and ICB representatives to submit SSCIs and Tile 10 333 Funding Proposals for the Defensive Cyber Skills Training Environment (DCSTE) (a.k.a Cyber Range) for a multitude of developing countries in the AOR.	https://www.pacom.mil/Contact/Directory/J6/

CENTCOM- Cyber staff/Division	Focuses on building and enhancing cybersecurity with partners in the AOR. Works in conjunction with the Command & Control Interoperability Board (CCIBs) Country Desk Officers. Focus on enhancing DCO and capacity building to operate effectively with partners to reduce risk and advance shared US interests.	Work in conjunction with CCIBs and coordinate efforts through Security Cooperation Offices at Embassies.	CCJ6-01, Theater Interoperability & Engagement Branch Centcom.cll.cent com-ha.mesg.ccj6-oi-branch@mail.mil
EUCOM-Cyber staff/Division	Manage Country Plan objectives, milestones, and tasks from strategy, organizational requirements (NATO/Pfp), and Line of Activity references. Create Cyber SC roadmap and coordinate assessments, exercises and train and equip programs that support critical partners.	For 333 development or integration efforts that have Cyber requirements, copy eucom.stuttgart.ecj58.list.ecj5-scp-authorities@mail.mil that tracks SSCI requirements and coordinates with Cyber OPR: Eucom.stuttgart.ecj6.list.jcc-engagements@mail.mil.	EUCOM Stuttgart ECJ6 List JCC Engagements: eucom.stuttgart.ecj6.list.jcc-engagements@mail.mil
AFRICOM - Cyber staff/Division	Focuses on building and enhancing cyber security with partners in the AOR. Works in conjunction with the Command & Control Interoperability Board (CCIBs) Country Desk Officers and ICB of the J5 to move the partner up the Cyberspace Security Cooperation Maturity Model with the desired published end states.	The CCIB, The Country Team, and the International Capacity Building team from the J5 work together under cyberspace objectives to ID and reduce risk and advance US and partner strategic cyberspace objectives.	https://www.africom.mil/about-the-command/directorates-and-staff/j3-operations-and-cyber
NORTHCOM-Cyber staff/Division	Conducts deliberate planning to develop Cyber and Network Operational concepts for the United States Northern Command (USNORTHCOM) and Concept Plans for a broad range of activities supporting Homeland Defense and Defense Support of Civil Authorities. Synchronizes J6 Theater	USNORTHCOM utilizes an "oficio" process to coordinate any TSC events with the Mexican Military. An "oficio" is an official correspondence	https://www.northcom.mil/Contact.aspx

	Security Corporation (TSC) activities with USNORTHCOM's capacity development plan for regional mission partners in order to increase Cyber capabilities and interoperability.	coordinated through the Office of Defense Coordination at the US Embassy, Mexico City to Mexico's Army/Air Force Secretariat (SEDENA) and Naval Secretariat (SEMAR). For any US entity interested in taking part in Cybersecurity capacity development events with Mexico or the Bahamas, submit requests through the J6 TSC team.	
SOUTHCOM-Cyber Staff/Division	Focuses on building and enhancing cyber security with partners in the AOR.	Submit requests through the SOUTHCOM Cyber Division.	southcom.miami.sci3.mbx.omb-scicc@mail.mil
SERVICE CYBER COMMANDS			
US Fleet Cyber Command	Delivers a Cyberspace Security Cooperation Team that provides assistance in activities that strengthen partner networks and facilitates joint interoperability, cyberspace security, and information sharing (i.e., assessments, subject matter expert exchanges). Engages with USCYBERCOM, USINDOPACOM, and USSOUTHCOM to generate roadmap developments for cyberspace security and information-sharing plans for Partner Nations. Provides advisement and oversight for	MOD - DoD level request for support will be submitted by COCOM via USCYBERCOM for USINDOPACOM and USSOUTHCOM Areas of Responsibilities. Navy to Navy level, request will be submitted through the respective Numbered	FCC_C10F NSAH_N5_N54 @navy.mil

	all foreign engagement activities conducted at the task force level (i.e., agreements, foreign engagement determinations).	Fleet or Regional Command Task Force (CTF 1040 in SOUTHCOM, CTF 1070 in INDOPACOM AORs.	
Army Cyber Command	U.S. Army Cyber Command plans and executes Cyberspace Operations related security cooperation activities in support of USCYBERCOM and Army ASCCS. ARCYBER Security Cooperation Division (SCD) develops, plans, and coordinates SC activities aimed at shaping the cyberspace security environment while assuring access and enhancing interoperability across US Allies. Primary focus on Network Defense (DC) and Interoperability.	Receives training requirements through Cyber Center of Excellence (CCOE), US Army Training and Doctrine Command (TRADOC) channels as assigned by the Department or the Army G-3. Submit requests through GCC CO-IPE or ASCC to ARCYBER G5 SCD	usarmy.gordon.a rcyber.mesg.g5.s cd@mail.mil
Air Forces Cyber	Plans and executes Cyberspace Operations related security cooperation activities in support of EUCOM and STRATCOM.	Submit requests through the GCC.	https://www.16a f.af.mil/
ACADEMIC/TRAINING INSTITUTIONS			
National Defense University - College of Informatio n and Cyberspace (CIC)	The College of Information and Cyberspace (CIC) is one of National Defense University's five component colleges. The CIC educates joint warfighters and national security leaders to lead and advise national security institutions and advance global security within the cyberspace domain through the use of the information instrument of national power. The College provides Joint Professional Military Education that focuses on the information and cyberspace aspects of national security, as well as graduate education (MS degree, certificates, and	Countries desiring to send representatives to attend CIC must request a seat allocations through the country's Security Cooperation Office (SCO). The SCO will then forward the request to the Combatant Command Security Cooperation Education and Training	College of Information and Cyberspace, Office of Student Services: CICOSS@ndu.e du SATFA Contact: TRADOC SATFA (ATTG-TRI-SXX), Bldg. 950, 950 Jefferson Ave., Fort Eustis, Va. 23604-5724 157-501-5031

	courses) offered in-person, online, and hybrid.	Office who will validate, prioritize, and submit it to the Army Security and Assistance Field Training Agency and the NDU International Student Management Office SATFA.	
Air Force Cyber College	The AFCC empowers warrior leaders through education, partnerships, and innovative research to integrate cyber in support of US National Defense Strategy	Non-Us. citizens who are members of the defense agencies of other countries must apply through their governments. Applications should be in the form of an education and training request for approval and processing through the appropriate Security Assistance Training Field Activity (SATFA) country program manager, who should forward the request to: SATFA Contact: AFSAT- Randolph AFB, TX	awc.cybercolleg e.org@us.af.mil
Air Force Institute of Technology (AFIT)	Offers cyberspace education and training and supports numerous research and development efforts in partnership with various defense organizations.	Submit requests through the website.	https://www.afit. edu/CYBER/

US Army Cyber College	The Cyber School's mission is to acquire America's most talented and innovative citizens and develop them into the world's most lethal. professional, ethical, and technically competent Cyber Warfare and Electronic Warfare Workforces. The Cyber School's vision is to become the world's leading organization in educating, training, and developing DoD's Cyber Warfare and Electronic Warfare forces of choice through focused and purposeful career paths and academic programs with tour core strengths: intellectual curiosity. Operational competency, mental agility, and persistent collaboration.	Receives training requirements through Cyber Center of Excellence (CCOE), US Army Training and Doctrine Command (TRADOC) channels as assigned by the Department of the Army G-3. Coordinates with operational forces and Arm Futures Command to maintain technical relevance Serves as the Army's primary training resource for Cyber, CEMA, and EW.	https://cybercoe. army.mil/CYBE RSCH/index.htm l
US Department of Defense (DoD) Cyber Crime Center (DC3)	Delivers cyber technical training to approved allies and foreign partners in residence at the DC3 Cyber Training Academy or through Mobile Training Team (MTT) in the foreign partner country. The highly specialized training provides students with the solid working knowledge necessary to conduct incident response and digital forensics of digital media, including networks.	All foreign partner training activities are coordinated through the AFSAT. NETSAFA, or SATFA Country Manager for each applicable foreign country. This includes confirming enrollment for in-residence training or to inquire about an MTT. Additionally, inquiries can also be coordinated through the International Military Student Office at the DC3 Cyber Training Academy.	https://www.dc3. mil/ info@dc3.mil

Naval Postgraduate School	The Naval Postgraduate School contributes to mobile and residential short courses organized/MASLed by ISG. In addition, PS provides hybrid delivery of longer cybersecurity graduate coursework via NPS MASL	Both ISG and PS MASLed courses are programmed via NETSAFA. Requests for NPS faculty support should be directed to the Director, Center for Security Cooperation Support.	https://nps.edu/web/c3o
ISG	The Defense Security Cooperation University's (DSCU) Institute for Security Governance (ISG) is the Department of Defense's leading implementer of Institutional Capacity Building (ICB) and one of its primary international schoolhouses. As a component of the Defense Security Cooperation Agency (DSCA), ISG is charged with building partner institutional capacity and capability through tailored advising, education, and professional development programs grounded in American values and approaches.	Please reach out directly to the email address provided.	isginfo@nps.edu
REGIONAL CENTERS			
Marshall Center- Program on Cyber Security Studies (PCSS)	Program on Cyber Security Studies(PCSS) is strategy and policy-focused and offers a 2 1/2 week resident course [SMC0023] in December and Nonresident courses and specialized workshops at the Marshall Center In Garmisch or in a host nation keyed to strategy and policy development, regional cooperation and information sharing. More about the Marshall Center and the Program on Cyber Security Studies at: https://www.marshallcenter.org/en/academics/college-courses/program-cyber-security-studies-pcss	Work through the German-American embassies, the Department of State, COCOMs, and Program Leadership at the George C Marshall European Center for Security Studies to request support. Country Teams, Combatant Commands, and Military Departments can always request direct support from the GCMC. Ideally, events should be planned within the USG POM submission cycle.	(Please address to all): cyber@marshallcenter.org GCMCPSD@marshallcenter.org registrar@marshalicenter.org scci@state.gov

		(next USG FY) and 6-18 months in advance tor specialized events and outreach activities. External requests require discrete requesting agency funding and the GCMC PCS team partners with partner nation national-level cybersecurity organization(s).	
Asia-Pacific Center for Security Studies (APCSS)	1) Provide cyber executive education for partner nations to advance cyber governance; 2) Provide tailored support (workshops, dialogues, and other tailored virtual events); and 3) Mentor/support partner nation long-term cyber capacity-building projects via "fellows projects" (initiated in coordination with country team/defense attaché and designed during a course).	Work through the in-country embassy representatives, Daniel K. Inouye Asia Pacific Center for Security Studies leadership (APCSS), and Combatant Commands to request support for attendance to courses. Country Teams, Combatant Commands and Military Departments can always request direct support from the APCSS for workshops, dialogues, and virtual education (webinars). Planning timelines for activities should be coordinated and scheduled well in advance, and ideally within the USG POM submission cycle (next USG FY). Events	ColofSecStudies Ops@apcss.org

		should be planned 6-18 months in advance for specialized events and outreach activities. External requests require discrete requesting agency funding.	
William J Perry Center	The William J. Perry Center for Hemispheric Defense Studies offers courses, seminars, workshops, and lectures related to cybersecurity in Washington, D.C., and in Latin America and the Caribbean. Focus: policy and strategic levels. Courses are MASLed. Offered in-residence, with a virtual course.	WJPC works in coordination with OD, US Southern Command, and US Northern Command. DSCA is executive agent. The WJPC program partners with numerous organizations, including National Defense University, the Inter-American Defense Board and College, the Organization or American States, the Joint Staff, ISG, and partner institutions throughout the Americas	Academic Affairs chdsacademics@ndu.edu
Africa Center for Strategic Studies	The Africa Center's academic programs focus on strengthening security sector institutions and equipping uniformed and civilian security sector leaders to design, implement, and monitor strategies that are country-owned, effective, and sustainable. The Africa Center's cyber capacity-building efforts include strategic policy and planning and executive cyber leadership, with a focus on applied, evidence-driven analysis and peer learning.	Work through the embassy representatives in African countries and Africa Center leadership to request support and attendance for courses. Country Teams, Combatant Commands and Military Departments can likewise request direct support from the ACSS for seminars, dialogues, and virtual webinars or	https://africacenter.org/

		roundtables. The planning timeline for events should begin at least six months, and preferably a fiscal year beforehand.	
Defense Institute of International Legal Studies (DIS)	Legal institutional capacity building (ICB) to support partner cyber-security capacity-building plans, including with respect to legal authorities, standard operating procedures, development of cyber rules of engagement (ROE), and integrated cyber legal reviews. Four-week Cyber Law & Hybrid Warfare resident course provides an in-depth global perspective of the domestic and international legal aspects of cyber operations and the emerging technologies present in Hybrid Warfare, and their impact on modern state governance, including application of international law to issues such as sovereignty, intervention, and due diligence in the cyber domain.	For legal CB support, requirements must be developed, validated and resourced through DSCA's CB requirements planning and review process. Work through COCOM J5 ICB Specialist and DIILS Regional Program Director for relevant COCOM. POC listed can provide appropriate contact information. For Cyber Law & Hybrid Warfare resident course, work through relevant COCO J5 International Military Education and Training (IMET) or Regional Defense Fellowship Program (RDFP) coordinators, and DIILS Resident Course Director (POC at right).	www.dills.org

SERVICE SECURITY COOPERATION ORGANIZATIONS			
Navy International al Programs Office (NIPO)	The Navy International Programs Office (Navy IPO) is responsible for managing and implementing International Security Assistance programs, Cooperative Development programs and Technology Security policy.	Submit requests through the NIPO POC.	NIPORECEPTIONIST@NAVY.MIL https://www.secnav.navy.mil/nipo/Pages/About/Security%20Assitance/Security-Assistance. aspx
NETSAFA	NETSAFA is the U.S. Navy's agent for international education and training, including cyber training/education. NETSAFA coordinates training support for international governments and international organizations. As a field activity of the Naval Education and Training Command (NETC), we serve as a focal point for all Security Cooperation training program issues, coordination, and advice within the U.S. Navy.	Initial country program requests for Navy training should be presented at the annual Security Cooperation Education and Training Working Groups (SCETWG) sponsored by the Unified Commands. This allows advance planning and maximum flexibility to accommodate country requests. The Navy will make every effort to accommodate country requirements as long as space is available in the course requested. Host Nations can view and Search online for all services training available using the I-SANweb. An |-SANweb account for the Host Nation may be obtained by Security Cooperation Officer (SCO).	https://www.netc.navy.mil/NETSAFA/

Air Force Security Assistance Training Squadron - AFSAT	The Executive Agent for all Air Force-sponsored international training and education. The command implements and approves Air Force-sponsored security assistance training monitors the progress of training and the welfare of U.S. Air Force-sponsored international students, and provides guidance for the implementation of the DoD Informational Program.		https://www.33fw.af.mil/
Air Force International Affairs Office - SAF/IA	Advances US national security by cultivating deep, enduring relationships through security cooperation with our Allies and Partners in support of US Air Force and US Space Force global operations.		OFFICE SAF.IA.Workflow@us.af.mil https://www.safia.hq.af.mil/About-Us/Directorates/
US Army Security Assistance Command (USASAC)	Leads the AMC Security Assistance Enterprise; develops and manages security assistance programs and foreign military sales cases to build partner capacity, support COCOM engagement strategies, and strengthen U.S. Global partnerships.		https://www.army.mil/usasac

STATE/INTERAGENCY ORGANIZATIONS: INTERNATIONAL CYBERSPACE CAPACITY BUILDING			
ORGANIZATION	DESCRIPTION OF CYBER PROCESS FOR MISSION/SERVICES IN SUPPORT OF PN COORDINATING SUPPORT CB EFFORTS	PROCESS FOR COORDINATING SUPPORT	ORGANIZATION CONTACT INFORMATION
US DEPARTMENT OF STATE / Office of the Coordinator for Cyber Issues (State/CCI)	The Office of the Coordinator for Cyber Issues (S/CCI) integrates diplomatic efforts across the full range of international cyber policy issues that impact U.S. foreign policy, national security, human rights, and economic imperatives.	Generally, there is a designated Department of State Cyber Officer at each Embassy that can serve as the POC on cyber capacity building efforts at the host-country level. Additionally, cyber capacity building	SCCI@state.gov

		efforts at the host country level can be coordinated at Embassies through country team meetings, including whole-of-Embassy cyber working groups. If there are any additional questions/requests related to the Department's cyber capacity-building efforts, please reach out to S/CCI.	
DEPARTMENT OF HOMELAND SECURITY / Cybersecurity And Infrastructure Security Agency (CISA)	CISA builds, sustains, and advances international partnerships to: 1) strategically cultivate international support for the Directorate's objectives, priorities, and core functions as well as broader DHS national security goals; 2) increase situational awareness and guide strategic communication on vulnerabilities and risks; 3) facilitate information sharing to help prevent, mitigate, and manage cyber and physical risks to enhance the security and resiliency of the Nation's critical infrastructure; 4) bolster operational capacity and address identified capability gaps and technological and information requirements; 5) share expertise and best practices to build and strengthen network protection, risk management, and incident response capacity; 6) help manage systemic risks, bolster the security of U.S. critical infrastructure, and maintain international stability; and	Please reach out directly to the email address provided.	CISAInternationalAffairs@hq.dhs.gov

	7) broadly shape the evolving cyber ecosystem to support its overall cybersecurity mission.		
United States Coast Guard	Ensure the security of our cyberspace, maintain superiority over our adversaries, and safeguard our Nation's critical maritime infrastructure through: - Defending and Operating in Cyberspace; - Protecting Infrastructure; - Enabling USCG Operations through Cyber	Please reach out directly to the email address provided	HQS-SMB-CG-791-CyberspaceForces@uscg.mil
United States Coast Guard Cyber Command	Enhance the resiliency of MTS Critical Infrastructure against cyber disruption through consistent, proactive engagements with public and private industry organizations.	Please reach out directly to the email address provided	MaritimeCyber @uscg.mil

*Credits for This Guide

The invaluable contributions and expertise of the Institute for Security Governance (ISG) have been instrumental in the creation of this guide. We extend our heartfelt gratitude to the entire team at ISG for their collaboration, insights, and dedication to excellence. Their knowledge and support have greatly enriched the content of this guide, ensuring that it serves as a comprehensive and authoritative resource for readers. For more information about ISG and their impactful work, please visit their website at https://instituteforsecuritygovernance.org/

APPENDIX H: Cyberspace SC Abbreviations List

Abbreviation	Expanded Term
A&A	Advise and Assist
AFCC	Air Force Cyber College
AFCYBER	United States Air Force Cyber Command
AFLCMC	Air Force Life Cycle Management Center
AO	Area of Operation
AOR	Area of Responsibility
APCSS	Asia-Pacific Center for Security Studies
ARCYBER	United States Army Cyber Command
AC	Austere Challenge (AC) Military Exercise
AM&E	Assessment, Monitoring, and Evaluation
BLE	Bi-Lateral Engagement
CAATSA	Countering America's Adversaries Through Sanctions Act
CAT	The FBI's Cyber Action Team
CBRN	Chemical, Biological, Radiological and Nuclear
CCB	Cyber Capacity Building
CCP	Contingency Planning Process
CENTCOM	United States Central Command

CERT	Computer Emergency Response Team
CIC	College of Information and Cyberspace
CISA	Cybersecurity and Infrastructure Security Agency
CO	Cyberspace Operations
CPG	Contingency Planning Guidance (CPG)
CRIF	Country Regional Information Fund
CSIRT	Computer Security Incident Response Team
CIKR	Critical Infrastructure and Key Resources
CNA	Cyber Network Attack
CNE	Cyber Network Exploitation
CYSFAM	Cybersecurity Focus Area Maturity Model
CYBERCOM	United States Cyber Command
DATT	Defense Attaché
DCO	Defensive Cyber Operations
DDoS	Distributed Denial of Service
DDS	Deployable DCO System
DIILS	Defense Institute of International Legal Studies
DOD	U.S. Department of Defense
DODIN	U.S. Department of Defense Information Network
DOS	U.S. Department of State

DTAP	Development, Testing, Acceptance, and Production
ECJ	European Command Joint
EDR	Endpoint Detection Response
EU	European Union
EUCOM	United States European Command
FMS	Foreign Military Sales
FMF	Foreign Military Financing
FS	Foreign Security Forces
GCC	Geographic Combatant Command
GDP	Garrison DCO Platform
HFOs	Hunt Forward Operations
ICE	In-Country Event
ICB	Institutional Capacity Building
IMOs	Intermediate Military Objectives
INF-L-BNG	NATO Light Infantry Battalion Group
ISG	Institute for Security Governance
IRM	Incident Response Management
JP	Joint Publication
LEGAT	Legal Attaché
JFHQ	Joint Force Headquarters
MARFOR	United States Marine Corps Forces
MLE	Multi-Lateral Engagement
MoD	Ministry of Defense
MTG	Meeting
MTT	Methods, Techniques, and Tools
NATO	North Atlantic Treaty Organization
NSS	National Security Strategy

NETSAFA	Naval Education and Training Security Assistance Field Activity
NIPO	Navy International Programs Office
NMS	National Military Strategy
NORTHCOM	United States Northern Command
OAIs	Operations, Activities, and Investments
ODASD(SC)	Office of the Deputy Assistant Secretary of Defense for Security Cooperation
ODC	Office of Defense Cooperation
OCE	Out of Country Event
OE	Operational Environment
OPT	Operational Planning Team
OUSDP	Office of the Under Secretary of Defense for Policy
PCSS	Program on Cyber Security Studies
PEO C4I/PMW	Program Executive Office Command, Control, Communications, Computers, and Intelligence/Program Manager for Warfare
PEO EIS/AIT	Program Executive Office Enterprise Information Systems/Allied Information Technology
PNs	Partner Nations
PM	Prime Minister
RBAC	Role-Based Access Control
SA	Security Assistance

SAF/IA	Air Force International Affairs Office
SARIMAX	Seasonal Autoregressive Integrated Moving-Average with Exogenous Regressors
SCO	Security Cooperation Organization
SC	Security Cooperation
SCOs	Security Cooperation Organizations
SDO	Security Defense Officer
SME	Subject Matter Expert
SOC	Security Operations Center
SOCOM	United States Special Operations Command
SOUTHCOM	United States Southern Command
SPP	State Partnership Program
SSCIs	Significant Security Cooperation Initiatives
TCP	Theater Campaign Plan
TCO	Theater Campaign Order
ToD	Test of Design
ToE	Test of Effectiveness
UCP	Unified Command Plan
UN	United Nations
USAREUR-AF	United States Army Europe and Africa
US Fleet Cyber Command	United States Fleet Cyber Command
USCG	United States Coast Guard
USCG Cyber Command	United States Coast Guard Cyber Command

USAID	United Station Agency for International Development
USASAC	U.S. Army Security Assistance Command
VLAN	Virtual Local Area Network
VMS	Vulnerability Management System
WJPC	William J. Perry Center
WMD	Weapons of Mass Destruction

Bibliography

---

[i] Political-Military Affairs, US Dept of State on X. (n.d.). X (Formerly Twitter). https://twitter.com/StateDeptPM/status/1587195595852234754?t=vnjSqUZMPORDb7yMFnoeyg&s=40

[ii] Inaugural USEUCOM exercise Cyber Unity: True to its name. (n.d.). https://www.eucom.mil/article/42481/inaugural-useucom-exercise-cyber-unity-true-to-its-name

[iii] murkyware-scanner/help: How to Use Murkyware™ Scanner. (n.d.). GitHub. https://github.com/murkyware-scanner/help

[iv] NRK Troms og Finnmark. (2022, January 20). Politiet tror det er en menneskelig årsak bak bruddet på sjøkabel på Svalbard. NRK Troms og Finnmark. https://www.nrk.no/tromsogfinnmark/politiet-tror-det-er-en-menneskelig-arsak-bak-bruddet-pa-sjokabel-pa-svalbard-1.15850988

[v] Submarine Networks. (n.d.). SEA-ME-WE 4 Submarine Cable System. Submarine Networks. https://www.submarinenetworks.com/systems/asia-europe-africa/smw4

[vi] BBC News. (2013, March 27). Egypt arrests as undersea internet cable cut off Alexandria. BBC News. https://www.bbc.co.uk/news/world-middle-east-21963100

[vii] Recorded Future. (2023). TA-2023-0627: The Escalating Global Risk Environment for Submarine Cables. https://go.recordedfuture.com/hubfs/reports/ta-2023-0627.pdf

[viii] All Ransomware Attacks, https://ransomwareattacks.halcyon.ai/

[ix] All Ransomware Attacks, https://ransomwareattacks.halcyon.ai/

[x] Active Cyber Defense Certainty Act, https://www.congress.gov/bill/116th-congress/house-bill/3270

[xi] FACT SHEET: Biden-Harris Administration Announces National Cybersecurity Strategy, https://www.whitehouse.gov/briefing-

room/statements-releases/2023/03/02/fact-sheet-biden-harris-administration-announces-national-cybersecurity-strategy/

xii Principal Deputy Assistant Attorney General Nicole M. Argentieri Delivers Remarks at the Center for Strategic and International Studies, https://www.justice.gov/opa/speech/principal-deputy-assistant-attorney-general-nicole-m-argentieri-delivers-remarks-center

xiii Use of Cryptocurrency in Ransomware Attacks, Available Data, and National Security Concerns; https://www.hsgac.senate.gov/wp-content/uploads/imo/media/doc/HSGAC%20Majority%20Cryptocurrency%20Ransomware%20Report_Executive%20Summary.pdf

xiv National Cyber Security Centre. (n.d.). Early Warning. www.ncsc.gov.uk. https://www.ncsc.gov.uk/information/early-warning-service

xv Conflict in Cyberspace: Parsing the threats and the state of international order in cyberspace, https://www.clingendael.org/pub/2019/strategic-monitor-2019-2020/conflict-in-cyberspace/

xvi FBI Efforts Since the Russian Invasion of Ukraine. (2023, February 24). Federal Bureau of Investigation. https://www.fbi.gov/news/press-releases/fbi-efforts-since-the-russian-invasion-of-ukraine

xvii "Microsoft Exchange Server Attacks," Cybersecurity & Infrastructure Security Agency (CISA), United States, May 2021. [https://us-cert.cisa.gov/ncas/alerts/aa21-110a]

xviii CISA and CNMF Analysis of SolarWinds-related Malware | CISA. (2021, April 15). Cybersecurity and Infrastructure Security Agency CISA. https://www.cisa.gov/news-events/alerts/2021/04/15/cisa-and-cnmf-analysis-solarwinds-related-malware

xix All Ransomware Attacks, https://ransomwareattacks.halcyon.ai/

xx All Ransomware Attacks, https://ransomwareattacks.halcyon.ai/

xxi Hybrid Conflict Neither war, nor peace, https://www.clingendael.org/pub/2019/strategic-monitor-2019-2020/hybrid-conflict/

---

xxii The data presented in the graph is based on publicly available sources and reports up to September 2021. Some specific sources include: Official announcements and press releases from the Russian Ministry of Defense and NATO official statements and press releases.

xxiii The data presented in the graph is based on publicly available sources and reports up to September 2021. Some specific sources include: Official announcements and press releases from China's Ministry of Defense and the U.S. Department of Defense.

xxiv "Pro-Sudan hackers attack digital services in Kenya" - TechCabal, https://techcabal.com/2023/07/27/pro-sudan-hackers-attack-digital-services-in-kenya/

"Kenya ICT minister admits cyber-attack on eCitizen portal, insists data secure", TheEastAfrican, https://www.theeastafrican.co.ke/tea/news/east-africa/cs-owalo-admits-cyber-attack-on-ecitizen-portal--4317894

xxv Albania weighed invoking NATO's Article 5 over Iranian cyber attack, https://www.politico.com/news/2022/10/05/why-albania-chose-not-to-pull-the-nato-trigger-after-cyber attack-00060347

xxvi https://www.state.gov/attribution-of-russias-malicious-cyber-activity-against-ukraine/

xxvii Oldsmar Water treatment Facility attack – Westoahu Cybersecurity. (n.d.). https://westoahu.hawaii.edu/cyber/ics-cybersecurity/ics-weekly-summaries/oldsmar-water-treatment-facility-attack/

xxviii Significant Cyber Incidents | CSIS. (n.d.). https://www.csis.org/programs/strategic-technologies-program/significant-cyber-incidents

xxix CCDCOE. (n.d.). https://ccdcoe.org/incyder-articles/nato-summit-updates-cyber-defence-policy/

xxx NATO. (n.d.). Cyber Defence Pledge. NATO. https://www.nato.int/cps/su/natohq/official_texts_133177.htm

xxxi NATO. (n.d.). Cyber Defence. Retrieved from https://www.nato.int/cps/en/natohq/topics_78170.htm

xxxii Public Safety Canada. (2023, June 29). Five country ministerial. Retrieved from https://www.publicsafety.gc.ca/cnt/ntnl-scrt/fv-cntry-mnstrl-en.aspx

xxxiii CCDCOE About us. (n.d.). https://ccdcoe.org/about-us/

xxxiv Inaugural USEUCOM exercise Cyber Unity: True to its name. (n.d.). https://www.eucom.mil/article/42481/inaugural-useucom-exercise-cyber-unity-true-to-its-name

xxxv Mujahedin-e Khalq Organization (MEK or MKO) | Encyclopedia.com. (n.d.). https://www.encyclopedia.com/politics/encyclopedias-almanacs-transcripts-and-maps/mujahedin-e-khalq-organization-mek-or-mko

xxxvi Rogin, J. (2023, October 2). This tiny European nation could collapse without U.S. aid — to Ukraine. Washington Post. https://www.washingtonpost.com/opinions/2023/10/02/popescu-moldova-ukraine-russia-war/

xxxvii Modern Diplomacy. (2024, January 19). Russia preparing to ban Britain from fishing for cod and haddock in Barents Sea. https://moderndiplomacy.eu/2024/01/19/russia-preparing-to-ban-britain-from-fishing-for-cod-and-haddock-in-barents-sea/

xxxviii Mattis, J. (2018). Summary of the 2018 National Defense Strategy of the United States of America. Department of Defense. https://dod.defense.gov/Portals/1/Documents/pubs/2018-National-Defense-Strategy-Summary.pdf

xxxix Description of the National Military Strategy 2018 The Joint Staff. (n.d.). https://www.jcs.mil/Portals/36/Documents/Publications/UNCLASS_2018_National_Military_Strategy_Description.pdf

xl House, W. (2022, November 8). FACT SHEET: The Biden-Harris administration's national security strategy. The White House. https://www.whitehouse.gov/briefing-room/statements-releases/2022/10/12/fact-sheet-the-biden-harris-administrations-national-security-strategy/

xli Pike, J. (n.d.). Defense policy. https://www.globalsecurity.org/military/library/policy/intro.htm

[xlii] National Strategies: Security, Defense, and Military, https://www.dau.edu/acquipedia-article/national-strategies-security-defense-and-military

[xliii] USEUCOM 2019 Posture Statement, https://www.eucom.mil/article/39546/useucom-2019-posture-statement

[xliv] The Unified Command Plan and Combatant Commands: Background and Issues for Congress, https://crsreports.congress.gov/product/pdf/R/R42077/11

[xlv] DEVELOPING A COMBATANT COMMAND CAMPAIGN PLAN: LESSONS LEARNED AT US CENTRAL COMMAND, https://mwi.westpoint.edu/developing-a-combatant-command-campaign-plan-lessons-learned-at-us-central-command/

[xlvi] CLIMATE, INFRASTRUCTURE AND ENVIRONMENT EXECUTIVE AGENCY / ENERGY; https://ec.europa.eu/energy/infrastructure/transparency_platform/map-viewer/main.html

[xlvii] Map of Submarine Cables; https://www.submarinecablemap.com/

[xlviii] DEVELOPING A COMBATANT COMMAND CAMPAIGN PLAN: LESSONS LEARNED AT US CENTRAL COMMAND, https://mwi.westpoint.edu/developing-a-combatant-command-campaign-plan-lessons-learned-at-us-central-command/
[xlix] DEVELOPING A COMBATANT COMMAND CAMPAIGN PLAN: LESSONS LEARNED AT US CENTRAL COMMAND, https://mwi.westpoint.edu/developing-a-combatant-command-campaign-plan-lessons-learned-at-us-central-command/
[l] EUCOM concludes Austere Challenge 2023. (n.d.). https://www.eucom.mil/article/42377/eucom-concludes-austere-challenge-2023

[li] Security Cooperation Bulletin, https://api.army.mil/e2/c/downloads/2023/01/19/7d7e0e33/16-09-security-cooperation-lessons-and-best-practices-bulletin-mar-16-public.pdf

[lii] Comparison of Platforms, https://www.rand.org/content/dam/rand/pubs/research_reports/RRA1300/RRA1357-3/RAND_RRA1357-3.pdf

liii Defense Security Cooperation Agency, Research, Development, Test & Evaluation, Defense-Wide, https://comptroller.defense.gov/Portals/45/Documents/defbudget/fy2021/budget_justification/pdfs/03_RDT_and_E/DSCA_PB2021.pdf

liv Security Cooperation Automation Appendix, https://dscu.edu/documents/publications/greenbook/20-Appendix-1.pdf?id=1

lv Defense Budget Overview - FY 2024 European Deterrence Initiative (EDI), https://comptroller.defense.gov/Portals/45/Documents/defbudget/FY2024/FY2024_EDI_JBook.pdf

lvi Justification for Security Cooperation Program and Activity Funding, https://open.defense.gov/Portals/23/Documents/Security_Cooperation/Budget_Justification_FY2021.pdf
lvii Traditional Combatant Commander Activities Between U.S. Special Operations Forces and Foreign Non-Military Forces, https://tjaglcs.army.mil/mlr/other-security-forces-too-traditional-combatant-commander-activities-between-u.s.-special-operations-forces-and-foreign-non-military-forces

lviii [Ukraine Security Assistance Initiative] (https://www.congress.gov/114/plaws/publ92/PLAW-114publ92.pdf)

lix Justification for Security Cooperation Program and Activity Funding, https://open.defense.gov/Portals/23/Documents/Security_Cooperation/Budget_Justification_FY2021.pdf

lx [10 U.S.C. § 321] (https://www.law.cornell.edu/uscode/text/10/321)

lxi 10 U.S.C. § 321 - Training with friendly foreign countries: payment of training and exercise expenses, https://uscode.house.gov/view.xhtml?req=granuleid:USC-prelim-title10-section321&num=0&edition=prelim#:~:text=%2DThe%20armed%20forces%20under%20the,United%20States%20to%20do%20so./

lxii [10 U.S. Code § 312] (https://www.law.cornell.edu/uscode/text/10/312)

lxiii [NDAA FY16 §1251] (https://www.congress.gov/114/plaws/publ92/PLAW-114publ92.pdf)

---

lxiv [10 U.S. Code § 164] (https://www.law.cornell.edu/uscode/text/10/164)

lxv Defense Primer: DOD "Title 10" Security Cooperation, https://sgp.fas.org/crs/natsec/IF11677.pdf
lxvi Congressional Role, https://sgp.fas.org/crs/natsec/IF11677.pdf

lxvii U.S. AND MONTENEGRO STRENGTHEN SECURITY COOPERATION RELATIONSHIP, https://www.dsca.mil/news-media/news-archive/us-and-montenegro-strengthen-security-cooperation-relationship

lxviii Foreign Military Sales Cybersecurity Assistance Framework. (2024, January 9). MITRE. https://www.mitre.org/news-insights/fact-sheet/foreign-military-sales-cybersecurity-assistance-framework

lxix ASSESSMENT, MONITORING, AND EVALUATION POLICY FOR THE SECURITY COOPERATION ENTERPRISE, https://open.defense.gov/portals/23/documents/foreignasst/DODi_513214_on_am&e.pdf

lxx AM&E Framework, https://open.defense.gov/portals/23/documents/foreignasst/DODi_513214_on_am&e.pdf

lxxi DOD Security Cooperation: Assessment, Monitoring, and Evaluation, https://www.everycrsreport.com/reports/IN10726.html

lxxii Sections 333 and MSI Program Execution Monitoring and Milestones (PEMMs), https://samm.dsca.mil/policy-memoranda/dsca-22-38

lxxiii Özkan, B. Y., Van Lingen, S., & Spruit, M. (2021). The Cybersecurity Focus Area Maturity (CYSFAM) model. Journal of Cybersecurity and Privacy, 1(1), 119–139. https://doi.org/10.3390/jcp1010007

lxxiv International Organization for Standardization (ISO)/International Electrotechnical Commission (IEC). ISO/IEC 27032:2023- Cybersecurity Guidelines for Internet security. Available online: https://www.iso.org/standard/76070.html.
lxxv International Organization for Standardization (ISO)/International Electrotechnical Commission (IEC). ISO/IEC 27032:2023- Cybersecurity Guidelines for Internet security. Available online: https://www.iso.org/standard/76070.

lxxvi International Organization for Standardization (ISO)/International Electrotechnical Commission (IEC). ISO/IEC 27032:2023- Cybersecurity Guidelines for Internet security. Available online: https://www.iso.org/standard/76070.

lxxvii International Organization for Standardization (ISO)/International Electrotechnical Commission (IEC). ISO/IEC 27033-1:2015-Information Technology—Security Techniques—Network Security—Part 1: Overview and Concepts. Available online: **https://www.iso.org/standard/63461.html**.

lxxviii International Organization for Standardization (ISO)/International Electrotechnical Commission (IEC). ISO/IEC 27033-1:2015-Information Technology—Security Techniques—Network Security—Part 1: Overview and Concepts. Available online: https://www.iso.org/standard/63461.html.

lxxix International Organization for Standardization (ISO)/International Electrotechnical Commission (IEC). ISO/IEC 27035-1:2016-Information Technology—Security Techniques—Information Security Incident Management—Part 1: Principles of Incident Management. Available online: https://www.iso.org/standard/60803.html.
lxxx International Telecommunication Union (ITU). ICT Security Standards Roadmap. Available online: https://www.itu.int/en/ITU-T/studygroups/com17/ict/Pages/default.aspx.

lxxxi European Union Agency for Cybersecurity (ENISA). *National Cyber Security Strategies: An Implementation Guide*; ENISA: Heraklion, Greece, 2012. **[Google Scholar]**

lxxxii International Electrotechnical Commission (IEC). *Industrial Communication Networks: Network and System Security. Pt. 3,3: System Security Requirements and Security Levels*; International Electrotechnical Commission (IEC): Geneva, Switzerland, 2013; ISBN 978-2-8322-1036-9. **[Google Scholar]**

lxxxiii Nieles, M.; Dempsey, K.; Pillitteri, V.Y. *An Introduction to Information Security*; National Institute of Standards and Technology: Gaithersburg, MD, USA, 2017.

lxxxiv Swanson, M.; Guttman, B. *Generally Accepted Principles and Practices for Securing Information Technology Systems*; National Institute of Standards and Technology: Gaithersburg, MD, USA, 1996.

lxxxv North American Electric Reliability Corporation (NERC). *Critical Infrastructure Protection Standards*; NERC: Available online: https://www.nerc.com/pa/Stand/Reliability%20Standards/CIP-002-5.1a.pdf.

lxxxvi North American Electric Reliability Corporation (NERC). NERC Security Guidelines. Available online: https://www.nerc.com/comm/RSTC_Reliability_Guidelines/Physical_Security_Guideline_%20Assessments_and_Resiliency_Measures_for_Extreme_Events_June_2019.pdf.

lxxxvii International Organization for Standardization (ISO)/International Electrotechnical Commission (IEC). ISO/IEC 27032:2023- Cybersecurity Guidelines for Internet security. Available online: https://www.iso.org/standard/76070.html.

lxxxviii Information Security Forum (ISF). *The ISF Standard of Good Practice for Information Security*; ISF: Surrey, UK, 2018. [**Google Scholar**]

lxxxix Souppaya, M.; Scarfone, K. *Guide to Enterprise Patch Management Technologies*; National Institute of Standards and Technology: Gaithersburg, MD, USA, 2013.

xc International Organization for Standardization (ISO)/International Electrotechnical Commission (IEC). ISO/IEC 27032:2023- Cybersecurity Guidelines for Internet security. Available online: https://www.iso.org/standard/76070.

xci International Organization for Standardization (ISO)/International Electrotechnical Commission (IEC). ISO/IEC 27032:2023- Cybersecurity Guidelines for Internet security. Available online: https://www.iso.org/standard/76070.html.

xcii International Organization for Standardization (ISO)/International Electrotechnical Commission (IEC). ISO/IEC 27033-1:2015-Information Technology—Security Techniques—Network Security—Part 1: Overview and Concepts. Available online: https://www.iso.org/standard/63461.html.

xciii International Organization for Standardization (ISO)/International Electrotechnical Commission (IEC). ISO/IEC 27033-1:2015-Information Technology—Security Techniques—Network Security—Part 1: Overview and Concepts. Available online: https://www.iso.org/standard/63461.html.

[xciv] International Organization for Standardization (ISO)/International Electrotechnical Commission (IEC). ISO/IEC 27034-1:2011-Information Technology—Security Techniques—Application Security—Part 1: Overview and Concepts. Available online: https://www.iso.org/standard/44378.html.

[xcv] International Organization for Standardization (ISO)/International Electrotechnical Commission (IEC). ISO/IEC 27035-1:2016-Information Technology—Security Techniques—Information Security Incident Management—Part 1: Principles of Incident Management. Available online: https://www.iso.org/standard/60803.html.

[xcvi] SANS Institute. *Security Awareness Roadmap*; SANS Institute: Bethesda, MD, USA, 2016. [**Google Scholar**]

[xcvii] International Organization for Standardization (ISO)/International Electrotechnical Commission (IEC). ISO/IEC 27001:2013-Information Technology—Security Techniques—Information Security Management Systems—Requirements. Available online: https://www.iso.org/standard/54534.html.

[xcviii] Office of the Superintendent of Financial Institutions (OSFI). *Cyber Security Self-Assessment Guidance*; OSFI: Toronto, ON, Canada, 2013. [**Google Scholar**]

[xcix] Souppaya, M.; Scarfone, K. *Guidelines for Managing the Security of Mobile Devices in the Enterprise*; National Institute of Standards and Technology: Gaithersburg, MD, USA, 2013.

[c] SANS Institute. *Critical Security Controls for Effective Cyber Defense*; SANS Institute: Bethesda, MD, USA, 2018. [**Google Scholar**]
[ci] International Organization for Standardization (ISO)/International Electrotechnical Commission (IEC). ISO/IEC 27032:2023- Cybersecurity Guidelines for Internet security. Available online: https://www.iso.org/standard/76070.html.

[cii] Souppaya, M.; Scarfone, K. *Guide to Enterprise Patch Management Technologies*; National Institute of Standards and Technology: Gaithersburg, MD, USA, 2013.

[ciii] Information Security Forum (ISF). *The ISF Standard of Good Practice for Information Security*; ISF: Surrey, UK, 2018. [**Google Scholar**]

[civ] Information Security Forum (ISF). *The ISF Standard of Good Practice for Information Security*; ISF: Surrey, UK, 2018. [**Google Scholar**]

[cv] CAPABILITY MATURITY MODEL AND METRICS FRAMEWORK FOR CYBER CLOUD SECURITY https://opus.lib.uts.edu.au/bitstream/10453/121301/1/CSCMM-SCPE-01-5-2017.pdf

[cvi] State Partnership Program, https://www.nationalguard.mil/Leadership/Joint-Staff/J-5/International-Affairs-Division/State-Partnership-Program/lang/en/

[cvii] Department of Defense State Partnership Program (SPP), https://www.nationalguard.mil/Portals/31/Documents/J-5/InternationalAffairs/StatePartnershipProgram/NG-SPP-Map-Nov-2024.pdf

[cviii] National Guard State Partnership Program, https://www.nationalguard.mil/Portals/31/Documents/J-5/InternationalAffairs/StatePartnershipProgram/National%20Guard%20State%20Partnership%20Program%20Map%2017%20MAY%202023.pdf

[cix] The National Guard State Partnership Program: Background, Issues, and Options for Congress, https://sgp.fas.org/crs/misc/R41957.pdf

[cx] Cyber Platforms and Systems (CPS), https://www.eis.army.mil/sites/default/files/2023-03/CPS_Collaboration%20Day_2023-03-28%20%281%29.pdf

[cxi] Robert-W-Brauchlehii-Co-Com. (2023, August 14). HII-LED team develops prototype cyber threat hunting kit to support defensive cyber operations. HII. https://hii.com/news/hii-cyber-threat-hunting-kit-saberhunt-2023/

[cxii] Cyber Precog packs data center power in a flyaway kit. (2022, June 13). https://www.boozallen.com/expertise/products/cybersecurity-products/cyber-precog-incident-response-threat-hunting.html

[cxiii] Forrester Reprint. (n.d.). https://reprints2.forrester.com/#/assets/2/2562/RES178480/report

cxiv Forrester Reprint. (n.d.). https://reprints2.forrester.com/#/assets/2/2562/RES178480/report

cxv 960th Cyberspace Wing. (2022, November 15). Cyber 101: Hunt Forward Operations. https://www.960cyber.afrc.af.mil/News/Article-Display/Article/3219164/cyber-101-hunt-forward-operations/

cxvi Politics, G. B. F. N. (2020, April 22). U.S. Cyber Command's Malware Inoculation: Linking Offense and Defense in Cyberspace. Council on Foreign Relations. https://www.cfr.org/blog/us-cyber-commands-malware-inoculation-linking-offense-and-defense-cyberspace

cxvii Politics, G. B. F. N. (2020, April 22). U.S. Cyber Command's Malware Inoculation: Linking Offense and Defense in Cyberspace. Council on Foreign Relations. https://www.cfr.org/blog/us-cyber-commands-malware-inoculation-linking-offense-and-defense-cyberspace

cxviii CYBER FORCES AND COMMAND AUTHORITIES, https://ctip.defense.gov/Portals/12/operational-law-handbook_2017.pdf, Page 133,134

cxix U.S. Cyber Command. (n.d.). CYBERCOM's "Under Advisement" to increase private sector partnerships, industry data-sharing in 2023. https://www.cybercom.mil/Media/News/Article/3444464/cybercoms-under-advisement-to-increase-private-sector-partnerships-industry-dat/

cxx Bureau of Cyberspace and Digital Policy, https://www.state.gov/bureaus-offices/deputy-secretary-of-state/bureau-of-cyberspace-and-digital-policy/

cxxi All Ransomware Attacks, https://ransomwareattacks.halcyon.ai/

cxxii NATO. (n.d.). NATO member countries. NATO. https://www.nato.int/cps/en/natohq/topics_52044.htm

cxxiii Significant Cyber Incidents | CSIS. (n.d.). https://www.csis.org/programs/strategic-technologies-program/significant-cyber-incidents

cxxiv Iranian state actors conduct cyber operations against the government of Albania | CISA. (2022, September 23). Cybersecurity and Infrastructure Security Agency CISA. https://www.cisa.gov/news-events/cybersecurity-advisories/aa22-264a

cxxv   Significant   Cyber   Incidents | CSIS.   (n.d.). https://www.csis.org/programs/strategic-technologies-program/significant-cyber-incidents

cxxvi   Cyber   Capacity   Building   in   Ten   Points,   April   2014, https://dig.watch/resource/cyber-capacity-building-ten-points

cxxvii Mapping the Cyber Terrain: Enabling Cyber Defensibility Claims and Hypotheses to Be Stated and Evaluated with Greater Rigor and Utility, November 2013, https://apps.dtic.mil/sti/citations/AD1107342

cxxviii Report: Integrating Cyber Capacity to the Digital Development Agenda, NOVEMBER 2021, https://thegfce.org/tools/report-integrating-cyber-capacity-to-the-digital-development-agenda/

cxxviiii The Design of Focus Area Maturity Models, June 2010, https://link.springer.com/chapter/10.1007/978-3-642-13335-0_22

cxxix ECJ6/ JCC, Security Cooperation Engagement Strategy, Feb 2020, https://community.apan.org/cfs-file/__key/docpreview-s/00-00-14-88-27/ECJ6-Cyber-Security-Cooperation-Overview.pdf

cxxx Cyber Science 2020 - Advancing a Multidisciplinary Approach to Cyber Security, 2020, https://www.sintef.no/en/publications/publication/1819400/

cxxxi The Cyber Defense Assistance Imperative – Lessons from Ukraine, FEBRUARY 16, 2023, https://www.aspeninstitute.org/publications/the-cyber-defense-assistance-imperative-lessons-from-ukraine/

cxxxii THE NATIONAL STRATEGY TO SECURE CYBERSPACE, February 2003, https://www.energy.gov/ceser/articles/national-strategy-secure-cyberspace-february-2003

cxxxiii New CNAS Report: No I in Team: Integrated Deterrence with Allies and Partners, https://www.cnas.org/publications/reports/no-i-in-team

cxxxiv National Defense Strategy Of The United States Of America, 2022, https://apps.dtic.mil/sti/trecms/pdf/AD1183514.pdf

cxxxv Cyber Defence - Built on European cooperation, 08 SEPTEMBER 2021,   https://eda.europa.eu/publications-and-data/brochures/cyber-defence---built-on-european-cooperation

---

cxxxvi DRAFTASEAN CYBERSECURITYCOOPERATION STRATEGY, 2021-2025, https://asean.org/wp-content/uploads/2022/02/01-ASEAN-Cybersecurity-Cooperation-Paper-2021-2025_final-23-0122.pdf

cxxxvii Cyberspace Solarium Commission (CSC), March 2020, https://drive.google.com/file/d/1ryMCIL_dZ30QyjFqFkkf10MxIXJGT4yv /view